# Beyond the Wall

A Novel of Post-Roman Britain

Jason Kyle

# Prologue

## Caer Gurcoc, Isle of Mona. 549 A.D.

The small town of Caer Gurcoc sat not far off the western coast of the Mona, the largest island off the coast of Britain and part of the kingdom of Gwynedd. Within this town was a modest, Roman-style villa, one of the few in the region. Inside this villa, two young children sat at a large, old, round wooden table, following their grandfather's every move as he shuffled about the dining room. Their grandfather, Peredur, was head of the family and lord of the villa and its surrounding lands. He was an old man in his sixties, balding, and sported a thick white beard, though his mustache retained much of his original brown color. A scar ran across one cheek and bisected a dark, bushy eyebrow.

In the corner of the room was his armor stand: a simple, wooden cross upon which a chainmail shirt was draped, along with an ornate, iron helmet with nose and cheek guards. A horsehair crest jutted out from the top of the helm. Behind the armor stand rested an oval shield, painted white with a bold "P" and an "X" overlapping each other in neat, red strokes across the surface. It was the Chi Rho, a symbol of good luck and devotion to Jesus Christ, used by Roman soldiers and their allies for the past two centuries. Behind the shield rested a tall spear with a gleaming tip and a sword in a worn but well-maintained scabbard. The old man passed by the display with barely a glance. A third child, walking behind the man, picked up the helm, plopped it onto his head, picked up the shield with a slight grunt, and then walked proudly behind his grandfather. The boy, Cadoc, was only eight years old and had to cock his head back in order to peer out from under the rim of the oversized helm. He had to use both hands to carry the shield and struggled to keep it off the ground. This comical attempt to walk under these conditions drew a laugh from his older brother, Rhys, and his sister, Enid, who was twelve and the oldest of the three.

Their grandfather walked over to a shelf and pulled down a simple clay jar and a colorfully painted wooden cup made by Enid. He poured himself a cupful of mead, made locally by Gilbert, his lifelong friend and comrade-in-arms, carefully stepped over a large hound that lay sleeping on the floor and shuffled over to join the children at the table.

"Will you tell us a story now, grandfather?" asked Enid eagerly.

"Yes! A story!" chimed in Cadoc, who was banging the shield against Rhys' leg.

"Stop hitting me," Rhys growled.

"I'm not touching you," Cadoc grinned.

Peredur sipped his mead, smiling through his mustache. He said nothing but glanced sideways at Enid, who took her cue.

"Boys!" she snapped. "Do you want to hear a story or not? Settle down before Grandmother puts you two to work. Again." As she said this, she leaned over, yanked the shield away from Cadoc, and returned it to the armor stand.

Peredur winked at Enid. *She'll make a fine mother herself in a few more years,* he thought approvingly.

"So, what story would you like to hear?" he asked. "Maybe one about that terrible winter we had back when your father was your age? That was a frightful time, I can tell you!"

"You have," Rhys said, rolling his eyes as he and Cadoc shared a bored look. "Tell us about King Arthur," he exclaimed as he wrapped his knuckles against the helm his little brother was still wearing. It had fallen forward, and only the lower half of Cadoc's face was visible. The two giggled.

"Yes, tell us about King Arthur," Cadoc echoed his brother.

2

"*King* Arthur, eh?" The old man said. "Well the first thing I should tell you right now is, he was no 'king'. Not rightfully speaking, anyway. Of course, there's some nowadays who call themselves kings who aren't rightfully such, either," he muttered. "But Arthur was a very fine commander, I can tell you. The finest I ever knew. And a good man."

"Tell us about Arthur when he slew the giant!" Rhys prompted.

"A giant?" Peredur chuckled. "Where did you hear *that* tale?"

"A bard sang for us last month," Enid said.

"Bards and their tales," snorted the old man. "Can't believe half of what comes out of their mouths."

"You can't believe half of what your grandfather says, either!" a woman's voice called out from outside.

The children giggled at their grandmother's remark.

"Hush, woman," Peredur barked playfully.

Cadoc was not letting his grandfather off the hook. "You knew Arthur. Tell us about your battles with him," he pleaded.

Peredur's gaze became unfocused for a moment as he stared over at his armor stand. Memories of hard-fought battles and friends, now gone, echoed in his mind.

"His battles, eh? I'm not sure your mother would like me telling you those stories," he said, glancing warily out of a window as though the mere mention of his son's wife would summon her forth like some bothersome pixie bent on mischief.

"We won't tell her if you don't," Cadoc said slyly.

The old man smiled. The boy was just like his father, he mused. Then he glanced over at the armor stand, shuddering slightly, as other memories surfaced. "Maybe I don't want to tell those stories, either," he muttered, taking another sip of mead.

"Please, grandfather?" Enid pleaded. "You don't have to tell us about the terrible parts. Maybe you could tell us about how you and Grandmother met? Was it romantic?"

The boys glanced at each other, clearly not liking Enid's suggestion. Peredur smiled at that and glanced over towards the door, where his dear wife of forty years was outside, tending to some flowers.

"How about," the old man pondered. "I tell you about my first campaign against the Picts when Arthur took us all the way up to Caledonia. I wasn't much older than you," he looked at Enid.

"Cale...dona," the girl cocked her head, unfamiliar with the Latin name.

"The lands far, far to the north," Peredur clarified. "North of Hadrian's Wall."

"Grandmother calls it 'Alba,'" Enid said with a bit of smug authority.

"Yes, Alba is another name for the Picts' land," the old man conceded.

"And you had to fight them?" Cadoc asked eagerly. "The Picts?"

"A few times," Peredur nodded. "My first real scrap with them was just a few months after I joined Tribune Arthur's *numerus*, shortly after I turned sixteen."

Peredur shook his head in wonder. How time has escaped! "That was forty-five years ago now!" he muttered. "That year, we fought them in the forest, and again at the Battle of Guinnion's Fort. Well, that was what we called the place. The fort was just some old Roman ruins, really, under the command of Guinnion. I've no idea what the proper name for the place was ..."

"What's a numerus?" Enid asked, tactfully interrupting his musings.

"When you were sixteen!" exclaimed Cadoc in childish astonishment. "That long ago? Was that when the Romans were here?

Peredur gave his grandson a fierce glare. "Just how old do you think I am, boy?" Then he grinned, unable to even maintain the facade of being angry with his grandson for long.

"The Romans left Britain nearly a hundred years before I was even born! But some things have stayed the same since those days. As to your question," the old man said, looking at Enid. "A numerus, or more properly a 'numerus equitum' was the Romans' word for a cavalry unit. The Romans were powerful enough to have many numeri within their armies, but here in Britain, we had to learn to make do with what we could. Arthur's Red Dragons were the last serving numerus in Britain, and he commanded it, personally, for a long time."

"How many men did Arthur have?" Rhys asked.

"Well, that varied," Peredur said, scratching his beard. "The Red Dragons numbered close to a thousand men at total strength, but we were rarely ever mustered at one location, all at once. And for bigger battles, such as at Mount Badon, Arthur was made Dux Bellorum and commander of whatever forces were present."

Peredur started to elaborate, but he saw the fleeting looks of dread the two boys gave each other, and he chuckled, "Arthur usually commanded about three hundred men."

"Three hundred?" Cadoc asked, amazed. "So many?"

The old man nodded proudly. "We could do that because the numerus was made up of noble lads throughout all of the Briton-held kingdoms. And we were well armored, highly trained, and could travel fast, moving across Britain in mere weeks if needs be. The larger the army, the slower it can move on account of its supplies. They have to be fed, after all. Large armies take a long time to mobilize, too."

Peredur saw the children's eyes start to glaze over as he talked about logistics, so he stopped and took another sip of mead. "Anyone need to get a drink or go relieve themselves before we begin?" he asked, glancing quickly from child to child.

The children giggled but shook their heads and remained seated at the table.

"Well then," the old man said. "It all started a long, long time ago...."

# Map of 6th Century Great Britain

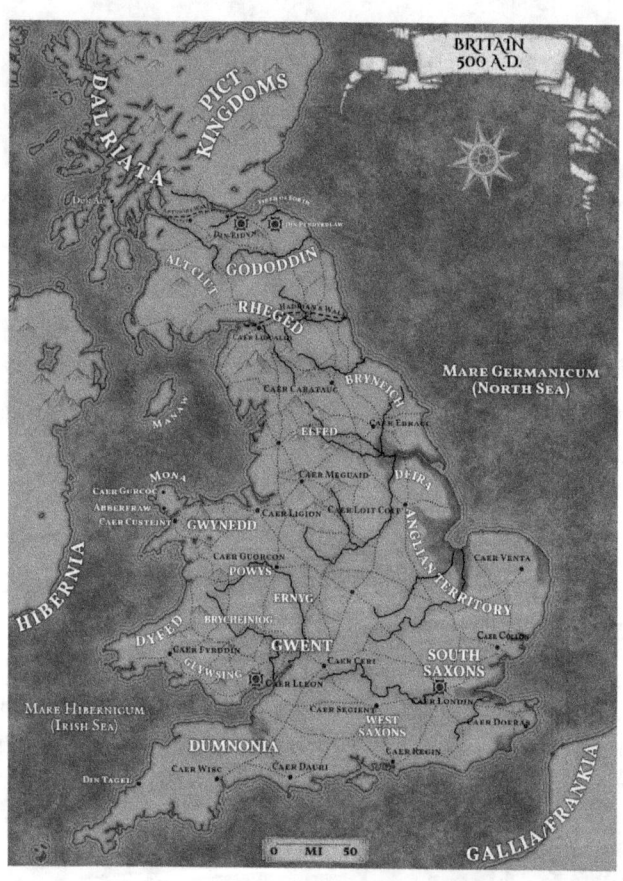

# Map of 6th Century Caledonia (Scotland)

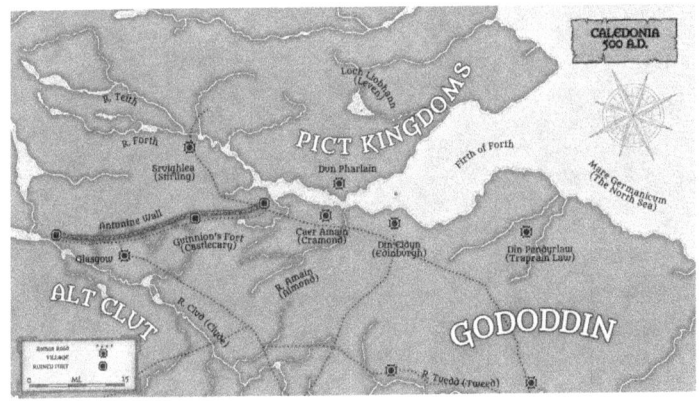

# Chapter One

M y father, Pelinor, was a soldier who fought under the banner of Ambrosius Aurelianus in his campaigns against the Saxons. For his exceptional service, Pelinor was given enough gold to return home to the newly formed kingdom of Gwynedd and purchase our family's estate in Caer Gurcoc, a small town near the northwestern shores of the isle of Mona. Due to its proximity to the island of Hibernia, it was a walled town and always watchful of Scoti raiders. It was a fine home, nonetheless, that provided us with an income in fishing and trading.

Pelinor married and sired three sons with my mother, Yglais, of which I was the youngest. I was born about eight decades since the Romans left Britain and thirteen years after the Western Empire finally fell to the Ostrogoths. We weren't as wealthy as the lords in Aberffraw, south of us, but with the fishing and trading that my father did, combined with the rent of our tenants in the form of goods and services, we lived comfortably. My father even became a horse breeder and occasionally sold stock to the retinue of our current King, Cadwallon Longhand.

Being the youngest of my father's sons, I was more or less allowed to choose my own path. Like my brothers, I was educated by a tutor and learned to hunt from my father and how to fight, mostly under the rough tutelage of my brothers. The most impactful part of my education, however, was sitting at the hearth with my brothers as our father regaled us with war stories from his younger days when he was willing to tell them.

He told me the tales of how the warlord Cunneda, formerly of Gododdin, had retaken this island of Mona from the invading Scoti of western Hibernia. He regaled us with stories of his own past, fighting in the ranks of Ambrosius Aurelianus, and his fight against the Saxons. The stories that most captivated my boyish imagination though, were those my father, and later my brother Aglofael, eight years older than I, told me about the elite Red Dragons Cavalry, led first by Uther, and more recently, his son Arthur.

Aglofael joined their ranks and died to a Saxon blade a short time after becoming a member of that unit himself. I was eleven years old then, and it was a day I will never forget. Word was spreading of a spectacular victory Arthur had won, at the River Glein, somewhere far to the east. My brother Lamorac, our friends and I were running around, fighting each other with sticks, reenacting the battle, when a red-cloaked soldier rode up to our villa. I paid him no mind once I saw that it wasn't my brother. I stopped when I heard my mother's screams from inside the house. A shiver ran down my spine, and I bolted for the villa. Lamorac ran beside me.

We found them in the atrium, beside the shallow pool. Mother was on her knees, wailing. Her face was buried in her hands. Father knelt beside her, rocking her. To my astonishment, he too was sobbing. I don't think I'd ever seen my father cry before. The soldier glanced around, looking very uncomfortable, then slowly turned around and left.

"What did he do to Mother?" I demanded, gripping my stick tightly as I looked from her to the departing soldier. I didn't know whether I should feel angry or scared.

Our father looked up at us, wiping his eyes, and gestured for Lamorac and me to come over. We did, and he wrapped us up in his free arm. Then he took a deep breath and slowly told us the news.

"Your brother is dead," he said in a hoarse, strained voice. "The Red Dragons have been fighting the Saxons all over the edges of their territory. Aglofael was slain."

My brother and I shared looks of horror before turning back to our father. My eyes instantly welled up with tears, and I began to cry.

"Was it at the Glein?" Lamorac asked.

"They don't know for sure," Father said. "The Glein, Portus Adurni, or somewhere else. He was buried ..." he choked, cleared his throat, and continued. "They buried him where he fell."

We grieved together for some time. Father, and especially Mother, was never the same after that day. Lamorac was made Father's heir as the now-eldest son. Especially after Aglofael's death, Mother fussed over me much more and made it clear that she hoped I would become a clergyman, or at least a scribe or some other such profession, as was common for younger sons.

Unfortunately for her, I was determined to honor my brother by following in his footsteps. I wanted to join Arthur's Red Dragons. So once I turned sixteen in the month of Augustus, I begged and pleaded with my father to give me his consent to join. Given his own military background, and the pragmatic view that as a younger son, I needed to find some form of employment, my father didn't seem to mind my decision. Mother was horrified by it however, and begged me to change my mind. When I did not, she demanded that Father forbid me from going. He looked from me to his sobbing wife, and back to me.

"I'm sorry, son," he said. "She has already lost one son. If you want to fight so badly, I'll write up an endorsement and you can join the King's guard, here on Mona." He glanced at Mother. "Will that satisfy you, Yglais?" he asked, taking her hand.

My mother wiped her tears and, after thinking about it for a moment, nodded.

"That's settled then," my father said, sounding pleased. "You may join King Cadwallan's guard- assuming his commander approves. He'll have the final say in the matter of course. But I shall write up an endorsement for you. In the meantime, we should visit the armorer in town and see if he has anything available that either fits, or can easily be adjusted to fit you. Can't have you show up to the palace looking like some country-born commoner."

"But father, we do live out in the country," I said, smiling.

"Yes but…. It's not the same thing," Pelinor said, looking a bit flustered.

From his own days as a soldier, Father had a small collection of weapons and armor. We found a simple, but good quality spangenhelm that fit me. It even had cheek guards, if not a nasal, like more and more helmets are being made with these days. I already owned some thick tunics that served well enough to soften blows in sparring. In fact, many levied commoners went to war with nothing but padded or layered cloth tunics for protection. But I needed a coat of mail or something to go over that, so we went into the town's center to see the blacksmith at Caer Gurcoc. He wasn't the sort to make elaborate pieces of armor; for that we would have needed to visit one of the more expensive shops in Gwynedd's capital city of Aberffraw, over a day's journey to the south of us. Thankfully, he did indeed have a shirt of mail that fit me well enough. "It's perhaps a little looser than it ought to be," the smith said as he examined the fit, "but you're a young man. I suspect you'll be able to grow into it, eh?" he nudged me with a wink.

Father agreed and paid the man with an agreed-upon weight of hacksilver-miscellaneous old Roman silver siliquae coinage, either whole or in bits, even older coins, jewelry, and whatnot. Even raw ore could and was used, as long as the metal was of the same type and quality. This type of transaction along with bartering, had become Britain's more common means of making large purchases since Roman coin had stopped flowing in so long ago.

While Father and I assembled kit for myself, I admit I felt guilty, for I still intended to join Arthur and his Red Dragons. King Cadwallan's guard offered a fine position, but they stayed local and only focused on protecting Gwynedd. That meant fighting off occasional Scoti raids and maybe ensuring that neighboring kingdoms like Powys to the east, or Dyfed to the south, didn't encroach upon our borders, as was prone to happen from time to time. I hated hearing of these petty squabbles between Britons and had no interest in being forced to take up arms against my own neighbors. Like my older brother Aglofael, I was much more concerned with the threat posed by the Saxons. And it was Saxons who killed him! So I quietly made plans to take my bay mare, Carys, and ride to Caer Lleon, where the Red Dragons were garrisoned.

I'd never left Mona before. In fact, I rarely even went as far as Aberffraw. There just wasn't any need for it. I reasoned that surely a large, important place like Caer Lleon couldn't be that hard to find though. I knew it was generally southeast of us, in the kingdom of Gwent, I even knew that it was near the shoreline of the Afon Wsyg. With that information, I was confident I could find my way there. I doubted it was more than a few days' of travel.

I decided I needed to leave soon, as Father intended to personally escort me to Aberffraw and present me to the king's guard. He saw it as doing me a favor, but that just wouldn't do. If I let him have his way, I'd be presented to their commander and, if he approved my petition, I'd be sworn to the king's service. By then it would be too late to leave and join up with Arthur, unless I wanted to break my oath and desert the king's guard. That would bring shame to my family and dishonor upon me, so that option was out of the question.

My best option was to sneak away some night. It would break Mother's heart, I knew, and I felt terrible. I loved her more than anyone else in the world, but I was a man now and had to do what I believed was best for me, too. I could only hope that, eventually, she would accept my decision. I was less worried about Father. I believed he would understand, though that would depend in part on how Mother reacted.

The next day, Father wrote out my endorsement. I asked to see it, and noticed that the letter he wrote wasn't addressed to anyone specifically. It simply verified our identities, acknowledged my intent to swear an oath of service, after which he mentioned the training I had received and vouched for my qualities on his honor, as well as assured "whoever was concerned" that I had the means to pay for my own arms and equipment, and keep it in good working order. I glanced up at him after reading the letter and thanked him, while trying to keep my expression blank and sound as nonchalant as possible. His own look as he passed the scroll to me was equally unreadable.

That very night, after my parents and even the servants had gone to bed, I quietly got dressed, packed up my things, being careful not to wake Lamorac, sleeping on the other side of the room, and crept out to the stables. I was just cinching down Carys' saddle when I heard soft footsteps behind me. I spun around, and to my horror, there in the soft moonlight stood my father and older brother Lamorac. Father was scowling, while Lamorac had an amused smirk on his face. I glared at him.

"Lamorac, you ratted me out?" I said, accusingly.

He made to speak but Father cut him off with a curt laugh. "Son, I know you much, much better than you must realize. And besides, you may have your mother's gentle nature, but where do you think your thirst for adventure and your stubbornness comes from?" He jabbed a thumb at his own breast. "I wasn't much older than you when I left home to answer Ambrosius and Uther's call for troops after they returned to Britain to sort out Vortigern and his Saxon allies."

Lamorac glanced at father then back to me. "What was your plan, little brother? Were you going to just ride all the way to Caer Lleon with no money, not even a sword, walk up to Lord Arthur and say 'Here I am!' and hope they didn't discover that you're little more than a runaway boy? And besides, you've never even stepped foot off Mona, let alone made a trek like the one you'd be making to get to Caer Lleon."

I flushed. That *had* basically been my plan, in fact. But it sounded so much worse when he said it. "I was going to also mention that Aglofael served and died under the draco standard and that I wanted justice for his death," I grumbled.

Lamorac lost his smirk at the mention of Aglofael, and backed off a step. Father's face softened a bit too. He sighed. "Per," he said using a family pet name that I absolutely despised. "That's not going to impress Arthur, nor his officers. The Red Dragons aren't some household guard who will take just about anybody able to wield a sword. They are an elite unit, led by battle-hardened veterans who earned their way up the ranks. They're a last, dying echo of what the Roman legions were at their peak. They've neither the time nor desire to nursemaid some runaway nobleman's boy out for revenge."

I hated how they kept referring to me as a "boy" but had to admit, if not out loud, that I hadn't been thinking, or behaving very maturely. Father must have read my mind. From behind his back he pulled out an old sword. Its small ivory guard and pommel were nicked and scratched, and the scabbard looked equally worn. He slowly unsheathed it and showed me the blade. Contrasting with the hilt, the blade itself was in pristine condition.

"This spatha was mine, when I began my own service under Ambrosius. It's been in our family for generations, so treat it with respect," he said as he handed the blade to me. I took it, reverently, and admired the blade. "You'll want to obtain a newer blade at some point, then just hold onto this one and keep it safe. It's what I did. Your grandfather never even had to actually use this sword in combat at all," Father winked at me.

Lamorac stepped forward then with a pouch and handed it to me with a lopsided grin. It was heavy, and the contents jingled as I took it. "You'll need some silver," he said. "You certainly won't be able to sweet talk your way onto a ship, or talk an armorer to repair your weapons and armor down the road."

"That's your inheritance, providing your brother lives long enough for me to pass on our estate to him," Father said dryly as he glanced over at Lamorac. "Spend it wisely and guard it well. Don't let some pretty young alewife use her wiles on you and fleece you of your silver."

I laughed at that one.

He continued, "Go down to the port at Caer Gybi. Trading vessels come and go pretty regularly this time of year. You should be able to buy your way onto one of them that's heading south, and can drop you off at the mouth of the Afon Wysg, which feeds into the sea. You should be able to follow the river north easily enough until you come to the fort. You might have to wait a day or two for a ship, but even so, a week at sea still beats nearly two weeks over open road, by yourself."

"Caer Lleon is two weeks away?" I asked, startled. Father and Lamorac shared an amused look.

"By land, without wearing out your horse? Just about two weeks, yes," Father chuckled. I winced. I had grossly underestimated the distance involved, apparently.

"Thank you, Father," I said, and impulsively reached out and hugged him.

After a moment, he returned my hug and squeezed me so tightly that I half thought he would break my ribs. "God go with you, my boy," he told me.

We separated, though one of Father's large hands lingered on my shoulder. "Make sure you write your mother, when you're able," he said. "You've silver enough to pay for an occasional messenger. And visit when you can."

"I will, father," I promised.

He patted me a couple of times, which I knew from long experience was the closest he would come to saying "I love you," then turned and walked slowly away.

I watched him leave for a moment, then looked past him and up to our villa. It was a fine home, and I would miss it.

"I'll miss you, little brother," Lamorac said as I strapped my belongings securely to Carys' saddle.

"Look at the bright side," I grinned. "You might finally be the best spearman on Mona once I'm gone."

Lamorac snorted. "I wish I could be there, hovering over your scrawny little shoulders when you realize that being a great spearman here doesn't amount to much on the mainland."

I waved dismissively. "Take care of Mother, will you? I know she's taking it hard."

"You could make it easy for her and stay. It's not too late until you've actually on the ship and it's left the harbor."

I rolled my eyes. "I've made up my mind, Lam," I said. "Saxons killed Aglofael. I won't make it my focus, but I do want justice for him! And if somebody doesn't stop them, we're just as likely to have them on our doorstep as the Scoti one of these days! Only I think the Saxons are by far the greatest threat, and I think Arthur is the man to stop them."

My brother had no response to that, and after giving me a hug of his own, he suddenly grabbed my head in a vice-like headlock and rubbed the top of my head with his knuckles, then released me.

"Take care of yourself then, Per," He said with a grin.

I returned it. "You too," I said, then at the last second my hand darted out and smacked him hard between his legs. He doubled over, cursing me. I laughed, hopped up onto Carys' back, and departed.

It wasn't a long ride to Caer Gybi, thankfully, and there was enough moonlight that I had little trouble on the winding road. On top of that, this was a journey I'd taken fairly often, so both Carys and I were comfortable riding it, even at night. We arrived there in about three hours. Caer Gybi was larger than Caer Gurcoc, with a population of over three hundred, and it was indeed busy this time of year, as my father had stated. Mona produced a decent amount of grain so that, along with fish and other trade goods, it made Gybi a popular stopping point for merchants, in spite of the risk from raiders. Everyone there was asleep by this time, so I pulled out my bed roll right on the edge of town, picketed Carys, and slept the rest of the night.

I awoke the next morning just after sunrise to the sound of men calling out to each other and to birds chirping and squawking as they dove for fish and hunted for prey along the beach. I purchased some food from a vendor then sat by the docks. A couple ships did come by that day. The first was continuing on north. The second, that arrived later on as I was eating supper, was indeed traveling south the following day. I haggled with the ship's master, an Eastern Roman named Stephanos, who finally agreed to deviate off his planned course slightly, enough to drop me off where I needed to go.

Since I would need to stay one more night at Caer Gybi, I went to the largest house in town, owned by a man known to my family named Idwal. For a couple pieces of silver, they were happy to let me board with him for the night and share his dinner table.

The next morning, after eating a hearty breakfast with Idwal and his wife, I boarded my ship. It was good-sized and had a single mast with a large, rectangular sail. Thirty men manned the oars, and another ten milled about, performing other tasks. All of them looked tough, and they were armed, which was reassuring. I lashed Carys to the mast. We created a straw bed for her, then a short time later, we put to sea.

Having lived on an island, short trips by boat were nothing new to me, so I was comfortable through most of the journey. I admit, I became a bit queasy a couple of times, when we encountered a bit of rough weather and were tossed around a bit in the deeper water between Gwynedd and Dyfed on our way south. That was the first day. Once it grew dark, I bedded down beside Carys and went to sleep.

The next day, we rounded the jagged stretch of Dyfed's coast that thrust out to the west. I was admiring the beauty of the tall cliffs, just barely visible from our position, when one of the deckhands came over and introduced himself as Zahir. He was a sailor from North Africa, I learned, with skin that was as dark as ebony, and he had an odd yellow tint to his eyes, which fascinated me. I'd never seen men like him before.

I asked Zahir about the extent of his travels, and what a tale he told. Stephanos frequently made voyages all throughout the Mediterranean Sea, Britain, and elsewhere. Merchants such as Stephanos were how we in Britain retained contact with the wider world, though it had become much less common since the Western Empire's collapse. The eastern half, at least, was stable under Emperor Anastasius, I was told.

"Have you been to Rome?" I asked, eager for news. It had been some time since I had heard news of that once illustrious city.

"I was there two years ago," Zahir nodded. "They trade, as they always have. On the docks, in the towns, the people go about their business as in any other city I visit, in other places."

"I thought it was burned down?" I asked. That was certainly what some had said over the years, that barbarians had sacked and destroyed the city.

"Parts of it, the palaces, temples, and such, were looted and destroyed to some degree," Zahir agreed. "But on the whole, the people seem to be surviving well enough under this Goth king, Theodoric."

That, I admit, gave me mixed feelings. I was certainly glad that Rome was 'surviving' as Zahir put it, but it saddened me to hear that a Goth ruled there. A barbarian now ruled a city that had once overseen one of the greatest empires known to man. I shook my head at the bitter irony of it.

*****

On the morning of the third day, we encountered Scoti raiders. We were sailing around the coast of Dyfed, where it jutted out to the west when a cluster of small vessels with dark sails appeared from out of the mouth of a cove. To my consternation, I saw that they were very clearly on a course to intercept us.

Zahir swore as the shipmaster began bellowing orders in what sounded like Greek and sailors scrambled about. Having never been on a ship this size, I simply did my best to stay out of their way. The oarsmen pulled out helmets from under their benches and then went back to work at a faster pace than before. The ship also angled south into deeper waters. Those not pulling oars put on armor and readied weapons. I decided to don my own chainmail shirt and was just working into it when Zahir came over to me and lightly grabbed my arm.

"Can you swim in that?" he asked.

I thought about it for a moment. "Probably not?" I responded.

"Best keep it off then. If things go badly, and you end up in the water, you won't want that extra weight," he advised.

I glanced around again, and this time, I saw that while the men were indeed putting on armor, it was the lightweight stuff made from layered linen or wool. Even the shipmaster only wore an older-styled but well-made linothorax, complete with leather strips around the shoulders and hips. I put my chainmail back away and followed suit, donning a thick wool tunic that I often wore under my mail. Then I put my sword back on, along with my helm, and gripped my spear and shield. My heart beat faster as I did, anticipating the potential battle ahead.

"Can they catch us?" I asked, feeling anxious. I felt my hand grip the soothing pommel of the spatha at my hip.

"Oh yes." Zahir grinned at me. "Over time, we could outdistance them. That's why they waited for us in that cove. It gives them an opportunity to head us off. We'll try to lose them on the wind. Wouldn't be the first time we've had to evade raiders. Probably won't be the last. And if we can't evade, we'll fight." Being capable of fending off or evading raiders simply went with the job. Zahir winked at me, adding, "I myself have spent a bit of time as a raider. So have many of the crew."

The next hour passed with agonizing slowness as the Scoti currachs continued towards us. The shipmaster tried to angle us out into deeper water, away from them, but the smaller boats were too fast. When they were close enough that an encounter became certain, more orders were shouted, and the crewmen not rowing oars loaded up slings, went to the edge of the ship and began hurling stones at the approaching raiders, who were close enough that we heard them yell and curse as they started getting hit. The raiders in the boats who weren't pulling oars brought up shields, but otherwise, they kept coming. There were five boats, and each one had at least a half dozen men in them. Some prepared knotted ropes attached to large hooks as they got closer, while others brought out javelins.

The realization that we were likely to get boarded and actually have to fight caused my heart to race and my stomach to tighten into knots. I tried to calm myself down. I'd fought boars before with my father and brothers. Boars could be terrifyingly dangerous, too, especially if a spear only grazed them. This was why I was traveling to Caer Lleon, I reminded myself- to join the Red Dragons and defend my homeland from barbarians just like these men. I gritted my teeth and forcefully pushed my fear to the back of my mind.

Sailors around me continued to pelt the raiders with slingstones, focusing on the boats in the lead. The raiders were taking numerous casualties from the barrage. Then, several javelins were hurled up at us. One of the oarsmen grunted and toppled backward! To my horror, I saw a javelin had caught him where his neck and shoulder met. He sprawled out, coughing, as his blood spilled out of him. My knees buckled, and I stared down at the man. No hunt, no matter how messy, could have prepared me for this! Another javelin flew up and over the side of the ship and buried itself into the deck, only a few feet from where I stood. I yelped and jumped away. Again, fear flared up, and I wanted nothing more than to find a corner somewhere and hide.

Zahir ran up to me and grabbed my arm. I about jumped out of my shoes in fright.

"Hey!" He barked. I turned toward him. His face was inches from mine, and his eyes bore into me.

"Either throw something at them or grab that oar! Make yourself useful!"

I looked again at the bench where the dead oarsman lay, then took a step forward, intending to replace him, however frightening I found the prospect. Just then, a grappling hook was lobbed over the railing. And then two more. The raiders were attempting to board us!

In my mind, I rushed to the railing, sword in hand, and helped the sailors fend off the raiders, but my legs refused to move! I looked down, terror flooding into me again. *What's wrong with my legs?* I thought. *Why can't I move?*

I turned to Zahir, but he had already dashed off. He had an axe in hand and was chopping at the rope while his comrades thrust spears at the raiders, attempting to climb the ropes and board our ship. To my intense frustration and confusion, my legs finally started working again, but I found myself going backward! It was like I'd lost control of my own body, and contrary to what I knew I needed to do, what I had every intention of doing, I stumbled back, away from the fighting! My heart was pounding so hard that I felt like it was going to burst. Then I heard the *thunk* of metal striking wood behind me.

I spun around, instinctively drawing my sword. Another grappling hook had tethered itself to the ship's right side, towards the rear, while the crew were focused on the raiders attempting to board on the left side! An oarsman cried out in alarm. A jolt of terror shot through me, and without thinking, I rushed to the railing, sword raised. Leaning over, I saw two men already climbing the rope, with several more in the boat below. With all the strength I could muster, I hacked at the rope and cut right through it. There was a split second when I made eye contact with the two raiders on the rope, who flashed looks of alarm that, in that moment, struck me as extremely funny. Then, the rope, along with the raiders, dropped into the water.

The fight dragged on, and by the grace of God, we began to outdistance the raiders, who'd failed to board. We exchanged javelins, then sling stones again for a few minutes, then the raiders were left in our wake, and we were safely beyond their reach. Only the one oarsman was killed, but several more were wounded to various degrees. Zahir found me by the railing where I'd cut that line and patted me on the back with a grin. I grinned back, relieved that he apparently believed I'd moved to the far side of the ship in order to defend it rather than what actually happened.

We continued sailing south, and that evening, the crew had a short, simple ceremony for their fallen man. He was bundled up, a weight was attached to his body to ensure that he sank, and he was dropped overboard. Master Stephanos even brought out a barrel of wine and allowed the men to have a few drinks.

*****

On our fourth day at sea, we swung east, around Glywysing, and finally a short distance northeast, past Gwent. We saw one other merchant vessel and a few small fishing boats. I disembarked at a point only a few miles from the fort, at the mouth of the Afon Wysg, just before dusk. I thanked the ship's master for our safe journey and said goodbye to him and to Zahir, who'd been a most entertaining companion on my journey and disembarked.

It was too dark to ride on to Caer Lleon, and the region immediately inland was too marshy for a settlement, so I found a dry spot on some high ground, made a fire, and bedded down there for the night. I hadn't any food, so I rigged a simple fishing line and, after a bit, caught a couple of nice fat salmon. I wrapped my thick wool cloak around me, for the air was a bit chilly, so close to the river, and fell asleep a short time later, listening to the sounds of birds calling to each other.

When I woke up the next morning, I spent about an hour fishing again, caught some breakfast, then rode off, mostly following the river northwest toward the famous fortress of Caer Lleon. I grew excited as I got closer. The moment I'd dreamt of for years now was finally nearly upon me. I envisioned myself riding beside Arthur amidst a great host of horsemen, with gleaming armor and flashing swords, following the fluttering banners of the draco standards as we rode down Saxons, Scots, and whoever else dared to challenge us. When I'd first set out from home, I'd imagined myself returning as a hero, full of epic tales, as my father had, when he chose to speak of them. After that fight on the ship, though, I felt a twinge of doubt. Did I have what it took to ride and fight beside heroes such as Arthur? I wasn't as confident of that answer as I'd been just a couple of days ago, but now I felt like I needed to join the Red Dragons. I needed to prove to myself that I was as brave and strong as any man. I thought back to my actions on the ship and felt my ears burn with shame, and resolved that I would never act so weak or give in to my fear as I had then!

The remaining miles went by, and I saw more and more travelers emerging onto the road I myself was using. Most were merchants, pulling carts or driving wagons loaded down with their wares, heading to Caer Lleon or the surrounding area, I guessed. Finally, after about three hours, I arrived at a large, cozy-looking village. It could even be called a town. There must be hundreds of people living here, all enjoying the security that Arthur's presence brought. In the distance, on high ground overlooking both the village and a good portion of the river, I saw the fort.

# Chapter Two

From the outside, there wasn't much to see but a large wall that extended for hundreds of feet in both directions. It was an odd-looking wall, about twelve feet tall, made from old stone and newer logs. A few square wooden towers were interspaced along the walls, about thirty feet high and roughly a hundred feet apart. The gatehouse that protected the two massive, arched gates into the fort was an even taller, wider tower, still fully made of stone. The gate was open, as most fortified towns were during the day, though a handful of armed guards loitered around the entrance. A muddy ditch, about six feet deep and up to twelve feet wide in places, encircled the fort, with the only break that I could see being where the road led up to the gates.

My heart pounded with excitement as I approached. I'd dreamed of this day for years! Now, finally, I was about to join the same numerus equitum that my brother had served in. *Unless they decided not to accept me,* I suddenly thought. I felt a chill run down my back. I knew I was a good rider and a good fighter. My parents and tutor both assured me I was smart. My parents were wealthy enough to have afforded to pay for my armor and weapons and give Carys to me. So there was no real reason why Arthur shouldn't accept me. Right? But what if he didn't? What would I do? I'd bragged to all my friends that the next time they saw me, I should be one of the famed Red Dragons and maybe even a proven warrior. My mouth became dry at the terrible thought of rejection.

I drew closer to the gatehouse and pushed my fears down. A trio of guards manned the gatehouse, and I waved up at them as I approached. They waved back. As I got closer, one of the guards called out, "What's your business here, lad?"

"I've come seeking admittance into Arthur's cavalry!" I replied.

"And who are you? The Red Dragons don't let just any boy into their ranks," the guard said.

I did not like his tone and shouted at him. "I am Peredur, son of Pelinor, the Lord of Caer Gurcoc! You will admit me!"

"Are you now," the guard said, plainly irritated but a bit wary.

"Caer Gurcoc?" I heard one of the other guards say. "I've never heard of it."

The three talked amongst themselves for another moment, and then one of them called down to me, "Wait here, young master."

The other guard disappeared from the tower. A minute later, a soldier in simple armor stepped forward and approached me, his hand resting casually on the pommel of his sword. He didn't bother saying anything; just looked me up and down. He eyed my bay mare, Carys, before his gaze lingered on the sword at my hip for a moment, then finally up at me. Apparently, he decided I was no danger and waved me through. "Follow me," he said.

Upon entering, I realized that the fort looked essentially like a village, a very organized, very uniform village. Streets were smooth, perfectly straight, and laid out in a grid. Most of them were even made of paved stone. There were clearly designated areas for houses and others for shops or food storage. Some were stone, but most were wood, or wattle and daub; the wattle being tightly woven wooden strips, with the daub, a hard layer of mud, animal dung, and straw, packed around them for insulation. Most of the buildings, even the stone ones, had thatch roofs. A few had nicer, reddish-brown tiled roofs. Several structures had obviously been cannibalized; the stones they had once been made of had been removed and used to repair other structures. Women and children were all over the place, socializing, cleaning, and going about their business.

I commented on this odd state, and the guard shrugged. As we walked up the street to the great hall at the center of the fort, he explained, "The Romans who built this place abandoned it ages ago. When Uther brought the Numerus here, they had to restore the fort. They did the best they could."

He pointed to the ground where we stood. "Wait here," he said before walking up a flight of stone stairs and going inside. I gazed up at the hall, impressed. It was a large, single-level building of smooth stone, with a row of columns along its face. Though many of these were cracked and chipped, they still supported the overhanging roof.

Beside the entryway, I noticed a tall stone statue of a man in old-fashioned Roman armor. The statue had seen better days. It had once been vibrantly painted, but now most of the coloring was faded and worn away by the years. An outstretched arm was broken off, and it was chipped and worn in various other places, bearing the marks of time. I dismounted so I could get a better look at the monument. There was a plaque below the feet of the man that read:

*In Honorem Titum Flavium Vespasianum, Legatum Legionis Secundae Augustae, Conquestoris Britanniae, Conditoris Arcis apud Iscae Augustae Anno tertio Tiberii Claudii Caesaris Augusti Germanici Imperatoris.*

"In Honor of Titus Flavius Vespasianus, Legate of the Second Legion Augusta, Conqueror of Britain, Builder of the Fort at Isca Augusta in the third year of Emperor Tiberius Claudius Caesar Augustus Germanicus," I mumbled as I translated the plaque.

"You read Latin," a nearby man said in surprise.

I jumped slightly. I hadn't heard him approach.

"Yes, sir," I replied, looking him over. "My father had a tutor teach me," I added proudly. The man before me looked to be a few years older than I and a head taller. He had dark, shoulder-length hair and a neatly trimmed beard. His clothing looked expensive, as did his dagger and sword.

He leaned casually against the arched door frame of the great hall, munching on an apple. "Do you have business here, or have you simply gotten lost," the man's eyes danced around as if to emphasize where we were standing.

"I'm here to join the *Draconis Rubri*," I said, using their formal Latin name. The man half smiled.

"Ah. So you're the lad the guard was just talking about. By the way, it's '*Numerus Equitum Draconum Rubrorum Ultimae Spei*'," he corrected. "That's the unit's full designation.

"Cavalry Unit of the Red Dragons - Last Hope," I translated. "Unusual name. And a bit sorrowful sounding."

"They were formed by King Ambrosius Aurelius and Uther the Pendragon almost forty years ago," the man said.

"Right about the time the Goth barbarians sacked Rome," I finished, understanding the name.

The man nodded, adding, "Not to mention that the Saxons had just seized a lot of territory here in Britain." Then he asked, "What's your name, boy? The guard said it was Pereter, Perci...?"

"Peredur, son of Lord Pellinor, of Caer Gurcoc."

"Caer Gurcoc? Never heard of it," he said. Then he looked at me, pointing at my cheek. "Does your father know you're here, boy?" he asked skeptically. "You don't look like you've ever even shaved, but you want to wield a blade in combat?"

"I shave," I replied, annoyed. That was true enough. I'd shaved once, about a month ago. "And I know how to fight! Anyway, just who are *you*?" I asked. His demeanor and continued reference to me as "boy" was beginning to rankle.

"Oh, I didn't tell you?" the man asked. "I'm Cai, Vicarius of the Red Dragons." He smiled, though it seemed more condescending than friendly.

I wasn't sure what a Vicarius was, but this man, Cai, seemed to think himself important, and as I didn't want to make any enemies so soon after arriving, I minded my manners. "Nice to meet you," I said and extended my hand. He hesitated a moment, then reached out and shook it with a nod.

"As to your question, I got his blessing before I sailed here from Caer Gurcoc. He gave me a letter for Lord Arthur and even gave me his old spatha!" I showed Cai the long, elegant blade, for him to inspect.

"Old is right," Cai said dryly, looking at it. "You know how to use that thing?"

"Not as well as I can the spear," I admitted, sliding the blade back into its scabbard.

"Not much occasion to use a sword against small game, I'd wager," Cai said with a slight smirk.

"Not so much," I agreed, a bit begrudgingly.

He bade me to tether my horse to a hitching post staked nearby. As I lashed Carys' lead rope to the post, Cai commented, "That's a nice mount."

I looked over at Carys proudly and patted her neck. Carys was young and muscular and stood fourteen hands tall. I always liked that her dark, reddish-brown hide seemed almost the same color as my own hair. "Raised her myself," I told Cai. "She was bred and trained to be a warhorse."

Cai nodded. "Well, come on. I'll take you to the officer in charge, Castellan Bedwyr. He runs the day-to-day operations within Caer Lleon and will decide what to do with you. I was about to head over and talk to him anyway when the guard found me. So you can follow me over there."

"My father was a soldier," I told him. "He marched with the Pendragon against Oisc. And my brother, Aglofael, died fighting with the Red Dragons."

The man grew serious. "Aglofael? The name doesn't ring a bell."

I noticed that he dropped his condescending tone now, at least. He continued, "The numerus has about a thousand members in total, rarely in the same place at the same time. I know more members of the numerus than most, but I certainly don't know everybody by name. When did your brother fall?"

"Five years ago, at the Battle of the River Glein, I believe. It was shortly after that battle that my family was given the news," I said.

"Ah. Arthur's first major victory, against the Anglians," Cai flashed a grin before growing serious again. "Yes, I was there then. A lot of the numerus was, though. Your brother could have fought fifty paces from me, and I would not have known it."

We fell silent, and Cai took me to the entrance of the great hall, which, I have to say, looked very underwhelming at first sight. The floor was mostly paved, but there were patches where the stone had long since been removed, and only earth remained. Servants bustled about, ignoring us as they went about their duties.

I was surprised and confused when Cai took us not into some chamber in the hall but through it. As we did, I realized I had grossly misjudged the scope of the great hall. It was not just the building I had seen from out the entryway, but virtually a small fortress in its own right! Behind what I thought was the great hall, separated by a large, grassy courtyard that led toward a much larger and far more grand structure. The courtyard itself was large enough to fit hundreds of people. To the left and right were jagged stone walls that looked to have been enclosed corridors connecting the two structures. Rows of broken columns and a few intact arches along the courtyard further hinted at eaves that might have extended from the roof, providing a significant shaded area within the courtyard.

The second building, or wing, of the great hall still left me in awe as we approached, cutting across the courtyard. There was a wide flight of stairs leading up to the double doors. The entry was flanked by a row of stone columns as thick as trees that supported the overhanging roof. The structure itself was a massive, square building, also made of stone that seemed as big as a mountain. It was carved with decorative murals along the top of it. Bits of paint still clung to the surface, and I tried to imagine how glorious and vibrant this building must have looked when it had first been completed. Above the entrance, a rectangular banner, depicting a red dragon on a white field, hung from a window ledge.

My companion paid no attention to the effect the building was having on me, and kept up his brisk pace toward the structure, which was still magnificent to me despite its obvious degradation. "We conduct training as soon as we have about eight new men," he informed me, "so if you gain the Castellan's approval, you could begin in a few days. We have a few other lads who've also shown up to enlist over the past couple weeks."

We went inside and I saw that most of the floor still retained its original stone. The rearmost portion of the great hall was relatively well lit inside; the Romans liked large windows. Shelves lined portions of the walls with scrolls and wax tablets. In one distant room I could hear a group of low voices, speaking in Latin. There were too many voices and being spoken too quietly for me to make out many words. Occasionally somebody laughed. In another room I heard a voice speaking my own Brythonic, but with an odd accent.

My guide finished his apple and tossed the core outside a window as we passed by, then guided me to an office where a thickset man with a receding hairline and a blonde mustache and beard sat behind a desk. He wore a decorative tunic, a heavy silver chain, and was hunched over a wax writing tablet in his left hand. His right, I noticed, was missing. Behind him was an armor stand, displaying an exquisitely made suit of lamellar, a type of armor consisting of thumb-sized iron plates sewn side by side in rows. Atop his stand rested an ornate helm with nose and cheek guards, and a bright red plume. A sword and shield were propped up nearby.

Cai paused at the doorway, knocked on the wooden door to get the man's attention, then stepped in when the man looked up.

"Castellan," Cai nodded to him. "Brought you somebody- the son of some island village lord who wants to join the Red Dragons. He has a letter from his father, verifying his identity. He also says his brother, a man named Aglofael, died with the Dragons five years ago."

"Hm," the castellan said, thoughtfully. "The name does ring a bell, but I didn't know him. Sorry lad."

I shrugged. From my conversation with Cai I was beginning to realize how unlikely it actually was that I might run into anybody who did.

"So you want to join the numerus, do you?" the man asked with a sigh. He set down the tablet he'd been reading and looked me over.

I gave him my name and told him everything I'd told Cai, along with showing him the scroll my father had written on my behalf. Despite missing one hand, Bedwyr deftly removed the wax seal from the scroll and skimmed its contents.

"Well," he said after a moment. "Your father vouches for your good character, and your martial training. And you can read and write Latin, as well? That alone makes you potentially useful, at least," the castellan said. "Cai. Would you do me a favor and see if my duplarius, Drystan, is around? He can put Peredur through the paces. If he paces muster, he can join the other recruits."

Cai nodded, and we left the room and went back to the smaller building at the front of the great hall. Cai snagged up one of the servants, told him to find Drystan and meet us at the training yard, then gestured for me to follow him.

The three of us zigzagged our way past the row of officers' houses lined up along a central street that bisected the fort, passed by some workshops and storerooms, and out to a corner of the fort, where there was a large open area.

As we walked, I couldn't resist asking, "So, you and Castellan ... Bedwyr? Who outranks who?"

Cai smiled. "Depends," he said. "On matters of logistics, training, and all other matters related to the men of the numerus, I am. On matters of the fort's operations, security, provisions, and recruits," he looked pointedly at me. "He is. And everyone answers to Arthur."

"And he's no king ... so who does *he* answer to?" I asked.

"A lot of people, actually," Cai chuckled, "And that also depends on the situation. When he's at home, and acting as a landowner in Dumnonia, he answers to King Geraint. I assume of course that you mean in his capacity as our Tribune."

I nodded.

"Well, in that case, he answers to the will of the Council, made up of the majority of the kings in western Britain. We stay out of local squabbles, but when a threat rears up from the Scoti, Saxons, or other external sources, if the Council decides local forces aren't enough to deal with the threat, they call on

Arthur to muster the Red Dragons and assist. Then most likely he'll be named Dux Bellorum and take command of all forces on the ground, both the Red Dragons and whatever soldiers can be mustered.."

I nodded again, and we kept walking, and I continued to look around, fascinated with the fort. Once, there would have been several barracks buildings here. Now, most of the stone that had been used to make the barracks in this area of the fort had been repurposed and used to repair other, more important buildings. Bits of wall were still present here and there, however. Many of these remaining walls were used to prop up rows of training weapons and crudely made, unpainted shields. Cai brought me over to one particular ruin where two walls were still mostly intact, forming a corner that was nearly twenty-five paces long and six paces wide. The corner of the ruin was about ten feet high. Against the shorter wall was a row of several straw-filled dummies that stood on wooden crosses. We squared up to the targets, about thirty feet or six Roman paces away. Cai folded his arms across his chest, leaned up against the longer wall, and gestured to a rack of spears and smaller, lighter javelins.

"Drystan will be along soon," he said.. "Until then, you can satisfy my own curiosity. "Let's see how you do with those," he said with a small smile.

I grabbed a handful of spears, selected one, held it up to get the balance of it, then hurled it at the target. The spear punched through the center mass of the dummy's torso. I did the same thing with the next two.

"Not bad," Cai acknowledged. And just as I started to smile, he added "for that short range."

I sighed.

"Can you do that with javelins, as well?" He asked.

I nodded. He was right of course. A well thrown spear should be accurate up to sixty feet at least. Javelins on the other hand, were for closer targets. Back home, I had occasionally skewered large rabbits with the javelin, while hunting with my brothers. These straw dummies would be little challenge.

As I selected a handful of newer-looking javelins from the rack, another man walked up. He glanced at me, then over to Cai. "I miss anything?" he asked, looking at Cai.

Cai shrugged, gesturing to the dummy. "The lad's just tested on spears. Did well enough. He's on to the javelin now." He turned to me. "Peredur, this is Drystan. Take your directions from him now."

I nodded, and glanced at Drystan. He saw the javelins already in my hand, and told me to proceed. I did, and one after the other, I launched the missiles at the dummy. Two went into the chest, and one, I was satisfied to see, went straight into the dummy's head. I looked over to Drystan and Cai, who'd stuck around. To my surprise, neither seemed all that impressed.

"You look pleased with yourself," Drystan said.

"My javelin went straight through the dummy's head," I said. "Shouldn't I be pleased?"

"It was accurately thrown, I grant you, but tell me something," Drystan replied. "Could you have done so well if the dummy were an enemy and actively trying *not to* get hit?"

"Maybe?" I replied.

"If the head is all you have to target, then go for the head," Drystan said. "But if you have sight of the enemy's chest, aim for that. The chest is a much bigger target, and not as easy for an enemy to dodge."

I nodded and told myself to remember that.

After javelins, Drystan pointed to a basket full of peculiar, dart-like weapons about a foot long. Like arrows, these darts had feathered fletching at one end. Instead of a simple arrowhead however, a full third of the shaft was made of iron, with a weighted ball at one end of the iron piece, where the wooden shaft fitted into, and the other end coming to a nasty looking barbed tip. These were called *plumbatae*, I learned from Drystan. They were primarily used for infantry, and he acknowledged, were becoming used less and less here in Britain, but they were still useful weapons, and Arthur wanted his men to be familiar with them.

I failed horribly with this accursed weapon. I did not know where to hold it or how to throw it. I threw it into the dirt several feet in front of me. Cai burst out laughing while Drystan just cringed.

"It's easy," Drystan said. He picked up a handful of the darts in one hand. In the other, he selected one of the darts, and grabbed it lightly around the fletching, holding it out for me to see. "The weight near the tip makes these little beauties correct themselves in flight. You can throw it overhand, underhand; however you like. Beyond that, it's not much different than how you would throw a rock." He hurled his plumbata at the target, sinking it all the way up to the weighted ball. One after the other, he threw the other four. All of them stuck into the target in a tight grouping.

Drystan gave me three more plumbatae. I tried to hold it as he did, and focused hard on the straw-filled target only a few paces in front of me. One dart sailed a foot over the target before skittering off into the brush behind it. Another one flew to the right, and finally, a fourth one clipped the target.

Drystan chuckled, probably amused by the look of horror I must have had on my face over my poor performance. "Don't let that rile you up too much," he said. "Very few recruits have ever used plumbatae back home before coming here. Being bad at throwing them won't disqualify you, though it was amusing to watch, I admit. This next weapon however, you do need to be proficient with," he said, and scooped up a wooden sword from a small pile. There was also a row of shields leaning against a wall. Drystan snatched one up, then turned to face me. I walked over and did the same. I saw a row of simple helmets laid out on a table, selected one with a padded liner attached to it, and put it on. Glancing over to Drystan, I realized that he hadn't put a helmet on, himself.

He must have seen me hesitate, for he grinned at me. "Go ahead and wear it. You'll want it."

"But you don't?" I asked, surprised.

Drystan and Cai exchanged looks, and then Drystan replied, "I think I'll get on without one."

I had an ill feeling about what I was getting myself into, but I got into a fighting stance then rapped my sword against the edge of the shield to signify that I was set.

Drystan winked at me, then attacked with measured blows, circling left, then right, testing my reactions. I dodged or parried most of his attacks, but several slipped past my guard, and he wacked me hard on the arms, legs, and helmet when I was too slow, or fell for a clever feint. After a few minutes, he dropped his blade. I'd barely hit him more than once or twice. I was sweating profusely from the bout, while Drystan wasn't even breathing heavily.

"What do you think?"Drystan asked Cai.

"No great swordsman, as he said," Cai acknowledged. "But he's not likely to hurt himself or any of his *cymbrogi*, either, at least.. He's terrible with darts, but good with the spear and javelin." Then he looked at me. "How are you with the sling?"

"Good," I replied. Assuming he would want a demonstration, I pulled out a sling I happened to keep in a pouch hanging off my belt along with my dagger. Glancing around, I picked up a small rock nearby, loaded it into the leather pouch of my sling, and twirled it at my side. There was a smaller shield about ten paces away, propped up against the wall surrounding our training area. I loosed my rock, and it ricocheted off the brass boss of the shield's center with a satisfying *clang* that left a dent in it.

I looked over to see how Drystan and Cai reacted. They both nodded in approval.

"Alright, you can join the other trainees, starting tomorrow," Cai said. "Your horse can be put in the stable against the far wall, on the other side of the barracks. You can take your kit and put it in the trainees' barracks. Men of the numerus are served two hot meals a day; a light breakfast before noon, and a larger meal in the evening. At first light, tomorrow, you will form up in front of your barracks with the other trainees with whatever armor you brought with you, your sword and dagger. There's a shield and spear rack outside your barracks block if you do not have either of those items."

As the layout of the fort was so organized, all the Vicarius had to do was point me in the direction of the barracks and I had but to follow the street out towards the wall, where rows upon rows of stone buildings in various states of disrepair stood. I shook my head, marveling at the enormous number of Roman soldiers that must have been garrisoned here, to require so many barracks. I kept walking, and soon found the trainees barracks. It wasn't hard. It was one of the only buildings in the immediate area that was fully intact, if not entirely of stone, and had a straw roof.

The barracks designated for the trainees was one of the closest to the training area and the corral. The building was not as nice as the villa I grew up in, but it was as good as the homes in most villages. The lower portion of the building was stone, but the rest was wattle and daub. It was about twenty by fifty feet, and had a dirt floor, with a thatched roof. A couple stools were set up outside against the wall, under the overhanging eave. Inside was dark; there were only two small windows built into the walls, on the short walls to the left and right of the entrance. In the very middle of the building was a small fire pit, and the ceiling above it was black from the smoke of hundreds of fires. On both sides of the firepit were six simple wooden bed frames, lashed together with rope, which also provided the woven netting to support the mattress, which was a large, linen sack, that I would need to stuff full of straw later. There was just enough room under the bed frames to store my belongings. There were also a few more stools inside, along with two small tables. A small wooden box was tucked away in one corner where clay cups, plates, and the like were stored, and a weapon rack against one wall that contained several spears and javelins. A neat row of large, oval shields also lined the wall, and several plumbata laid in a pile near the weapons rack. I picked an empty one, shoved my gear under the bed, and then introduced myself to the group.

There were seven others that shared the barracks with me. They'd all joined within the past month, and they gathered around to introduce themselves after I made my way to the barracks. Two red-haired brothers named Rhun and Ewan came from the southern region of Dyfed. They had a telltale Gaelic accent, which wasn't surprising given the recent, if somewhat brief history Dyfed had as a Gaelic colony. The brothers had been here the longest and had already done a bit of training, they told us. Besides them were Bran, Madog, from the surrounding region of Gwent, and Dewi, a short, stocky twenty-year old with light blonde hair who came from Powys, to the north of us. Then there was Tutwal, a muscular man about Rhun's age. His people were the Dobunni tribe, and lived in the southwest region of Ergyng, dangerously close to the Saxon territory. The last to introduce himself was a fellow with dirty blonde hair and an odd name, Gilbert. At sixteen, I was the youngest, while Rhun was the oldest among us at twenty-two years old. Rhun was the only one of us with any facial hair- he had a short beard that was growing in quite nicely, which I admit I envied just a bit.

When Gilbert introduced himself, I picked up an unfamiliar accent in his speech.

"Gilbert?" I asked, curiously. What sort of name is that?

"It's an eastern name," he shrugged. "You can call me 'Gib' if you want. It's what my family often calls me."

"Eastern?" Madog chuckled. "That's one way of putting it. Tell him how *far* east."

"It's Frisian," Gilbert answered, looking a little uncomfortable.

"Isn't that in Germania?" I asked.

"He's a Saxon," Dewi confirmed, with a look of disdain.

I started at that, and studied Gilbert anew. A Saxon? Here? Would Arthur really allow Saxons into the Red Dragons? My heart began beating faster, and I felt my hands twitch as anger built up inside me.

"No. I'm a cymbrog, just like you!" Gilbert protested. Clearly this was an argument these two had had more than once since their arrival here. "So was my father. My grandfather came from Frisia. He settled our family in Caer Badon."

"Saxon, Frisian. Same thing. You're no cymbrog. You're a trespasser," sneered Dewi.

I nodded, standing beside Dewi. To me it made no difference. Saxons, Frisians. Jutes. Angles. They were all Germanic invaders.

"Lumping Frisians in with Saxons is about the same as if I said there was no difference between Britons and Picts or Scoti," Gilbert growled.

Dewi jumped off his seat and stood over Gilbert, glaring at him for that remark. Gilbert stood up as well, looking down at the shorter youth. That made me notice how everyone, in fact, was taller than Dewi.

"My brother was killed by a Saxon dog!" I spat.

"Sorry to hear that," Gilbert said. "Again, I'm not Saxon! Neither I, nor my family had anything to do with that. I was born here! As was my father! And my grandfather came here from Frisia to join the *foederati*, soldiers sworn to serve King Vortigern along the eastern shore forts in exchange for land. Land we paid for with our blood, fighting against raiders and pirates. We *earned* the right to be here," Gilbert said, firmly.

"Vortigern," Madog scoffed. "Saying you earned the right to be here because your grandfather swore an oath to that Saxon lapdog will earn you no respect here."

"How about the fact that I'm here, joining Arthur's cavalry, same as you?" Gilbert shot back. "Doesn't that earn some respect?"

"It does with me," Rhun chimed in, moving to stand beside Gilbert. "I don't know about you," he said, staring at Dewi and I, "but my own family is Gaelic. For that matter, my home in Dyfed has had long ties with the Gaels of Hibernia. So if Gilbert has no right to be here, then I would say neither do my brother and I. Yet here we are, preparing to help defend our homeland against invaders, the same as every other man present. If being born in Britain, and more importantly, the willingness to stand and fight in her defense means nothing to you, then just how *do* you decide who deserves to be here?"

That gave me pause. He made a good point. My own family was certainly native to Britain, being descendants of the Ordovices tribe. The Ordovices had been one of the tribes that had never accepted Roman rule and been all but exterminated for it, but I knew that many families were mixed Roman, and even Gaelic stock. Once, the Romans had been the invaders. The Gaels still were, at times. How long did a person or family have to live in a land before they could justify claiming to be a native of it? Maybe, as Rhun and Gilbert said, simply aligning with the values and interests of that land, and being willing to shed blood in its defense, was enough. However conflicted I now felt, Gilbert's argument had no effect on Dewi.

"Fah!" Dewi grunted. "Guess we'll see how well you do," he said. "I wonder what you'll do when you're called upon to fight your fellow Saxons?"

"They're not my fellow anything," Gilbert snarled, stepping closer to Dewi. "But if you want to know how well I'll do in a fight, you're welcome to find out, right now!" He shoved the short youth backward. I lunged forward, as did Dewi, ready to jump the Frisian.

Quick as could be, Rhun, the oldest and biggest of us, jumped up and pushed us apart. "Hey now! We don't need you two to fight here in our barracks! You want to risk being thrown out of the Red Dragons before you've even been sworn in? I'm sure you'll have plenty of opportunity to settle this in training, *later*," he stressed.

"So who are your people?" I asked Dewi, curiously. "Mine were Ordovices."

"I'm Cornovii," Dewi responded proudly.

I cocked an eyebrow at him. "Ah. A well-known tribe," I acknowledged.

Dewi smiled proudly, until I continued.

"The Cornovii raised an entire auxiliary unit for the Romans quite a while back, and were stationed here in Britain, as I recall."

"So? Lots of tribes eventually supplied recruits for the Romans," Dewi shrugged. "Britain was part of the Empire for over three hundred years."

"So the auxiliaries from your tribe were the only ones allowed to remain in Britain. Most were deployed to other parts of the Empire."

"What are you implying?" Dewi asked me, with narrowing eyes.

I shrugged. "Nothing much. Just seems a bit odd is all. The Romans must have really trusted that Cornovii cohort to put their loyalty to Rome above that of their kin, is all."

"Oh, sod off," Dewi growled, but he dropped the subject after that.

Tensions eased, and we got to talking about what the earlier arrivals had been taught so far, how they liked it at Caer Lleon, and things of that nature until finally, a woman walked by the street shouting that supper was ready. We jumped up off our seats where we had all been lounging, grabbed our own cups and plates from the storage box, and made our way down the street, joining several other villagers along the way.

"Some of Arthur's men live here with their families," Rhun explained as we walked. "Particularly the single men, or men with families who just prefer living here as opposed to wherever they originally came from. The women gather at the courtyard and they all contribute food for the meals, make and serve the meals, and when the food is done, a few of them walk down the streets through the housing areas and yell at us to come get food. From that point, food is usually available for a couple hours before it's all eaten and the women go home."

"I can't imagine my own mother being willing to help make food for hundreds of men," I chuckled. Thinking back, I'm not sure I'd ever seen my mother do much cooking. We had a servant who prepared most of our meals. The only times I could recall ever seeing my mother get involved were if we were having a feast and the servant needed help.

"Then your mother wouldn't be given housing inside the fort," Dewi said. "The women aren't forced to cooperate, so to speak, but it's expected of them if they're going to be given space for a house inside the fort's walls. Anyway, it's not like they all help with every meal. They have some sort of rotation worked out amongst themselves. Some women make meals some of the time, some do it other times. I don't know how they sort it out, that's between them," he added with a shrug.

Once again, I found myself walking past the statue of Vespasian and into a large courtyard where dozens of Arthur's men, with their wives and children, were sitting down to eat. Off to one side, long tables full of food were arrayed in front of a large cooking fire. Several pots were being cooked over it. A dozen women worked to keep the fire going, stirring stew, turning spits of meat, and keeping the platters on the tables full of food for us to serve ourselves from. The usual staples such as large loaves of bread and pots full of porridge were available. Platters with lush, green cabbage, and purple carrots were on hand, along with large bowls of apples and nuts. Barrels of water and ale were also available to go with the meal.

Stomach growling, I loaded up my plate, and was about to walk over to the other side of the courtyard where everyone was eating, but when I turned around I nearly bumped into a thin old man, about the same height as myself. His long red hair was thinning and streaked with white, and looked quite unruly. He grew an unusually long beard and mustache as well, also more white than coppery red. The man wore a long, rough, dark blue tunic that seemed too big for him. I stared at him a moment, unsure what to make of him. Was he a beggar? Someone's servant? Before I could say anything, the old man, who scowled at me, spoke first.

"Watch yourself, child! You nearly made me spill my meal!" His voice was surprisingly deep, with a slight edge to it. I glanced down, perplexed when I saw only a large horn of what smelled like mead.

"Your- your meal, sir?" I asked. I addressed him as sir purely out of respect for his age. Although his hair and clothing suggested a man of lower status, his bearing suggested otherwise.

The man looked down, then up at me through thick, bushy eyebrows. He turned to a woman at his side. She looked to be in her late forties, though she was still beautiful, with large eyes, long dark hair and a voluptuous figure. "Do you suppose this child is simple, Nimue?" He asked her, then he turned back to me before she had a chance to react.

"You heard me. Yes! My meal! A fine, thin porridge with honey and hops."

"It's mead, though," I stuttered, still confused.

The man rolled his eyes. My friends, sitting at the table within earshot, snickered at my discomfort.

"Sounds like fine porridge, to me," Gilbert called out. "One my own father consumed at least as often as anything else," he added with a chuckle.

The old man winked at Gilbert. "A man of good taste, no doubt. Your friend here is a little slow, isn't he," he stated, rather than asked.

Gilbert grinned. "He certainly can be," he agreed.

"Only sometimes," I acknowledged weakly, then I shot Gilbert an angry glance. I really wanted to punch him, but this was neither the time nor the place. Instead, I focused back on the peculiar old man in front of me.

"And who might you be?" I asked him.

"I am Myrddin, of Caer Fyrddin," the man said. "And this is Lady Nimue."

"A pleasure, my lady," I said, bowing to her. She smiled and nodded at me.

"You're Myrddin? The bard, Myrddin the Wi-" Dewi exclaimed in surprise, cutting himself off at the last second.

Myrddin shot him a bemused glance, one eyebrow raised. "Myrddin the Wild? Yes. I am. Bard, sage, healer ... I've even been called a magician from time to time. Particularly by the ladies." He grinned and threw me a wink. The woman beside him snorted and rolled her eyes. "Just don't ever call me late for supper!" he said. "And who might you be? One of Arthur's lads, I presume?"

"I'm Peredur, of Caer Gurcoc, and yes, sir," I replied.

Myrddin took a drink from his horn and looked me up and down. "Finish your training yet? You look young."

"I've just arrived," I answered. "I begin training tomorrow."

"Ah. Well, good fortune to you," he said and strolled away, laughing at something the woman accompanying him said.

"So Arthur keeps a bard here at Caer Lleon?" I asked the other recruits when I sat down.

"He was being modest," Rhun said. "He's less a bard and more like one of the wisest men in Britain, who can *also* sing, and tell jokes and stories, and probably play just about any instrument capable of producing sound. As he said, he's also a healer."

"He probably speaks every language you've ever heard of and then some," Gilbert added.

"A bit of a drunk, too, I guess," I mentioned.

"Maybe," Gilbert shrugged. "I've heard a bit about him too. He's had a tough life. Not sure what happened but the story is he went mad for a while and lived like a wild man in the woods up north. That's why he's known as 'Myrddin the Wild'. Usually though, it's not something people call him to his face," Gilbert added, glaring at Dewi, who only shrugged in response.

Once we were done eating, we took our cups and bowls down to the river, washed up, then returned to our barracks in time to prepare our weapons and armor for the next morning. All seven of us had padded shirts of either thick wool or layered, quilted linen. These worked well in combination with mail or other, heavier armor. They were commonly worn by themselves too, and would offer protection against slashing attacks, and even some protection from arrows and sling shot. Only Dewi and Gilbert had to rely on just this, however. The rest of us had mail and all had helmets of similar design- open faced, with smooth, round crowns that included wide, flaring cheek guards.

Each of us had at least one spear, and a shield. These were center-grip shields with a single handle in the middle, which was protected by a boss, a semi-dome shaped bit of iron or brass that protected our shield hand a bit better, as well as provided the shield with a bit of offensive capability; there's nothing like smashing an enemy in the face with that shield boss to daze them a bit before you launch a second attack with your sword or spear.

We all had daggers and swords of our own, save for Gilbert, whose blade was too short to easily be classified as a sword but was double the length of most daggers. He carried a *seax*, the infamous signature weapon of the Germanic Angles, Jutes, Frisians, and Saxons, from which the Saxon people derived their name. It was a nasty-looking weapon, nearly twenty inches long from blade tip to hilt, and was single-edged, with the dull spine of the blade curving forward slightly towards the tip, making it look just a bit like a cleaver, but a cleaver that could also be used to stab.

Less than thirty years ago, the treacherous Jute warlord Hengist had taken advantage of the seax's ambiguity between being a utensil and a weapon by bringing their blades to a feast held by Vortigern that had been intended to end the long war between Britons and Saxons. Instead, Hengist and his men slaughtered hundreds of Vortigern's nobles, paving the way for the Saxons to seize an enormous amount of land in southeast Britain. From then on, to Britons, the seax became a tangible symbol of Saxon deceit and barbarity. I admit, seeing Gilbert casually wearing and handling his own seax angered me a bit. From the way the others looked at him, I know I wasn't alone.

As we cleaned and inspected our armor and equipment, Rhun explained the running of the numerus a bit to me.

"It's pretty simple, really," Rhun said. "The commander, or Tribune, of our numerus is Arthur, of course. You met Cai, his Vicarius, and second in command. Word is that Cai and Arthur are brothers, or childhood friends or something. Castellan Bedwyr manages the day to day running of the fort. The Castellan also has a lot of influence in the village outside of the fort. Below those three are the decurions, the officers who lead groups of about thirty men, called turmae. Arthur, Bedwyr, and Cai also have their own turmae though. Anyway, below the decurions are duplarii."

"Any others?" I asked as I ran a lightly oiled rag along my spatha's blade.

Rhun shrugged. "Informally, there are the contubernia, or small section of five to ten troopers who share a barracks together, or a tent, when we're in the field."

Rhun gestured around us. "That's us. And the most senior man of these tentmates are called a decanus. That's what I am, but neither the contubernium nor the decanus are formal elements, unlike the turmae. They're just..." Rhun shrugged, struggling to explain. "We exist for convenience. Like if the decurion or his duplarius needs a few men to assign to guard duty. The easiest way to accomplish that is for them to snag up one of their two or three decani and have them task a contubernium for that detail."

I nodded my understanding, and we finished preparing our equipment for the morning. The sun was nearly set, so we were expected to go to bed shortly. I had one extra task to do: I had to take my mattress out to the stables, find the stalls where the fresh hay and straw were baled, and stuff it. Gilbert volunteered to come help me.

"Why in the name of the Virgin would you do that?" I asked, suspiciously.

"Gives me a chance to take one last stroll before bedding down," Gilbert replied. "And maybe a chance for you to see that I am not your enemy. And if you can't see that," he smiled suddenly, though it was not a friendly one. "Well, we could always settle your issue with me out at the stables."

We walked down the stables in silence. Gilbert and I each filled a sack of hay, and we walked back. As Gilbert handed me the sack of straw he'd filled, I paused.

"Thank you for your help, Fri- Gilbert," I said, feeling awkward.

Gilbert gave me a wry smile. "Don't mention it."

I took the sack from him, made my mattress, and before long, my fellow trainees and I were sound asleep.

# Chapter Three

Training began the next morning, as the sun was only just beginning to show on the horizon. Our instructor introduced himself as Decurion Caradoc, a lean man of average height in his prime. He had dirty blond hair and a patch of beard on his chin, streaked with gray. The decurion started off by inspecting our kit, making sure we had everything, that it was in good shape, and that our weapons were sharp, and clean. Dewi's helmet was deemed unfit for service, and he was told to either get it fixed or replaced within the week, or be given extra duty, cutting firewood, digging cesspits when needed, and that kind of work.

"You can't do that to me, I'm the son of Lord-" Dewi tried to protest.

Caradoc cut him off with a harsh laugh. "Boy," he said. "Every man here is the son of some lord, ship's master, or the like. A couple are even princes. Otherwise you wouldn't have been able to afford that small fortune in weapons and armor. Your heritage means *nothing,* here. So get that helmet fixed!"

Dewi stared at Caradoc, who calmly stared back, as though daring the youth to argue some more. Dewi kept his mouth shut, and looked down. Caradoc continued on with his inspection.

We did physical training for the next two hours, which started with a long run around the perimeter of the fort, then pairing off to wrestle. I was unlucky and got Rhun, who beat me soundly. I'm not sure which annoyed me more whenever I had to train with Rhun, his constantly beating me, or the fact that he was so friendly while doing it! Once for example, I began our match by immediately lunging for his leg, in order to bring him down to the ground. He was faster though, and spun around behind me. Before I had time to think, the man had his legs wrapped around my hips and his arms snaked around my neck. Even as he started to choke me out, he was complimenting me!

"Good try for my leg," he said, in a casual voice while I struggled to break his hold. "Your technique looked good. I was just a bit faster is all."

Of course, I was unable to reply, given that I was gasping for breath. A moment later, I tapped his arm, and he released me and then helped me to my feet.

There was a short halt while we went to the dining hall and ate breakfast, then Decurion Caradoc had us back at it, with weapons training. We practiced with slings, bows, and javelins. Only Rhun and his brother, Ewan, were better at javelins than I. As it happened, with spears at least, I could and did best all the other lads in my section. My last match was against Dewi. Our "spears" were of course simply long staves with the ends wrapped in some cloth. He kept making the same thrusts at me, and always at my chest or stomach. It became too easy for me to sidestep or knock his spear out of alignment with me, then counter. Inspired a bit by Rhun, I pointed this out to Dewi.

"I know what I'm doing," he grunted, then he varied up his attack by executing two quick thrusts, one towards my stomach and the second toward my face.

I sidestepped and smacked the end of my staff against the back of his knee. When his leg buckled, I followed that up with a hard thrust to his chest. The thickset youth stumbled backwards and fell. I offered my hand to him, but he ignored it, giving me a glare as he stood up and dusted himself off.

Finally, the Decurion had us go at each other with swords. We trained the longest with this weapon. First we went through various forms of thrusts, parries, and other sword drills, then we took a quick water break. When our break was over, Decurion Caradoc had us pair up and fight each other, rotating partners periodically. It wasn't long before the match all of us had been anticipating happened. Gilbert faced off with Dewi, and I knew the instant the two squared up that this was going to get interesting.

Both were armed with heavy wooden swords, as we all were, and large, round shields. They circled a few times, sizing each other up. Gilbert made a quick step at Dewi, as though to lunge. The short Cornovii jumped back, raising his shield. Gilbert smiled slightly and kept circling.

"You two going to dance around in circles all day? Somebody do something," Caradoc grunted, impatiently watching the two. The other two pairs were already busy exchanging blows. In response, Dewi yelled, and chopped at Gilbert with his sword. The taller Frisian easily raised his shield and swatted the blow aside, thrusting his own sword at Dewi in the same motion, trying to make use of his longer reach. Dewi however, weighed more, and he braced himself, taking the hit on his shield. It was Gilbert who staggered back, and the shorter youth immediately followed up with a hard punch to the Frisian's chest with his shield's boss. Gilbert was knocked to the ground, and lost the grip on his own shield. He immediately rolled to one side, spun, and got to his feet, though Dewi stomped down hard on his shield, preventing Gilbert from scooping it back up.

Without thinking, I took a couple steps toward the two, holding out my own shield for the Frisian, but Caradoc stepped between us and shook his head. There would be no interference, no outside help.

"No shield for you, Saxon," Dewi sneered as he stalked towards Gilbert, putting himself between Gilbert and his shield.

"I don't need one, *wealh*," Gilbert shot back.

The rest of us stopped even trying to focus on our own bouts upon hearing that particular slur. My own hands instantly balled up in fists at Gilbert's use of that insult and I was suddenly glad Caradoc had prevented me from giving him my shield. I respected the Frisian's courage, but for him to use that term... "Wealh" was a term the Saxons had been using with increasing regularity over the past several years to refer to us native Britons. Ironically, it basically means "outsider". It was their way of essentially saying that Britain itself was *their* land now. Not ours. Even worse, the term was also used interchangeably to mean "slave". It had a predictable response from Dewi.

The blond Cornovii shouted in rage and swung his wooden sword wildly at Gilbert, slashing left, right, and every which way. One slash clipped his helmet, sending if flying towards Bran, who yelped and raised his shield reflexively. Gilbert bobbed and weaved and parried Dewi's attacks. Then, the moment Dewi let up, the taller Frisian countered. Trying again to make use of his height advantage over the shorter youth, he made a series of rapid, downward angled thrusts, which forced the blond youth to raise his shield to defend against. With Dewi blinded by his own shield, he wasn't able to see Gilbert dive at his legs, hook his sword behind the Cornovii's heels, and knock him to the ground.

The heavier youth landed hard on his back with a loud "*Oof!*" as he lost his wind. Gilbert scrambled on top of Dewi, who swung his sword up at Gilbert's head. Gilbert leaned back, dodging the swing, then using his left hand, he pinned Dewi's sword arm to the ground, trapping it awkwardly against his chest. The Frisian pointed the tip of his own sword against Dewi's exposed left armpit.

"Yield!" Gilbert barked.

Dewi growled something unintelligible and kept struggling. Gilbert dug the tip of his sword into the stocky youth's armpit a little. Dewi squirmed, and his face went from angry, to frightened.

"Alright, I surrender!" he conceded.

"Am I Saxon, or a cymbrog?" Gilbert demanded.

Dewi pressed his lips together defiantly. "You just called me a wealh!" he snarled.

Gilbert grinned. "To get you riled up. And you've been calling me 'Saxon' all this time. Fair is fair."

He tapped Dewi's chest with his wooden sword. "Now," he said again, "Am I Saxon, or a cymbrog?"

Then with a glance to Caradoc, who looked down at him and just shrugged, Dewi sighed. "You're a fellow countryman," he acknowledged.

Gilbert flashed a grin, and promptly released Dewi's arm as he stood up. Then he reached down, holding his hand out to the Cornoviii, but the stocky youth ignored it, rolled over onto his stomach, and got up.

"Are you girls done squabbling now?" Caradoc asked dryly.

Dewi glowered over at Gilbert as he dusted himself off, then nodded up at Caradoc. Gilbert also nodded, still smiling.

"Great. Now, let's continue training. Back to ranged weaponry." Caradoc walked us over to the ruin where the straw dummies were lined up. At the spot where we were to throw from were a row of wicker baskets. He nudged the lid off one of them for us to see the contents.

"We'll start with plumbatae," he said, grinning at me. Clearly, Bedwyr and or Cai had told Caradoc of my particular weakness. I sighed, and walked over to the basket.

We practiced throwing darts for an hour, before Caradoc called an end to my misery.

"Good work today, lads," he said. "Bran, you're a natural with those darts!" He turned to me. "Peredur ...." he shook his head. "Make sure you practice throwing the plumbata on your own time, in the evenings."

"Yes, sir," I acknowledged, feeling mightily embarrassed.

"You lads did well, for your first day," our Decurion told us, then added with a smirk, "You were almost as good as I'd expect the wives here in the fort to do. Anyway, it's almost supper time. Go wash up down at the river. Clean off your kit, then go eat. Expect the next few weeks to go like today has. Peredur, don't forget to go and retrieve the darts you threw over the wall."

"Yes, sir," I said.

Dewi raised his hand. "Yes, Dewi?" Caradoc asked.

"Sir, we're *cavalry*, right? Shouldn't we be training on horseback?"

"Oh you will," Caradoc assured. "But you need to be able to walk, before you can run." And with that he dismissed us for the night.

*****

The next morning brought more pain than I think I had ever experienced in my life. Every muscle in my body hurt. From the muffled groans of my tentmates, I wasn't the only one. As Caradoc had promised, the next day was conducted the same as the first. As was the day after that. After a week of this, Dewi quit. We all saw it coming. He was the slowest of us and the weakest, the first to complain about being hungry, thirsty, or cold.

"I can't deal with these insufferable conditions!" he finally gasped while we jogged the perimeter of the fort, our noses red and runny from the morning chill as our breath came out in thick puffs of warm air. It was now late in the fall, and the mornings and evenings were getting distinctly colder and colder. "If *this* is what being in Arthur's cavalry means, I want none of it!" And with that, he had abruptly stopped running, turned, and returned to our barracks.

"God's speed," said Gilbert with a wave as we left him behind and kept running. By the time we returned, his things were gone. This cycle continued for three more long weeks. Running, sparring, weapons training. In the evenings, Rhun helped me work with the plumbatae. I got to the point where I could at least impale the straw target with one of those darts from twenty, then thirty feet away, consistently. My accuracy still left something to be desired, though.

We learned to fight as individuals and in formation. The first day we were introduced to that, Caradoc showed up at dawn, as usual, but with him came what looked like a full turma, armed with tall spears and shields. As they got closer, we realized that the people with him were boys!

"Lads," he said. "Arthur likes having every male capable of holding a weapon to know the basics of fighting in formation, in case this fort ever gets attacked."

"Not the women?" Gilbert asked. "In Frisia, and other parts of Germania, it's not unusual for the village women to pick up a spear and fight, too, if a situation gets desperate enough."

"Our women don't fight," Caradoc said. "Not because they *can't*, but because in the event that Caer Lleon is ever besieged, there will be more tasks needing done than just fighting. Their role in a fight at the fort would be to tend to the wounded, watch out for fires starting inside the fort, and to bring us water as we man the walls. Tasks just as important as the fighting itself."

"So this morning will be a bit of a 'killing two birds with one stone' sort of situation. These boys need refresher training on fighting in a shield wall, and you lads definitely need to learn it. Most of them have trained with previous recruits. So don't take this training, or them, lightly." We nodded.

Decurion Caradoc continued, "We're cavalry, which means much more often than not, we will be expected to flank and break Saxon shield wall formations by charging into them from the side or rear while infantry fight them in the front. Nonetheless, there are times when the ground may be unsuitable for a charge, or even the use of horses, period. Ideally, this is where Tribune Arthur would summon additional infantry support from the nearby regions, but in a pinch, he expects us to be more than capable of getting our rumps out of the saddle and fight in shield walls as effectively and with as much discipline as any unit of foot soldiers."

Caradoc paused, casually jammed his little finger into his nostril, then flicked his hand away. Rhun and Ewan sniggered.

The Decurion glanced at them, and scowled. "This is serious stuff," he said. "The Red Dragons fought in a shield wall only a few years ago, fighting Saxons over in the boglands around the River Bassus. The crafty dogs thought they'd have the advantage of us if we had to fight them dismounted."

Caradoc smirked. "Arthur showed them otherwise."

He gestured to the group of boys, who came over to stand by the decurion.

"The essence of the shield wall is pretty straightforward," Caradoc continued. "We form up into at least two ranks deep, close enough together so that our shields form an unbroken, wooden wall. The first rank, or line, presents their shield directly to their front, and the men behind them raise their shields, ready to protect against arrows, rocks, and attacks from spears, axes, and the like once the formation gets stuck in. The spears of the first two ranks will be presented towards the enemy, while any further ranks will either continue to throw javelins or plumbatae over the heads of their cymbrogi to soften up the enemy as they advance. Ideally, a shield wall is a defensive formation, though men can be taught to march towards the enemy in tight formation; and you will."

He turned to the boys and barked, "Shield wall, three deep!" The boys sprang into action like a disturbed beehive as they transformed from an unformed group into a rectangular block, three ranks deep, with about eight boys standing shoulder to shoulder in each rank. He walked down the line, making adjustments, scooting a boy over here, raising somebody's shield there, until he got to the end, and turned to us.

"This is what you need to be able to do, in moments if need be," he said. We spent the rest of the day practicing getting into shield wall formation. We did it while starting in a column, lined up on the road, and immediately after a water break while everyone was sitting down, resting.

Caradoc had us practice for a while with long staves rather than metal-tipped spears, so we didn't accidentally hurt each other. Then we formed up into two small shield walls and, without even those staves, attempted to push the other team's shield wall apart with just our weight, and open-handed strikes at our opponents. Caradoc allowed us to slap each other, at least.

My group advanced slowly, with all of us constantly glancing around to make sure we were in line with one another. Rhun was on my left, Madog on my right.

"Stay together, cymbrogi!" Rhun yelled at us.

We inched forward, just as the other shield wall was advancing at us. My heart pounded in my chest with excitement, and I gripped the handle of my shield tightly with anticipation.

"Ready.... now!" Rhun called out. We rushed at the other group for the last several feet, hoping to use that spurt of momentum to knock them down. That was the trick to the shield wall, especially when attacking. We had to stay side by side, so that our shields, held tightly to our chests, could overlap, but we also wanted to use the weight of our formation, and momentum of a short range charge to try and disorient the other group, and break up their shield wall. They, of course, were doing the same thing to us. A youth not much smaller than me slammed his shield into mine, and immediately I felt the press of not only my opponent in front of me, but his two companions behind him, and my two companions behind me. I reached across my shield and beat at his helmeted head with my gloved hand, while warding off his attempts to do the same thing.

All across the line was like this. The lines held, though they shifted this way and that.

"This will give you some idea what it will look like if and when you have to do this against the Saxons," Decurion Caradoc called out loudly so as to be heard over our shouts and the clatter of shields being smashed into each other.

Finally, after several minutes of constant straining, a couple of their number near one end of the formation took a gamble and, rather than just continue to push against their fellows in front, they scooted around, and charged into our lads, slamming their shields into them. Without the weight of the boys behind him, our teammate on the end was immediately knocked over by the boys he had been pushing against. This caused a ripple effect, and within moments, my team's whole formation was getting knocked over and piled on with whole-hearted enthusiasm from the boys in the other team.

"And that is why flank attacks are so effective against formations," Caradoc said with satisfaction. "Good job, lads," he told the other team. "You couldn't push through these boys' formation head-on, so you rolled them up from the side. You took a gamble, and it paid off."

I felt dampness around my nose, and when I felt it, I realized that my nose was bleeding a bit.

"Awww, did we hurt you boys too much?" one of the lads from the other group called out, noticing my blood as well.

"Not as much as I'll hurt you if you all want another bout!" I snapped.

Boys from the other boys left, but continued on their way. I was ready to go after them, and force them into a rematch, but felt a hand on my shoulder. I spun around and saw Rhun.

"Forget them," he said. "They may be younger, but they've done this before. Don't take it personally."

I grunted, not particularly wanting to let them go, but Rhun was our decanus, and more than that, I genuinely respected him, so I did as he suggested.

We continued training until supper, by which time we were thoroughly exhausted.

# Chapter Four

Tutwal was the next of us to quit. He'd received word that his home in Ergyng had been raided. His older brother was killed and his family's livestock had been stolen. Now he was needed at home. We said goodbye to him and wished him well. His departure served as a grim reminder to me, and likely my companions, regarding just how tense the situation was between Britons and Saxons, especially in the midlands.

We trained hard every day, nearly all day it seemed, except on Dies Solis, the Sun's Day. As was customary in the Christian lands of Britain, Arthur was adamant that Caer Lleon observe the Lord's day, so nobody worked or trained that day if it could be helped. Even the meals were simpler on the Sun's Day to reduce the time spent cooking for the women. This allowed everyone the opportunity to rest, play games, and socialize, after morning mass of course.

The fort itself offered very little for us to do, as all of the structures within it were dedicated to either a military function or housing for the officers and their families. So after mass, we agreed to visit the village outside the walls to see what fun there was to be had there. All of us except for Bran, who actually opted to stay behind and talk with the priest about religious matters.

As we passed some of the villagers, Gilbert drew several looks, ranging from curious to outright hostile. I glanced over and saw that he was wearing his seax.

"Gib, are you trying to start a fight, wearing that, here?" I asked.

Gilbert shrugged. "You all wear your daggers. I don't see a problem with me wearing mine."

"It's not quite the same thing," Rhun muttered.

"We should go down to the river. We could cut some poles and go fishing," Ewan offered.

"Fishing? We have servants and slaves who can do that," Madog said.

Madog's family was the wealthiest in our group by far. He even claimed to be related to the king of Gwent.

As we talked, we strolled through the village's main street. At one shop, we admired some brooches decorated with gold and silver. At another, we examined well-crafted belts, boots, and other leather goods. The cobbler saw us looking at his wares and began extolling the quality of his wares.

"Come, come! Try these on! I guarantee you've never worn better," the man insisted. "Arthur himself gets his shoes here!"

We laughed and kept walking, seeing an alehouse not too far away. It was a small, modest-looking building, and the only thing that gave it away as a drinking establishment was the broom hung above the doorway, a customary sign in Britain. We were just discussing whether to go in or not when a trio of young ladies walking down the same street caught our eyes, coming from the opposite direction. A slave or servant, carrying a large wicker case, walked silently behind them.

"Good morning, ladies," Madog called out, grinning broadly.

The three glanced at us but acted like they meant to pass us by.

"Pardon us," Rhun tried. "We're new in this fair town, here to fight in Arthur's cavalry."

The girls stopped and smiled at him, then looked at each other and giggled. Of course they responded to Rhun, I thought. He had that "tall, dark, and handsome" look that girls all seem to love for some inexplicable reason. Moments later, Rhun, Madog, and Ewan were chatting away with them.

"Wait, how did we just become invisible?" I asked Gilbert.

"Don't get worked up over it," Gilbert muttered to me. "See the tall one with the blond hair?"

I nodded. "Of course! She's gorgeous!"

"And I've seen her before. At the fort," Gilbert said in the same, low voice. "Do you know who that is?"

"I do not," I said.

"That's Bedwyr's daughter!"

"Her?" I asked, surprised and disappointed. "You're sure?"

"Sure enough that I'd rather we weren't seen talking to her out here," Gilbert answered, glancing around warily as though he expected the castellan to appear at any moment, which was entirely possible, I concluded.

We followed the group, who were continuing down the street, still chatting away. The girl Gilbert pointed out as Castellan Bedwyr's daughter was laughing at some story Rhun was telling her. At one point she boldly put her hand on his arm. Alarmed, I glanced at Gilbert, who clearly saw it too.

"Ooh, this could end badly," I said.

As though I'd just cursed us, almost no sooner had I said this than Gilbert looked down the street and asked, "Uh, where did they just go?"

"What do you mean?" I asked, startled. "They're right ..." I looked down the street where the group had just been walking through the busy street. They were gone!

"Bollocks," I swore. "They can't have gone far. Let's split up and find them. The last thing we need is having Rhun piss off the Castellan for sullying his daughter's reputation."

We continued on the street we'd been on, then took a right at the first street we found going that way. If only this town wasn't so big, I fumed. There must be at least three hundred people out here, all out and about, shopping and gossiping and doing what villagers do on a Sun's Day when no work needed to be done. Just our luck!

The two of us spent an hour, methodically going up each and every street, poking our heads into the public buildings, and even asking street vendors. Rhun and the group may as well have vanished. We did however, begin to get

59

a clearer picture of the situation, though that didn't make us feel any better. Apparently, it wasn't uncommon for Bedwyr's daughter to be seen socializing with men around town.

"Downright shameful," one woman said disapprovingly. "She's at least fifteen! If Lord Bedwyr doesn't marry her off soon, and she keeps being so bold with the lads, he'll never find a suitable husband for her!"

We kept looking, and soon the crowded market gave way to individual homes surrounded by fences that contained the family's chickens, pigs, and the like. Eventually we came to an older section of the village on the outskirts. The buildings were old, broken stone, and layed out in the organized Roman manner. Looking around, we saw a few people that seemed to be living in some of the buildings, but they were clearly the poorer people. A few old men and women with missing or deformed limbs sat around, doing nothing much. Here and there a pair of small children ran by, wearing rags or nothing at all.

"Let's go back," Gilbert advised in a low tone, glancing around. "There's now way our friends ended up here."

"Agreed," I said, feeling a mix of pity and apprehension as I glanced around at the residents of this area. We had just turned around and begun to head back to the village when a voice spoke, off to our left.

"Well, would you look at that, lads. A Saxon dog, right here in our own village. And a lordling."

Gilbert and I slowly turned. There were three teens, dirty and dressed in rags, staring at us with open hostility. The biggest of them, with shoulder-length black hair, carried a stout cudgel in his hands. A second youth, nearly as big, had a quarterstaff. His face was covered in freckles and he had reddish-brown hair.

"Apologies if we've disturbed you," I said. "We were just leaving."

"Go ahead," the boy with the cudgel said with a smirk. I guessed he was the leader. "We'll just have your belt pouches, daggers, and those fine shoes you're wearing."

"Bollocks to that," Gilbert grunted. I shot him an annoyed look. The last thing I figured we should do was antagonize these three. I figured our chances weren't terrible if we had to fight them, but who knew if they had more friends in the area. This was their home, after all.

"Give us what we want, or we take them off you, after we've knocked some sense into you," the boy with the cudgel growled. He slapped the stout cudgel against his open palm.

"We were just going to get some food," I said, making a last effort at avoiding a fight. Why don't you three join us? I'll pay."

The third member of the group was small, looked about fourteen, and had no visible weapon. He looked intrigued by the offer, and glanced up at their black-haired leader, but the big youth with the cudgel was eyeing me up and down, no doubt recognizing the good quality of my clothing and dagger.

"Bah! With everything they're carrying, we could treat ourselves to enough food to last a month! And I want that seax."

"Come and take it," Gilbert growled.

The leader shrugged. "Get them, lads!" He snarled, and stepped forward, raising his cudgel.

I started to raise my hands to defend myself, but Gilbert reacted first. With a shout, he lunged forward and grabbed the leader's cudgel before he'd barely raised it and punched him squarely in the nose. The youth staggered back, and used the space to swing his cudgel at Gilbert, who tucked his arm against his side to protect his ribs, and absorbed the blow, then struck the leader again.

The lad with the quarterstaff yelled, and brought the weapon up to swing at me. His mistake. He should have thrust with it. Instead, he signaled his attack so early that I darted in and struck him with an uppercut to his jaw. He staggered backwards, and I kept on him, delivering a flurry of punches to his stomach.

Ever since I was a boy, I tried to be a good Christian and avoid fighting whenever I could. However, whether it was my brothers or neighboring boys, I always found that once a fight was forced upon me, something came over me, and I relished the physicality of it. I didn't go mad with battle lust, as some do, but I did find the challenge a bit exhilarating, if I'm being honest.

To my right, Gilbert was still snarling and cursing, and exchanging blows with the leader, now without his cudgel. The third and smaller of the three made to jump on Gilbert's back. I grabbed a fistful of his tunic and yanked him to the side before he could, then continued to spin him around, and shoved him into the boy who still wielded the quarterstaff. They tumbled to the ground, and I seized the quarterstaff but did not attack the two immediately. Instead I glanced over to where the Frisian and the group's leader were fighting. I was alarmed to see that Gilbert was straddling the other boy and raining punches down on him, while he could do nothing but squirm left and right with his arms up, frantically trying to protect his head. I looked again at the other two. As they sat up they looked up at me, holding their quarterstaff, then they looked over and saw their leader, getting the stuffing beat out of him. The smaller boy lost all heart and scrambled to his feet, then took off running. The freckled youth jumped up and made to attack me, but the instant I discerned his intent I thrust the end of the staff into his stomach once, twice, then swung the end of the staff in a tight arc, smacking the side of his head. He collapsed with a groan, clutching at his head. He was still conscious, but I'd hit him hard enough to draw blood. He showed no intent to get up, so I turned my attention back to Gilbert and the black-haired leader.

"Gilbert, that's enough!" I snapped at him. He glanced up at me with wild eyes. I saw that his nose was bleeding, but otherwise he looked fine. The other boy looked far worse.

The Frisian didn't say anything but turned back to the other lad, still laying on his back. He cocked his fist back, but I intervened, and thrust the quarterstaff between the two. Gilbert's fist hit the staff instead. That got his attention.

"Enough!" I said again.

Gilbert stopped, and stared at the other boy, his breath coming in ragged gasps, and blood dripping from his nose and mouth. When the attacker showed no sign of continuing the fight himself, Gilbert nodded, and stood up. I crouched down and checked on the other boy. He was conscious, and I saw him peek out from behind his forearms. He looked absolutely terrified.

I walked away, and Gilbert followed, only turning to look back once, as the leader slowly got to his feet, and ran off with his friend. Gilbert gave me a feral grin. "We sure showed them!"

"Yes," I agreed. "I wonder if they would have still confronted us if you'd not been wearing that bloody seax."

"Probably," Gilbert said, wiping blood from his face with his tunic sleeve. "They were just as attracted to your bloody nice clothing and fat pouch. What's in it? Silver? Gold?"

I scoffed. "Gold? Just how rich do you think my family is? It's hacksilver."

"Silver?" Gilbert stared at me.

"Yes," I said. "So?"

Gilbert rolled his eyes. "Just how sheltered were you on your island? Do you realize how many people around here might go years without seeing silver? And you think nothing of the fact that you have a small fortune of it, and carry it around with you?" He shook his head.

"At home, most people I know have silver, and yes, some have gold too," I admitted. "Most of the men in the Red Dragons are much wealthier than my family is."

"And you would still be among the most wealthy people of any village or town you happened to visit," Gilbert replied.

"What about you?" I retorted. "You wear nice clothing. You had enough money for a horse, armor, and if not a sword, then that nice seax, at least. You're no pauper, either!"

"You're right, I'm not," Gilbert acknowledged. "My grandfather came to Britain with next to nothing. He earned enough coin to buy some land, which he nearly lost in Vortimer's war. Many of my kin did. My father became a merchant in Caer Badon. We do all right. Better than many. I'm aware of my good fortune. Your problem is you don't seem to be."

I wanted to argue his point, but realized that he was probably right. Mona wasn't a particularly large island, all things considered. I'd rarely needed to interact with many people aside from my own family and our servants. My father, I believe, was a kind and generous lord, who took care of his servants.

"Never give a servant cause to resent you," he cautioned me and my brothers. "They prepare our food, handle our belongings, and hear our private conversations. Should a servant displease me, I could have them whipped, thrown out of their homes, and utterly ruin them, should I have cause, but," he would always pause and make sure he had our complete attention before adding, "they have the same power over us! A hateful servant could poison our food, ensure that 'accidents' destroy our possessions, and tell our secrets to other families."

Even with that kind of upbringing however, I'd never really traveled far from home before. I'd never seen poverty, not like I had even in the short time since leaving home, like the boys we'd just encountered. I had thought it hard when I camped out in the woods with my brothers or father on hunting trips, and endured the cold or the rain for a day or two. A few times we'd even gone an entire day, even two, with little food, when father wanted us to be able to travel light. He said hunger would motivate us to hunt better. My brothers and I had of course thought he was being absurd, and overbearing. I thought I knew hardship, until I came here to Caer Lleon. I didn't like thinking on this too much, so I changed the subject.

"Just how did you end up here, Gib?" I asked while we walked. "You insist that we regard you as a cymbrog, but you're clearly proud of your Germanic blood, too." I gestured to the seax at his belt. "I don't get it. Hengist's grandson, Octa, is pretty well established back east, I hear. Cerdic has quite a bit of influence in the midlands. That's not far from Badon, right? Why didn't you join *his* warband?"

"Why don't you join the Scots?" Gilbert asked. "Hibernia's not far from your island home, right? The Gaels and Britons even live together pretty peacefully in Dyfed, as I understand it.."

"The Gaels aren't my people. Arthur is," I objected.

"There's men of Dyfed in the Red Dragons," Gilbert pointed out. "Including Rhun!"

"The people of Dyfed are cymbrogi now," I argued. "They get raided by Gaels as much as any Briton kingdom does. Truly, they were Gaels decades ago, but they're as much Britons as you are ..." I stopped as I realized what I said. This was actually a lot more complicated than I'd ever really considered before!

Gilbert chuckled. "Exactly. I'm as much a Briton as I am Germanic. And the Frisians fight Jutes and Saxons as often as they ever did Britons, maybe even more. You do know when the first Saxons came to Britain, right?"

"Everyone knows that," I said. "There were a few brought over with the Roman army, and then boatloads more came over with Hengist and Horsa!"

Gilbert laughed again, then idly scooped up a rock lying on the road, and threw it at a nearby tree. It hit, then flew off into the woods. "You've got it backwards, man," he corrected me. "The Romans started bringing over hundreds, if not thousands of my people as foederati, a long time ago, to defend against other, hostile tribes. Why do you think the southeast coast is called the 'Saxon Shore'? That didn't happen with the small warband that Hengist and Horsa brought over! So just like how men of Dyfed are both Gaelic and Briton, so it is with quite a few of my kin, as well. I decided, and my father agreed, that Arthur and the Britons are closer to being my people than the Saxons are. Britain is my home. Every time Cerdic of the West Saxons expands his holdings, he has no regard for who's in his way. Briton or German, anyone who doesn't swear fealty to him is killed or driven off in order to make room for his own kin. He doesn't care if they're Briton, Anglian, or Frisian. My father told me his men have even fought Octa's from time to time, and everyone back home is pretty sure it was Cerdic, or his son Cynric, who did in King Aelle of the South Saxons a few years ago. Arthur is the only one trying to establish some kind of peaceful existence for *all* Britons, not just his own little kingdom. He's from Dumnonia, right?"

"I believe so," I acknowledged.

"See? If Arthur was like everyone else, he'd stay put there, protect Dumnonia in the name of whoever rules there, and everyone else be damned, but he doesn't do that. And everyone respects him for it."

"Except the Saxons," I grinned.

Gilbert grinned back. "Except the Saxons," he agreed. "Cerdic and Arthur will have to fight, one of these days. Everyone at Badon knows it. And I want to be in Arthur's numerus when those two meet!"

"That would be a fight for the ages," I agreed.

We arrived back at Caer Lleon a short while later, and waited with no small amount of trepidation for the return of our friends. Bran was already at the barracks when we showed up, deeply involved in a dice game. Rhun, Ewen, and Madog didn't arrive until after sunset, when the rest of us were preparing for bed.

"Where have you three been?" I demanded the moment they came in.

"We were out, with Nest, and her friends," Rhun replied, startled. "Why?"

"Nest? The tall blond girl?" Gilbert asked.

"Yes. Why?" Rhun repeated.

"Did you happen to discover who her father is?" I asked.

"No. Should I have?" Rhun asked.

"Normally? Maybe not," I conceded. "Here? Yes! She's Castellan Bedwyr's daughter," I said.

Rhun paled a little.

"What did you *do* today?" I asked.

Rhun exchanged guilty glances with his brother and Madog. "Nothing," Rhun said, rubbing at his neck. "We just went down to the river and chatted."

I grabbed at his shoulder as he began to move towards his bed and turned him around. At the base of his neck, just barely visible from under his tunic, was a dark reddish-purple mark.

"Nothing?" I asked, tapping his neck.

Rhun pulled up his tunic to hide his neck. "Nothing that concerns you!" he said.

I shook my head. "Do as you will," I conceded, "I just hope you don't live to regret 'nothing'."

Rhun smiled smugly as he began preparing for bed. "I'm fairly certain I won't."

Ewan and Madog chuckled. Nothing more was said by anyone, and we laid out our kit for the next day's training, then went to bed.

# Chapter Five

A month into our training, we finally progressed to mounted drills, but if we thought that would be easier, we were wrong. Every day Caradoc had us spend several minutes simply mounting and dismounting, over and over again, as well as having us compete to strap on our horse's equipment. The slowest of us to get into the saddle had to run the perimeter of the fort while carrying it.

Two weeks into mounted training, in late October, tragedy struck. We were practicing a wheel turn at a gallop not far from the fort when Bran's horse stepped wrong and took a spill. In an instant he went flying into the air over his horse's head. He landed hard with a loud *thud*, and his horse slammed down on top of him, then rolled away, neighing shrilly and thrashing its legs in agony. One leg was shattered and he lay unconscious where he'd fallen. My stomach knotted up in terror and revulsion at the horrible sight.

"Bran!" I cried, as my friends and I dismounted and raced over to him. Although I reached him first I froze, looking down at him, unsure of what I could do to help. The others were right behind me.

"Help me get his kit off!" Rhun immediately barked at us. I knelt down, unfastened the ties to his helmet, and removed it, along with the wool cap worn underneath the helmet for padding. Decurion Caradoc was only moments behind us. He saw that we were being productive and assisted in pulling off

Bran's belts, and then his chainmail shirt. Bran moaned softly as we worked. I felt a wave of relief that at least he was still alive.

Blood was spreading in a growing pool across his legs. I pointed this out to Caradoc. Madog stepped away, doubled over, and retched. Rhun, whose father was a healer, had picked up a few things and helped Caradoc. He started by gently patting Bran's left arm, then worked his way down his chest, and hips, methodically checking for injuries. Caradoc was doing the same with the right side. "His leg is broken!" Rhun pointed out to Caradoc, quietly.

"It looks pretty bad," Caradoc acknowledged, scrutinizing it. "I've seen injuries like this. We need to stop the bleeding quickly before he dies." As he said this he unbuckled his belt and quickly strapped it around Bran's thigh, high up near the groin, then cinched it down tight. Bran gasped in pain. The belt hurt, but it would cut off the blood flow to his leg, and stop the bleeding, maybe saving his life. While they worked I knelt beside Bran, cradling his head in my lap, and just talked to him. If he could hear me, I hoped I could be of at least a little comfort to him while Rhun and the decurion worked.

Once the belt was secure, Caradoc grabbed Gilbert's shoulder. "Gib, can you take care of Bran's horse?" He stared intently into Gilbert's eyes as though searching for weakness.

Gilbert glanced over at the mortally injured horse. "I can take care of her," he sighed. The look on his face made his distaste for the job clear.

"Get it done quickly, then join us at the hospital," he said. "We'll put Bran on your horse." With that, Caradoc, Rhun, and I carefully picked Bran up and mounted him onto his horse. We tried to be careful, but Bran still let loose with a blood-curdling scream of pain as we got him mounted, then he passed out again. We lashed a belt around Bran and attached him to the saddle to help keep him from falling off, then all of us but Gilbert accompanied Bran back to the fort. We rode on either side of him to further ensure that he did not fall from his horse. The last I saw of Gilbert as I glanced over my shoulder, he was kneeling down next to the stricken horse and stroking its neck as he drew his long seax from the sheath at his hip.

The ride back to the fort, down the street, and to the small hospital seemed to take forever, though in reality it probably only took about ten minutes. Caradoc rushed ahead to find our medicus while we brought Bran inside and gently laid him onto an empty bed with a fresh mattress. He was fading in and out of consciousness, and once, while he was awake and mostly alert, he asked for water. Seeing a small barrel of mead that our medicus kept in the hospital gave me an idea and I poured some into a cup for Bran, to help dull the pain. While I was doing that, Rhun cut away the bloody leg of Bran's trousers so by the time I returned with the water, his leg was bared, and we could all see the extent of his injury. I cringed as I handed the cup to Bran and helped him sip it down.

Within a few minutes, Caradoc returned, practically dragging a heavyset, middle-aged man with brown hair streaked with gray behind him. The man, who I presumed was the medicus, had a large leather satchel slung across his shoulder. He also had a roll of linen cloth tucked under one arm. The moment he entered the room, the man batted Caradoc's hand aside and pulled out a toolkit from his satchel. He assessed Bran's injuries and got to work.

"Someone's been working on this boy already," he noted and looked around at us.

We all pointed to Rhun.

"Good lad. You have any experience with treating injuries, do you?"

"Some," Rhun replied. "My father is-"

The medicus didn't let him finish. "Good! You can help me. The rest of you will get in my way. Remove yourselves."

We did and found stools outside of the hospital to wait for the medicus to finish. In the meantime, Decurion Caradoc went to find Tribune Arthur, to report Bran's injury to him. We heard Bran moan from time to time, and once he screamed. We heard the medicus yell "Hold him down!" Then it went silent. Gilbert joined us while we waited. There were flecks of blood on his tunic and trousers, and his hands had a reddish tint. He'd clearly tried to wash the horse's blood from him, but had been in a hurry to get to the hospital, and therefore had been a bit sloppy. Dirt on his cheeks was streaked, and his eyes had a reddish tint to them. I said nothing, but put a comforting hand on his shoulder. Gilbert liked horses nearly as much as I did, but then, that was probably true of most men who spent enough time on horseback.

Caradoc returned, with another man following close behind him. He was tall! And he was big. He was the kind of man that only took a glance for someone to never forget, and the kind of man I can't imagine any sane warrior would ever want to have to face in one-on-one combat. He had closely cropped, short blond hair, and a neatly trimmed, equally short mustache and beard. His clothing consisted of a white tunic with embroidered edging, white trousers, shoes, and a wide leather belt. He wore an ornate dagger and sword, slung from a baldric in the standard military fashion. A crimson cloak was fastened across his shoulders, and a golden torc, sculpted in the semblance of a dragon hung around his neck. Walking along beside the man was a young, gray wolfhound, barely more than a pup by the looks of him. The decurion started to announce the man's presence but Gilbert had already put two and two together, and jumped to his feet, bowing to the man. The rest of us were starting to rise as well when the man waved at us. "Sit, sit, lads." The tall man had a pleasant voice. I was startled at how young he sounded though. I looked more closely at his face, and realized that while the beard made him look a bit older, I suspected he was still in his early twenties. "Leave formalities to formal occasions," the man continued. "It's good to meet you all, though, of course, it could have been under better circumstances. I'm Arthur, by the way. Uther's son."

"And our Tribune," Decurion Caradoc growled softly while staring mean-ingfully at the rest of us. His eyes made the rest of his statement clear as day, *"So make sure you watch what you say and be respectful, or else..."*

"And what are your names?" Arthur asked, looking over each of us.

We gave them as I stared up at him.

71

"How's your contubernalis?" His pronunciation of the old Latin term was flawless; I couldn't help but notice.

"He broke his leg, my lord," Ewan said, glancing briefly over at our decurion.

"The medicus has been treating him for ages now, Tribune," Madog chipped in.

"Rhun's in there with him, helping the medicus, Tribune," I added.

Arthur looked us over, one to the other, as we answered him, sizing us up as he did. His eyes lingered a moment on Gilbert's seax, but whatever his thoughts, his face betrayed nothing, and he said nothing about it. "And how are the rest of you doing?" he asked.

"We're fine, my lord," Madog answered for us.

The wiry, gray wolfhound pup that had been by Arthur's side came up and sniffed at us, lingering the longest on Gilbert, particularly his hands and the dried blood on his clothes. Gilbert started to pet the dog but hesitated, glancing up at Arthur. The large man smiled and nodded.

"This is my pup, Cavall," Arthur said. His eyes twinkled as the corners of his mouth pulled into a faint smile. "Duplarius Cavall Magnus Augustus," he pronounced, as Gilbert reached back and scratched the pup between his shoulders, and his tail immediately began to wag. "Duplarius?" I asked, noticing the rank, even above the very regal name Arthur had apparently given this dog.

"That's right," Arthur said. His smile broadened, and he glanced at Caradoc. Even the gruff decurion seemed amused. "So he outranks you lot."

All the tension over the day's tragedy eased a bit, and we couldn't help but laugh. But Arthur wasn't finished.

"I think, for the time being, Duplarius Cavall will be this section's responsibility," he said thoughtfully. "You lads will make sure he is fed, watered, exercised, and trained. Am I understood?"

"Yes, Tribune," we said in unison.

"Looks like right now, your duplarius wants pets," Arthur said. Then, with a nod at Caradoc, the two of them strode into the hospital.

"Tewdrig." Arthur greeted the medicus with a brisk nod. "How's Bran?" he asked, hesitating only the briefest moment to recall Bran's name.

We all leaned towards the door, listening.

"He's resting now," the medicus, Tewdrig said. "He's got a couple fractured ribs and his leg is broken in two places. One splinter of bone went through the skin. I've pushed the bone back in place, cauterized the wound, and stitched it up. Me and the lad here wrapped his leg in a splint that he'll need to wear, probably for a few weeks."

"Will his leg heal properly?" Arthur asked.

There was a moment's hesitation. "I can make no promise of that," Tewdrig said with a sigh. "He should heal, with time and rest, but with a break like his, I can't promise *how well* it will heal."

"Thank you," Arthur said. "Should we have Myrddin look at it?"

"You can," the medicus said, "I doubt he'll be able to do any more than I've done, though."

He must have looked insulted, because Arthur responded by saying, "Don't worry, old friend. I wasn't doubting your abilities. Sometimes second opinions can still be helpful, eh?"

I heard them talk a bit more, in a lower voice, then he and Caradoc came outside.

"Well, lads," Arthur told us. "Looks like your friend, Bran, will be recovering for a while; long enough that we've decided to let him go back home to Powys. He'll be more comfortable with his family than he will in any barracks here at Caer Lleon. So right now I want you to gather up his belongings from the barracks, bring them here. You can say goodbye to him then, and you'll resume training in the morning. Any questions?"

When we affirmed that we had none, Arthur nodded and walked away with Caradoc. Cavall watched them go for a moment, then decided to stay with us while we petted and scratched him.

We took care of Bran's belongings, wished him well that evening, after he was feeling a bit better, and were allowed to see him off as a small group of Arthur's men escorted him home in a wagon, as his leg made it impossible for him to ride. After Bran left, our training resumed in earnest. We learned how to conduct scouting maneuvers in small groups- like what kind of information our decurion needed, how to hide properly, and how to use hand and arm signals if we needed to.

For the final phase, we were attached to a turma of Arthur's men and practiced maneuvers as a formation. We practiced throwing javelins and plumbatae at straw dummies. As has been the case throughout my training, I did fine with javelins, but that skill seemed not to carry over with plumbatae, and any time I was forced to throw mine at the targets as we galloped past them, it was always followed by hoots of laughter from my contubernales. I got good enough to at least hit the dummies, most of the time, but only God could predict where. It might hit the dummy's head, an arm, a leg, or rarely, a direct hit to the torso. Although I never admitted this to either my friends or especially to Decurion Caradoc, many of the times that I had hit a target with one of those accursed weighted darts, it wasn't actually the target I had been aiming for.

Finally, we practiced moving in and out of a wedge formation, and charging at a line of straw and wood dummies. We used spears for our initial attacks. These would usually splinter on impact, after which we dropped the broken shafts, drew our swords, and made a few more slashes at the dummies. Then the decurion would shout for us to withdraw about fifty to a hundred feet away, reform, wheel about, and charge again.

"The reason we continually charge, withdraw, and charge again," Caradoc explained one afternoon, "is because the enemy will usually outnumber us. We cannot afford to give them time to encircle us, or we're doomed. Cavalry trapped by infantry have very poor defense; our strength lies in our ability to outmaneuver an enemy infantry force and hit them from on the flank or rear, or wherever they are weakest. We charge, we kill a few, we break up their formation, and before they can encircle us, we pull back, far enough away that they can't chase us down, then we look for another vulnerable spot to attack them."

"What about cavalry against cavalry?" I asked.

"Well, Peredur," he answered. "That's why we do so much training in one-on-one combat. That's where that particular training really comes into play. Fortunately, the Saxons don't have a lot of cavalry. Only their nobles and their retinues generally have mounts, so they rarely field more than a hundred cavalrymen. In fact, they usually have much fewer- no more than a turma's worth.

We continued on with mounted training through the rest of October. It felt strange, without Bran beside us. Tutwal had been a quiet lad who kept to himself, and he'd had to leave early on. Dewi had gotten on everybody's nerves and hadn't stayed with us very long either, but we missed Bran. He'd been a bit of a clown, and was devilishly good at dice. Being given a bit of responsibility for taking care of 'Duplarius' Cavall proved to be the perfect distraction for us, one I suspect the Tribune knew we could use. We took to waking up extra early in the mornings to go to Arthur's large house, next to the great hall, and bring Cavall whatever scraps we'd saved from supper the previous night and feeding him, along with making sure he had a bowl of water, and that it wasn't iced up, as it was beginning to do, with winter getting closer.

For the most part, Cavall had the run of the fort. With Caer Lleon only housing a few hundred men, plus their families, everyone knew Cavall, and since he had been brought to the fort as a very small pup, he was well suited to life here. Now that we began visiting Arthur's house and feeding him, Cavall likewise began to spend time at our barracks, particularly just after meal times, when he knew we would be able to feed him the freshest morsels of food. Sometimes he even trotted along with us when we did our morning run around the fort, and he loved playing in the river while we bathed or washed our clothes or other belongings.

We were allowed to stop training on October 31st for the festival of Samhain. Like many of our holidays, Samhain is an interesting blend of the old Pagan festival that our ancestors held to praise their gods for a bountiful harvest and a hopefully mild winter, hundreds of years ago, with newer, Christian activities now included. As winter is the season of the dead, our ancestors also used this festival to venerate the deceased, offer sacrifices, and wear masks and costumes to hopefully confuse spirits into not lingering and haunting the people, but the druids who conducted these rituals were nearly all killed off when the Romans conquered our island, and Britain has become a mostly Christian land for over two hundred years now. So while we still celebrate Samhain, we really have only a vague idea of how it used to be conducted, and many of the Pagan elements have been forgotten.

Our morning began with a church service where our priest reminded us of the Christian martyrs who have died for their faith and called on us to take inspiration from the saints, such as the recently deceased Bishop Patrick, who had brought Christianity to the heathen Gaelic tribes in Hibernia, and of the miracles performed by the likes of Bishop Germanus, on our own island. Finally, he called upon Michael the archangel to bless and protect us. Michael was becoming known as the patron saint of warriors, particularly mounted warriors, and his image was a favorite on many shields.

After mass, the women gathered in the courtyard of the great hall and prepared a fantastic feast for the fort's population. For festivals such as this, the villagers in the surrounding area were also encouraged to visit the fort, and the women from the nearby village also brought food and drink and aided in preparation for the evening feast.

The main gates were wide open, and people trickled in, carrying baskets, with only the briefest of delays as the four guards on duty checked them over before allowing them entry.

"Maybe we should have volunteered for guard duty today," Madog joked, as we watched a good-looking, buxom woman pull an apple out of her basket and give it to one of the guards, along with a light peck on his cheek as she walked through, laughing musically.

We weaved through the streets, pausing briefly to watch a man in a colorful, brightly painted mask juggle several balls high into the air.

"Big deal," Gilbert shrugged. "I've seen a juggler do that, but with *knives*!"

"I once saw a man swallow a knife," Rhun offered.

We continued on and snagged up some honeyed cakes. Gilbert pulled out a drinking horn he liked to carry and allowed a woman to top it off with a mild, fruity ale she'd brought to Caer Lleon for the festivities. From there, we weaved our way through the crowded streets, towards Arthur's house. A small child nearly slammed into Gilbert as he was taking a swig.

"Hey! Watch yourself!" Gilbert scolded, as he raised his horn in the air. Only a few drops were spilled. After several minutes, we made it to Arthur's home, and more specifically, to the small shelter other soldiers had made for Cavall. It was just like a normal wattle-and-daub roundhouse, complete with a thatched roof, but sized for a dog. Cavall was lying at the entrance, head on his paws, though he sat up immediately upon seeing us. We all produced samples of the treats we had acquired at the various stalls and fed him.

"We should make a vexillum for Cavall's fine little house," Madog said, thoughtfully. He was looking at the rectangular pennant planted into the ground at the steps leading up to Arthur's house. We looked too. It was white, with gold trim, and depicted a red dragon in the Celtic style stitched on it, encircling a small Chi Rho. It was clean, and of good quality, but it had clearly seen some use.

We finished with our snacks, saw that Cavall had a bowl of fresh water available, and continued on our way. Cavall came with us. We played games of chance and listened to an old man in a long, dark blue tunic sing for a crowd in a strong, clear voice that belied his age. He was good!

As we got closer, I realized it was the man I'd bumped into when I first arrived.

"Hey look! Rhun exclaimed. "Myrddin's performing!"

And perform he did. He sang several songs; everything from Brittonic ballads to more bawdy, drinking songs in Latin. At some of the lyrics, I glanced around. The men were all laughing, clapping, and stomping their feet to the rhythm. I saw a few mothers glancing down at their children, who didn't seem to even understand the words and realized that many of the children probably didn't speak Latin. Likely, some of the adults in the crowd didn't, either. Hence the reason Myrddin probably thought it safe to sing such songs. I laughed in appreciation of his clever antics.

We could have listened to Myrddin all evening, but after a bit, Cavall decided he wanted to join in and started yipping. This caused Myrddin to play a sour note on his lyre. Although he himself took it in stride and continued playing, even smiling over at us and at Cavall, I noticed we were getting a few annoyed looks from the people closest to us.

"Let's get Cavall out of here," I suggested to Rhun and the others. They agreed, and we eased away from the crowd.

"I think I just saw somebody I wanted to talk to, anyway," Rhun said with a grin, and before any of us could ask for further detail, he faded into the crowd. I got a glimpse of a tall girl with long blond hair, however, and groaned. Rhun was sure to bring down the wrath of our castellan upon his head one of these days, I thought.

The rest of the day passed by far too quickly. At some point, Cavall wandered off, but we weren't worried. Everyone in Arthur's cavalry knew him. There was a great feast that evening. Then, once the sun started setting, a giant bonfire was built in the large, open training ground. We danced and sang. Children ran around, shrieking and laughing.

Towards the end of the night, Cavall came up to me with a stick in his mouth, as I sat drinking some watered-down wine, while seated on a log near the bonfire. He nudged my arm. I ignored him. He nudged me again.

"Recruit," a voice said, startling me. I looked over. It was Duplarius Drystan, looking amused, and a bit drunk. He sounded and smelled like it, too.

"Yes, Duplarius?" I asked.

"It appears that my fellow duplarius is ordering you to play with him."

"Sir, he's just trying to get me to throw that stick, which he'll have me do for half the night if I oblige him," I protested.

"So you're telling me that Duplarius Cavall is instructing you to engage in training with him; training that seems to me could directly aid in your skills, or more accurately lack thereof, in your accuracy with the plumbata? Smart thinking, Duplarius!" He grinned down at the wolfhound and reached down to scratch the dog. Cavall stood and wagged his tail in appreciation for the attention.

I sighed. Clearly, I was not going to win *this* battle. I took the stick and started to simply throw it. Then I thought better of it, glanced over at Drystan as he walked off, and specifically held one end of it, as I would the feathered end of a dart, and hurled the stick into the woods. Cavall immediately took off after it in a streak of gray. Moments later, he was back in front of me, tail wagging, with the stick in his mouth. I sighed again, took the stick, and hurled it again. And again. And again.

The rest of the night passed uneventfully, and one by one my friends and I returned to our barracks room and went to sleep. Mercifully, although training resumed the very next day, we were allowed to sleep in a bit and did not actually begin training until close to noon.

*****

Two weeks later, we completed our training. My tentmates and I were brought before Tribune Arthur in the great hall. A soldier stood off to his left, holding Arthur's standard. On their right was the fort's priest, who held before us a tall staff with a golden cross mounted on it. We stood straight and proud, in our best clothes, and with our swords sheathed at our hips. Off to one side stood our instructor, Caradoc.

"The Red Dragons are unique in the kingdoms of Britain," Arthur stated. "It is the last military unit here modeled in the Roman style on this isle and is the best trained, and best equipped force. It is made so because its coffers are filled with a tithe from all the kingdoms of western Britain, and its ranks are filled with Britain's noblest sons. In exchange, the Red Dragons ride to the defense of all of these kingdoms, whenever we are needed. The only conflicts we will not involve ourselves in are internal ones, between Brittonic kingdoms," Arthur stressed.

I admit, that was some relief to hear. Even during the course of our training, we'd heard of a small, but heated border dispute between Dyfed and Gwent, a thing that wasn't all that rare, and they weren't the only kingdoms that squabled. A few years ago, my own king, Cadwallon, had sent troops into our southern neighbors of Powys. In some instances, disputes weren't even between kingdoms, but between kings and the lord of some hillfort who was powerful enough to challenge their king's authority over some matter. None of us were anxious to be drawn into such internal conflicts. We were here because we wanted to focus on the greater threats shared by all Britons.

Arthur continued. "Neither I, and by extension High King Conanus Aurelius, nor any of your officers, will ever issue you an order that will place you in the predicament of being forced to take up arms against your homes. If there is ever a situation where you are given an order that conflicts with your honor, or vows sworn to the kings from whose lands you come from, you shall be permitted to leave the Red Dragons with your honor intact. Once you swear your oath here, before myself, and to our Lord Jesus Christ, you shall be a member of the Red Dragons. You will be expected to garrison the walls of Caer Lleon with your turma for one season each year, which is established by rotation. During that time you will be required to live within the walls of the fort. During the seasons in which your turma is not called to service, you are released to your homes. The gates of Caer Lleon are always open to you however, should you choose to reside here. As a member of the Red Dragons, even when your turma is not already on garrison duty, should the need arise, you may also be called upon to muster here in response to various threats to this fort, or to any of the kingdoms united under the banner of King Conanus. You will be expected to always maintain yourself, your arms and equipment, and your horse, and be ready to answer the call to arms within three weeks of receiving the call."

"Are there any who do not understand what I have said, or who now have any doubt in regards to your commitment to the Red Dragons?" Arthur looked at us, his eyes boring into ours one after the other.

We all answered, "No, Tribune!" as he did.

With that done, Arthur commanded us to take a knee and place our right hands over our hearts. Before him, as the priest held the cross aloft, we swore our oaths. We swore to obey our kings, Arthur, and our officers, and to do our duty, even until our last breath, and to never abandon a cymbrog. We swore to always uphold the honor of the tradition of the Red Dragons, and to never do anything that could bring shame upon the unit, our families, or ourselves.

"And now," Arthur said with a smile, gesturing for us to rise, "Let me be the first to welcome you into our brotherhood, as a brother." He walked down the line, beginning with Rhun, shaking our hands and offering us words of praise and encouragement. When he got to me, he grasped my forearm firmly and looked down into my eyes with sincere warmth.

"Welcome, brother. I know you will do your father, Lord Pelinor, proud and serve the Red Dragons with the same valor as he served."

"Tha- thank you, Tribune," I stammered, as I clasped his thick forearm. Looking up at him as he welcomed me into the Red Dragons, I determined that I would charge into hell for him, should he ask it of me. I was now a soldier of the Red Dragons.

How little did I know at that moment that in the years to come, I would practically do that. At Agned and at the Tribruit. At Badon. And more directly, in the woods of Caledonia.

# Chapter Six

Following our formal induction into the Red Dragons, Decurian Caradoc had us form up one last time at the training barracks and assigned us into turmae. Madog was assigned to a turmae under the command of Decurion Galhault, while Gilbert and I were assigned to Decurion Owain's turma. Rhun and his brother Ewan were placed into Castellan Bedwyr's turma. There was a brief look of panic in Rhun's eyes when he discovered his assignment. The rest of us just smirked at his discomfort, and we all wondered the same thing. Did the castellan know of Rhun's involvement with his daughter? When he glanced our way, all we could do was shrug and try not to break out laughing at his predicament.

As Bedwyr's turma was coming off garrison duty, Rhun and Ewan were allowed to return home to Dyfed. I learned later that Bedwyr and his family lived within the fort, so for him, 'going home' simply meant shifting his focus from running his turma to spending time with his family. He also owned some lands in the surrounding area with livestock as well as orchards, which provided some of the food we ate here at the fort. These were maintained by a workforce of hired servants and Saxon slaves who had been taken in the wars against them.

Rhun and Ewan packed up their gear, we said our farewells, and they left the training barracks. Then Decurion Galhault's duplarius came and collected Madog. A short time later, a man walked up to Gilbert and me as we sat at our bunks. A second man accompanied him, hanging back. The man who approached us had a scar across his jaw that parted his short beard.

"I'm looking for Gilbert, son of Wulfstan, and Peredur, son of Lord Pelinor?"

"I'm Peredur," I said, raising my hand.

Gilbert identified himself as well. "I'm Gilbert. Or Gib, if you prefer."

"I'm Decurion Owain. This is my duplarius, Harri. You've both been assigned to my turma. Grab your things. I'll take you to your new quarters and introduce you to the rest of the men."

As we walked over another section of the fort, Owain talked. "I was glad to get you two. My turma's only had twenty men in it since the Battle at the River Bassus, the summer before last. Most turmae have three contubernia. I've got two. I'm putting you both in with Decanus Cornelius. Maybe if Arthur can find me a couple more men, I could go back to three contubernia."

Owain and Harri passed us off to Cornelius, and left Gilbert and I to get settled in. Cornelius in turn introduced us to the others in our section. Cornelius was the oldest, at twenty-four. He was a typical younger son to a nobleman from Elfed, a small kingdom northeast of my own homeland. There was Marcus, whose family was from Caer Londin, on the edge of what used to be a major Roman city, but Saxons had all but driven off the native Britons. They had resettled in the village right here surrounding Caer Lleon. He was the tallest of us, and had darker features that displayed his Roman heritage.

Next to be introduced was Quintus, of Portus Adurni. His father owned a small fleet of fishing vessels and did moderately well, though life had become a bit precarious for Britons living there, as it was on the fringes of West Saxon territory. In fact, Quintus had admitted, his own father actually had to pay taxes to Cerdic.

"He doesn't have a choice!" Quintus defended his father when he saw our startled looks at that revelation. "No Brittonic king is willing or able to fight for Portus. Cerdic controls it. If my father doesn't pay the Saxons, they'd drive him and the rest of my family out of the town with nothing but the clothes on our backs. And if we crossed his son Cynric, that evil bastard might just have us all killed instead. That's why I'm here. I'm hoping that some day, Arthur will liberate Portus from the Saxons."

A tough-looking blond lad was Idris. He was from all the way from the northern kingdom of Alt Cut, the same region our decurion hailed from and had practically grown up defending his land from Gaelic and Pictish raiders. So even at nineteen, he was a seasoned veteran and had the scars to show for it.

"If you ever need to acquire something," Cornelius told us with a smirk, "Idris is the lad for it. He can get you just about any kind of food or any piece of kit that you might need, and for a reasonable price. Just ah... don't pester him too hard as to *how* he acquires it."

Idris just grinned and gave us a wink.

Another of my more interesting tentmates was an odd, stocky fellow with a shaved head named Aylmer. Aylmer came from south central Britain. Calleva, Caer Calemion. Something like that. In either case, he'd picked up an amusing accent as a result of growing up hearing Latin, Brythonic, and Germanic. Though only twenty-three, Aylmer's hairline was already noticeably receding. And unfortunately for him, he loved telling tall tales, particularly about beasts he'd hunted or encountered. It made the rest of the contubernium feel like he was just a bit mad. There were others, but these were the most memorable of my tentmates.

"Just like when you were recruits, we train every day," Cornelius explained. "Only we don't train as long; usually from shortly after dawn until about noon, with a meal in between, but don't think you get to loaf around the rest of the day. Arthur has some funny notions about slaves- he doesn't like having them in the fort. I think he finds the notion of it distasteful or something," Cornelius shrugged. "So while we're serving our time on rotation, *we* do the work around here. We fix up the walls, repair the thatch roofs as needed, and keep the brush from creeping up to within arrow range of the fort's walls. Arthur doesn't want any enemies stupid enough to attack us here to have any cover or concealment. We also dig fresh latrine pits, fill in the old ones; though that's usually reserved for soldiers on punishment details. There's also servants to assist with some of the labor. And then of course there's security details at night. There's twenty-three guard towers on the walls; one tower every one hundred and forty feet. So each night a different turma is on duty and we man the towers. Local militia man the towers during the day."

\*\*\*\*\*

This was how my first two months as a soldier went. I got into the rhythm of it quickly enough. Since September, when I joined, I knew I'd gained weight. I grew stronger and faster, and became much better with the sword than I was five months ago. How that time flew. I continued to work on the plumbata, and got at least .... proficient at it. Not great by any stretch of the word, but proficient.

One night in late Januarius, I found myself on tower duty. That winter, there were eight turmae on duty. A different turma took over guard duty on the walls each night, from sunset to sunrise, so I'd pulled this duty numerous times by now. That night was just the darkest and coldest maybe in my life, up to that point. The section of the wall I was assigned to happened to overlook the river, facing east, making that section of the wall seem even colder than elsewhere. A torch in its stand beside me gave my tower just a bit of light, illuminating the fifteen square feet of my platform. A dozen javelins were stacked up against one corner. I had a small table to set a jug of water and some food, and a chair. I could see my breath every time I exhaled, so I knew it was freezing, or near freezing temperatures. I pulled my cloak a bit tighter as I stared off into the dark. Cornelius warned me, the first time I'd been assigned to one of the towers facing the river, that if the Saxons ever attacked this fort, the river would be their most likely route.

I always kept this in mind whenever I was on that wall. Occasionally, I heard an owl hooting off in the distance. Midway through the night, I heard a faint clacking noise coming up the stairs, and the sounds of breathing. I spun around, hand reaching for my spatha. It was just Cavall. He glanced up, but otherwise paid no attention to me. Instead, he trotted past, out of the tower, and over to a section of wall. Then he stood up on his hind legs and rested his forelegs on the ledge of the wall, between the crenelations, and growled.

"What is it, boy?" I asked, tensing. Something was out there. I pulled the torch off its stand and joined Cavall on the wall. Holding the torch out, away from my head and slightly behind my head, I stared off into the night. Cornelius taught me to hold the torch this way so that if there were enemies outside, it would be harder for them to use my torch to target me with slings or arrows. Torches were both necessary, but dangerous, he told me. I held it slightly behind me so that the torch's light wouldn't destroy my night vision. There was nearly a full moon out, but it was a cloudy night, and much of it was obscured. I scanned left and right, looking for any hint of metal glinting off the torch, but saw nothing. Nor did I hear anything. And yet, Cavall continued to growl and whine. I walked along the wooden rampart and over to the guard tower next to mine that shared the section Cavall was at. As it happened, Gilbert was on the same wall as I was tonight.

"Gib, you see anything? Cavall's acting weird."

Gilbert looked over past me and at Cavall. Then he walked over to the window of his tower and stared out. "I don't see anything, either," he said softly, at last. He kept scanning, though. "Do you think we should alert the Decurion?"

"I don't really want to disturb Owain unless we have something to actually tell him," I said, reluctant at the idea of reporting to him that something may or may not be outside the walls, purely based on Cavall behaving a bit odd.

Gilbert nodded. "Fair enough. Keep an eye out, though." I nodded in agreement and quietly walked back to my tower. Then the torch illuminated the silhouette of a man on the wall with me! I yelped and dropped into a crouch, sword out and ready before I'd even thought about it.

The man in my tower emitted a low chuckle and took a step forward, raising his hands so I could see that they were empty. For his part, Cavall merely glanced over his shoulder at the man, then resumed his growling and whining as he stared off into the darkness over the wall.

"You should trust Cavall more, Peredur," the man said in a friendly tone. I recognized him immediately.

"Tribune," I bowed my head to Arthur. Arthur nodded to me, then walked over to the wall, joining Cavall.

"Dogs have much, much keener senses than we do," he said after a moment. "And they can be surprisingly good at providing you with information, if you take the time to learn their language. You've been around Duplarius Cavall for some time now. What do you think he's trying to tell you right now?"

I smiled a little at Arthur's use of Cavall's 'rank', then looked over at the wolfhound. "He's just ... growling and whining," I said after a moment.

"He's doing more than that," Arthur corrected, still speaking softly. "His ears are up and forward. He hears something out there. Those growls tell you he's feeling aggressive. His whine tells you he's also feeling excited and eager to be out there. The hair on his neck and spine is raised. More indicators of aggression. And finally, his tail is straight out. So, *something* is out there. He's focused on it. It's exciting to him, but he's not scared of it."

Arthur was silent for a moment, then spoke again. "Your initial thought to alert your decurion was the correct one, but I suspect I know what's out there. So why don't you grab the other soldier you were just speaking with and escort Duplarius Cavall outside. I'll keep an eye out up here."

"Yes, Tribune," I said, and turned to get Gilbert.

"Peredur," Arthur stopped me.

"Yes, Tribune?" I asked.

"Take these. You might need them." Arthur fetched a couple of javelins from inside the tower and handed them to me with a slight smile.

A few minutes later, Cavall, Gilbert, and I jogged out through one of the small doors of the south wall. I leashed Cavall before heading out so he couldn't tear off into the darkness and leave us behind. I carried the javelins in my other hand. Gilbert had a torch in his left hand and a spear in his right. The moment we were outside the wall, Cavall began whining in obvious excitement. His tail wagged slightly, and he strained at his leash. He strained so hard that the leather cord snapped, and Cavall raced off into the darkness with an excited bark. I swore, and Gilbert and I ran after him. My heart was racing, and I gripped my javelins tightly, switching one to my throwing arm as I ran. My head whipped around left and right, looking for the enemy or whatever had gotten Cavall excited.

Moments later, we saw three shapes running away. Gilbert identified them before I did.

"Deer!" he yelled.

I stood still for a moment, in absolute relief that it had just been deer, and let out a long sigh. I thought about trying to bring one down, then, but in the time it took me to register what Gilbert and my eyes were telling me, and bring up a javelin to throw, the deer were out of sight, and we could hear Cavall barking as he chased off after them. From up on the wall, a guard at one of the other towers called down, "Who's down there? What's going on?"

"It's Peredur and Gib!" I called up. "Cavall just chased off some deer!"

"Should have killed one!" the guard called back down. "It's been awhile since we had deer meat."

I shrugged up at him.

"Should we go after Cavall?" Gilbert asked.

"We'd never catch him. Especially at night," I decided, looking off into the dark, in the direction Cavall had run. "Let's go back and report to Tribune Arthur."

We followed the wall until we found the small, narrow door, ducked our heads, and went back inside the fort, climbed up the step to the rampart, then back to our towers. True to his word, Arthur was waiting for me. He was seated at the small table, with a scroll in his hand, and a faraway look on his face. Then he noticed me.

"So, what did you find outside?" he asked.

"At least three deer, maybe more," I replied. "Tribune, I'm sorry! Cavall broke his leash and ran off after them. I didn't think it would be a good idea to chase after him."

Arthur glanced at the leash I held up, and nodded. "You're right. It would be stupid. We need you here, on the wall. Cavall can take care of himself. So ... " he made a show of looking me over. "Where's the carcass?"

"The ... carcass, Tribune?" I asked, confused.

Arthur rolled his eyes. "You said Cavall found some deer. I gave you a pair of javelins before you left. I would assume you made use of them and killed at least one deer. So where's the carcass?"

I cringed, sensing I'd made yet another mistake tonight. "I didn't think to kill any deer, my lord."

Arthur sighed. "So, your duplarius identified a band of enemy deer, just outside our walls. An alert you might have ignored, I'll remind you. He led you to them, and you let them escape. You also lost track of him."

I hung my head. "Yes, Tribune."

"A pity," Arthur said with a shake of his head. "Venison would have made a great addition to tomorrow's supper. Well. I'll leave you to the rest of your watch. I expect Cavall will have returned by then. If not, we can go find him in the morning."

"We, Tribune?" I asked, surprised.

"Yes. 'we'. I gave you the task of taking Cavall outside to investigate the disturbance. You let him get away by using a leash that was too weak to restrain him. Ultimately though, he is *my* hound. He is *my* responsibility. Leaders are always responsible for those under them." Arthur stared intently at me, and I understood he was talking about more than just Cavall's escape.

He continued, "Since Rome left this land a hundred years ago, a dozen kingdoms have sprung up. All of them have soldiers they can call upon. A few of them even still try to hold to the old ways, and fight as the Romans did. The Red Dragons are unique. It is not formed out of whatever young men happen to just live in the surrounding villages. It is made up of the nobility of Dumnonia to the south, Powys, Dyfed, Gwynedd, Elfed in the Old North, and others, all the way up to Gododdin and Alt Clut, who border the Pict lands. Everyone in this numerus is hand-picked. Everyone chosen already knows how to ride, how to fight, and has the discipline to obey orders, even before they came here. Most even have a strong enough sense of honor, and courage. For most warbands and even most kings' retinues, that is enough, but I need more than that. I need men that can be sent out on a mission alone, or in small groups, who may or may not have all the necessary equipment and supplies, and still find a way to achieve their goal. I expect my men to be quick enough to think on their feet and improvise, and to seize opportunities when they present themselves. The Red Dragons won't retain men who are unable to do that. Do you understand, Peredur?" His eyes bore into mine.

I stared up at him, trying to gauge just how badly I had messed up, but his expression was unreadable. He didn't seem angry with me. Annoyed? Disappointed, maybe? Yes, that seemed to be most likely. I hadn't failed in my duties, after all. But neither had I taken initiative to obtain food for the unit when chance had provided itself.

"Yes, Tribune," I answered, feeling foolish and a bit angry at myself for disappointing Arthur, even in this small matter.

"Good. Because I need as many such men as I can," Arthur said, "And there are never enough." He smacked the scroll against his open hand repeatedly for a few moments as he stood to go. "Learn your lesson well, Peredur. You may have a chance to show me what you've learned, sooner rather than later." He moved to the stairway and walked back down the stairs. I barely heard his final words. "Much sooner ..."

We were each left to our own thoughts. The rest of our watch passed uneventfully, finally relieved sometime later, and we went back to our barracks and our soft beds.

*****

Arthur made the announcement the next afternoon. Everyone formed up in a rectangular formation. I noticed that he had a scroll in his hand and wondered if it was the same one from the previous night. Cavall had returned and sat not far from Arthur.

"Men," our Tribune said in a loud, clear voice. "Our friend, King Leudon, of Gododdin, is in trouble. Picts have been raiding his lands since the end of the harvest. Villages have been burned. Men, women, and children have been killed. King Leudon has attempted to bring these barbarians to heel, but they attack, and fade into the wilderness before he has a chance to respond in force. He has called for assistance, and the Red Dragons shall answer. Vicarius Cai, Decurions Galhault, Owain, Morcant, Titus, and Delwyn; your turmae will ride with me." The decurions named by Arthur nodded in acknowledgement as Arthur called them off. "The remaining turmae will stay and continue to garrison the fort. If your turma is riding out, get your affairs in order and get your gear packed. I want to be on the road in a few days. Decurions, see me after the formation. The rest of you are dismissed."

Having heard our decurion's name called off, Gilbert and I rushed back to our barracks and began to pack, along with the rest of our section, knowing that we would be among those going north. Packing our few belongings would be done the night before we actually rode out, but in the meantime we could make sure our spare clothing, blankets, and the equipment we planned to bring were all freshly cleaned, and serviceable. Later that day, Owain came by and spoke with us as we were putting an extra sharp edge to our swords and daggers, reminding us that if we were missing anything we needed, now was the time to go buy it.

"The ride north will take a month, this time of year. There will be towns we can stop and resupply at along the way, but there's no telling what supplies they'll have on hand, the further north we go. Also, we're gathering men along the way. Arthur's sending out messengers in the next day or so to muster more of our men. So we should be up to at least ten turmae by the time we reach

King Leudon at Din Pendyrlaw. And that means each stop we make from here on out, dozens of fighters will probably be competing for the same supplies you yourselves might wish to buy."

We nodded our understanding. Before he returned to his home, Owain inspected our weapons and armor, pointed out a couple of deficiencies, and then left.

The next three days flew by. Each of our six turmae had two to three wagons of varying sizes in which we loaded tents, spare weaponry, extra blankets, canteens, and sacks of food, particularly grain from the fort's granary. Each man had a blanket rolled up and strapped to the back of his saddle, along with a canteen, and a long case that contained a half dozen javelins. Each of us made sure that the leather loops on the inside of our large shields were filled with a row of plumbatae, as well. On the evening of the third day, Owain did a final inspection of our turma. All twenty-two of us formed up in two ranks, with our mounts, as he went down the line, scrutinizing our weapons and armor, and checking over the horses to make sure that they too were ready for the long ride ahead. Each of us had also painted the leather shells of our shields white, with a large, red Chi Rho over that.

At dawn the following morning, we formed up in a long column at the northern gates. It was a cold, February day, and raining, so only a few wives and other family members stood by the gates to wave to us as we waited for the signal to depart, wrapped up in heavy woolen cloaks. Then Arthur and his own turma trotted past us, to take their place at the head of the formation. I saw his standard bearers with the draco standard of the numerus as well as his personal vexillum go by. Some of the men cheered at the sight of the brass headed draco with its long, red tail fluttering by. As they passed me, I saw that each man of Arthur's turma wore a deep red hooded cloak, and all of their shields were painted white, as my turma's was, but emblazoned on their shields were elaborately painted red dragons in varying styles. Some also incorporated the Chi Rho. Arthur himself had an image of the Virgin Mary, encircled by a dragon, on his own shield.

Moments later, we heard the distinctive blast of a horn, called a lituus, that our numerus used to signal it forward, and our column moved out. The lituus, like many other elements of our numerus, was part of our Roman heritage, and therefore one more relic of a past that was quickly being forgotten in the chaos of this present, dark age. I must admit, I felt some disappointment that we would not be fighting some Saxons or Angles, but at least this still sounded like it would be an adventure worthy of my father's own tales. I looked back once at the fort, then fixed my gaze forward, anticipating the coming battle, and the glory I was determined to win.

# Chapter Seven

O ur detachment followed the winding Afon that flowed northward, and then the Afon Hafren from there. These rivers marked the borders of the Britonnic kingdoms of Gwent and Powys to the west, and Anglian territory to the east. Along the way, traveling on one of the Roman roads, we came across some sprawling ruins off to our left. These weren't the first we'd seen since leaving Caer Lleon, but they were some of the largest. There had clearly been a fortress, and a surrounding village, once. Not far from the road I saw a simple, stone slab. I nearly passed by without a second glance, until I noticed that it had words carved into it. I scrutinized it as I rode by.

"What's it say?" Gilbert asked from behind me.

"This place was called Bravonium... Bravinium, maybe?" I replied. "The wording was a bit rough and hard to read, especially without dismounting for a closer look."

"This place did not die quietly," Marcus muttered, riding beside me.

I glanced his way. He must have seen my confusion because he gestured at the ruins.

"Look at the walls. These ruins look old, but there's still traces of ash everywhere. I'd wager that if we really looked around, we'd find bones, broken weapons, and all sorts of things."

I did look, and a shiver went down my back. It was mid-Februarius, so it was naturally cold, and a bit overcast. Skeletal trees dotted the landscape. Now that Marcus had pointed out the ash, I couldn't help but see the landscape differently. Some of those smooth, round stones that littered the ground here and there could actually be human remains. How many people had died here, I wondered, and who had killed them? I thought back to my history lessons. Rome had never fully solidified its hold in the mountainous western regions, where my people lived. Could my ancestors have rebelled against the Romans here? Maybe. But then, Romans fought numerous civil conflicts as well, particularly in its later years. A few of those had even affected us here, on the fringes of the Empire. At least one Romano-Briton officer had made a play for the throne, and even reigned as emperor for a short while. The last one was Constantine III. Many Britons had tried to forget him though, as he was the man ultimately responsible for pulling the last of the Roman troops out of Britain in order to seize Rome, at the expense of our security.

I found it remarkable that even in their ruined state, these buildings still commanded a sense of awe. Such artistry went into their making. And such effort. Bits of color were still visible on some of the carvings, near the top of the buildings. These must have been so colorful and beautiful once upon a time, I thought. One such building looked to have been a temple. I thought about what had replaced these great stone monuments to Roman culture, and felt a bit wistful.

"I would like to have seen the Romans in Britain at their peak, maybe two hundred years ago," I said. Marcus nodded, looking at the burned, roofless temple and its jagged columns.

Gilbert made a noise "I bet your ancestors would disagree. I know mine did. They always resisted Rome's attempts at subjugation," he said proudly. "Yes, the Romans built beautiful monuments to their own glory. And they paid for it with the blood and sweat of *our* people."

I shrugged. "Empires are like people, I think. Most are neither wholly good nor wholly evil. I can appreciate the talent, ingenuity, and hard work the Romans put into places like these without condoning everything they did as a people. However, I could point out that the Romans really weren't much worse than anybody else, past or present. That includes your people, as well as mine. At least the Romans left us with usable roads," I said and gestured to the very one we currently rode on.

We continued on for the rest of the day and rode until nearly sunset. When we stopped, we pulled tents out of the wagons each turma had allotted to it, and just as the Roman legions had done for centuries, each contubernium of eight men shared a tent. Pickets were posted. Even in Briton-controlled territory, there were still outlaws to consider, and wild animals that might try to get into our food stores. There was also the possibility of Saxon raiding parties.

Each morning we broke camp, quickly putting our tents away back in our wagons, ate a light breakfast, donned our armor, and got back on the road. Only a few days after we passed by the ruins we came upon a large homestead. My turma was riding point, ahead of the main body that day, so we were the first to arrive. It was a well-furnished place, with a notable well, a mill, and a modest-sized flock of sheep. A youth who'd been with them apparently saw us, then ran towards the house, gesturing back at us.

Owain looked over the place approvingly. "Let's pay our respects to the land-holder. Maybe we can purchase some of his stock to supplement our rations." Gilbert and I grinned at each other and my mouth watered, just thinking of some fresh lamb for supper.

Owain gestured. "Harri, with me. Sawyl, Cornelius, sit tight. I wouldn't want to frighten this family by riding right up to their doorstep with twenty armed men," he said with a smile.

Harri nodded, and the two rode up to within a few paces of the house. It was a large, rectangular structure of wattle and daub. Smoke curled lazily from a small hole near the peak of its thatched roof. Uncommonly, I noticed the timber beams extending into the foundation, a detail I had rarely seen before. Nearby, a smaller outbuilding stood to one side, built in a similar style. Beyond it, a pig pen lay muddy and stinking, the animals grunting softly as they rooted in the muck. Beside me, Gilbert stared at the house, scowling slightly.

"What's wrong?" I asked, looking at him.

"Something feels....off about this place," he said slowly.

I shrugged. "The man's home looks extra sturdy. Most people don't bother using thick timber around the entire house." I cocked my head as I suddenly noticed something else. "And most people don't build rectangular houses. Roundhouses are the traditional style. Though Romans preferred this of course."

"So do my people," Gilbert said, and his scowl deepened. His hand slowly moved to rest on the handle of his seax, and he glanced around, studying the landscape around us.

I was just about to say something more when I heard a yelling at the house, then a door slam shut. We weren't close enough for me to hear what was said, though it had sounded oddly harsh and guttural to my ears. I watched as Owain and Harri quickly mounted up and rode back to us at a trot. Owain's hand rested on his sword, and both men were looking around, as though expecting an attack.

"What happened?" Cornelius asked the moment Owain and Harri reached us.

"They're Saxons!" Owain exclaimed.

"Saxons? *Here*?" I asked, startled, looking over at Gilbert. His lips pursed together and his jaw muscles flexed.

"God's blood!" Sawyl swore. "Do we kill them?"

"Maybe," Owain said, also glancing over at Gilbert. "Sawyl, take a couple of your men and go back to the column. Inform the Tribune of the situation. Cornelius, I want you to take your section of men to sweep the immediate area to see if there's any more of these people. Gilbert, you'll come with me back to the house. I couldn't speak with that 'landholder' so I want you with me to translate." The way he said 'landholder' made me think that at this point, our decurion didn't quite believe the man's status. "Harri. Peredur." He gestured at us. "You two come along as well, and just keep an eye out. Be ready for trouble.

The rest of you," he gestured to the remainder of Sawyl's section, "Check out the structures around the house. If you see anything suspicious, come get me."

The men nodded, then everyone rode off in separate directions in accordance with their assigned tasks. As we rode back up to the house, I asked Owain about the Saxon and what his presence might mean.

"Nothing good, no matter how you look at it," Owain replied. "He might be the first of a wave of Saxons willing to risk encroaching into Briton territory in order to get a good piece of land, if all the prime farmland in the east has already been claimed. I refuse to believe there's *that* many Saxons here. It's possible that he had a falling out or had some other reason to break with his own people, and is here with the knowledge and permission of the Britonnic lord of these lands, whoever that is. That's possible, but also unlikely, I think. And even if he is, I'd say the most likely explanation is that he's a spy."

By that point, we'd arrived at the house, and Owen banged hard on the door. From inside, a gruff male voice shouted, but the door didn't open. Owen sighed, and looked over at Gilbert. "Did you understand him?"

Gilbert nodded, and flushed slightly. "He, uh, told you to go away."

Owain cocked an eyebrow. "I'm guessing he said that a bit less politely than you did."

Gilbert nodded again, looking embarrassed. "He suggested you should go and ah... spend some quality time with your mother, Decurion."

Owain actually snorted. "Tell him he can either come out and talk like a civilized man, or we can burn his house down around his head."

I felt a jolt go through me. This had just gotten serious! Apparently Gilbert felt the same way, because his eyes widened. "You mean that, Decurion?"

Owain's face hardened. "I do. Now tell him."

Gilbert shouted at the man. There was a pause; then we heard a number of voices speaking- angry voices that spoke rapidly. At least one was a woman.

Gilbert cocked his head, listening. "A woman inside is berating the man, telling him to cooperate..." He winced as we all heard the man shout the word

"Wealh," among other things. Then, abruptly, the door opened, and a tall, surely-looking man with long blond hair and a thick beard stepped out of the house, folding his thick arms across his chest. He growled something in his language. We glanced at Gilbert.

"He asks what we want," Gilbert translated.

"For starters, civility," Owain said, matching his tone with the Saxon's. "So if I hear the term 'Wealh' again, I bash in the teeth of whoever's mouth uttered that word."

Gilbert translated. The moment he'd begun to speak, the Saxon's head whipped around and he focused his intense stare at my comrade. He scowled, spoke again, and nodded, looking over at Owain.

"He agrees. And asks why you're bothering him and his family," Gilbert said after a moment.

"Ask him if he's aware that the giant river off to our east is the generally accepted boundary between Britonnic and Saxon lands," Owain said, a bit sarcastically.

Gilbert spoke. The man glanced eastward, then back at us, and spoke again.

"He says he is aware of the fact, but he was exiled by his ealderman, a high-ranking noble, for killing another man in a dispute. He says he pays rent to Lord-"

Just then, Sawyl's contubernium rode up. Two of them held weapons in their hands. They dismounted, and showed their find to Owain. One held a sturdy-looking spear with an odd feature- a set of crossbars a couple inches below the blade. Another produced a bow.

"We found these in that smaller building," a man named Lucius spoke up. He fixed the Saxon with a wary glance as he showed us his find. "They were rolled up in a blanket."

Owain casually dropped his hand to rest on the pommel of his sword as he turned back to face the Saxon. The large man's eyes flickered from Lucius to

Owain, noting his hands. The Saxon unfolded his own arms, and now held them loosely at his sides. He said something.

"He demands to know why we're going through his belongings," Gilbert translated.

"Does he now?" Owain said, chuckling, though there was no humor in his tone. He took the spear from Lucius, examining it. His fingers tapped on the small crossbars, before he ran his thumb across the edge of the spear and nodded with approval. "This spear is in good condition. And sharp. Very sharp. It could probably punch right through a coat of mail, with a bit of force." He glanced at the Saxon's large arms as he said this.

"Ask him why he has these weapons," Owain directed to Gilbert.

He did, and the Saxon responded, gesturing emphatically out towards the countryside. "He says they're for hunting game," Gilbert relayed.

"Game!" Owain echoed, sounding incredulous. He snatched up the bow, flexing it. "This bow has a damned heavy draw weight. This isn't needed for *hunting!*" He practically spat the words. "This is a warbow!"

Gilbert hesitated. "Should I translate that, Decurion?"

Owain glared at the Saxon. "Do it. Let's see his reaction."

Gilbert did, and the big man actually laughed a little. He gestured to his large arms, then to Owain. Gilbert flushed a little as he turned back to our decurion.

"He, ah..." Gilbert winced.

"What did he say?" Owain demanded.

"He insists that it is for hunting and that maybe the draw weight only seems too heavy because you're too weak."

Owain barked a laugh. Whatever he might have said next, I don't know, for at that moment, hearing horses approaching, we all turned, and saw that Arthur, along with Sawyl, had arrived. Owain paused his questioning as we waited for our tribune to dismount and join us.

Arthur was in full armor, with his crimson cloak fastened about his shoulder and carrying his crested helm tucked under one arm. He glanced at the Saxon and then at us as he approached before resting on Owain. "Report," he said.

Owain relayed everything that had transpired over the past few minutes and showed Arthur the weapons Sawyl's men had found on the premises.

"What's his name?" Arthur asked, glancing at the man, who was staring warily at him. Arthur was even taller and larger than he.

Owain paused, and the expression on his face told Arthur the answer. He glanced at Gilbert. "Ask him," he ordered as he returned his attention to the Saxon.

There was a quick exchange. "His name is Eadric," Gilbert relayed.

They conversed for a few minutes, during which time Arthur took the spear from Owain and examined it with interest. He asked Eadric about the crossbars on the spear. The Saxon's demeanor relaxed as he talked, and made a number of gestures.

"He says it is a boar spear. The crossbars, or 'wings' help prevent the spear from penetrating too deeply into the beasts, where the shaft might break, or the boar might continue charging while impaled."

Arthur nodded, impressed. "I like this design! May have to get one of these for myself."

Eadric, seeing Arthur's body language, began to relax. He even smiled slightly, and spoke again. Gilbert translated. "Eadric says these are becoming more common, back home, and more popular than regular spears."

Arthur nodded again. "Has his lord here seen this yet?" Arthur asked casually, but I saw his eyes sharpen a bit as he studied the Saxon's face.

Eadric shook his head and spoke. "He has not. His lord, Callum, rides out here every summer after the lambs have been born and takes twenty percent of the flock. He says he's been on this land for the past four years."

"I see," Arthur murmured. He handed the spear back to Eadric with a polite nod. Eadric actually smiled as he took it. Owain's eyes widened and his jaw dropped a bit. I suspect that because I was standing on the Tribune's left side, I was the only one who noticed that Arthur had handed the spear back to the Saxon with his right hand while his left casually rested on the handle of his dagger. Then he turned back to Owain. "Aside from the weapons, did your men note anything suspicious here? Was this man or anyone actually spying on the road?"

"Not that we saw," Owain acknowledged.

"Then I think we're done here," Arthur replied.

"But he's still a Saxon! On Briton land!" the Decurion protested.

Arthur shrugged. "Owain, we're in Powys. This man doesn't represent any clear threat to our column, and we have no real authority here."

"Are you serious?" Owain asked. "We may not have official authority here, but you and I both know that King Cyngen wouldn't care if he found out we'd dealt with a Saxon spy, colonizer, or whatever he is. It wouldn't matter even if he does have the permission of the land's lord. That just makes him look bad, too!"

"You prefer I kill this man and his family? Or maybe just drive them off this land in the middle of winter, purely because the man is a Saxon, not unlike our cymbrog, here," he said, looking pointedly at Gilbert. Then he continued, "That's also ignoring the fact that he's probably a known landholder to the lord of this territory. Would you like to explain to him, or to King Cyngen, why we chose to evict or slaughter his subjects on little more than a whim? For the last time, Owain, there is nothing to be done here. That's final. We're done here."

Owain gave a respectful nod, and Arthur turned away.

"We'd originally thought to buy some of the man's stock to supplement our rations," I decided to risk mentioning.

Arthur looked back at me, then to Owain. Then he glanced out over the man's flock approvingly. "Not a bad idea." He turned back to Eadric, still standing in his doorway. "Would you happen to have any sheep you'd be willing to sell? I can offer a fair price, in copper ore."

Gilbert translated, and the man actually grinned and nodded. They conversed for a few minutes as they negotiated a price, with the result being that Eadric and his son helped us sort out twenty of his sheep, while our quartermaster was brought up from the column with a few small sacks containing ore and a scale to measure out the landholder's payment. The man's wife came out to watch as we made our transaction. I noted that she was large with child. Servants who were attached to the supply train came and rounded up the sheep and herded them into the trail end of our column.

As we prepared to leave, Eadric approached Gilbert and said something, gesturing down the road. Gilbert's eyes widened a bit, and he said something to the man. They shook hands, and Gilbert called out to Arthur.

"Tribune! Eadric wanted to warn us. If we stay on this road, there's a town, a few days up the way, along the border of Elfed. They've come down with plague!"

Arthur and Owain exchanged glances. Then Arthur walked back over and also shook the Saxon's hand with a firm grasp. He nodded to Eadric's wife, threw the boy a wink, and then we mounted up and rode away. We continued on our way, enjoying fresh mutton for many nights as we slowly progressed northward.

After riding through Powys, we passed into the small kingdom of Elfed nearly two weeks into our journey, marking the halfway point. Had our column been making this trek in the summer, and we didn't need to bring so many wagons of food with us, we could have made much better time. As it was, the weather slowly became colder as we rode north. We passed a few towns along the way, but they rarely had food to sell us, not at this time of year.

We knew the town in question when we approached. It was the only one straddling the border with Elfed, and we immediately noted the rows of freshly dug graves, just beyond the town's shallow defensive wall. I shivered as we silently rode past, noting a few of the townsfolk watched us go by. Some were coughing loudly. A few waved at us. Many of us made the sign of the cross, hoping to ward ourselves against evil spirits. Saxons and other barbarians were one thing. However savage and numerous they were, we could see them. We could occasionally negotiate with them. We could *fight* them, but short of avoiding people when they were sick, and praying to God for deliverance, there was no combating plague. When it struck, populations were decimated.

From Elfed, we passed through the kingdom of Rheged. The main road that traveled almost the entire length of Britain, made by the Romans, of course, unfortunately passed through the Kingdom of Bryneich. Bryneich was supposedly still a Brittonic kingdom, but so many Saxons had moved in over the past few years that Arthur decided that our presence would likely stir up trouble, which we had neither the time nor the inclination to deal with. So we split off of the main road and used other roads north, and crossed into Rheged. The ground was more rugged, and the roads more degraded and less direct, but the worst threat on these roads were bandits, which weren't stupid enough to attack a column of armored horsemen our size.

When we came to Hadrian's Wall, Gilbert gave me a critical look. "This is the famous wall you wouldn't shut up about for the past few days?" he asked, gesturing. The wall was impressive, if somewhat less so than I had imagined, and consequently described to my friends. Of course, the wall I had grown up hearing about was the version of it that was well-maintained, and garrisoned by Roman legionnaires.

"This wall was made hundreds of years ago, and has been abandoned for the past century," I protested. "Even now, look at it, man. Look at how thick it is! And it's still a dozen feet tall in places. Nobody builds like this these days. And this wall spans the entire width of this isle!"

"Well now it's an impressively big pile of rocks, loosely resembling a wall, and has so many many weeds and bushes sprouting from it that in another century I doubt anyone will even realize what it was," Marcus snorted.

"Sure they will!" I argued. "Even if most of the wall itself wears down, look at how tall the rampart is. Look how steep the defensive ditches are. An army could still defend this ground, if need be. These earthworks won't disappear for a long time!"

"All these facts you keep spouting at us, nonstop..." Idris commented, "I can't help but wonder, you didn't spend much time with girls growing up, did you?"

"Says the man who's always checking his reflection anytime he comes across something shiny?" I retorted.

Idris shrugged and smiled. "It isn't easy being as good-looking as I am."

We argued and teased each other like this constantly while we rode, if only to ease the monotony. Thankfully, Hadrian's Wall marked the beginning of the end of our journey, for the wall represented the southern border of the Kingdom of Gododdin, though I'd heard from a couple of our men from this region that the Anglians of Bryneich were slowly settling into the area, which was causing some friction.

Gododdin was one of the larger kingdoms in Britain at this time. Its eastern border extended to the sea known as the Mare Germanicum, as the Romans had named it. Its northern border was established at the Firth and Forth, where the sea nearly cut straight through our isle. Gododdin's western border was the most ill-defined. It was honestly impossible to truly distinguish on a map where Gododdin ended and where Alt Clut, to the west, began. Partially this was because Gododdin was as much a reference to a tribe by the same name as it was a kingdom with defined borders. It was more common to simply speak of 'the Gododdin' for example, than it was to say the 'Kingdom' of Gododdin. Fortunately for us, King Leudon of Gododdin and King Domgal of Alt Clut got on well enough. They were both too busy fighting off Picti and Scoti raiders to worry too much over who owned a few small villages in the central region at the fringes of their two kingdoms.

Upon reaching the River Tueth, Arthur rearranged our column a bit.

"We've entered the area the Picts have been raiding now," Owain told us on that first night. It's possible that we're already under their observation. So for these last few days of travel, we're to wear full kit and be ready for anything. Our baggage train will be placed in the middle of the column to ensure its safety. From here on out we don't light any fires at night either. Arthur wants noise and light discipline. God willing, we'll slip through here and up to Din Pendyrlaw without the barbarians realizing that King Leudon's been reinforced."

We acknowledged our decurion's orders, and kept a close lookout of the surrounding terrain as we rode the last leg of our journey. A few times we saw thin columns of smoke in the distance, but of course we had no way of knowing whether the smoke came from a villager's hearth, or a Pict encampment.

Whether we were seen or not is impossible to say. Given how events transpired, I suspect they did not, God be praised. At the very least, if we were seen, they chose not to attack us, and we arrived safely at the hillfort of Din Pendyrlaw, the most impregnable city in Gododdin. The city was built upon a truly massive hill. We'd seen it from miles away, but I was in awe as we approached its walls. It boasted tall, thick walls of stone and timber, as well as impressive earthworks, and a great hall at its peak. Sentries manned tall guard towers, and dozens of houses crowded around the outer walls.

King Leudon himself came out to greet Arthur, at the head of our column. The two walked up and shook hands. I saw the king grin broadly. Beside him, a woman with long dark hair walked up and hugged Arthur.

"That's Morgause, the queen of Gododdin," Owain told us as we watched them greet our tribune. On the ride north, rumors had circulated that Arthur had family in Gododdin. Owain had addressed this to the turma, as other decurions had probably done. Yes, his half-sister was married to Leudon, and they had two sons, Gawain and Medraut, and a daughter named Tenue. Certainly, this family connection was a reason for Arthur's ride north, but it was absolutely not a primary factor, Owain stressed to us. "Remember, first and foremost, this mission was a directive from the Council. So don't anyone get any idea that we're just riding to Caledonia to save Arthur's family. Not that any one of us wouldn't likely do exactly that if it were our own families in danger," he'd added dryly.

Seeing her in the flesh now, I stared at the woman with a bit more interest, trying to compare her to Arthur, to see if I could spot a family resemblance, but aside from her slightly taller than average build, I saw nothing remarkable about her. She carried herself well though. Even under different circumstances, I suspect I would have realized she was royalty. She had that proud look about her. By contrast, King Leudon was shorter; in fact he was a bit shorter than Morgause. He was thickly built and had a warrior's look to him. Their children weren't with them.

We watched them for a bit; then orders were passed down for us to fall out and set up camp. The village didn't encompass the entire hillfort, so we found an open area near the outermost wall and set up our tents and picket lines for our horses. Our wagons were positioned in the center of our camp. Having finally reached Din Pendyrlaw, we were also allowed to celebrate with hot food and sponge baths within the privacy of our camp.

It was hard, going to sleep that night. As content as I was to finally be at our destination, I knew we should expect to be in combat before too long, maybe even within the next few days. Dueling dreams of glory and the fear of behaving dishonorably played out in my mind. When the time came, how would I behave in the face of the enemy? I both dreaded and longed to find out. I shoved the incident at sea out of my mind. That one didn't count, I reasoned. I'd been trained to fight with the sword and spear, and expected to fight in a shield wall or with cavalry, *not* on boats, out at sea.

# Chapter Eight

"After conferring with King Leudon and his advisor, Guinnion, Arthur has decided to deploy the Red Dragons into a series of outposts," Decurion Owain told us. We had been encamped outside the hillfort for two days, while Arthur and our senior leaders met in council with the king and his advisors, discussing our strategy. Now our turma was gathered around a large, crude map of the region composed of lines drawn in the dirt, rocks and sticks to represent various villages, patrol routes, and the like.

"King Leudon will be sending out messages to his lords to muster whatever men they can spare and assemble at a village eighteen miles west of Din Pendyrlaw, called Caer Amon, here," he said, gesturing to a rock on the map with a javelin in his hand. "We believe that the Picts number no more than about eighty to a hundred men, operating in groups of twenty to thirty raiders. They attack villages a few hours before dusk, burn what they can, steal what they're able to make off with, kill any who resist, and scurry back into the woods south of here. By the time the men of the village, or King Leudon's levies can respond, it's near dark, and impossible to pursue the barbarians."

"Are they mounted?" Gilbert asked, studying the map. "They seem to be covering quite a bit of territory."

"Witnesses say that their leaders are mounted, but most of the raiding party is on foot," Owain answered. "We believe they could be using the River Clud, southwest of us, to make their escapes, and to move quickly from village to village. Either they have boats hidden away, or they're crossing at fording sites.

My bet would be boats though. So, each turma has been assigned a ten-mile patrol route from here... to here," he said as he drew a line in the dirt from where the River Tuedd flowed into the eastern sea, to a point west of the Firth of Forth.

"Decurion Galhault's turma will cover the ground between the Tuedd and the Clud, east of us. Along with our patrols, once they are mustered, King Leudon will start moving supply convoys between villages, particularly villages the Picts haven't attacked yet. This will serve two purposes. It will move supplies west, where we'll need them for the second part of this operation, but also these convoys will be bait. When the Picts attack them, the guards will signal us with horn blasts, and hopefully we can respond in time to destroy the raiders."

"And if we aren't?" one of the other soldiers asked.

"The wagons will have additional men hidden within," Owain answered. "Each convoy should have about twenty men, but only half will be visible. Any fewer, and the raiders might suspect that it's a trap, but with twenty men, even if we aren't able to respond in time, King Leudon's levies should at least be able to hold their own against these raiders. Anyway, between our patrols, and the convoys, we believe we can eliminate the raiding parties," Owain paused, then looked around at us.

"That's Part One. To make sure that we've wiped out all of the barbarians, once the raiding has stopped, we'll consolidate our turmae south of Din Pendyrlaw and do a thorough sweep west and then north, up to the River Forth, which is the border to King Leudon's domain. That's Part Two. From that point, depending on how long it takes, and how we're doing on supplies, we will either return to Caer Lleon, or pull back to an old Roman wall, here," he gestured to an area just south of the river.

With a start, I realized that I recognized the area from maps I'd seen as a boy. "That's the border wall built by Emperor Antoninus Pius, hundreds of years ago," I mused aloud.

Owain glanced at me. "Thanks for the history lesson, Scholar Peredur," he said, dryly. Then he looked around at the rest of the turma. "I don't expect this

... Antonine Wall to become any kind of defensive position for the Red Dragons. If any of the structures there are at least intact enough for us to get a bit of shelter from this cursed rain and wind, that's likely all we might want it for, aside from an easy location to use as a reference point while we scour the woods clean of barbarians."

"So, where's our patrol route?" Gilbert asked.

"Our turma is to patrol from here," he gestured at the eastern end of the Antonine Wall, "down to here, near the River Clud. It's a bit more than ten miles, but we'll also be the closest ones to King Leudon's levies, which will be just a few miles east of us, should we need their assistance."

The briefing ended then. Owain pointed out that the Red Dragons would be breaking camp at first light the next morning, with each turma going to its designated position.

\*\*\*\*\*

From Din Pendyrlaw it took us two days to reach our assigned region. I was surprised and a bit disappointed when we reached the Antonine Wall. I'd imagined something more like the one built by Emperor Hadrian some hundred miles to the south, but this one was less of a wall and more like a very tall, steep berm. It was an impressive feat to be sure, to create a berm that ran nearly forty miles and that completely walled off the northern portion of Caledonia, but still less impressive than the southern stone wall with its numerous guard towers and forts connected to it. Some of those were even still lived in.

My turma rode along the Roman road that ran parallel to the wall, seeking out a likely spot to set up our outpost. Many areas along the wall were marshy, and unsuitable for an outpost without spending considerable time in constructing one. We found areas where someone, presumably the Romans, had once done precisely that. Here and there, land was leveled, and we saw the low, stone foundations of what were once buildings.

Almost midway between the east and west coasts, we finally found a spot along the Antonine border wall where the ground was a bit more elevated, making a natural land bridge between the north and south. There was a break in the wall, which allowed a road to run through it, making use of this higher ground. Ruins indicated that a sizable Roman fort had also been built here.

"This place might work," Owain said, and called for us to go investigate. We turned off the road and rode through what would have been the fort's southern gate. While it was mostly cleared away, with nothing more than the usual stone foundations of buildings remaining, this fort at least, had a few stone structures. The rectangular great hall was designed similarly to the one in Caer Lleon, though smaller in scale. It had an enclosed courtyard, was constructed of stone, and was mostly intact. Granted, the wooden floor, ceiling, and previous levels that would likely have existed in such a tall building had long since rotted away, but even the skeletal remains of the hall were at least usable. We inspected two or three other buildings, also made of stone, and deemed them serviceable.

As we inspected the old fort, we saw that the ground was littered with animal and even a few human bones. We also found bits of old equipment scattered about, and several small statues and alters. A real treasure, found by Marcus, was an old-style, rusted Roman helmet. It was missing one of the hinged cheek guards, but still had the flaring neck guard, and the ridged piece that protected the forehead. A bit ominously, when he showed his find off to us, Owain pointed out that a dented tear in the side of the helmet looked suspiciously like it had been made with an axe.

Although the fort had greatly deteriorated with the passing of time, and much of it was now gone or functionally useless, we were pleased with the walls. Aside from gaping holes where the gates would have been, this fort actually had stone walls about ten feet tall, with earth ramparts behind them and a defensive ditch dug around it. A second, more shallow ditch, further down the slope, protected the first, on its northern wall.

Walking over to the section of the fort where it joined with the border wall, I peered down. The northern wall was about fifteen feet tall, thanks to the ditch at the base of it. It wasn't impregnable by any means, but it surely wouldn't be a terrible location to defend, either. And it had a good view of the surrounding area, as well.

After walking around a bit, we gathered at the entrance to the great hall in the center of the fort. Gilbert cradled a human skull in his arms and gave us all a grin.

"Anyone need head?" he asked and held the skull up as he wiggled his eyebrows.

"I'm not desperate enough yet," Marcus replied. "But give me another week..."

"By then he'll have turned that thing into his new drinking goblet," I grunted.

Gilbert looked back at the skull thoughtfully and turned it to face him as he did so. "You know, I might at that," he mused.

"Quit messing with the skull," Owain said. "What do you lads think of this place?" he asked.

"Good walls. Good view," I said.

"It's certainly big enough for King Leudon's levies," Decanus Sawyl said. "Maybe not big enough for them, and the Red Dragons though."

"We'd need to build up the gatehouses, or block them off for this place to be truly useful," Gilbert pointed out. "Otherwise there's four easy access points into the fort."

"That shouldn't be too hard to do, once the levies get here," Decanus Cornelius mused.

Owain nodded in agreement. "I think we'll use this spot," he said. "We'll gather the wagons and supplies here, by the great hall. We can set up our tents inside the stone foundations where some of the buildings used to be."

Besides our horses, we had three wagons we'd used to transport our turma's tents and supplies, not to mention the mules we'd used to haul the wagons. Every turma was also given a small cage containing a trio of homing pigeons that could quickly relay important messages back to Din Pendyrlaw, if we really ran into trouble. Otherwise, for routine reports, one of the men was to ride east to

Caer Amon, where another messenger would continue on to Din Pendyrlaw, or to Arthur, to relay whatever message we needed to pass on. Those same messengers also relayed information back to us.

We set to work, and by the end of the day, we had chopped down some trees and made a crude but functional corral for our horses, and unloaded our wagons. While we waited for our levy infantry support to arrive, we continued chopping down trees and shaping them into usable logs. We also stored barrels of water along the wall to put out fires should the fort ever be attacked with fire.

Owain worked us hard, but once the sun was down we set up our tents in case it decided to rain, and built up a large fire. We cooked rations, and sat around telling stories or playing dice. Throughout the day, we'd caught glimpses of a pack of wild dogs roaming the area. They kept their distance, but didn't seem to fear us either. Now, at night, we heard them barking and yapping at each other, on the other side of the wall. Fortunately, they hadn't looked like they were starving, so they weren't desperate enough to come after our horses and mules with us camped so close by.

I seemed to have terrible luck with dice, so while some of the others played, I simply enjoyed the comforting warmth and the spectacle of the flames of our fire dancing and flickering. Gilbert sat beside me, whittling some kind of animal from a chunk of wood. My mind drifted, and I thought of home, and what my family would be doing now. I hoped Mother had adjusted to my absence, and that my father and brother were getting along. I wrote to her and the rest of my family after becoming a Red Dragon and sent the letter off with a merchant heading toward Mona, shortly before the winter solstice. Not very surprisingly, by the time we left Caer Lleon, I hadn't received a reply. Then I started thinking of current events, which in turn led me to the long chain of events that had led up to it.

If the stories were true, the balance of power between we Britons and the Saxons had all begun to shift sixty years ago with the arrival of just three ships full of Saxon mercenaries under the command of the brothers Hengist and Horsa.

"It's said," I spoke up, still staring into the fire, "that the warlord Hengist's daughter was so beautiful that when King Vortigern saw her, he became completely obsessed with her, and that's the leverage Hengist used to trick Vortigern into giving him the land of Cantia."

Cornelius looked over at me, pausing as he was about to cast his dice, and laughed. "That's believable! Seems to me that some of the stupidest things men have ever done usually involve a woman. Look at the tale of Samson and Delilah Father Marcellus told us about at mass."

The lads chuckled at that, and Cornelius cast his dice, whooping in pleasure a moment later.

The others groaned.

"What's the stupidest thing you've done?" I asked.

"Lied to a girl about being one of Arthur's Red Dragons. She adores Arthur," Cornelius replied.

That got our attention. "Did it work?" Marcus asked.

"Too well," Cornelius grunted. "Her father caught us together one evening, out in the woods. He was ready to kill me, but she calmed him down by telling him I was a Red Dragon and that we were in love. Her father backed off, but demanded I marry his daughter."

"So, how's your wife these days?" Gilbert asked with a grin.

Cornelius shot Gilbert a disgusted look. "We didn't get married. I left home, joined the Dragons for real, and by the time I returned her father had decided to marry her off to some local lord whose wife had recently died. He paid her father a nice bride price of sheep, and as I heard it, paid her a dowry in gold jewelry." Our decanus chuckled humorlessly. "Guess the wealth she was offered was more attractive than my status as one of Arthur's Red Dragons."

"You couldn't compete and pay a higher dowry?" Gilbert asked.

Cornelius scoffed. "My father's lands provide us a comfortable living, but not enough to compete with that lord. Anyway, if a little gold was all it took her to forget about me, I probably dodged an arrow with her."

The rest of us nodded our heads in agreement. Just then, Idris came walking over to the fire. He carried his clothing in one hand, dripping wet from a fresh washing, and wore nothing but a cap and his shoes.

"Greetings, lads," he said casually in his odd accent and held his clothes out near the fire. Those nearest to him scooted away, giving him space.

Marcus swore. "Put some clothes on if you're going to come over here with us!"

Cornelius just smirked at him. "You cold, Idris? Or is that your normal look?"

Idris grinned. "Don't be jealous," he said as he continued to dry out his clothes by the fire. "After all, your mother was fine with it when I visited her before we left."

Cornelius said nothing but scooped up a small rock and threw it at Idris, who yelped and turned to the side in order to avoid getting hit where it really could have hurt.

Ignoring them, Gilbert turned to me. "What's the craziest thing *you've* done that involved a girl?" he asked.

I laughed, and glanced over toward our makeshift corral. "I taught Carys to bow on one knee. Then when a girl I liked walked by one day, I dismounted, and Carys and I bowed to her."

Gilbert just looked at me. I noticed Cornelius and a couple others glance my way, too.

"What?" I asked.

"That's it?" Gilbert asked. "Was she even impressed?"

I shrugged, suddenly feeling a bit self-conscious. "She laughed. She had a very charming laugh."

"Peredur, she was laughing *at* you," Marcus sighed.

"You've never... been with a woman before, have you?" Carnellius asked, though his tone made it sound like more of a statement.

"That's none of your business," I replied, and felt my cheeks and ears growing hot. The men chuckled at my answer, so I grumbled "I'm going to go visit the woodline," I grumbled, and walked away, ignoring the remarks of "Peredur the Innocent" being thrown around.

\*\*\*\*\*

The next two days went about like the first. We worked on improving the fort while the sun was up, and relaxed during the evenings. Over four hundred levies marched up on the third morning following our own arrival. Owain spoke with their commander, named Garwlwyd, and the men settled in, pitching their own tents and consolidating their supplies with ours in the courtyard of the great hall. Garwlwyd was a penteulu, or clan leader, as well as the commander of these levies, and he was a frightening-looking man. He was lean and hard-eyed, with a blond beard streaked with gray. The most distinctive thing about him though was that he wore a wolf's pelt for a cloak over his sleeveless chainmail shirt. The skin of the front legs wrapped across his shoulders, and the wolf's head was draped over his helmet, so that he reminded me of carvings I'd seen of the Romans who, once upon a time, were depicted carrying the legions' banners. I was just glad he was on our side. Upon his arrival, Garwlywyd was quick to inform us that more levies would join us later. The smaller, front wing of the great hall was used as the headquarters and barracks for the levied troops' leaders, while the larger wing in the rear was set aside for the field hospital.

With our levies now on hand to begin restoring the old fort and providing small patrols of the immediate area around the fort, we started up our patrols of the region. On our third day of this, a courier was waiting for us at the fort upon our return. He was one of King Leudon's levies, and spoke with a northern accent.

"The raiders struck again," he informed us bitterly. "They hit a small village and killed the men who tried to defend it. Several of the children were killed or injured as well."

Owain swore. "And the women?" he asked.

The levy looked away, and his hands clenched into fists. "The barbarians violated several of them. A couple that resisted were killed as well."

Owain nodded, as though expecting that answer. "How many killed?" He asked in a curt voice. He was maintaining his composure, but I knew he was seething. We all were.

"About ten men. Nearly double that in women and children," the courier replied.

Our decurion asked a few other questions regarding the incident. Meanwhile, I reflected on the news. I had been disappointed when Arthur had first told us that we were riding all the way to the north end of Britain to aid the Gododdin, rather than fight the Saxons. I knew revenge for my brother wasn't supposed to be my primary motivation for riding with the Red Dragons, and I had tried to shift my priorities since joining the numerus. The entire point to the existence of the Red Dragons was to aid *all* of the various Brittonic kingdoms against our many common enemies, after all. And I was fine with that. I'd just hoped we would be fighting Saxons in particular. Hearing the courier's lurid report of the raiders' savagery had a sobering effect. I could easily imagine the devastation they had inflicted upon that village. That in turn made me remember that these raiders had been terrorizing villages all along the Gododdin's southern border for months now. How much more pain and suffering had they caused in that time? Surely they were as brutal and barbaric as the Saxons. That thought made my need to avenge a single man, even if it was my brother, seem almost petty in the grand scheme of things.

The courier's next bit of news snapped me out of my introspection. Cai's turma had made first contact with the Picts, he relayed with some satisfaction. "They attacked one of our 'supply' convoys, between the rivers Clud and Tuedd, last evening! They ambushed it, and killed two of the guards outright with slings, then rushed in. Your men jumped out of the wagons and joined the fight. We killed four, and wounded several more before the raiders broke off and scurried back into the woods, including the man we assume was their leader. He was the only one on horseback. And he had a sword, shield and helmet. The rest only had spears and shields. They think that band had twelve to fifteen raiders."

"None of our men were killed, then?" Owain asked.

"No Red Dragons were killed," the messenger replied, and we sighed with relief.

"Any further instructions for us?" Owain inquired.

"Take a prisoner, if you can," the man responded. "Lord Arthur said they need to know how many more warbands are out here, and where they are camping at night. He also asked if you've had any contact with the blue-painted barbarians yet?"

"One of our sentries heard some suspicious sounding bird calls last night," Owain answered. "But we've seen nothing yet."

The messenger nodded. "That was probably them. I'd wager they've seen you. Keep a good lookout. Now that we've bloodied them, depending on their intentions, they'll either bugger off back north, or get even more aggressive."

Owain nodded, and looked off into the woodline to our north. I did too, and a shiver went down my spine. For all I knew, the Picts were out there right now, watching us. As it happened, the fort's isolation, combined with the miserable weather that kept most people close to home this time of year, was likely our salvation, though we cursed it at the time.

Only a day later, we were riding patrol and had reached the southernmost portion of our route. It was a mostly clear sky, and it felt nice to have the sun shining down on us for a change. Then we saw a thick column of smoke appear in the woods to our south. We pulled up, all eyes staring into the trees.

"Should we check it out, Decurion?" Gilbert asked.

Owain looked around, then at the smoke. "Not yet," he replied after a moment, scratching his jaw. "That's Galhault's section, but let's not return to camp just yet, either."

We watched in silence for several more moments. Whatever was burning was dying out, which wasn't surprising. Although it was sunny today with only a few clouds, the area was rather wet from the frequent rain we had been getting for the past week. Then we heard a horn blast. Everyone in the turma tensed up at that. It wasn't one of ours!

"Let's check it out, lads," Owain decided. He raised his arm high and in his deep, command voice he shouted, "Wedge formation. At the canter, forward!" The moment he started moving, we followed, automatically fanning out into a wedge, with several feet of distance between each other.

My heart pounded as we rode towards the woods, and I scanned left and right, expecting a horde of half-naked, blue-painted barbarians to come charging out at us. I gripped my spear tightly in my right hand. We got to within two hundred paces of the woodline. I licked my lips nervously. I realized though that, unlike the battle on the ship months earlier, I wasn't terrified of *this* fight. I'd trained for this. And this time, unlike on the ship, I was surrounded by cymbrogi who rode side by side with me. I would rather risk death in battle than fail in my duty now, and earn the disdain of my peers, or even worse, of Decurion Owain.

I was near the rear left of the formation, along with Gilbert, which made me feel a little better. We got to a hundred paces, and then we saw them! Dozens of men came running out of the woods towards us. It took me a second to process who they were, because they didn't look how I expected them to. Some were shirtless, true, but most wore tunics, just like ours, and trousers, too. Like us, many also had on cloaks with checkered and striped patterns. What made them stand apart the most was their long, shaggy hair and bushy facial hair that nearly all of them grew. Even more than that was their shields that most of them brandished. The patterns painted on them looked a bit similar to ours, but somehow also foreign. They were also smaller than ours, and mostly square.

I processed these differences in an instant. My next thought, assessing the scene, was the fact that I could see horsemen, deeper in the woods, also coming our way.

*They weren't supposed to have horsemen*, I thought. My heart was pounding and my mouth went dry as fear coursed through me. Was there a whole Pict horde about to come pouring out of those woods? My mind went blank. What were we supposed to do? I thought, frantically. Then Owain bellowed "Turma, *chaaarge*!"

On reflex, I dug my heels into Carys' flanks, and she surged forward. I tossed my spear up into the air, intending to catch it in a reversed, underhand grip so that I could be ready to throw it, but I fumbled and accidentally batted the spear away instead. I swore to myself as I watched it fall to the ground in horror.

*Lord Jesus, please don't let anyone have seen that!* I thought as I reached down and drew my spatha from its scabbard. We were almost upon them when the situation exploded into chaos. First, the riders that had been to the barbarians' rear burst out of the woods, veering to our right, cutting down Picts as they rode past. In the same moment, Owain shouted the command "Angle left!" and our wedge formation turned to the left, avoiding a collision with the riders coming from the woods. Men in front of me swung their swords down, and more Picts fell to the ground.

Something Decurion Caradoc taught me came to mind. "Drills are bloodless battles, and battles are just bloody drills," I repeated that in my head, and raised my own sword, preparing to slay the first Pict that came within reach, but none did. My comrades in front of me had already cut down the Picts in front of us, like so much wheat before the scythe.

We made a wide circle, and made ready for another pass at the barbarians, but the other group of horsemen, who I realized were Galhault's turma after spotting my old friend Madog, were completely mixed in amongst the Picts, hacking and slashing. I recognized Galhault too. He was so big it was impossible to miss him. He wasn't quite as tall as Arthur, who was one of the tallest men in the unit. But the decurion was easily the largest, and strongest man in our numerus. Adding to that, he wore a crested helmet, which made him seem as tall as Goliath, to my eyes. I watched, slack-jawed as Galhault, who had apparently lost his sword, literally picked one hapless barbarian up by the cloak nearest his neck as he rode past. He smashed his own helmeted head into the Pict's face, then threw him aside. The barbarian flew through the air for several feet before his limp body tumbled from the momentum, and lay still. All around the Picts were being slaughtered.

I was so overwhelmed by the carnage and the noise around me that I scarcely knew what to do with myself. My heart was racing, and I felt myself grow lightheaded, as I had once long ago when I'd nearly slipped from the edge of a cliff back home. Cornelius moved over beside me, leaned over, unhooked my canteen from the back of my saddle, and handed it to me.

I grabbed it, though my hands were shaking slightly, and I took a long drink before putting the stopper back and putting the canteen away. My lightheadedness went away, and I nodded gratefully to Cornelius.

"Happened to a lot of us, the first couple of times," he said. Then an evil grin crossed his face and he held out a spear to me. "Oh, and I think you dropped this."

My face burned with embarrassment, and I snatched the weapon out of his hand. Glancing around, I saw knowing smirks on the faces of several of my tentmates. So much for nobody seeing my mishap during our charge.

"Check for survivors!" Galhault called out. "We need at least one prisoner who can talk!"

We dismounted and fanned out, slowly working our way back through the woods as we checked over the bodies. I felt sick, but took another sip of water, a few deep breaths, and the feeling went away. There weren't nearly as many bodies as I'd expected. In fact, I only saw a half dozen, as I looked around more closely. "I'd swear there were dozens that came out of the woods," I muttered.

"Fear does that," one of my tentmates, Quintus, said. "Every threat seems more frightening and more dangerous than it is. Some people get too used to the danger, though," Quintus mused. "Then their minds deal with the fear by downplaying the danger. That's almost worse. It can lead to recklessness or complacency. There are also several more bodies in the woods, though."

"Or worse than that," Owain chipped in. "They get to enjoy the excitement too much. That can turn men into monsters, along with making them reckless."

"So what happened here?" I asked, seeing a member of Galhault's turma.

"We were on our patrol when Galhault thought he saw movement in the woods. We went in, and in a few minutes we came upon a campsite. It was empty though. So Galhault had us start up a fire and toss their bedrolls and anything we couldn't use onto the fire." The man chuckled at that, and I thought it was a bit funny myself.

"That got the Picts' attention because practically as soon as we started burning their stuff, they came out of the woods and attacked us. They must have gotten overconfident, being that we were in the woods and dismounted, because there were more of us than them. And they didn't factor in Galhault." The man laughed, shaking his head. "He's like the champions the bards sing about. The rest of us dropped our stuff and jumped onto our horses, ready to get out of there and take the fight out in the open. We couldn't stop them from tooting away on a horn though. So there were probably other raiders in the area. Anyway, Galhault didn't mount up with us. He just roared, and charged them with his bare hands! I swear he killed half of them with just his fists. That sort of knocked the fight out of them and they took off to the west. We chased after them. The woods slowed us down a bit but we kept on them. Then your turma showed up and these poor devils were caught between us. So, there's bodies scattered around from here all the way back to the campsite of theirs we found."

We continued to search the area, but only found dead bodies. A couple were still alive, but were so close to death that we knew we wouldn't be able to get anything out of them before they died.

"Do we have somebody who speaks this.... 'bar-bar-bar' language of theirs?" One of the men called out, several minutes later. A few chuckled, though I didn't quite get the joke. "I found one alive, but he doesn't speak any of the Brythonic languages that I know."

"Did you try Latin?" Someone called out. Several more men laughed. I joined in for that one. We all gathered around the wounded Pict was, sitting upright on the ground at their campsite. The fire set by Galhault's men still smoldered nearby. The prisoner looked to be in his early twenties, had swirling blue tattoos painted on his face and arms, and a patchy beard. He was wounded across his back, and it was clearly causing him pain. Owain walked over and examined the man. He spoke to the man in a language I'd never heard before. The Pict glanced at him, then looked away, saying nothing.

"I"m from Alt Clut, west of here," Owain said, bending over to look the prisoner in the eyes. "I've encountered these people from time to time. My people even trade with them. I know a bit of their language, or at least one of them. Like us, the Picts have more than one. You'd be surprised how many of these Picts also speak Brythonic, when they want to."

Without warning, he lashed out and punched the man in the jaw. The Pict grunted, but said nothing.

"How many more of you are out here?" Owain asked, slowly and clearly.

The prisoner didn't respond. He just looked up at the sky, and sighed.

Owain punched him again. And again. By now, the rest of our men had finished checking the bodies, both to see if any were still alive, as well as looting them for anything worth taking and were gathering around, watching the scene. A few, on their own initiative, faced outward, with spears and shields in hand, in case there were further enemies nearby.

"We need to be heading back soon if we're to make it before sunset," I commented, looking from Owain to Cornelius. "Should we be returning to our own camp?"

"Probably," Owain acknowledged. He scratched his jaw, and looked around and spotted something, half buried in the ashes. He walked over, and pulled out a stained, bronze cooking pan and walked back to the Pict, acting as if he planned to hit the man with it. The Pict flinched, but did nothing else aside from glancing from the pan, and up to Owain, who gave the Pict a thoughtful look.

"I think this barbarian can speak our language. We could torture him, and probably get him to talk. Problem is, people in pain will say about anything that they think will make the pain stop, even if just temporarily," he said, to nobody in particular.

"Hey, Galhault," Owain finally called out. Galhault strode over. I saw the Pict's eyes go wide when he saw the big man approach. So did Owain, who smirked. He handed the pan to Galhault. "Do the thing."

Galhault grinned, and took the pan in his massive hands. Then, while he stared down at the barbarian, he slowly curled the pan up like a scroll! The men of Galhault's turma, who had seen him do this trick, chuckled. The rest of us, to include the prisoner, stared wide-eyed and slack-jawed at the display of sheer, brute strength from Galhault.

"Just imagine what he could do to your hands. Your arms .... your head," Owain said in a low, sinister tone to the Pict, tapping the man's limbs and head as he spoke. That got him, clearly terrified at the sight of Galhault and what he had just done. Galhault grinned down at the prisoner, showing him the pan, and tossed it aside. Then he looked the Pict up and down and slowly grabbed him by the foot and ankle. Both were completely enveloped in Galhault's hands.

The prisoner, whose breathing had been increasing rapidly as Galhault did this, suddenly yelled, "I'll talk!"

"How many of you are out here?" Owain asked, immediately.

The Pict was silent for a moment, his eyes flitting around. "There were two hundred men in my warband, when we came south," he finally answered.

"Liar," Owain sneered. He nodded to Galhault, who clamped down and pushed his foot sideways, about to snap the prisoner's ankle like a stick.

"It is the truth!" The Pict shouted and attempted to free his leg, to no avail.

Owain and Galhault exchanged glances, then walked away from the group to talk privately for a few moments. When they returned, Owain gestured to us. "Mount up, lads, we're riding back to the fort. Galhault's men will take the barbarian to Arthur, and find out what else he can tell us about his friends.

We formed up on the draco standard in column formation and made the ten-mile ride back to the fort. The sun had set by the time we got within sight of it, but we had some moonlight, and the levies who guarded the fort had torches lit. Once we were within a hundred paces, Owain held his right hand up in the air so the guards could see he had no weapon. He called out our identity. The guards shouted their acknowledgement and opened the gate.

Once inside, we removed our mounts' bridles and saddles and took them for a short walk in an open area of the fort. Owain talked with us while we walked.

"Some of you may have heard me question that Pict earlier today. You may have heard that he *claims* there were two hundred of his countrymen out in these woods. Even if that were true, we just accounted for thirty of them today, mostly thanks to Galhault's turma. Recall that just the other day, Cai's turma defeated another band. That accounted for a dozen or so enemy fighters. That means, in a matter of days, we've destroyed nearly a quarter of their combat power, but there's still more out there, so don't let your guard down in future patrols."

"Do you think we'll encounter any Picts here?" Cornelius asked.

"Yes," Owain said immediately. "At some point, probably sooner rather than later, these barbarians are going to realize they're being hunted, and more than likely they'll want to go home then. This wall we're on stretches across this entire land, from coast to coast. The Romans built it here because it's the narrowest stretch of land in this region, maybe the whole island of Britain. It's only forty miles wide. That's it. In order for them to get home, these Picts have to cross over this wall, somewhere."

"About that Pict," I said, walking up to the Decurion.

"Yes, Peredur?"

"Would Galhault really have crushed that man's leg?" I asked, feeling just a bit afraid of the answer.

"Of course," Owain answered. I must have looked shocked, because he sighed, and went on. "Peredur, if our situation had been reversed, and the Picts had overwhelmed and captured us, what do you suppose they would have done to us?"

125

"Tortured us?" I asked, sensing that was where he was leading the conversation.

"Oh yes," Owain replied. "Assuming they had the time, and weren't afraid of our people catching them, they would have absolutely tortured us, especially if they felt we had information they needed. Then they would have killed us, and maybe stuck our heads on spears as trophies. And so would the Saxons. And the Scots. That's war, Peredur. It's how war has always been, at least as far back as the days of Joshua and King David that the priest talks about at mass."

"If we practice the same barbarism that our enemy does, what right do we have to regard ourselves as the better men?" I asked.

Owain stopped then, looking at me in silence for a moment. Then he chuckled softly. "I must admit, you're clever, Peredur. You sound like Arthur, when he gets going. He dreams of the Britons all being united as one glorious, Christian kingdom. But that's all it is, a dream. As for us being 'better', I'd say that's yet to be determined. Maybe we were, once, but look around. We're in a ruined fort, built by the Romans, who abandoned this island ages ago. And now even the Western Empire is gone. It's like we're living in those 'end times' the priests speak of, before the return of the Christ. War, plague, death, cities being abandoned and destroyed everywhere we turn. We're in a fight for survival, Peredur. All of us. The Scots raid my homeland in Alt Clut, and are crowding the Picts so hard that they've carved a full-fledged kingdom into Caledonia's coast. This is causing the Picts to push south, into Gododdin and Alt Clut. They figure they must conquer, or die. I can respect that. I really can. They're strong and brave warriors, but if they have their way, our people would be driven off, enslaved, or slaughtered. And by the way, those Pagans don't care about Jesus Christ or his teachings or things like peace and loving your neighbor."

We had approached the stable now and began unbuckling the kit from our horses. Owain continued. "That applies to the Saxons, too, most likely. I don't know whether they're coming here simply because they're greedy, bloodthirsty wretches or whether some other people, meaner and more bloodthirsty than they are, are driving the Saxons west, but the end result is the same. They're here to stay, which means if we don't maintain our dominance of this island, it's likely that it will fall to those Woden-worshipping Saxons, eventually. Do you understand, Peredur?"

"You're telling me that we can't afford to fight in a way that befits a civilized, Christian people probably ought to," I said, resenting the very idea even as I spoke it.

"That's pretty much it," Owain agreed. "We're surrounded by barbarians who are coming at us with the mindset that they will conquer us or die trying. We have to fight just as hard. That means that, like them, I won't hesitate to kill however many of them I have to. I'll torture whomever I have to ensure our own survival. Were I Arthur, I would probably march against the biggest Pict settlement I could find, burn it to the ground, kill or enslave every Pict I could find between here and that village, and line Gododdin's border with Picti heads on spikes as warning against further encroachment. That was how our ancestors did it."

I stared at him, unnerved, not just at what he was saying but the intensity in his tone.

"You are a scary person," I said at last.

Owain grinned. "Yes. I am. I wish every barbarian in Britain knew that. Maybe they would think twice before attacking me or the people I care about. Who knows. Maybe if I were scary enough to make them surrender, then I could try acting as the good Christian you and our Tribune Arthur would wish me to be. Of course, they might perceive that as weakness and take up arms again ...."

I just shook my head, sensing that he was teasing me now. We brushed our horses, fed and watered them, then headed back to our barracks, and stripped out of our own armor and equipment. The levies who guarded the fort while we patrolled had also gone out and killed a pair of deer, so that night we had the luxury of deer rib for supper. I wasn't feeling very talkative anymore after my conversation with Owain, so once I had gotten my food, I went over to a low portion of the southern wall which was only a few feet high, and sat down to eat.

As I did, I looked out into the woods and saw a couple of our local wild dogs, no more than thirty paces away. The smaller of the two, a tawny colored thing with a white muzzle and belly, and large ears, slowly inched toward me, only stopping when it got to within a dozen paces of me. It stared intently at the food in my hands. I stared back at it, unable to determine the dog's sex, and continued eating, until there were only a few scraps of meat left. I could have eaten all of it, but decided not to, and tossed the bone to the tawny dog, who jumped and caught it in the air. The other dog bolted over then, but the first one growled fiercely at it, causing it to back off.

Along with my deer rib, I also had a chunk of bread. I ate most of it, then had an idea, once I was down to just a small morsel. I stretched out on the wall and leaned down, holding just a tiny bit of the bread. The more timid dog backed off, seeing me lean over the edge of the wall. The tawny one backed off a step, but fixated its eyes on my bread. It took a couple steps closer, then a couple more. It got to within a pace of me, then stopped. It looked at the bread, and at me, and actually whined. I couldn't help but chuckle.

"Alright, I guess you've earned it," I decided, and tossed the bread at it. Again, the dog leapt up and caught it mid-air. The bread was gone practically before the dog even landed, but this time the dog was close enough for me to see its belly.

"Enjoy, girl," I said.

My food was gone now, and the sun was all but gone. Normally, we returned from our patrol a few hours before sunset, and used this time to make small improvements on the fort, prioritizing the walls. There was none of that, this evening, given how late we returned. So once I finished eating, I washed up, made sure my weapons and armor were ready for tomorrow, and laid down onto my bedroll. It was nearly freezing cold outside, but thankfully, the air in our barracks, with our entire turma inside, was comfortably warm. I drifted off, still thinking about Galhault and his Picti prisoner.

# Chapter Nine

---

Two days after our fight, a levy patrol led by Garwlwyd himself, returned from the surrounding woods as the sun was going down. He carried a pair of decapitated heads by their long hair in one fist and held them up for Owain to see.

"Caught these two watching our camp," he informed the decurion in his gravelly voice. "We managed to surround and kill them before they could escape and tell their friends about us being here."

"Good work!" Owain nodded his approval. "Think any other Picts have managed to spot us? It would be a shame if they knew to avoid using this route when they eventually try to return home."

The levy commander spat on the ground and shook his head. "Not likely," he replied. "I've been leading the patrols myself, with men I've trained. We're woodsmen who live along the Forth. We're as good in these woods as any Pict. Probably better."

Owain thanked Garwlwyd, who nodded in return, and walked away, still carrying the heads. None of us asked what he was going to do with them. I for one was just a little scared by him. He was nearly as much of a barbarian as the Picts, it seemed to me, but he was our barbarian, thankfully.

The next few days passed slowly, and without further incident. We woke up, ate, and conducted our patrols. Although we had entered the month of Martius, it was still freezing cold throughout most of the day this far north. Despite that, every couple of days, we braved the icy temperatures of a nearby stream to bathe ourselves and wash our clothing. While we rode on patrols, the levies continued to work on the fort, and kept up their patrols as well. Beginning with the northern opening, gatehouses were built from freshly cut logs, as well as watchtowers. The Romans had dug rows upon rows of small pits in front of the northern wall. Freshly made wooden spikes were planted in these pits, to help strengthen our defenses, should the Picts ever actually attack the fort. These would also pull double duty as our latrine pits. When the levies showed up, they dug pits too. So now the entire northern wall was lined with rows of hundreds of holes, with stakes planted into the base of them, and partially filled with human waste. Should any Picts be unlucky enough to fall into those holes, well, they would be in for a bad time.

Once, Gilbert pondered the likelihood of Picts actually attacking us here, now that we had built the fort up. "I wouldn't bet on it," Owain told us on the first day. "We're not digging these defenses because I think the Picts will attack but because, in my experience, the very appearance of a well-prepared fortification can make the enemy less likely to attack."

I'd also started eating my suppers on the wall with Mel, the dog I had, unoriginally I admit, named after her honey-colored fur. I discovered that she and the other dogs of her pack seemed to prefer relaxing along the south side of the fort, probably due to the fact that the ditch along that wall was the most overgrown with brush and had numerous puddles. That stretch of wall was littered with animal bones as well. At first, Owain warned me against "messing with the wildlife" when he saw me feeding the dog, but gave up when he caught Gilbert, and others, tossing scraps out into the ditch for the pack as well. Mel quickly became comfortable enough to nearly take food right out of my hand.

The one day we didn't ride out on patrol was on the Sun's Day. We, and more importantly our horses, were allowed to rest on that day. As it happened, this particular Sun's Day, a storm rolled in from the southwest. There was no clergy to lead us in a service here at the fort, so Decurion Owain allowed us the luxury of sleeping late.

The lowered temperature roused me, or maybe it was the sound of Cornelius, snoring loudly, not far from my own bedroll. I tried to tune him out and go back to sleep, but it was no use, and now that I was awake I needed to relieve myself. Reluctantly, I sat up and pulled on clothing that had just been serving as my pillow. I threw my fur-trimmed woolen cloak over my shoulder as I headed outside and blearily trudged up to the north gate, nodded to the guards, who opened the door, and walked out to the latrine pits. This morning, most of these pits were half filled up with frozen puddles, made from the freezing rain the previous night. I amused myself by melting a small, yellow hole in the middle of one such puddle.

I finished my business, then headed south, to the great hall, where we kept our food, and talked the man guarding our food and supplies into giving me a small wheel of cheese. I ate a bit of it, hard as it was from the cold, and continued south. I walked over to my favorite spot on the southern wall, sat down, and scanned the scenic landscape. Everything had a white sheen to it, as frozen vegetation does, and there was a blanket of fog surrounding the fort, hiding much of the landscape that was normally visible. I glanced up at the early morning sky and sighed, noting the puff of vapor my breath created in the freezing air. The sun was only just peeking up over the horizon, though as cloudy as it was, the sun itself was hidden. This overcast sky, the fresh snow, and heavy fog had the effect of making me feel as though I were in a cold world of gray, one in which all color had seeped away. I ate another bite of cheese, then whistled, scanning the brush for movement. I saw nothing, so I whistled again. This time I heard brush rustling, and looked out. Mel came bounding over, gracefully weaving her way through the bushes. As usual, she stopped a couple paces away, and sat down.

"Well good morning, Mel," I said, happy to see the dog. She cocked her head at me, but otherwise remained still, until I broke off a piece of cheese and held it up. She stood up and tensed, eyes on the morsel of food. I chuckled, then tossed it to her. She jumped, caught it and devoured it, then licked her lips and stared at me, clearly expecting more. I had just torn off another piece when Mel's head suddenly swiveled around, facing the woods, about two hundred paces off. I looked towards the woodline, barely visible in the morning fog.

"What do you see out there, girl?" I asked, softly. She growled then, soft and low. The hair along her spine rose, as well. Barely even conscious of it, I flattened myself out on the top of the old, moss-covered rock wall where I'd been sitting. My cloak was a light tan color, and so it blended in well enough with the stone, if I held still, which I did.

Mel began barking, but stayed where she was. A couple other dogs, somewhere in the ditch, also started barking. My heart began beating faster.

*What was in those woods?* I wondered. Then I noticed movement off to my right. A moment later, a man came out from the trees. He wore a fur cloak and a plain tunic over checkered trousers. He also held a spear and a small, rectangular shield. For a moment, I considered the possibility that he was a local, northern Briton. Then he turned my way and I noted his long, wild hair and beard, and more tellingly, he looked to have blue markings on his face. *Pict!* I realized with a jolt. I forced myself to remain still as he moved out into the open. He looked back into the woods and waved. More Picts came out of the woods.

*Why aren't the sentries sounding the alarm?'* I wondered. Then I realized-there was a sentry tower on the western wall, but only a tall gatehouse on the southern wall. Where these Picts were emerging, particularly with the fog, must have been in the perfect spot to not be immediately noticed by either the sentries on the western watchtower or the southern gatehouse. I kept watching, afraid of making a move and being seen. Then I saw an older, balding man emerge, leading a horse. He walked over to the first man I'd seen, and gestured at the fort, while jabbing the man in the chest. His subordinate raised his hands up in a placating gesture. This was my opportunity, and I took it. I rolled off the wall I'd been laying one, and sprinted to the rows of tents my turma occupied. Thankfully, most of the men inside were awake and dressed.

"There's Picts outside the fort!" I exclaimed the instant I was inside. My voice cracked from the excitement and fear.

Everyone sprang to their feet, strapping on their weapons and bombarded me with questions.

"How many?"

"How close are they?"

"Are they attacking?"

I was just about to answer when a loud, deep braying sound of a horn sounded. It came from one of the levies on a watch tower.

"To the walls!" Owain bellowed, and our turma scrambled to grab spears, shields, and hand weapons as we sprinted to the sound of the horn. From other tents and makeshift shelters, our levy auxiliaries were doing the same thing. We surged up the embankment along the wall and saw dozens of Picts on the move, to the west of us. They weren't attacking, however. We saw that straight away. Several Picts were lined up, facing us, some two hundred paces away, but the rest, even further off, were streaming past the fort, angling northwest. Even though the Antonine Wall ran across their line of march, without men defending it, the wall merely slowed them down as they climbed up and over it.

"They're trying to get home," Owain determined, looking out at them.

"Why would they march right past us, then," Cornelius asked him. "Surely it would have been safer to cross over the bogs than risk being spotted by us."

"I don't think they intended to," I chipped in. "Or maybe they didn't realize we've reoccupied the fort. I saw that old man on horseback talking with the first of the Picts who came out of the woods. He seemed pretty angry. Maybe that first man was the one who led them past us?"

"Doesn't matter now," Owain cut in. "They're here. These are the raiders who've been attacking King Leudon's folk. They don't get to just slip through our fingers." He whistled sharply, getting the turma's attention. "Get to your mounts, quick as you can, lads! We're going after them."

"There's dozens of them!" one protested.

134

"And twenty-two of us. Sounds like good odds to me," Owain countered. "Now get mounted!"

Turning to the levies, Owain spotted their leader. "Garwlwyd! Get one of your people to send a bird to Din Pendyrlaw! Tell your king we've made contact with the Picts and require reinforcements. Then get your people ready to march. Leave a third here to man the fort. We're going to do what we can to either destroy or at least slow these raiders down for a few days until Arthur can get here."

Garwlwyd nodded, then sprang into action, as did we. Racing back to the barracks, we helped each other get into our armor, then ran to the stables, or rather, the barracks near the bath house on the southeast corner of the fort that we had turned into a stable. We got our horses ready, then Cornelius and Sawyl checked us over. The moment they reported to Owain that we were ready, we mounted up and rode out of the gate.

It took us about twenty minutes to kit up and ride out. In that time, the Picts, which our sentries estimated to number somewhere around one hundred and fifty men, would likely have only been able to travel a couple of miles at most. Under ideal conditions, locating the raiders within a two or even a three mile area wouldn't have been difficult, but we were in far from ideal conditions. The fog had not lifted, which limited effective visibility to no more than a couple hundred paces. Also, the farther north we rode, the thicker the woods became, as the region north of the wall wasn't as populated and therefore hadn't been deforested to the extent that the southern regions had. Not only would this make them harder to locate, but harder to travel through. Our horses would become both an asset and a liability, but we were going to try.

We rode northeast initially, believing that the Picts would eventually angle that way as well. Garwlwyd gave us one of his men, Brynn, as a guide. Brynn grew up in a village about twelve miles northwest of our fort, and knew the region well. We rode there using the Roman road that snaked its way northward, and made it in three hours. We were slowed down by the levies, but were unwilling to ride too far into the wilderness without them. The levies were exhausted by the time we reached the village though, not being professional soldiers accustomed to forced marches. The notable exception was Garwylwyd himself. That man was barely even breathing hard. I glanced behind him. Most of the men were dripping with sweat and panting profusely from their march. Many of them collapsed to the ground, exhausted. I seriously doubted they would be traveling anywhere quickly for a good bit.

The village was located on top of a large hill, overlooking the River Forth. The moment we rode into the gate, Brynn asked the guards if they'd seen the Pictish raiders. They shook their heads, and assured Brynn that they'd neither seen nor heard anyone all day.

Owain swore in frustration. He looked around. "These villagers scarcely paid any attention to us as we rode up. Are they loyal to King Leudon, Brynn? How friendly are they with the Picts?" He asked.

Brynn chuckled. "This village is officially a border town of Gododdin. They pay their taxes to King Leudon, but a lot of that tax money comes from trade with the Picts. There are people here who were born in the north, and Picts come through this village at least as often as we do."

This didn't sound all that surprising. Even in the south, I knew that borders distinguishing one kingdom from another were often in a state of flux, and that towns or villages that happened to be located in such areas often found themselves unable to be properly protected by any king, and so had to wall up, protect themselves as best they could, and try not to anger any of their neighbors, regardless of who that neighbor happened to be.

Ever since the Romans had withdrawn, kingdoms based on the provinces they had carved Britain into, or ancient tribal territories, were constantly forming, expanding, and merging with neighboring kingdoms, either through peaceful means or by conquest. The situation was such that had any monks decided to draw a map showing the multitude of kingdoms that had formed over the past century, that map would probably be obsolete in a couple of decades. The best that could be done now was what we had- a loose alliance of those kingdoms, mostly in the west, who were still under the control of other Britons.

Brynn gestured towards the countryside. "From here, on a clear day, we would be able to spot the raiders if they're attempting to head back north," he asserted, as we ourselves scanned our surroundings. "We would also just be able to see the River Forth, north of us, if not for the fog." He gestured again, "It's only about half a mile away."

Owain scratched his jaw, then turned to Brynn. "You mentioned a large lake in the mountains to the west, earlier. What's the distance between that and this village?"

Brynn thought for a moment, then answered, "As the crow flies, the loch is about thirty miles west of here."

"Are there many places they can cross the River Forth?"

"Not many," Brynn answered. "The one just north of us is the safest, most reliable one. They probably crossed that ford on their way south, and might have been hoping to cross back north this morning. Doubtful they'd try for it now though, with us about. There's another one east of here, closer to the Firth, the mouth of the river. Unlikely that they'd try that one either though, under the circumstances."

"Then we'll ride northwest along the Forth until we reach the next ford. With God's blessing, we'll intercept the Picts before they can cross the river." Turning to us, Owain called out, "Let's ride, lads. Keep your heads on a swivel and your weapons ready. If we don't run into these barbarians on the way, we'll set up an ambush for them at the ford."

He turned to Garwlwyd. "Penteulu, your infantry will slow us down now. Stay here. If we need you, I'll send Brynn back for you. If we either don't find the Picts, or are able to deal with them ourselves, we'll return here for you, then return to the fort."

"I'll have them ready to march," Garwlwyd affirmed, glancing around to give his men a hard glare.

We took the opportunity to refill our canteens, then rode out, into the woods and the fog. For the next hour, I felt like I was in that valley of the shadow of death that David spoke of in the scriptures. Every shadow became a Pict, hiding in ambush. Thin trees and branches seemed to resemble spears, and I questioned whether the bird calls I heard in the distances were in fact birds at all, or actually Picts, signaling to each other. I pulled the cork from my canteen and brought it up to take a drink.

"Don't." Cornelius quietly advised, riding ahead of me. "You're not actually thirsty. You're scared. Don't waste the water now."

"Aren't you scared, Decanus?" I asked.

Cornelius turned in his saddle to look at me. "Keep your voice down," he answered, speaking softly. "And yes, Peredur, I'm scared. We all are. Welcome to being a soldier. Ninety percent of the time you're bored to tears. Ten percent of the time you're absolutely terrified. The trick is to push the fear down. Focus on what's going on around you, and how you've been trained to respond to it. Don't focus on the fear."

I nodded. "But Decanus, it's the stuff around me that's making me scared."

Cornelius chuckled. So did a couple of the other riders. "No," he corrected. "It's the stuff you *think* is around you that's making you scared. Being alert is good. It can keep you alive, but you also have to learn to filter out what's actually out there from what you're imagining is out there. If you let your imagination get out of control, you'll see a Pict behind every tree, and your mind will become so exhausted, you'll miss the moment there actually is a Pict. And yes, Peredur, somewhere out here is a Pict warband, so being alert isn't a bad thing."

We reached the closest fording site a bit under an hour later. We were less than a hundred paces away from the river when we heard Owain cry, "There they are! They're already crossing! Red Dragons, caracole to the right! Charge!"

The caracole was a classic cavalry maneuver for launching ranged attacks against an enemy; one perfected by light cavalry who used javelins and bows as their primary weapon. It was one of many tricks in our arsenal. Our turma maintained its column formation and galloped up to the near side of the river. As we got within range of the Picts, we hurled javelins at them, and continued to ride on, angling in a wide arc to the right. This enabled us to inflict casualties upon the barbarians, while still maintaining our distance, and preventing them from effectively counter-attacking. They barely even had time to throw javelins of their own at us before we had galloped away. Even better for us was that we'd caught the bulk of their party still crossing the ford and they were completely exposed.

As I was near the end of the column, by the time I was in range to throw my javelin, the Picts were reacting. Those in the rear turned to face us and raised their shields, doing their best to form a hasty shield wall. Those in the front rushed up the bank on the far side of the river, anxious to clear the ford. My mouth went dry and my heart raced as we galloped by. To ease my fear, I unleashed a loud warcry and threw my javelin into their masses, and saw it strike deeply into a shield as I followed the column away. The man went down, but whether it actually penetrated his shield deeply enough to hit him, or simply knocked him down from the force of my throw, I have no idea. One of them threw their own javelin in my direction. I ducked instinctively, and it sailed behind and past me. Several Picti bodies lay strewed about, many with javelins jutting out from their bodies.

"Reform on the draco!" Owain called.

We reformed, back into column. All of us had a second javelin in hand, ready for another pass. The downside of catching the Picts already crossing was that, while they had been extremely vulnerable to our first attack, the ford itself wasn't wide enough to allow us to ride alongside of them. And now they were far enough away that a second pass would have been a waste of time. We would have to wait until they crossed. Brynn called out after them, in their own language.

I've no idea what he shouted at them, but it must have been a taunt. Those closest to us hurled javelins at him. Brynn easily dodged to one side and the javelins planted themselves into the mud where he had been standing. Gilbert laughed loudly, and wagged his middle finger at them.

The Picts, for their part, cleared the ford, but didn't continue on. Instead, they bunched up into a crude shield wall. We heard several horn blasts from them as their leadership attempted to reestablish order. Owain, meanwhile, instructed Brynn to ride back to the village with all haste to bring up the levies.

"They're in a bad situation, and they know it," Cornelius chuckled, looking over at me. "We can't cross the ford with them right there on the far side, but they can't leave their position either, because once they start off up the road we can cross and continue harrying them. And of course Garwlwyd and his levies will eventually catch up to us as well. So the longer this stalemate goes on, the better our odds get."

Then we heard a faint, whistling sound, followed quickly by a loud, metallic *clang*. From the rear of the column, a sense of horror washed over me as I saw our draco standard waver, then start to fall. Chaos erupted as Harri, our standard bearer and Duplarius, toppled to the ground, and those around him scrambled to grab the draco standard before it could hit the ground. That would have been a bad omen! At the same time, several more men cried out, and the sound of more objects hitting helmets, shields, and mail rippled through the column.

"Incoming sling stones! Fall back!" Owain shouted to us.

Our trained response to reacting to sling missiles kicked in, and we all immediately wheeled our horses around and galloped fifty paces to the rear. Upon turning back around, we saw that two of our men were still sprawled out on the ground, unmoving, Harri being one of them. A third lay on the ground, cursing, and clutching his arm, obviously injured. A rock kicked up dirt near the wounded man. Another hit him in the leg. He screamed. This was followed by laughter and jeers from the far side of the river.

"Sawyl, get your lads over there! Retrieve our wounded! Cornelius, have your lads answer those barbarians in kind!" Owain ordered.

Instantly, Decanus Sawyl and the men of his contubernium dismounted, held up their shields, and rushed for our wounded cymbrog. Rocks pinged off their shields as they advanced back towards the river bank. My tentmates and I pulled pouches full of sling stones from our saddle. We loaded our slings and got them spinning as we scurried up to the water's edge, then hurled our missiles the instant we caught sight of the Picti slingers.

I was still scared, but I realized that as odd as it sounds, I was becoming used to the sensation. As I did that, the fear became easier to suppress. Adding to that, I was confident in my abilities with the sling, and the overriding sense of urgency to shut down the slingers who were pelting Sawyl's men helped me completely disregard the fear for my own safety and focus entirely on doing my utmost to deal with the Picts.

Slings weren't our primary weapons, and we didn't hunt with them as often as the Picts, so we weren't as good as they were, but we were still proficient, and with our volley, a half a dozen of the barbarians fell to the ground with yelps and cries of pain. More Picts broke out of the shield wall to join the slingers at the river bank. I know I personally dropped two of them.

"Pull back!" Cornelius called out to us after a minute or so of us exchanging sling stones across the river. There were now at least a dozen Picts lining the river bank, crouching down low to the ground behind their shields, while a dozen more were loosing stones at us from behind this second, smaller shield wall.

We slowly backed away. Cornelius was limping from where a Pict had scored a grazing hit to his left leg. We'd accomplished our mission however, and gave Sawyl and his men the time they needed to retrieve our casualties. Harri was dead. He'd been the first one targeted, and so the Picti slinger had had all the time he needed to make a well-aimed throw, nailing Harri in the head. The rock had hit his helmet on the rim, just above his eye, and struck with such force that it dented his helmet. It was a gruesome wound. The armor the other two were wearing kept them alive, but the impact of the stones had still fractured ribs or collarbones. They were still able to ride, if agonizingly, so Owain draped Harri over his horse, and the two wounded men trotted off, back to the fort on the wall, with one of them also taking the reins of Harri's horse.

The stalemate continued, with both us and the Picts slowly lowering our weapons and getting comfortable on our own respective sides of the river, just out of slinger range of each other.

Once, they began to edge away from the ford. We let them get a whole fifty paces away before we mounted up and prepared to go after them. They immediately sprinted back to the river bank, forming their shield wall, spears thrust towards us.

"Will you Romans sod off already?" a thickly accented voice called out to us from within the shield wall.

We all looked at each other, uncertain whether we should even humor the barbarians with a response. Normally, I probably wouldn't have. I don't think of myself as particularly hot-headed, or attention seeking, but I was sad and angry over Harri's death, though I hadn't known him all that well. Their taunting angered me further, so I responded, "Quit running like rabbits, and we could settle this, now!" I surprised myself by shouting back.

"Rabbits?" the voice shot back, indignantly. "We're the wolves that have been tearing your lands up. Now we're returning to our den! But if you want to try and stop us, come on over!"

"Returning to your den?" I scoffed. "Is that where you thought you were going when you walked right up to our fort this morning?" That got a chuckle from my turma.

Slowly, a gap appeared in the Picts' shield wall, and I saw the Pict who belonged to the voice. He wasn't much older than Gilbert or I, and he made a crude gesture at us.

"We smelled something absolutely foul, and decided we should go and see what manner of creature that could possibly be! That led us to you!"

"*Us?*" I responded. "You barbarians smell worse than a pen full of pigs! Have you even heard of bathing?"

"We have!" the Pict answered. "I bathed with your sister just the other night! And by the way, what *is* that on your chin? Is that a beard you're trying to grow, Roman? My little brother has a better one. And he's ten!"

I heard Gilbert snicker beside me, and felt my cheeks growing warm. I actually was trying to grow my beard out. Did it truly look that bad? I started to bring my hand up, then stopped myself, but the Pict saw my reaction and laughed.

"We're not Romans, you ignorant, Pagan dog!" I shouted, changing the subject. "We're Britons! There haven't been Romans on this land in a hundred years!"

"That was the best you could do?" Cornelius asked, from where he was sitting, not far away.

"I don't see you doing any better," I grunted.

"Ho! Roman!" The Pict called again. "Your mother is a rat! And your father smells of elderberries!"

"I've got some elderberries you can choke on!" I offered, and wagged my middle finger over at him.

"You're offering me your small, blueberries, are you, Roman?" The Pict laughed. "Ha, that sounds about right for your kind!"

I was working on a response to him in my head when I heard a commotion from their side of the river. I caught movement too, just barely visible in the fog. The rest of my turma must have noticed, too, for they all stood up, glancing towards Owain. Then, slowly, the Pict shield wall expanded. Not only did it get wider, but we saw their formation deepen. More of their standards carved in the semblance of various beasts appeared, and more spears bristled out from behind them.

"Hey, Romans!" the Pict who'd been exchanging insults with me called out. There was a smug glee in his tone that hadn't been present before. "You want us to come to you? Fine! Here we come!"

143

Owain swore. "They've been reinforced! Back, two hundred paces!" he shouted, as all Hell broke loose. A swarm of blue painted barbarians rushed us, screaming war cries as they came. There were *hundreds* of them now. We scrambled to our horses, even as javelins and long spears began thudding into the ground where we had just been.

"Fall back!" Owain shouted again.

As ordered, we sped away at a gallop, but only as far as we needed to in order to create distance and reform. Even as we rode off, the faster Picts were catching up to us. One grabbed my foot a moment after I'd mounted up. On instinct, I thrust my spear at his head, but he dodged to one side and I missed. He did however release me, and Carys took off in an instant. A javelin flew past me. It came so close to skewering me in the back that the spear tip actually grazed my mare's right flank and she neighed shrilly.

"Run, Carys!" I urged her. I'd raised her since she'd been a filly. The thought of her dying in these woods to some barbarian blade made me more afraid than I'd ever thought to be for my own life. Carys darted through the woods as we avoided fallen trees and barbarians alike. We moved back two hundred paces, then wheeled around and faced the oncoming horde in a neat formation of two staggered ranks, with Owain in the middle front.

"Ready javelins!" Owain called, and each of us withdrew one of the light spears from the quivers attached to our saddles. Those of us who still had them transferred our spears to our shield hands.

As the barbarians got to within about thirty paces of us, Owain shouted, "Throw javelins!"

We hurled our javelins into the closest screaming Picts and a dozen of them staggered back and fell to the ground, impaled. Several more had their shields punctured, and had to discard them as they continued their charge.

"Fall back, two hundred paces!" Owain yelled. Again, we spun around and galloped away down the road, just as Pict spears again began to sail towards us. We reformed another two hundred paces away, hurled javelins again, and fell back again. We repeated this maneuver two more times, until all of our javelins had been thrown. Though we were leaving a trail of dead barbarians in our wake, the horde coming at us didn't seem in the least bit diminished, though they were at least beginning to slow down.

"Fall back, three hundred paces," Owain commanded.

We galloped to the rear again, maintaining our formation. It was a loose formation, on account of the sporadic trees and rocks in the area, but with our small number, we at least maintained a sense of cohesion. Owain looked over his shoulder and called out, "Column formation. At the canter, forward!"

Owain moved out first, along with Cornelius, who'd taken up the draco standard, then the rest of us folded in toward the middle, forming a column of two riders abreast, leaving the Picti horde behind us as we headed back to the hillfort. As we rode, I glanced back, checking Carys' flank, where the Pict javelin had grazed her. The blood was already drying though, and didn't look too bad. Although the rest of the movement was uneventful, I kept alert, constantly scanning our surroundings for signs of movement. I wouldn't feel safe again until we reached the walls of our fort.

We encountered Garwlwyd and his levies not far away on the road south. The warrior looked quite put out to discover that he and his levies had missed the fight, and had to simply turn around and march right back to our fort with us. Once we returned, we took care of our horses, bandaged up the few injuries we'd sustained, then buried Duplarius Harri outside the fort's walls. His weapons and armor were stashed in one of our wagons, to be returned to his family upon our return to Caer Lleon.

# Chapter Ten

T hree days later, more reinforcements arrived. Gilbert and I were on sentry duty on the eastern gate when the long column of the Red Dragons, followed by a few hundred additional levy infantry, marched up. While they were still a hundred paces off, my friend grinned beside me. "I dare you to challenge them," he said.

"It is what Decurion Owain instructed us to," I reasoned, grinning back at him.

We waited until the column got to within twenty paces, as instructed. I stood at the position of attention up on the modest gatehouse Gilbert and I shared, sucked in a deep breath, and shouted down, "Halt and identify yourselves!"

Below me, Arthur cocked his head and looked up at me with what I hoped was amusement. He held up his right hand, and shouted up at me. "Arthur, Tribunus of the Draconum Rubrorum Ultimae Spei, and the Dux Bellorum. I've come with the Red Dragons and levied forces of King Leudon to reinforce the garrison, and demand entry."

"As you command, Tribune," I called down. Gilbert was already nodding down at the second pair of guards, located at the double doors of the gate, who immediately swung them open. Arthur, the numerus' decurions, and a handful of others rode in. The rest dismounted and began stretching or jogging off to the woodline to relieve themselves as they waited for further instructions on where to set up.

Arthur glanced up and over at me as he walked past, and flashed me a quick grin. "Good job, sentry," he said, then turned to face Owain, who had come over from the fort's great hall, along with Garwlwyd.

"Owain, good to see you again," Arthur said, slapping him on the shoulder. "Guinnion," he said to a clean-shaven, middle-aged man with long, white-blonde hair beside him, "This is Owain, one of my decurions. He and his turma already bloodied the Picts as they tried to slip over the wall and get home a few days ago."

Turning to Owain, he said, "You met Guinnion when we first arrived, I believe? He's King Leudon's equivalent of a Magister Militum, and commander of the levy infantry. He's going to take over management of the fort, and manage logistics here. That leaves us free to find the barbarians' winter quarters and end their raiding for good. Vicarius Cai and his turma will serve as messengers, and coordinate between our two forces."

The two clasped forearms and exchanged greetings. "I saw you at our first council of war, what, nine days ago?" Owain said.

"I think I remember you, though we didn't have a chance to talk before," Guinnion replied. "Well met, Decurion."

"Now," Arthur continued, "Why don't we go inside the great hall and figure out how we're going to sort these Picts out," he said.

He turned to a pair of men beside him. One I knew was Vicarius Cai. I'd seen the other man at Caer Lleon a few times, but couldn't place his name. He looked remarkably similar to Cai though, making me wonder if the pair were related. They were of the right age to be father and son, I mused. Both were broad shouldered and muscular. They also shared the same, dark brown hair, though while the older man was clean shaven, Cai sported a fashionable beard and was nearly as tall as Arthur.

"Would you two see to it that the men tend to their horses, get fed, and know where they can set up their tents, then join me at the great hall?" Arthur asked.

He didn't order them, I noticed, but that didn't necessarily mean much. Arthur rarely seemed to phrase his commands as such, but rather as requests. It was simply a subtle show of respect that Arthur demonstrated to his men, who reciprocated it in kind, many times over.

The three made to walk away. "Oh, and on your way up, see if you can rummage up some wine and food for us while we talk," Arthur added.

Cai and the older man nodded and strode away.

A few hours later, a pair of levies relieved us on the tower, and we made our way back to our tents. It was a beehive of activity. With Harri's death, Cornelius became the new duplarius, and he was directing everyone to get their gear packed up back into our turma's wagons.

"Glad you're back," he told Gilbert and I the moment we walked in. "Help the turma out. We're relocating. This fort is too crowded with both the Red Dragons *and* a thousand levies, now that there's even more of them, so their infantry are taking over the fort, their handful of cavalry are setting up camp in the woods behind the fort on the east side, and we're to set up on the west. Once we've done that, Arthur wants us to go out and dig more pits with stakes. The fort needs to be prepared in the next two days. Once that's done our entire numerus, plus the mounted levies, are going north to destroy the Pict warband. Ideally that will take no more than a week or so. Then we can go home, hopefully before some Saxon warband starts getting froggy with us absent and decides to push west again."

As instructed, we set up our tents on the edge of the woods some two hundred paces southwest of the fort. This allowed us to selectively clear enough trees to create a makeshift corral for the numerus' horses. Since we didn't plan to spend much time there, we didn't do anything too elaborate. We were set up in a day and a half. The conscripted levy infantry however, took a full two days to unload the supplies brought from Din Pendyrlaw and Din Eidyn, get sleeping quarters arranged and latrine pits dug out before Arthur and the other officers deemed them ready.

In that hustle and bustle, there was an incident, and Decurion Owain called our turma into formation. I noticed the other turmae were doing so as well, in their own areas.

"Men," he said with a sigh, "It would seem that since the arrival of the levies' main body, somebody has taken it upon themselves to carve phalluses on the door of the great hall, and some of the barracks being made by the levies."

The formation erupted into fits of barely suppressed snickering and laughs that suddenly became coughs. Owain glared at us until the noise died down. "It's no secret that there is some mutual...scorn... between the Red Dragons and the levies of Gododdin," He continued, choosing his words carefully. "But the great hall is the headquarters of the levies, and Counselor Guinnion is not taking this perceived insult to himself or his men well. He was in fact quite vocal regarding his desire to see the offending 'artist' flogged, should that man's identity be discovered."

That got our attention. Many scowled. The idea of one of us being flogged over something so petty was grossly disproportionate.

Owain nodded slowly. "I won't bother to ask whoever did this to come forward. But if any of you know who it is, please keep an eye on that person and ensure that they don't do it again. We need these men of Gododdin, and we don't want to piss them off."

He dismissed us after that, and as we worked, we laughed and speculated as to who the culprit could be. There were no further incidents until the night before we were set to leave the fort. The sun had already set, and we stamped our feet and held our cloaks tightly about us as we tried to stay warm as we stood in formation. This time the formation was for our entire unit, rather than by turma, and it was Arthur and Cai who scowled at us.

"God's blood, what happened now?" Marcus grumbled, standing beside me.

"A fight with a levy?" I speculated quietly. I had certainly seen at least one fight nearly break out the previous night over a game of dice between a pair of levies and one of Galhault's lads. We didn't have to wait long.

Cai lashed out at us almost immediately after all decurions reported that their men were all present. He swore at us and called our professionalism, maturity, and our lineage into question. "Whoever the bastard is who drew phalluses on the walls, you should know, you came this close to making Guinnion take his levies and quit the fort!" He gestured with his thumb and finger. "You're lucky we're riding out tomorrow! I'd have every one of you outside, doing log drills until you dropped!"

I winced, thinking about the times my tentmates and I did various exercises as a group, using a large log. They were brutal, and everyone's least favorite form of physical training- aside from one or two very fit men who actually enjoyed it. Everyone had seen Galhault happily do log drills by himself, for example. He had a whole routine that he did often, back in Caer Lleon.

I snapped out of my reverie as Cai finished his rant, and Arthur stepped up to us. While Cai had been loud and angry, Arthur looked us over quietly, hands folded across his chest, with more disappointment than fury.

"Men," he said, calmly, "I know there's been a bit of tension with the levies. Some of you have complained that they're lazy, and not pulling their weight. I've also heard the complaints directed at Counselor Guinnion himself. You don't have to approve of him, nor even respect him or his men. But soon enough the time will probably come when you will have to fight beside them, likely in the next few days. So if you're spending your evenings carving phalluses on their walls, and depicting... scenes of things being performed by a man and labeling that man 'Guinnion'..." there was a ripple of snickers and shocked gasps throughout the formation, "you should consider the effect such things could have on our allies," Arthur continued, still calmly, but with more force, making himself heard over the clammer. We got the message and the noise died down.

"We display images of the Saints and the Chi Rho on our shields that represent our faith and trust in our God. Some of you display images of dragons and other beasts, in the style of our ancestors. Men of the Gododdin and warriors all over Britain depict these same images upon their own shields. The Chi Rho and the Saints are even common sights in the eastern lands."

Arthur walked over to his standard bearer and took the draco standard, then he held it up before us. "Take a good look at this," he said, shaking the standard. "These used to be a common sight as well, in Britain. Now, we're probably the last unit on this entire isle still using it. So when people up and down this land see this standard, they know they're seeing *us*. Over two decades ago, when my father fought the Saxons under this standard, he became known to his friends and enemies on this isle as the Pendragon- the Dragon's Head. His name and reputation were tied to this symbol, just as our numerus is. Everyone knew when they saw this standard that it spelled doom for whatever foe it flew against, and hope for those it protected.

"I have done my best to keep that reputation alive. This draco represents the best of our people- our strength, our honor, and our professionalism," he stressed the last word as he looked us over. "It shames me when men under this standard insult our allies and behave like undisciplined barbarians, and it tarnishes the legacy of the draco," Arthur concluded. He handed the standard back to his red-cloaked duplarius. He nodded to Cai, and strode away, followed by his standard bearer.

"Decurions," Cai growled. "Dismiss your men. See me at the great hall afterwards." Then he turned and followed after Arthur.

In front of our turma, Owain looked at us like a disapproving parent, with his fists resting on his hips. "Well lads, I guess I've nothing that needs to be added to what our Vicarius or Tribune said. So get out of my sight and go to bed. We're going to have a busy week or two." With that, he joined the other decurions and headed off toward the great hall.

The mood was somber as we crawled into our bedrolls. I doubted that whoever the offender was, and I had a couple suspects in mind, felt overly guilty. Guinnion had in fact been developing quite the reputation around the fort. So it was little wonder that he would be targeted for public mockery. We all had great respect for Tribune Arthur, but even he rarely stood on formalities. He was almost like a friendly uncle or older brother. As long as we obeyed him and stayed respectful, he was approachable, friendly, and frequently worked shoulder to shoulder with us, leading by example. Guinnion was precisely the opposite. Doing nothing to earn our respect, he demanded the utmost deference to everyone he perceived as being lower status than himself, constantly. Even some of the other levies had made a few comments to that effect. Now Garwlwyd on the other hand; *he* commanded, and was given respect. He reminded me a lot like Arthur. The levy chieftain was a bit quieter and rougher around the edges than Arthur, but he was also a leader, through and through. I'd even seen him sparring with Cai the other morning, and the two seemed equal, to the surprise of my comrades and I, who'd slowed in our work on the fort to watch the intense match.

That last night at the fort, I tried to go to sleep straight away, but I was too restless, knowing that we would be riding north in force in the morning. I thought of my family back home and laid there in my bedroll, praying.

"Heavenly Father," I whispered, "Please don't let these pagans take my life in the coming battle. It would break my mother's heart. She's already lost one son, your servant Aglofael." I hesitated, afraid of sounding selfish, so I added, "But should it be Your will that die in the coming days, please let me die with honor, facing the enemy ... and if it's not too much trouble, maybe let it be a quick death? In Your name I pray, amen."

"Amen," I heard a whisper nearby. Startled, I glanced over and saw Gilbert rolling away from me in his own bedroll.

"Good night, Gib," I whispered, smiling slightly.

"Good night, Peredur," he whispered back.

I don't know how long I continued to lay awake, but eventually, I fell asleep. As tired as I felt when I woke up to the braying sound of the buccina, I decided it surely couldn't have been that long.

"Come on, girls. Up and at them! Time to get ready to go!" our new decanus, Aylmer, called out.

"Shhh. Be vewy, vewy quiet. We'a hunting wascally pagans," Gilbert muttered, in a high-pitched imitation of Aylmer. The rest of our tentmates laughed. With Cornelius' promotion to duplarius, Aylmer was selected to be our new decanus. He still looked a little weird, and definitely talked weird, so decanus or not, we still felt it our duty to make fun of him from time to time.

"I don't sound like that!" Aylmer growled, sounding almost exactly like that. We laughed again, even as we complied with his demand and rolled out of our blankets, hurriedly got dressed in the chilly air that even our large tent didn't protect us from, and made our preparations to depart.

We collapsed our tents, packed up the rest of our gear, fed our horses, and were formed up on the western gate in less than two hours from the time we'd awoken to the buccina. The guards let our column through the gate, and we rode into the fort, and up to the northern gate, which led out into the wilderness. The levies, I noticed, were barely stirring. Sunrise had been over an hour ago and they were only just waking up. I wanted to look down on them for being undisciplined, but deep down I envied them in this one thing, at least.

We rode past the village overlooking the Forth and stopped for our first meal on the south side of the river. As we ate, Owain came by to brief us. He drew lines in the dirt with the butt of a javelin as he spoke. "The north side of the river belongs to the barbarians." He drew a squiggly line representing the Forth. "We're here," he said, stabbing a spot in the dirt. Then he drew another line, splitting off of the Forth. "This is the River Alain, a tributary of the Forth. "Before the main body crosses, Arthur wants three turmae to move a couple miles ahead." He stabbed the javelin into the dirt at three spots. "Ours is securing the left flank. We're to follow the Alain west a ways, then swing around north along that range of hills there. Brynn called them the Ochil Hills-"

"Monadh Ochail," Brynn corrected.

"Yeah, those," Owain said. "We're sweeping the far side of those hills, ensuring that there is no enemy presence in that area. Our objective," he dropped a small rock in a spot northeast of us, "is a spot called Loch Liobhann. It's a nice large lake, and a perfect staging point for the Picts. It's Garwlwyd's strongest guess. Decurion Galhault is taking his turma there, approaching from the south. Arthur and the main body are trailing him. Finally, on the right flank, Decurion Tyree is taking his men east along the Forth, then turning north, and approaching the lake from the far side, to the east. Once we're set, we're to send runners letting Arthur know we're in place."

"That only leaves the north unobserved," Gilbert mused.

"Can't be helped," Owain responded. "The further north we go, the more likely we'd be to stir up more barbarians than even we could handle. Anyway, that's the plan. If we run into the enemy before we reach the lake, we're to displace and link back up with the main body. Once Arthur knows he's got eyes on the approaches to the east and west, he and troops will move up and assault the Pict encampment from the south. Once they do, that will be our cue, and Decurion Tyree's, to ride up north a ways and ensure there are no reinforcements coming in. At that point, we will turn back south and engage the enemy from the rear, probably alongside levy light cavalry, if I know Arthur."

Owain had been drawing our route in the dirt as he spoke. Now he looked up at us. "Anyone have any more questions? No? Good. We leave as soon as everyone's done eating. Don't take too long, Brynn," Owain called over to the levy. As before, the local was attached to us as a guide. The scout, with his mouth full of food, just nodded and waved his acknowledgment.

Before we dispersed, Owain added, "If all goes to plan, everyone should be in place within two days. We have the longest route, about forty miles, so we need to get going as soon as possible. I want to clear as much of that small mountain range as we can before we have to make camp tonight."

"Sounds easy enough." Aylmer nodded.

Gilbert slowly turned to face him and spoke for all of us. "Why in the name of all that is Holy would you say that? You know it won't be easy, now, right? You've just put a curse on us."

Most of the numerus were Christian, as I was, or at the very least prayed to Jesus Christ as well as their other, pagan gods, as I was fairly sure Gilbert did. But one thing we all had in common was a soldier's firm belief that uttering such phrases as "things can't get any worse," or "this is too easy," or variations of those statements inevitably incurred the wrath of God. It was a universal superstition. And Aylmer had spat in the face of that.

"Shame on you, Gib, for having such a ... Pagan superstition," Aylmer chided. As if some god were mocking his hubris, a peal of thunder sounded ominously in the distance. Everyone stared at Aylmer, who rolled his eyes and walked away. Right then, looking at that mountain range again, partially obscured by a layer of fog, I felt a shiver go down my spine, and made the sign of the cross.

Once we'd finished eating we mounted up and rode off. As we crossed the bridge and over the Forth, I couldn't help but think about how badly our last crossing, or rather attempted crossing, had gone only a few days ago. At least this time if we ran into too much trouble Arthur and nearly our entire numerus was only a few miles away, but then Aylmer had said those dreaded words.

The mood of the turma was somber as we mounted up and rode off on our route, in column formation. Though our path detoured off the Roman road, thankfully there were still numerous trails crisscrossing the region that we could use, and therefore allowed our wagons to roll along without too much difficulty. We were tense, and not in the mood for idle chatter. Instead, we listened to the birds chirping as they alerted each other to our presence. Once we heard a wolf howl some distance off.

The last two days had been nice, mostly cloudless, with mild wind. It had even been pleasant. Naturally, the morning we left the fort, the wind picked up, and clouds rolled in again. We reached the mountains without incident two hours later. At this point, progress slowed, as the terrain became more rugged, and the path more serpentine. We could have ridden along the ridge. That would have been easier, but it was also a sure way to announce our presence to anyone within a few miles. All they would have had to do was look up and they would see our silhouettes moving along. So Owain made sure that Brynn found trails for us to take along the side of the mountains.

I glanced up as we rode, periodically watching the weather. "I'd wager we'll have rain by tonight," I sighed.

Gilbert chuckled mirthlessly beside me. "That's a safe bet. You know, we've only been here in Caledonia for what, two weeks? I can already understand why the Picts are trying to push south. What I don't get," he flinched as the sky suddenly split with lightning, followed a few moments later with a crack of thunder, "is why in the world the Gaelic tribes like the Scoti are trying to move into this place. I mean, just how bad could Hibernia be?" he marveled.

I shrugged. "Bad enough that even the Romans left it alone."

"Just like this place," Gilbert grunted.

"Not true," I corrected. "Once they'd pacified the south, the Romans marched up here and attempted to conquer it. They followed the east coast though, if I recall my history lessons."

"Clearly, that didn't work out so well for them," Gilbert remarked.

"More's the pity," I said. "If they'd succeeded, these barbarians might be our northern, civilized cousins now."

"And what difference would that make?" Gilbert shrugged. "There would still be wars."

"Maybe. Maybe not," I protested.

"Plenty of fighting goes on between Britons in the south," Gilbert reminded me.

I was about to reply when Aylmer, riding three ranks ahead of me, let out a yelp and pointed off down toward the base of the mountain we were riding along.

"Something's down there, and it's following us!" he warned, trying not to yell. We were all too aware of how well sound can travel in the mountains.

Owain called a halt, and in a well-practiced maneuver, we all angled our horses outward, in a sort of herringbone formation. This enabled us to mostly stay in our column, but everyone faced outward, so that we had someone observing every possible angle around us. I spotted our mysterious follower first. "It's Mel!" I called out with a suppressed laugh.

"Mel?" Owain echoed, riding over to us. "Who in Hell is Mel?"

"Mel's a dog I found hanging around the fort we've been staying at."

"Wait, you mean that scrawny, mangy dog you've been feeding?" Owain asked, cocking an eyebrow and looking from me to Aylmer.

"Yes. And I named her Mel," I repeated.

"Clever," Owain said flatly, glancing pointedly at the dog, staring at us from about thirty paces away.

"Aylmer, good looking out, I guess," Owain said, shaking his head. "Peredur, I've told you before to quit messing with the wildlife. Alright, lads. We've still got miles to cover. Let's get moving."

We headed out, continuing to scan our surroundings. There were no more false alarms, and we kept riding. Clouds rolled in, but thankfully, it did not rain. Not yet. A storm was definitely on its way though, we knew. The wind picked up, and we still got occasional flashes of lightning, accompanied a short time later by thunder. Owain kept us going though, until it was nearly dark, then he finally decided to have us take shelter for the night in a nice, heavy patch of woods. We'd covered roughly twenty-five miles, and cleared about half the length of the Ochail Hills.

Owain surveyed the area, and nodded. "Let's set up our tents here," he said, pointing to a mostly flat area devoid of trees, but still about twenty paces into the woods to the west. "Even with the concealment of the trees, we won't be hard to spot if any Picts wander by, but right now I think this blasted weather is a bigger threat. Duplarius, organize a watch rotation for the night. I want to be on the move again tomorrow morning the moment it's light enough for Brynn to guide us through."

"Yes, sir," Cornelius nodded. Then he turned to us. "Alright Sawyl. Aylmer. You heard the man. Let's get those tents up! One hour shifts. We should only need one contubernium for tonight. Sawyl. That'll be your people."

Sawyl nodded, then all of us scrambled to pull our tents from the four supply wagons we'd taken along, set up the frames and the coverings of the full enclosed tents for ourselves, and extra large blankets for the horses that we'd brought, anticipating that the weather would become bad. We also picketed the horses under the largest trees in the area, providing the most possible shelter for them for the night. With the twenty men of our turma, plus the half dozen levies who'd accompanied us as wagon teamsters, we were set up in no time.

Owain also decided we were safe enough to allow each section to dig out a fire pit and cook up some meat and porridge. We tore into our supper, having not eaten all day while conducting our reconnaissance, then went to sleep. Under normal conditions, I'd never been overly fond of our tents. They were small, compared to what I was used to, and felt cramped. As the temperature had been dropping these last few days however, I felt glad for the size of the tent for it became warmer from our body heat. It never really felt comfortably warm, but it was at least tolerable.

I woke up once, hearing a set of guards changing out from Sawyl's contubernium, sleeping in the tent beside ours. Beyond that, I had a mostly restful sleep. I suppose the long day's ride, broken up occasionally by the labor of us having to help the teamsters move the supply wagons up and down particularly steep portions of the trail, had exhausted me enough that even the anxiety of a looming battle wasn't enough to keep me awake. The fear began gnawing at me the moment I did wake up, however. As always, the routine of storing our gear, collapsing the tents and putting them back away in our wagons went quickly, and in less than an hour our turma was back on the sparse trail that led through the woods and towards Loch Liobhann.

The next morning was more of the same, only it was raining this time. It wasn't a heavy rain, more like a drizzle that turned into sleet. We huddled in our cloaks, pulled up our hoods, and rode on in silence. We saw more and more signs that we were in Pict country as we rode. Off to the southeast, in the direction of the lake, we thought we saw lines of smoke that could have been cooking fires. Once, we passed a clearing where a cluster of old, partially collapsed wattle and daub roundhouses stood.

We came upon the Pict encampment four hours after setting out. We weren't able to actually approach the camp itself, as the lake was in a vast basin, mostly surrounded by higher ground. It was over two miles wide, we'd been told, but because of the fog, at a point where the ground dipped down, all we could see past the reverse slope were the silhouettes of more trees, and then a wall of gray. It was as if the whole world were walled off in mist past that slope. Then Brynn spotted a guard while we were still about three hundred paces away. We all froze when he pointed the man out, sitting against a tree close to the ridgeline ahead of us, holding onto a spear and shield. He wore the hood of his checkered cloak well up over his head and didn't seem to have spotted us. We quietly dismounted and backed off, deeper into the woods until we were sure we were out of sight.

While the rest of us stayed with the horses, Owain, Cornelius, and Aylmer carefully went forward again, crouching low and using trees and foliage to conceal themselves. After a few minutes, they returned.

"Garwlwyd was right," Owain told us, speaking softly, but with an edge of excitement in his voice. "That's got to be their encampment, up ahead. There's a screen line deployed on that ridge facing us. Guards are posted about every fifty paces or so. We should be far enough away that they won't hear us if we stay hidden at the base of this hill right here. We'll keep people on watch, on the side of the hill, but they need to stay low while they're on duty. And nobody peek over the hill at the crest. If this hill is being watched, that's the part the enemy will be watching the closest. Everyone not on watch will stay down here at the bottom of the hill. Keep chatter and noise to a minimum.

"Peredur, Gib. You two go report to Arthur. Tell him where we were, that we're set, and that we've encountered no enemy presence west of the lake, until we made contact with this screen."

We nodded, mounted up, and turned to leave. "I won't let you down, Decurion," I promised him.

"Counting on you not to," Owain said. "God's speed."

Keeping the enemy screen line in mind, we rode off at an easy trot as we headed south, and made sure not to skyline ourselves by popping up too close to the ridge. The sleet turned into snow before we'd gone more than a few miles. We weren't surprised, the weather had been getting progressively worse all morning. I was worried though, that as we moved south, towards the Firth of Forth, where the River Forth emptied out into the sea, this fog was going to become even worse. At least from our observation post we'd established, we could see for a few hundred paces.

"At least the Forth won't let us stray too far south," Gilbert said, trying to be positive.

"But this *is* going to slow us down," I countered, glancing up at the small, white flakes lazily falling down around us. Then it got worse.

"I think I see movement off to the left," Gilbert said softly. I glanced over, and sure enough about two hundred paces away, as far as the fog would allow us to see, were the silhouettes of several riders. They were keeping pace with us, and riding parallel to us.

"They surely must be Picts," Gilbert murmured, glancing over at them again. "Wonder why they haven't attacked us yet?"

"I'd say either they haven't actually seen us yet, or they aren't sure if there's more of us that they can't see," I replied. "Either way, we have a problem. We need to swing around to the northeast soon, but they're between us and Arthur."

"Let's still angle away from them, and pick up the pace," Gilbert suggested. I agreed, and we turned more to the south, and increased our speed to a canter. The riders not only increased their speed as well, but angled to intercept us.

"They've seen us!" exclaimed Gilbert in alarm.

"Let's try to outrun them!" I yelled, and we swung away from the Picts, putting our horses into a full gallop, and they gave chase. After a few moments I turned to check on their progress and saw that they were fanning out, encircling us. There must have been close to a dozen of them, and although a few were lagging behind, several were either keeping pace or gaining on us.

My mind raced as I thought of a solution. We couldn't maintain this pace for long. Then I made a quick decision. I didn't see any way for both of us to get through the patrol, but this fog presented an opportunity for one of us to.

"Keep going!" I shouted at Gilbert. "I'll buy you time!" As I said this, I pulled my shield out from behind my back and gripped it tightly in my left hand.

"What are you going to do?" Gilbert asked, looking over at me.

"Whatever I can! Go! Link up with Arthur!"

Gilbert glanced over his shoulder, then jerked to one side as a javelin sailed past him. At least a half dozen of the Picts were definitely on the verge of catching us.

As my friend continued to race away, I slowed Carys down, allowing the closest Pict to catch up. Before he realized my intent, I whipped my spear out, striking him across the face with the wooden shaft. He fell and I spun to face the others. A second Pict was on me in a moment, and impaled himself on my spear, before I'd had time to even think of a proper course of action. Unfortunately, as he was knocked off of his horse, the barbarian took my spear to the ground with him. A third Pict rushed me, stabbing at my head with his own spear. I dodged, though the blade still glanced off my helmet. I hadn't even had time to draw my sword to counter attack yet, so I kicked my heels into Carys' flanks, getting her to surge forward and past the Pict, then kept going. At all costs I had to keep the group's attention on me for as long as I could, but also avoid becoming surrounded. I'd be dead in an instant if they succeeded in that.

I rode at an angle away from them, pulling out one of my six javelins from the case attached to my saddle as I did. A rider came up alongside me, on my left side, and I threw it at him. He jerked backwards and the javelin flew past him. I swore. Then, on impulse, I yanked Carys' reins, pulling her towards the Pict and punched him in the head with the iron reinforced rim of my shield. He went sprawling, and I yanked out another javelin. Picts were coming at me from all sides, so I picked out two that were sufficiently spaced out and bolted Carys through them. As I did, I thrust my javelin toward the stomach of the man to my right. He wasn't close enough, but the action still made him swerve away from me.

I felt a blow on my left shoulder that made my whole body feel like it was on fire for a moment. I spun around in time to see a Pict with a sword. It was the other man I'd ridden past. I kept riding, hoping to string them out a bit. We raced along like that for at least a mile, then Carys slowed down, getting winded. I looked behind me. There were several Picts on my tail, but only two that were dangerously so. I still had the javelin in my hand, so I spun Carys around in another tight turn and flung the javelin at the closest pursuer. This time I got lucky and it took him in the chest. He tumbled backwards off his horse and lay still. The second rider, the one with the sword, swung at me as he charged me. I brought my shield up, ignoring the burst of pain I felt, and blocked the attack. This barbarian was young, probably not much older than I was. I noticed that he also wore a helmet, and a gold torc around his neck. I pulled out my own sword and yelled "Raaah!" at him as I swung. He flinched, and barely parried my attack in time.

Over his shoulder I saw more riders were catching up fast behind him. I yanked back on the reins and Carys, who'd been bred and trained to be a warhorse, reared up, flailing her front hooves at the rider and even his own horse, who shied away. As she came back down, I struck again at the swordsman. This time I sliced through his right shoulder and sword arm. He screamed in agony, dropping his weapon. I would have finished him off, but in that span of time, two more riders caught up to us. I spun Carys around and took off again. One of them threw a javelin, which flew past me even as Carys was completing her turn.

I hunched down low, trying to make myself a small target, and took off as fast as Carys would go. A few moments later I glanced backward, and was startled to see that nobody was pursuing me. I slowed down, afraid that I was missing something, and looked closer at the group. They were gathering around the young swordsman I'd wounded. One started to separate from the group, as if to continue pursuing me, but someone called him back. I guessed that the rider must have been someone important, so I thanked God for looking out for me, then continued riding at an easy canter and put a few miles between myself and those Picts.

I thought about the swordsman. Though not necessarily rare, that Pict had worn a helmet and that torc looked pretty expensive. The fact that he even had a sword wasn't insignificant, either. They aren't easy to make, and not just anybody can afford them. Carys was a damn fine horse, too; in fact she was one of the fastest in the turma. That swordsman's horse was almost as good. He really must have been somebody important, I concluded.

As I rode, I doubled back a couple times and hid in some trees, watching to see if they'd decided to follow me after all. When I saw nobody behind me, I dismounted, groaning from the pain in my left shoulder. I slowly pulled my helmet off, filled it with most of the water from the canteen slung on my saddle and let Carys drink. She inhaled it all in a matter of seconds, then shoved her dripping wet muzzle against me as though asking for more.

"Sorry, girl," I apologized. "We don't have much more. "You'll have to eat some snow." I drained the last few swallows of water, then held out my empty canteen to show her. "We'll both have to."

Carys snagged the canteen out of my hand in her mouth, shook it up and down, then tossed it aside. "Harpy," I grumbled at her as I retrieved it. She nickered at me. I took a few moments to look her over. There were no new injuries, beyond the red, scabbed over cut she'd received the other day, and that didn't seem to be bothering her as she ducked her head down and pulled up some tufts of grass and snow to munch on.

I looked around, assessing the situation I found myself in. Because of the fog, I still couldn't see much more than one hundred and fifty to two hundred paces in any direction. I was surrounded by groves of trees and brush. A sense of dread built up inside of me as I realized that while we'd managed to shake our pursuers, we'd also become completely lost. My only consolation in that moment was the hope that I'd at least succeeded in keeping the Picts from catching up to Gilbert, and that he'd managed to report to Arthur. I looked up at the sky. It was impossible to gauge the time of day. Everything around me just seemed to be shades of gray or white.

"So. We're all alone in a God-forsaken wilderness. Any which way we turn could lead us head on into a pack of wolves or a warband of Picts. And it's freezing cold and snowing," I sighed, looking up at the sky again. "Carys, you've really gotten us into a mess this time," I said softly. She twitched her ears toward me but otherwise ignored me and kept eating.

"Eat up, girl. Then we need to find shelter and rest up a bit until the weather clears," I told her.

A few minutes later I saddled back up, and we rode off. I didn't go far. Having no idea which direction would take me to Arthur in this storm I simply picked a direction and rode until I found a particularly thick patch of woods with some especially large pine trees. I dismounted, removed Carys' saddle and bridle, then pulled out a simple rope harness from a saddle bag and tethered her to a low-hanging branch. Finally I unfolded her saddle blanket fully and draped it over her.

With her needs attended to, I unstrapped my thick bedroll from the back of the saddle and laid it out. I debated on whether to peel off my chainmail shirt and thick, woolen tunic to check on my shoulder, but decided against it. It was a bit of work to take that thing off by myself, and any movement I made with my left shoulder hurt, though the fact that I at least had full range of motion allowed me to confidently determine that the damage likely wasn't too serious. I wasn't feeling any worse than I had earlier, either, so I supposed my injury was probably no more serious than some heavy bruising from the sheer force of the blow. Had I not been wearing this chainmail, it would have been much worse for me. Having made that decision, I sat down and eased back against a tree trunk, then pulled out a wheel of cheese and cut a thin wedge out of it with my dagger. I supplemented that with a hard biscuit, and washed my supper down with a few handfuls of snow; at least water was plentiful here. I made sure I had my shield nearby and my spatha positioned on my hip so it could be drawn quickly if needed, and just for good measure, pulled out one of my four remaining javelins and laid it down within arm's reach as well. Getting comfortable was difficult, with my injury, but I did, and closed my eyes, slowly drifting off to sleep. I had to trust that if something approached, Carys would warn me.

My fight with the Picts replayed in my mind over and over, and I saw the spears thrust and thrown at me, and the sword blows that had nearly killed me. In slow motion, my mind replayed the moments I'd killed those men. Somehow, in spite of the previous fights I'd been in, going all the way back to the encounter with those Scoti raiders those months back, I'd never actually killed anyone before, at least not for sure. In those previous fights I'd only been throwing javelins or stones at enemies from some distance, and in most cases I wasn't even sure what damage, if any, I'd actually caused. This time I'd killed two men face to face. Technically of course, one of those men had practically done all the work himself in riding straight into my spear, but that scarcely mattered. The shocked, pained expressions of the men haunted me that night. They were the first of many men I would kill in my lifetime. I consoled myself with the knowledge at least that if I hadn't killed them, they would certainly have killed me, or Gilbert. And that would have compromised our entire mission here.

# Chapter Eleven

The sound of Carys nickering in my ear woke me up with a start, and I reflexively began to draw my spatha. I looked around, blinking. Though the sky was still overcast, I could see the telltale pinkish hue of the sun as it rose, and that it had stopped snowing. The songs and soft cooing of at least two or three different varieties of birds reached my ears. I relaxed, and slowly slid my blade fully back into its scabbard as I stood up. I stretched, and immediately remembered the injury to my left shoulder. I hissed as the flash of pain hit me, but stretched my arm anyway. I needed to know that I could at least move it. To my relief, I had full mobility. It just hurt, a lot. I walked over to the nearest bush and relieved myself, then dug out a bit of bread and cheese from my saddlebag. As I ate, I thought about the last time I'd seen Gilbert, racing eastward to deliver Owain's message to Arthur. I really hoped that he'd made it away from the Picts safely, and been able to accomplish our mission. There was nothing I could do about him though, I decided. For the present, I needed to consider my next move.

"All right," I told Carys, as I drew a crude map of the area into the fresh snow. "I was too busy just trying not to get skewered by barbarians to know for sure where in Hell we are, but I don't recall crossing any rivers, so it's a safe bet that we're still south of the River Earn, and north of the River Forth. We probably ran generally westward. The Red Dragons, then, should be somewhere east of us. I glanced again toward the rising sun, appreciating the stunning beauty of the scene for a moment, despite my situation.

"By all accounts, Loch Liobhann is rather large, so if we head southeast we should come upon either the lake or Arthur's men. We'll just have to keep an eye out for Picts as well, though."

Beside me, Carys munched on a clump of grass, paying no attention to me.

"With any luck," I concluded, "we could even cut across signs of the men, if not be in contact with them by tonight." I looked at Carys. She looked back at me and whinnied.

"Glad we agree," I said. I stood up, rubbed out my map with my foot, then saddled Carys and mounted up, gritting my teeth in pain. I guided Carys through the woods in what I believed was a southeastern route. Were the sky not so bloody overcast all the time, and the woods not so thick in places, I could have been more confident in my azimuth.

Since I wasn't sure what the Picts had decided to do after they'd ceased chasing me, I proceeded cautiously, and stopped every so often to listen and look around. I had a large canteen full of water, about two-thirds of my cheese wheel left, a few biscuits, as well as a small sack full of grain wrapped up inside one of my saddlebags. I'd lost my spear, but still had a few javelins left, as well as a sling, the plumbatae attached to the inside of my shield, my spatha, and dagger. As long as my journey didn't take more than a day or two I should be fine, I reasoned.

I noticed an odd smell in the air as I prepared to leave and looked around, sniffing. I smelled smoke, making me feel puzzled and uneasy. Smoke usually means people, and this far north it was unlikely that many people I might encounter would be friendly. I scanned the horizon, trying to determine the source of the smell. Then I saw a column of dark smoke rising above the treeline to the north, no more than a mile away, based on the fact that I could actually smell it. At first I wondered if this was Arthur's work. The Red Dragons were likely going into battle this morning after all, I knew, but the smoke seemed to be coming from too far north. After a few moments, I shrugged and urged Carys into an easy canter heading southeast, I hoped.

Another hour went by when my mare stopped and whinnied. Knowing her mannerisms, I became instantly alert. Something in the area made her nervous. My hand went to my spatha and I scanned the woods to my left and right. I made a clicking noise to Carys, telling her to continue on, and patted the side of her neck with my free hand. She complied, but her ears were twitching. That alone caused my heart to beat faster, and my palms grew a bit sweaty. I listened, but heard nothing beyond the usual noises. A light breeze rustled the leaves of nearby trees. All around me I heard the calls of a variety of birds, just as I'd been hearing all day, but Carys was uneasy. *Something* was out here. A shiver went down my spine. What was out here with me, I worried. Were Picts approaching? Wolves? Maybe a witch, or an evil spirit? My hand went to the small, silver cross I wore around my neck, and whispered a prayer.

I saw a glimpse of movement, to my right, barely fifty paces off the road. Carys caught it too, and snorted, sidestepping a bit to the left. Then I saw it. It was a huge brown bear. I froze, staring at it in awe and disbelief. I'd heard of the beasts and seen carvings of them on Mona. I knew a nobleman who even had the hide of one adorning his wall, but I had never actually seen one before. The bear was just ambling along, grunting and huffing periodically, and generally ignoring me. For my part, I was enthralled. The beast looked even bigger than Carys, at least in the body. I considered bringing it down with my remaining javelins, but I was traveling too light to make much use of the kill. The hide would certainly be too large and heavy to carry, never mind the time it would take to skin such a beast. And then there was the meat. How much of it could I even carry? Surely no more than a few pounds. And I had a hunter's loathing for killing animals where most of the remains would only be wasted.

Then I heard a somewhat high-pitched mewling sound, off to my left. It was like nothing I'd ever heard before- simultaneously amusing, but also somehow disconcerting. I nudged Carys forward, scanning the trees and bushes and reeds. I heard the odd, braying sound again, then saw two small bundles of brown fur shuffle out from the bushes and onto the trail. It took me a moment to realize what they were. Bear cubs. The sight of the small, almost fluffy-looking creatures and their soft mewling noise amused me. One even stood up on its hind legs and sniffed the air around me, curious, but that amusement dissipated almost immediately as another thought crossed my mind. Dogs and boars could become extremely protective of their young. What about bears?

I jerked my head around, back over to my right, scanning the area where I'd last seen the large brown bear. I quietly urged Carys back into a canter and started to ride away, but I was too late. A roar like I have never heard before ripped through the air and then, what seemed like a massive, furry boulder came crashing through the woods straight at me with unbelievable speed!

I spurred Carys into a gallop and admit that I shrieked a most unmanly cry as I urged her on to her full speed. My command was of course entirely unneeded, and likely irrelevant, for Carys' own instincts kicked in the moment that mother bear came barreling towards us, and she took off faster than I knew she was even capable of!

We sped away down the trail, but when I heard huffing and snarling behind me, I looked over my shoulder and felt like my heart was going to explode with terror, and a shock jolted through my body. The bear was sprinting after us and was only a few paces back! She was so close, I could clearly see her long, stained fangs and the shimmering strands of saliva that coated them. Horrified, I saw that she was even bigger than I'd realized. As she chased us, I saw that her huge, round head was actually level with Cary's own flanks, and she was broader! If she caught us, if she managed to get even one good swipe at Carys with her massive claws, we would be done for.

It could have been my imagination, but I will swear to my dying day before God that it felt as though the ground itself shook as that furious bear pursued me down the road for what seemed like an eternity. I hunched down low, practically pressing my face against Cary's neck as I screamed at her to run.

Finally, the distance between us widened, though she nearly caught us. At last, Carys' stamina and speed proved greater than the bear's, and she was left behind. The last I saw of that monstrous creature, she had given up and stood on her hind legs, as though to keep us in sight for as long as possible to ensure that we were absolutely not returning or something. She was truly massive. Even on horseback, I suspected that were she standing directly in front of Carys and I, I might still have to look upward to meet her gaze. I woke up to nightmares for a long time afterward where my mind provided vivid alternative realities where she did indeed catch us. I always woke up just as her toothy maw was filling my vision, preparing to swallow me whole.

We rode on for another couple miles before Carys was willing to stop. Her flanks were heaving, and she was exhausted. I dismounted, filled my helm with water from my canteen, and let her drink. She practically buried her muzzle into it and splashed water all over as she drank.

"I promised myself I wouldn't show weakness again after that ship battle awhile back," I grumbled to Carys after she'd drank her fill and bent down to eat at some grass, "but that bear absolutely does not count!"

Carys looked at me and knickered. "You were scared too!" I pointed out. "That bear was bigger than you, even. I doubt Arthur himself would have behaved any different. So don't you dare judge me."

She swished her tail and went back to grazing. I took a long drink from my canteen, refilled it with snow, then mounted up and began riding again. I hummed a bit as I rode, partially to ease the monotony, but partially to keep my mind calm, acutely aware that I was totally alone, in enemy territory. I kept my head on a swivel, constantly scanning left and right, as well paying attention to Carys, whose keener senses would more likely alert me to danger before my own would.

A couple hours into the morning I passed by a trio of stones. They were about as tall as I was, and intricately carved with geometric patterns using swirling designs as well as depictions of various beasts, partially obscured by patches of moss. The Picts were good carvers, I had to admit. The designs looked beautiful, though a bit foreign, in comparison to the statues of emperors, deities, and Roman-style architecture I was more accustomed to seeing.

I spotted a pair of rabbits, some twenty paces away, shortly before noon. I halted Carys, slowly dismounted, and dug out my sling and a small stone from a pouch on my belt. Taking a chance, I slowly crept forward a few feet as I slipped the middle finger of my right hand through the loop of one the cords of my sling. The other cord was knotted at the end, which I gripped between my thumb and index finger. I brought the sling up, loading my stone into the leather pouch with my left hand, and began spinning the sling overhead. The distinctive whirling noise the sling made caused one of the rabbits to look up and over towards me. Before it could decide whether to flee or not, I released the knotted cord and hurled the stone at my prey. The stone zipped through the air and killed the rabbit instantly upon contact. The other rabbit bounded away, so I went over to the one I'd killed, then skinned and gutted it on the spot.

I used snow to clean my hands off afterwards. Finally, the miserably cold weather here in the north became useful. The rabbit's meat wouldn't spoil nearly as fast as it would in warmer temperatures, so I didn't need to cook it right away. Instead, I scooped up some snow and packed it around the rabbit, using its fur to wrap the meat and keep it even colder. Then I lashed the bundle to Carys' saddle, mounted up, and continued riding, already excited for the meal I would have tonight.

"A man cannot live on bread alone," I smiled to myself. That reminded me, I did still have some bread left, stale though it was. I reached into a bag and snacked on another biscuit as I rode.

I kept scanning my surroundings as I rode, and the later the day grew, the more agitated I became. Aside from the stones, I'd seen nothing but hills and groves of trees all day. Even if I'd rode directly west in my attempt to escape the Picts yesterday, I'd only gone a few miles. Today, I'd traveled several miles. I should be encountering signs of the numerus' passing before too long. Then I realized, with the snow from last night, it would be possible I could ride right over their trail and never even know it. Right then I felt absolutely sick to my stomach. I might be doomed to wander these woods until I died! I fought down my rising panic and tried to focus. I remembered that smoke from this morning. Had that been them? They should have attacked the Picts today, if everything went to plan. I dismissed the notion. That had surely been too far north to have been my people. Nevertheless, I decided to keep an eye on the skyline, because at some point today, I should see ... something. Smoke, carrion birds, maybe even the column itself. Something.

When I finally did find that something, another couple hours later, I nearly broke down crying. There, on the top of a small hill devoid of trees, was a familiar cluster of stones.

"No, no, no," I groaned softly, feeling an overwhelming sense of despair. I rode up to the stones, to be sure, and scrutinized the patterns etched into them. There was no mistake. These were the same three stones I'd passed hours ago! I looked around, bewildered. I'd tried to keep the sun at my left until noon, then on my right as it continued its cycle. Granted, it was still overcast, and there were times when the sun was hidden behind clouds, but I thought I'd kept my bearings. I continually looked for points in the horizon to ride towards as I traveled, in order to not drift from my heading. How had I fouled up so badly? I should have found a trail by now, or if I'd overshot that I should have at least run into a river, or that small mountain range my turma had ridden through a couple days ago. My frustration boiled over and I completely lost my situational awareness, not to mention my Christian upbringing, swearing long and loudly for several moments. I used every profane curse and vulgar phrase I'd ever heard, and invented a few new ones to vent my frustration on the stones, these Hell-spawned trees, and the inbred, Pagan barbarians who lived here.

After a few minutes of this I sighed heavily and looked around. The woods around me weren't a single, massive forest. Rather, the terrain was hilly, with patches of trees scattered about. Some were little more than a large grove, other areas blanketed entire hills. In places, particularly from the vantage point of a tall hill, one could see for a few miles, in clear weather. as it mostly was this afternoon. I decided to ride over to a particularly tall tree on a hilltop not too far away, and see what I could from that vantage point.

I unslung my shield, stripped out of my sword belt and cloak, and took off my helmet in preparation. I'd grown up climbing trees and while my armor, and especially my injured shoulder made things harder, in short order I was several feet up and had a great view of the area around me. Again I was struck by the wild beauty of the landscape, in spite of the present circumstances. Scanning the skyline, I noticed that the smoke column I'd seen that morning was no longer visible. "Have we gone far enough away from the source of the smoke that we can't see it anymore?" I murmured, "Or has the fire gone out?" I slowly scanned the area in all directions, attempting to at least orient myself. Then I spotted a familiar mountain range. I glanced up in the sky, noting the location of the sun, then back at the mountain range, and swore softly to myself. The mountains were southwest of me, unless I was missing something. That put me about fifteen miles north of where I'd hoped I was.

I was still processing this when I saw a couple of men emerge from some woods to my north, about four hundred paces away. As I focused on the area, I saw more and more emerge. They were too far away to identify, but the fact that they were coming from the north made it unlikely that they were friendly. My first impulse was to get behind the hill with Carys, but the idea of losing visual contact with the group made me nervous. Instead, I shimmied down the tree as quickly as I could, while still being careful not to shake the branches too much. I didn't want to draw their attention to me, if they hadn't already seen me. Once down on the ground I hurriedly put my gear back on, except for my helmet. I didn't want to chance the men spotting the iron of my helm and giving my presence away. I guided Carys behind the hill, then crawled back around the side of it, far enough that I could keep an eye on the figures.

Time passed excruciatingly slowly as I watched them approach. When they were within a few hundred paces, I was able to count about two dozen of them. They were formed up in a wide skirmish line, with several paces between each man, and all but two of them were on foot, which was good for me if I was spotted. They weren't heading directly towards me, but rather sweeping through the open, low ground. The first thing I noticed were the small, square shields many of them carried. As they got even closer, I made out more details. The shields had swirling patterns on them. The men had long hair and beards. A few had blue designs painted on their faces. Their clothing was mostly earthy greens, browns, grays, and the creamy color of undyed wool and linen. There was no doubt about it, then. These were Picts. They wore no armor, so they were unnervingly quiet as they jogged by in the open field before me. The way they were spaced out, and how they looked around as they approached, made me realize that they were hunting for something, or someone.

A shiver ran down my spine as a fresh wave of fear washed over me. Had they seen me, after all? Were these Picts part of the group that had been at Loch Liobhann, or a different group? Maybe my cymbrogi had fought and lost the battle, and this group was hunting for survivors. Or maybe they were a simple hunting party from some village, like the one that I'd probably identified this morning by their smoke, I chided myself.

Carys nickered, still hidden behind the hill, and as quiet as the sound was it still nearly scared me half to death. I looked over and whispered soothingly to her. Fortunately, I'd taught Carys to lay down on command while she was a filly. I'd only done it to show the trick off to my friends, but now it might help prevent us from being detected. I crawled back over to her, pulled her into a depression below a large tree, surrounded by thick brush, and gently brought her down to the ground. I crouched down beside her, my left hand stroking her neck, and my right tightly clutching the hilt of my sword. I could no longer see the Picts approaching, but they were close enough now that I could hear them as they talked to each other in their foreign, lilting language. It was similar enough to Brythonic that I felt I could actually get a sense for what they were saying, though I only understood a word or two. They were angry about something.

Their tone alone betrayed that much. I heard the sounds of two of them moving through the brush on the far side of the hill Carys and I were pressed up against. Then I saw one of them! He was no more than a few paces away, and slowly walking down the hill. At any moment I feared he could stumble upon my tracks. Even worse, from a few paces away on my other side, I heard the other Pict. As they made their way down the hill and passed Carys and I, there was a howl. It was loud and clear, likely no more than sixty paces to my left, coming from another patch of woods. A moment later a few short barks responded.

Carys swiveled her head in that direction, ears forward. I quickly placed my hand over her muzzle, desperate to comfort her and keep her quiet and still. Even the Picts seemed unnerved by the howling and barking, as they began talking quickly and the one closest to the woods gestured with his spear. The pair continued down the hill, but they angled to my right, away from the howls. Thankfully, they weren't looking at the ground now, but at the woods where the howl had originated. In another minute, they were down at the base of the hill. If either of them looked behind them, they would almost certainly see me. My heart was pounding heavily in my ears and my hands became slick with sweat as I gripped the hilt of my sword. At any moment I might have to flee, or fight for my life. They didn't look back, however. Instead, they kept walking, focused on the land before them, or glancing off into the woods where the wolves were.

I pressed my forehead to Carys'. "Good girl," I whispered over and over in relief, and scratched her jaw. Slowly, my own heartbeat returned to normal as the Picts got further and further away. After a few more minutes, they disappeared all together as they walked up, then over another hill. That's when I noticed something else, in the woods. I squinted at first, then felt myself go almost giddy with relief and happiness. I saw four wolves, or at least hybrid wolves, just inside the woodline. Among the pack was one tawny-colored hound that I recognized immediately. It was Mel! I laughed, and called her name. Her head perked up as she turned towards me, and barked once.

Carys whinnied, almost in my ear, causing me to start. I looked around, ensuring for a final time that the Picts were gone, then stood up and gave her the signal to do the same. I looked over at Mel and called her again. She walked towards me, cocking her head, making me grin in excitement. She really did know her name, I was delighted to see. I tried to coax her to come towards me, and she did, but only a few feet closer. After a minute or so, she barked again, tail wagging, then rejoined the other dogs after one of them, the one that looked the most wolf-like, yipped and growled a couple times. They faded off into the woods. I wondered just how far they went though. We were surely a dozen miles, probably twice that far, from the fort where I'd first encountered the pack, yet they were clearly following me. Some of them had, anyway, I corrected my assessment. At the fort, I'd seen several more dogs than I did here.

Still cautious of heading out too soon, given that the Picts had walked off in the same direction I myself needed to go, I decided to stay on the side of that hill for the night. It was a good spot. It had concealment, cover from the weather, and offered a good vantage point to the area around me. Besides, I reasoned, I had that rabbit to cook at some point. The cold wouldn't preserve it forever. So while I waited for dark I removed Carys' saddle and bridle, placed her gear under a large, nearby tree, alongside with my shield, and tethered her to the tree. I unbuckled my helm and dropped it onto the ground beside the rest of my gear, followed by the padded cap I wore under it. After a moment's hesitation, I decided to remove my sword belt and propped it up against the tree, as well. I also gathered firewood, and dug out a fire pit to mitigate the amount of light my cooking fire would emit. I heaped dry pine needles into the bottom of the pit. These would make perfect tinder for my fire. Finally, I gathered up some dead sticks to sustain my fire with, to include one long, thin one that I would use as a spit for the rabbit.

By the time I'd made all my preparations for that night's feast, it was dark enough to start the fire. I hovered over the firepit, pulled out my iron striker along with my piece of flint from out of a saddlebag, and got busy. The striker looked a bit like a bracelet, but was shaped in an oval to fit around fingers rather than a wrist. I held it tightly in my left hand, and hit it with the flint, in my right hand. A moment later I gritted my teeth and cursed when I nicked my knuckle with the flint, drawing blood. I ignored it for the moment, and kept at it. A minute later sparks from the flint striking the iron striker ignited the pine needles, and started a small flame. I knelt down and blew on it, coaxing the flame to grow. It did, and I added bigger sticks into the pit. Once I had the fire going, I took a moment to scoop up some snow and clean the blood off my hand. One more little misery, I sighed irritably. Soon that was forgotten though, as I eagerly spitted my rabbit, and slowly rotated it over the fire, cooking the meat. When it was nearly done, I decided to spit a wedge of cheese on the end of the stick, as well, just to warm it up a bit. My mouth salivated as the meat got closer and closer to being done and the smell of cheese and rabbit meat filled my nostrils.

Not far away, I heard a noise. Carys heard it too, and she looked over, whinnying softly. I saw an animal's eyes reflecting the faint glow of the fire, and for a moment I was so startled I nearly dropped the spit. Then I saw that it was Mel. She was sitting, just a few paces away, tongue hanging out, eyes going from me to the rabbit. When I looked up, she whined. I smirked at her.

"Come to beg for food, have you, girl?" I asked her softly. She whined again. I sighed, carved off a large strip of leg meat with my dagger, and tossed it to her. I deliberately arched it so that she had to come close to get it. For once, the meat hit the ground in front of her. It landed only a couple feet in front of me. I pulled off my cheese and munched on it, enjoying the soft, warm, smoky flavor as I chewed, and continued to cook the rabbit. Mel crept closer, slinking low to the ground. She whined softly, then inched nearer. Finally, she darted forward, snatched the meat, and backed off a step, devouring it quickly. A moment later, she was looking at me again, noisily licking her muzzle. I chuckled, and shaved off another strip of meat.

"You have to earn this one, girl," I said. This time, instead of throwing it, I held it out to her by one end of it. Mel whined, staring intently at the meat, but didn't budge.

"Come on girl, you can do it," I encouraged her, softly. I wagged the meat at her.

She wrestled with the decision a moment longer, then she slowly inched forward, one step at a time. Finally, when she was close enough, she leaned forward and cautiously took the meat out of my hand.

"Good girl!" I gushed, happily. I wished I could have fed her the entire rabbit. I suspected if I could have kept feeding her, before long Mel would have actually let me pet her, but regrettably, I knew I needed the meat for my own sustenance. And it wasn't like she was starving, from the look of her. For all I knew, she'd been eating better than me these past couple days, and was only begging for my food because she took me for an easy prospect. I finished the rest of the rabbit while Mel lay down on her belly, watching me intently. As I ate, I tossed the bones to her, one by one. She licked them clean but didn't eat much off them. Instead, she carefully picked up each bone in her mouth and carried them back to the woods, where the other three dogs were likely still waiting.

Once I'd finished off my rabbit, and Mel understood that there were no more bones to be had, she faded back into the woods, giving me a last look over her shoulder. I enjoyed the cozy warmth of the fire, wrestling with whether I should put it out or not. Fire pit or no, the glow from the fire could still potentially be seen for a ways off, and I had no desire to draw any passing Picts to my position while I slept. On the other hand, I was in a nice thick grove of trees, and seriously doubted it could be seen from too far away. And it was cold. Also, I was more concerned about Mel's pack of wolf-dogs than I was Picts at the moment. They probably weren't that far away, and while I wasn't worried about Mel herself, the other dogs in her pack were another story. I had to trust Carys to warn me, I decided. As was becoming my custom, I laid out my shield and one of my javelins before wrapping myself up in my blanket and bedroll for the night.

Then I laid down, using my saddle as a headrest, trying not to think about how in the world I was going to get out of these woods the next day. I assumed the battle was over at this point, and the Dragons would probably be heading back south soon. That might be my last, best chance to link back up with them. I envisioned life here in these woods if I failed to find my way out, assuming I didn't starve or freeze to death first, and my stomach clenched into knots at the thought. At least if I died in battle, someone would probably be able to relay the news to my parents, but if I died out here, there would be no confirmed reports. My parents would only know that I disappeared, out here in the wilderness. I prayed, begging God to deliver me from this place, then attempted to go to sleep.

# Chapter Twelve

I was just nodding off, listening to the faint crackle and pop of the wood burning as the fire burned when Carys, who'd been dozing nearby, came alert, whinnying softly. Immediately, I came awake, grabbed my shield and javelin, and rolled to my feet.

"What do you sense out there, girl?" I murmured, scanning the darkness of the woods.

I heard a rustling noise in the woods, about ten paces away. Was it Mel's pack? Had some Picts seen my fire, after all? I crouched into a fighting stance and held my javelin underhanded, at shoulder level, ready to throw.

King David's book, the Psalmi, came to mind, and as I scanned the woods, I calmed myself down by reciting a bit of it. "... Even though I walk through the valley of the shadow of death, I will fear no evil, for You are with me; Your rod and Your staff, they comfort me. You prepare a table before me in the presence of my enemies...."

Carys snorted and neighed again, louder, and tugged on her tether. I tensed, ready to throw, as a silhouette emerged from the growing darkness of the forest.

"Please don't attack, Roman," a soft, feminine voice said. That caught me off guard, and my arm relaxed, though I still held my javelin up.

"Step into the light where I can see you," I commanded, trying to sound forceful rather than frightened.

Slowly, from only five paces away, a girl emerged into the faint glow of the fire. Her hands were raised, palms toward me, so I could see that she held no weapons.

I studied the girl. She wore a simple long-sleeved dress that was belted at the waist, and a hooded, wool cloak. She was a bit shorter than me, with a slight build.

"I mean no harm," the girl stated. She took another step toward me and pulled her hood away from her face, revealing a head of tousled, auburn hair, and a freckled face with full lips. She looked about my own age. Her next words really caught my attention. "We can help each other, I think?"

She'd spoken in Brythonic, but in a lilting accent that I couldn't quite identify.

"You're a Pict," I guessed, and scanned the woods around me, not ready to believe that she was alone.

She nodded. "And you're a Roman. And we both need help the other can give," she said and slowly lowered her hands.

"I'm not a Roman. I'm a Briton. And how do you think we could help each other?" I asked as I glanced at Carys, to see where her attention was focused. My mare was looking only at the girl, so I decided that this Pict was indeed alone, as improbable as it seemed. I lowered my shield, as my shoulder was beginning to hurt from the weight of it, but kept my javelin ready to throw.

"Roman. Briton. I see no difference," she shrugged. "You're lost, yes? I know this land. Maybe I could guide you. Where do you go?"

I thought for a moment, then decided it couldn't hurt to answer her. "I'm trying to rejoin the unit of cavalry that rode through here recently." I ignored her comment about me being lost, not wanting to acknowledge the truth of that, though it was a bit unsettling that she knew.

Her eyebrows furrowed a bit. "I know of the horsemen you speak of. I know where they were. I'm not sure where they are, now."

"How long ago did you come upon them?" I asked.

"They attacked a village not far from mine this morning. I did not see the fight, or your people, but I heard about it. I know where they were."

"Is it far? Where was this village?" I asked. I had a pretty good idea how far this should have been, but I wanted to hear her confirm it.

"Not far," she answered. "Maybe two or three hours away on horseback. The village was on the west side of a large loch."

The auburn-haired girl smiled. "I can guide you there. Can we go now?" She glanced over my shoulder, scanning the area where the other Picts had traveled.

I wanted to accept her offer. I doubted she herself was much of a threat, and I was definitely lost, but there was something off about her, and this situation didn't feel right.

"Why are you so ready to leave with me, an outsider? And who are you, by the way?" I asked.

"It doesn't matter why. I was treated badly in my village and ran away. Now I'm offering to help you out of here, which also helps me. My name is Maithgemm."

"But what will you do after I've rejoined my cymbrogi?" I asked in confusion. "We're all soldiers. Do you intend to become a- "

She cut me off, glaring at me. "I am a *good* girl. I can make myself useful. I can be an interpreter. I can scout, cook, clean. Many things, but my body is my own." She stressed this last part, her eyes boring into me as if she expected me to make advances on her.

"I had no such thoughts," I protested, mostly truthfully. In spite of her disheveled appearance, she was cute, and even her cloak failed to hide her distinctly feminine curves.

"Then it is settled," she declared.

"I don't know how well Carys will do, carrying both of us," I mused.

"I'm not heavy, and it's not far. We'll be fine," she said.

By this time I'd lowered my javelin. Now I sat back down on the saddle on the ground. "You don't have any weapons on you, do you?" I asked, scrutinizing

182

her again. I was tired, and wanted to go to sleep, but at the same time I really didn't want to risk getting my throat cut while I slept.

She rolled her eyes and sighed heavily. "No. And if I'd wanted to kill you, I'd have waited until you were asleep, then bashed your head in with one of those stones around your fire, which I smelled from some distance back."

I looked at her for a moment. That didn't sound particularly reassuring.

"Look!" she said, and gathered up her cloak, holding it away from her body. "No weapons!"

"You're a Pict who just showed up out of the woods," I said, then reluctantly added, "I'll allow you to accompany me, but I'm searching you for weapons first."

Her eyes narrowed. "Fine, but by all the gods, you had better not try anything!"

"I only worship one God, and He would not approve of me mistreating you, even if I were of a mind to. Which I'm *not*," I replied, feeling awkward and just a little indignant.

She stood before me, rigid and watchful, and held her arms out. As briskly as I could, I felt along each of her arms then circled around her waist. She was tense, and taut, clearly ready to fight or flee in an instant if she felt she needed to. I moved my hands down to her hips. Her breath caught, and I quickly slid my hands along the outside of her legs, feeling for the telltale lump of a weapon, or strap. I reached her ankles, and detected nothing. The process had only taken a few seconds, and as soon as I was done, I stood up. I knew I was blushing from even that brief bit of contact with her.

"Satisfied?" she asked in a flat tone.

I nodded.

"May I sit by your fire now?" she asked as she took a step forward and sat down next to the firepit.

"Be my guest," I said.

"Kind of you," she replied. If she picked up on my sarcasm, she ignored it. She held her hands over the pit, warming herself. I gently set my shield and javelin back down beside the rest of my gear, against the tree.

"Do you have any more of that meat you were cooking earlier?" she asked, actually sounding a bit shy.

"No," I replied, then faintly heard her stomach rumble. I sighed this time. My desire to be a good Christian host warred with my distrust of her being a barbarian.

"I have some food you can have, though," I said at last, and fished the cheese out of my saddlebag. I unwrapped it and pulled out the half wheel that remained, started to cut a thin wedge, then glanced over at her out of the corner of my eye. She looked tired and worn out. Her clothing was threadbare and torn in places, and I couldn't help but feel some pity for her. I cut off a larger wedge, put away the remainder of the wheel, and handed the wedge to her. She took it, smiled up at me, then focused on the food. I sat back down beside my javelin and shield, and wrapped myself back up in my blankets, watching her as she nibbled at the hard cheese, obviously savoring it. She was definitely hungry, I concluded. That only added to the mystery though. Had she come from a village only that morning, shouldn't she have been better fed? Shouldn't her clothing be less worn out?

She caught me looking at her, and stopped eating for a moment. "What?" she asked between bites.

"Just wondering what it is about you that you're not telling me," I answered.

"Says the boy who still hasn't even given his own name," she responded with a twinkle in her eyes.

"Boy-" I began to protest. Then started over, "I did tell you ...." I replayed our conversation in my head, and then felt annoyed at myself. She was right.

"My name is Peredur. I'm with the Red Dragons cavalry unit, under the command of Tribune Arthur," I said, proudly, then wondered if I'd told her too much. She could still be a spy or something.

"Arthur?" she echoed, eyebrows shooting up. "The son of the Pendragon? That Arthur?"

"Maybe," I replied, more cautious in my response this time.

"You are!" she exclaimed. "We have heard of him! He is a great warrior." Suddenly she eyed me up and down, looking doubtful. "You look too young to fight with such a man."

I felt a flash of anger. "Shows how little you know, girl," I growled. "I've been in a fight against Scoti raiders, and two fights against your kin now." She didn't need to know how that fight against the Scoti had gone.

The girl's eyes widened a bit. "I am sorry, great warrior. I did not mean to offend your manly pride."

I opened my mouth to say something, then shut it. I didn't know how to respond. Was she mocking me? I felt like she was, but her face revealed nothing. I decided to change the subject. "We should sleep now. I assume even you need light to take us to the lake."

She looked up at the sky. Clouds obscured much of the moon and stars, providing very little natural light. "I agree," she said after a few moments. "We should leave as soon as the sun rises."

I glanced again at her thin cloak and dress. "Will you be alright?" I asked after a moment.

The girl's eyebrow arched as she gave me an odd look. "Concerned for me, are you?"

"You're my guide out of here," I answered. "So yes, I'd prefer if you didn't freeze to death tonight."

She looked a bit suspiciously at me. "And what do you suggest?"

I sighed. "You can sleep *next* to me," I stressed the word, in order to avoid any misunderstanding. "We each have our own cloak, but I have my blanket. We can share that, and both of us will be a bit warmer."

The girl glanced out into the woods, down at the firepit, which was barely more than smoldering now, then back at me. "I accept the offer," she said. I

185

leaned back, resting my head on the saddle and opened my arm out. She ducked under the low-hanging tree branches and crawled over to me. Before she laid down next to me then looked me in the eyes, her face just inches away from mine and murmured, "Peredur, you have lovely green eyes. If you try to take advantage of me, I'll gouge them out."

I was taken aback, once again unsure how to respond.

"Well, don't try to rob me or something and make me kill *you*, barbarian, because, uh, you have a pretty ... mouth," I stuttered.

I felt more stupid than I ever had in my life and abruptly lay down and turned away from her.

Behind me, I heard Maithgemm muffling a laugh as she laid down beside me with her back to mine, then pulled on the blanket to cover herself with it as well. It seemed like only moments later, I heard the soft, rhythmic breathing of someone sleeping. She must have been exhausted, to fall asleep so fast. I was still trying to decide what to make of this mysterious girl when I too finally fell asleep.

# Chapter Thirteen

I was the first to wake up the following morning. I made Carys ready for another day of riding, gathered my weapons and belongings back up, then woke the girl up. Her eyes blinked open slowly and she looked around almost confused, as someone does when coming out of a deep slumber.

"Good morning," I greeted her. "Carys is ready to go. So am I. So we can leave as soon as you're ready. We can eat while we ride."

She nodded, still clearly groggy, and said nothing. Instead, she slowly stood up, stretched, and yawned loudly, then she shambled off into the woods, mumbling something about needing a moment of privacy. I went ahead and mounted up. I waited, and after a while I finally called out, "Maeve? Maith ...gwen? What was your name again?"

There was no response. I was just beginning to wonder if she'd heard me, or if she'd decided to ditch me for some reason when she came out of the woods. She looked much better, I noticed. Her wild mane of red-brown hair looked brushed, from what I could see under her wide hood. She'd cleaned her face and hands, as well.

"It's Maithgemm," she said, slowly, as one does to a small child. "If that's too hard, you can just go with 'Gemma'. That's close enough."

"Gemma it is," I said, and held out my hand. She grabbed my forearm, as I grabbed hers, and hoisted her up behind me in the saddle. She took a moment to adjust some of my equipment around, particularly my large canteen, and the case of javelins, then she banged on my shield, slung across my back.

"Can you do something about this? This metal part sticking out of your shield will be murder to deal with."

Images of the boss smashing into her sternum or face anytime Carys took a hard step flashed through my head, and I readily conceded her point.

"Can you carry it on your own back then?" I asked. "It's too big to strap on Carys' side with both of us riding her."

"Yes," she answered, and helped pull the shield off of my back. I grunted slightly as I moved my left arm. She heard it.

"Are you injured?" she asked, lightly tapping my shoulder.

I flinched, more from reflex than pain. "Yes," I admitted. "So please don't bump against my shoulder if you don't have to."

She agreed to try as she wrapped her arms around my waist, and told me she was ready to go. Not wanting to rely on her anymore than I had to, I pointed Carys southeast, and prodded her forward into a trot. Gemma said nothing to correct me. When she did finally guide me, it was to gesture occasionally towards some thin trail or towards some rock outcropping, or other such landmark.

Though partly cloudy, the sun was actually visible today, and I reveled in the warmer temperature. It still wasn't warm enough to remove our cloaks by any means, but it was at least warm enough that the thin layer of snow began to melt. As we rode, I pulled out two biscuits from my saddlebag, and handed one back to her. A short while later I offered her my canteen as well. We talked a bit. Mostly she asked the questions, asking me about my family, my home, and life at Caer Lleon. I tried asking her about her own life, but aside from picking up that her mother had died in childbirth, her father had died a few years ago, and she'd been miserable at the village she'd fled, I didn't get much from her. She loved swimming, was proud of her cooking and sewing abilities, and was good with a sling, but she evaded more questions than she answered, it seemed. A bit over two hours later she pointed to a ridgeline I recognized, a couple miles in the distance.

"The loch is over that ridge," she told me. I remembered my turma's encounter with the Pict screen line from a couple nights ago, and realized I was looking at the same low ridge, just from a point a bit further south. I became excited, and signaled for Carys to increase her speed to a canter. I kept my eye on the ridge, watching for movement or the glint of metal, in case there were Picts still occupying it, as there had been the last time I'd been here, but I saw no movement, until we got closer that is. Once we got to within about three hundred paces of the ridge I saw large, black birds flying around above the treeline. Huge ravens and crows, their smaller cousins, circled and dived at something on the other side of the ridge.

"There was a battle there, I'd say," Gemma said somberly. She, too was looking up at the sky.

I guided Carys past a particularly large hill, somewhat resembling a giant laying on his back. I half expected Picts to come bursting out of the woods at any moment, but aside from the cawing of distant crows, it was quiet. Several minutes later we cleared the ridge and the trees, and looked out into the basin below.

I'd read of great battles, and heard a few stories regarding what they were like, and their aftermaths, but the scene that lay before me was far beyond anything I'd ever imagined. I gasped at the sight. Hundreds of bodies lay scattered about the lake. Dozens of sheep and a few horses lay scattered about as well. These were concentrated around a cluster of wattle and daub homes, surrounded by a mostly destroyed wicker fence. Broken weapons, shields, torn clothing, and bits of armor lay everywhere, along with heaps of animal hides, used for tents. The blackened, charred remains of cooking fires dotted the ruined camp as well. Some of them still smoldered, and thin wisps of smoke rose into the bleak sky. There must have been an encampment along this entire stretch of the lake, I decided. Scavenger animals and birds, like the multitude of crows and ravens we'd seen on the way up the hill, swarmed the field. Then there was the incredible, terrible stench. Gemma and I both nearly gagged, and wrapped the hems of our cloaks around our faces.

Hesitantly, I started to urge Carys forward, but Gemma put a hand on my right shoulder, apparently mindful of my injury.

"Don't. Please don't go down there." I glanced behind me. Her eyes were wet with tears. Whatever she felt about her people that made her want to leave the north, this battlefield full of her dead kin was breaking her heart, I realized. Another thought hit me then, and though I obliged her and did not proceed down the slope towards the lake, I looked closer at the field. I saw no dead Britons. Only Picts. Though I'd never been in a true battle before, even I understood the significance of that. Arthur had won. Our men had buried our own dead, carted off the wounded, but left the enemy dead for the scavengers. I was flooded with a sense of relief, and sighed. I wanted to rejoice but I felt that wouldn't be very appropriate with Gemma riding behind me.

We rode north, around the edge of the battlefield. "I'd like to find the graves of my own people," I explained to her. I was anxious to determine how extensive our casualties had been.

"Bad idea," she said, clearing her throat. "We should leave this place."

"Why?" I asked.

"Many more will be coming here."

"Many more, what? More Picts?" I asked, feeling alarmed.

"Yes," she said. "I have seen warbands moving through the village I left. I've heard talk. King Drest has been uniting the tribes of the Caledonii, Fortriu, and others for an invasion of the south. This," Gemma gestured to the dead scattered below us, "was *not* Drest's army. These were maybe one or two tribal warbands. The ones that came south first, maybe."

"You mean the advance party?" I asked.

Gemma shrugged.

"Gemma, this is important. If I take you down there, would you be able to identify what tribe or tribes this group was made up of? Could you handle that?"

I felt terrible, asking her to do this, but if what she'd just told me was true, I knew Arthur would need all the information he could, assuming of course he didn't already know this somehow.

Gemma sighed and looked out at the battlefield for a few moments, then finally nodded her head. "Take me down there," she said softly.

I urged Carys forward and we rode down into the basin, amongst the bodies of her countrymen. Scavengers moved away as we approached, but they didn't go too far away.

Gemma pointed to a cluster of men. "Maeatae," she said.

I skirted the edge of the battlefield, reluctant to fully surround myself within the swarm of crows, ravens, rats and other creatures scurrying about. Even from the edge, I was beginning to get a sense for what happened. The largest cluster of dead were here, along the southeast edge of the lake. They formed a wide front, some hundred paces wide. This had been where the Picts encamped near a village and made their initial defense, I suspected. In the vicinity of the village I noticed a number of women and even a few children as well. My stomach clenched, and I felt sick upon noticing them. Gemma noticed them too, and I felt her stiffen as she let out a horrified sob.

I angled Carys over that way. I needed to see that part of the field, to better understand just what happened. As I did, I saw that the types of injuries changed. The piles of men I saw in the southern area had clearly died from the thrusts and cuts of bladed weapons. Those closest to the hovels however looked to have died from stones, arrows, and javelins. Many of the bodies, the ground around them, and even some of the roundhouses were riddled with javelins and arrows, and stones were embedded into the walls of some of the buildings.

While this was the first battlefield I'd ever witnessed, I found myself grateful to my father for encouraging me to go out hunting as often as I had. Because of those many hunts, the sight of dead bodies, of viscera, and the various types of wounds I bore witness to now all felt somewhat familiar. The fact that the bodies were human instead of game made the sight more disturbing however,

191

and I admit, I looked away from some of the more ghastly sights. I could appreciate of course that Gemma was viewing the battlefield in a very different way than I was.

"The people who lived here were Venicones," Gemma said. "And it looks as though Arthur is no different from other warlords. His men cut down women and children. I thought he was more noble than that," she spat, bitterly.

"We marched north with a large force of levy foot soldiers from Gododdin," I protested. This was more likely their work, not Arthur's."

I dearly hoped that was the case, at least. I really didn't like thinking about the alternative.

"Was he not in command?"

"Probably," I admitted. "I wasn't here though, so I don't know how this happened. Something's strange though," I pondered aloud, scanning the area. "The ground here isn't as torn up as it should be after a cavalry charge. I think this is where the levy infantry attacked the camp."

"And the village," Gemma added, unwilling to overlook that.

"And the village," I acknowledged with a grimace.

I envisioned a formation of infantry advancing towards the encampment from the south. If they had, Arthur's cavalry would have hit the flank, but the Picts had their left flank protected by the lake. I looked westward.

"There," I exclaimed. "See that torn up mud coming down that slope? That's where the Red Dragons made their charge!" I shook my head. What a sight that must have been! I could just envision it now- the Gododdin men coming out of the woods to the south, advancing into the Picts, probably in a surprise attack. They must have initiated the attack with a barrage of sling stones, arrows, and javelins, followed up by a charge, and engaged the Picts shield to shield, blade to blade. Once the Pict line was fully entangled, Arthur and the Red Dragons likely charged into their flank, as a hammer blow to compliment the infantry's anvil.

"They would have had the cover of these woods and this slope. The Picts wouldn't have had any time at all to react as the bulk of the Red Dragons swept down into them."

"Very heroic," Gemma said flatly.

I sighed. I felt like my very soul was being torn in two. On the one hand, envisioning Arthur's decisive victory here made my heart swell with pride, and even envy that I had missed it. On the other, there were the slaughtered villagers, and the company of the sorrowful Picti girl riding behind me. I was convinced the Red Dragons had not been the ones who had attacked the village itself, but that was little consolation.

"How can you tell which tribe this or that person belonged to?" I asked, trying to change the subject.

"The same way I assume you know if you're looking at a Briton or a Saxon," she said. "There are differences in clothing, in physical appearances, and other details."

We rode past the small village. There were more bodies sprawled around a low, stone wall. Another defensive position. Dozens of broken javelins lay strewn about, and impaled many of the bodies there. That wall clearly hadn't provided them as much protection as they'd hoped. At least these had been warriors.

Most of them Gemma decided were likely Caledonii, the largest tribe. She explained that the Caledonii controlled most of the land north of the wall. Probably why the Romans had named this land Caledonia in the first place, I decided. The second group, she declared, looked like Maeatae. They all looked the same, to me.

"So, Arthur cleared out several hundred camped here," I mused, as I scanned the battlefield, estimating the number of casualties, and noting the large numbers of tents and cooking fires. "But you say there's more coming?" I glanced over at Gemma.

"Probably," she nodded. "Maybe even twice as many. Word was put out last summer that everyone able to fight should gather here as the moon entered its first quarter. They expected to catch you southerners off guard by striking early in the year with a large force, drive your people away, and be done by early summer, in time to focus back on managing the livestock."

"They were going to indiscriminately attack and kill, enslave, or drive off farmers and their families, were they? To include women and children?" I asked, pointedly.

Gemma scowled at me, muttering something in her native tongue. I left the subject alone and glanced up at the sky.

"What tribe are you from?" I asked.

"I'm ... Dicalydones. We're a subtribe of the Caledonii."

"You seem to know a lot about this King Drest. Were you a village chief's daughter, then?" I asked, glancing over my shoulder at her.

She gave me a dark look, then nodded. "I was. My village was northwest of here. Some years ago, after becoming king, Drest rode from village to village, telling of his big plans to invade the south. He demanded that the other chiefs bend the knee. My father's village, and a few others, resisted. They thought the plan to invade the south in such numbers was mad. Drest's men came and burned our village down. The menfolk, and many of the women were killed. Those of us too young to resist were enslaved. Myself included," she said.

I frowned as I listened to her story. Something in the back of my mind was nagging at me, like something wasn't quite adding up, though what that was I couldn't identify.

"Now, for the past year or so, the invasion is practically all everyone's been talking about. Drest crushed any who opposed him, and united all the tribes under his banner," she continued.

I listened to her story in silence, getting a clearer image of the kind of man this King Drest was, and not liking it.

"I'm ready to go," I told her, finally. As uncomfortable as it had been for me, I knew that riding through the village had been especially hard for Gemma. I saw no reason to prolong her anguish by staying there. "Arthur needs to know what you've told me. He'll have gone south, to the border wall that the Romans built a long time ago. Do you know of it?"

"The one that cuts the land in half from east to west, just south of the River Forth?" she asked.

"That would be the one," I agreed. "We reoccupied one of the forts that was still in good condition. It's on a land bridge that cuts through a wide stretch of marshes. I need to get there."

"I think I know the one you speak of," she said. "Though it's hard to say. There's many ruins along that wall. Even the wall itself is fading back into the land in some places. We're about a day's walk from Sruighlea, the hillfort at the bridge crossing the Forth. From Sruighlea it's another few hours' walk to reach your wall.

"Carys should be able to get us there in a few hours. So let's just ride until dusk, then find a place to hole up for the night. We should be able to reach the fort sometime early tomorrow afternoon."

"Agreed," she nodded. Then she looked up, and froze. "Oh, now those could be Fortriu ..." she said. Her voice sounded strained.

"Where?" I asked, scanning the battlefield.

"Up there!" she exclaimed, pointing to the northeast.

A cold chill went down my spine as I looked where she was pointing, not on the battlefield, but in the woods overlooking it. A large column of people were converging on the basin, hundreds of paces off.

"You can identify them from here?" I asked, amazed.

"No, I can't!" she snapped. "Would you like to stay here until they're closer so I can?"

"We probably shouldn't," I said and turned Carys south, intending to ride away.

I gasped as I saw movement through the trees west of us. There was a pair of horsemen, leisurely approaching from the north. I urged Carys to the other side of a roundhouse, to hide from the riders. Another pair, riding through the battlefield and close to the edge of the water, were to our east. These two pairs of riders must be part of a screen line for the oncoming horde on foot, I realized. There was only a slim chance that I could outrun them, especially as Carys was carrying both me and Gemma.

Gemma heard my gasp, saw the riders, and came to the same conclusion as I. She dismounted, hissing urgently at me to do the same. I did, and she pointed to a large, wooden hatch on the ground. It led into a fogou; a deep, narrow hole in the ground that kept extra foodstuffs a bit cooler. She scrambled over to it and lifted the hatch by a rope handle.

"Get in!" she urged.

"But Carys- " I started to protest.

"Get in or get killed," she hissed, glancing towards the woods.

Hating myself for abandoning Carys, I had the presence of mind to snatch a pair of javelins from the scabbard at Carys' side, then scurried after Gemma down into the small man-made cave.

As we felt our way along shelves lined with clay jars, I whispered, "You realize if they find us down here, we're trapped."

"*If*," she said back. "You're welcome to go back up."

Even as she said this though, we heard voices approaching the entrance. We hurried to the rear of the long chamber, which angled deeper underground the further we went. The moment we felt an end to the shelves, we leapt to the side and hunched down low. My heart pounded in my ears, and I pressed a javelin against Gemma. "Here. Take this. You may need it if we're found," I whispered to her. After a moment of her pawing blindly at me, she found the small, slender spear and took it from me.

We heard excited voices, and horses snorting and whinnying. Then there were curses, and the sound of a horse galloping away.

"Some men found your horse. I think they tried to take her, but she fought them," Gemma whispered. I grinned, dearly hoping that she was right. Then the hatch of the fogou opened, and light streamed in. The chamber, little more than a large hole really, had wooden walls and a ceiling, was about ten paces long, and narrow. With the shelves lining both walls, there was only enough space for one man at a time to walk through. If we had to fight, Gemma or I could block the whole width of the narrow room with my shield that she'd carried down, slung across her back. We each had a javelin, and I still had my spatha. From behind the rows of urns, wicker baskets, and cloth-wrapped bundles, I watched as a man slowly descended into the cellar. I gripped my javelin tightly, my body tense as I prepared to spring out and throw it, should the man give me any reason to believe he'd spotted us.

The Pict, wearing a cloak over a loose-fitting tunic and checkered trousers and brandishing an axe, looked around briefly, then tipped over an urn slightly with his free hand and sniffed. He grunted, and tapped the sides of a few others. He stuck his axe into his belt, grabbed two of the urns, then turned and walked back up and out of the fogou. Gemma and I both sighed in relief.

I waited for several minutes, giving myself time to calm back down and hopefully for the Picts to clear out, then slowly crept my way up the entrance. Before poking my head out, I listened. I heard voices talking from several directions, and walking about. I heard at least one horse whinny. I walked back down to where Gemma remained hidden.

"We can't escape right now," I sighed. "They're all around us."

"As long as we aren't discovered here, we might be able to get away when the sun goes down," Gemma suggested.

"Maybe," I said. "Hopefully Carys finds me once we're away, or we can find another horse or two. Otherwise we're in for a rough go of it, trying to escape on foot."

We debated on closing the hatch that the Picts had left open, but I was afraid the man might walk by again. If he did, and he remembered leaving it open, that

197

could spell bad news for us. So we stayed hidden as best we could in the dark recesses of the hole and stayed silent.

We hunkered down then and waited for night to come. There was some cheese and dried meat in one of the wicker baskets, but it was so old and moldy that neither of us were hungry enough to attempt to eat it. The other urns within reach were empty so we had nothing to drink either. All we could do was huddle together in the deepest, darkest corner of the cellar and wait for the sun to go down. Gemma dozed a bit. Although I felt a bit tired as well, I was too worried that more men would come down and inspect the cellar for more usable food and drink. Thankfully, none did. It grew darker and darker, and slowly, voices and the sounds of the camp, which we'd heard off and on all day became fewer and fewer. Finally it became quiet, shortly after the sun went down. I gestured for Gemma to follow me, and we slowly crept up the sloped cellar floor and to the door.

I poked my head out, scanning for movement or any sign of guards and saw none. I could hear men at work, though the noise was faint. From the sounds, I guessed they were still burying their dead. In the moonlight I saw that dozens of small, hide shelters had been set up just outside of where the battle had been fought, and along the woodline, extending in a long strip along the western half of the lake.

Not seeing anyone nearby, I looked at Gemma and waved her forward. Together, we cautiously made our way out of the cellar, and through the silent village. It had been cleared of bodies and now so that aside from the absence of a few roving dogs, it looked like it could be any other totally normal village. At least one of them had even been reoccupied, we noticed. The faint glow outlining the door, and the smell of smoke indicated a fire was blazing inside one of the houses to my right. I kept an eye on the door of that house as we slunk past. Unfortunately, I was so focused on that one that I nearly pissed myself in fright when I heard a deep voice muttering just a few yards away, to my left front. I spun my head around just in time to see a figure emerging from another roundhouse. I froze. We were caught out in the middle of the open ground of the village, too far from any shelter to hide. Nor was it dark enough to avoid being seen, thanks to the moonlight. We were both wrapped in our cloaks, so my mail armor and sword were hidden and thankfully I'd left my helmet slung from Carys' saddle. That would have been an almost certain giveaway as to my identity as a Brittonic warrior. Gemma instantly tossed away the javelin she carried.

"Keep walking," Gemma whispered, so quietly I barely heard her. She surprised me by grabbing my arm and draped it around her shoulders just as the man looked up, straight at us, and stopped. He said something to us, speaking in a curious rather than challenging tone.

Beside me, Gemma giggled lightly, and rested her head on my chest as she spoke to the man. Her other arm slid up behind my back and lightly smacked the back of my head, just as she dipped her head to the man. Following her lead, I did the same. While she talked, I studied him. He looked to be in his late thirties, and had a shaggy head of light-colored hair and a large mustache. Around his neck was a braided metal torc and a thick bear hide fastened together with a chain, draped over his broad shoulders, which gave him an even more imposing presence. Beneath the hide, the warrior was shirtless, revealing a hairy, muscular torso. He wore typical, loose-fitting checkered trousers, secured with a leather belt that glittered with decorative metal discs. Clearly this was somebody important.

The man smiled, apparently amused by whatever she told him, then looked at me and said something. This time, the hand she kept at the back of my head squeezed momentarily on the small scarf we soldiers wear around our necks to prevent our armor from chafing. I nearly gagged, and said nothing. Again she spoke to the man, sounding earnest and even a bit sorrowful, and pointed to my neck.

The man nodded, and pointed at the shield slung across her back, and asked her something. My heart skipped a beat, but I focused all of my willpower into being as calm and relaxed as I could, and hoped that Gemma had this under control. She shrugged and looked down, even partially pulling the shield out from behind her back and rattled off something to the big man that evidently satisfied him. She looked back up at him, smiling shyly and put her free hand on my chest, leaning into me as she spoke some more. Under different circumstances, I could have found that experienc very enjoyable.

The warrior nodded at me, said something else to Gemma, then gave us a smile and a wink. He yawned, and to my intense relief, finally shuffled off towards the woods. Gemma held me in place for a moment longer, then spun us around in the opposite direction, and we set off at brisk walk. Without stopping, Gemma scooped the javelin back up off the ground where she'd tossed it and hid it within the folds of her cloak. Neither of us said a word until we were out of the village and were deep into the woods. Even then, we glanced around, listening for the sound of guards who were probably out here, somewhere.

"What was that all about?" I finally whispered. "Who was that man?"

"That was King Drest," Gemma sighed, shakily. I recognized the onset of fatigue that she was beginning to display. I'd felt it myself on enough occasions these past few weeks, so I helped her sit down. Shifting my sword around, I flopped down beside her, feeling a bit weak myself.

"*He* was King Drest?" I echoed in disbelief.

She wiped her forehead and nodded.

"What did you two tell each other? And how do you know that's who he was?"

She cleared her throat, suddenly seeming a bit embarrassed. "I've seen him before," she answered. "As you probably noticed, he's not very forgettable, once you've met him."

I nodded in agreement. Even had I never known the warrior's identity, the large man had a presence about him. He would have been a hard one to forget. Not unlike Arthur, I reflected. "So how did you get us out of that mess? What did you tell him?" I asked.

"I told him we were locals who had been away from the village when the Romans attacked us. I told him that you'd received a neck injury a long time ago and couldn't speak very well."

"Clever girl."

She smiled back thinly, then slowly stood up. "We should get going, yes? We need to either find your horse, or get walking. It would be best to be as far from this village as we can before dawn."

I agreed, and stood up with her. I desperately wanted to look around and try to find Carys, but knew it was too risky. If she had been snatched up by the Picts, she would be one among dozens of horses, and unlike the numerus, the Picts didn't keep their horses all stabled together. So to find Carys would mean wandering through the Pict camp at night, checking over every horse we came to. Their camp was just too large for that, and we'd barely escaped the village once, thanks to Gemma's quick wits. Leaving without her still made me feel absolutely terrible, as though I were abandoning a family member to the Picts. I had to accomplish my mission though, and return to Arthur. So, with a heavy heart, we started off and headed east. For the first mile or so, we focused on being as quiet as we could rather than fast, as we were more worried about the Pictish screen line around the encampment detecting us. We'd been traveling for about fifteen minutes when the sound of brush rustling, and then the soft stamping of hooves reached us.

I stepped in front of Gemma and braced myself, preparing to throw my javelin as the horse came closer. Then a silhouette emerged from the shadows, some fifty feet away. It was coming straight towards us, at a canter. I raised my arm up, javelin held at the ready as the horse came on. It slowed to a trot, rather than sped up, as I would have expected. Still there was no shouting or war cries to be heard. Something felt off. I hesitated, and the horse got to within ten paces of me. Then I saw- there was no rider! An instant later, moonlight illuminated the horse through the trees, and I dropped my arm in relief.

"Carys!" I laughed. I glanced quickly behind me to see Gemma also lowering her own javelin, only marginally slower than I had. Meanwhile, Carys whinnied softly as she approached, ears forward and prancing a little. She walked straight up to me and ducked her head, nudging me. I pressed my forehead to hers, happy as I could be to see that she was alright and had escaped the Picts on her own. I walked around her, making sure that she was unharmed and that all my equipment was still in place. She was fine and my gear was all there. All except my helm, I noticed in dismay. It must have fallen from the saddle where I usually kept it slung from either during or after her escape. I was sorely disappointed in myself for not securing it better, but in the end, I decided losing my helm was a small price to pay for the otherwise good fortune the three of us had been blessed with today. I leapt up onto Carys' back, then held my arm out for Gemma, who took it and climbed up behind me.

"Let's ride for at least half the night and put as much distance between us and the Pict army as we can before we get some rest," I said as we rode. She agreed, and pointed out the heading we needed to take.

"So you told him we were locals," I said, resuming my questioning. "But what did you tell him about us, and my shield, and javelin?"

I felt Gemma shrug. "That was easy. I told him we picked them up from the battlefield, as you needed them for the battles to come."

I noticed that Gemma seemed to be avoiding some of my questions, just as she had earlier, I realized. "What did you tell him about us though?" I pressed. It wasn't all that important, but the more she dodged the question, the more curious I became. And none of her answers thus far properly explained her behavior with me in the course of her conversation with Drest.

"It doesn't matter," she muttered.

Now I was fairly bursting with curiosity. "Oh come on! Tell me. What did you tell King Drest about us?"

"I told him," she sighed, and I realized she was embarrassed. "I told him we were... sweethearts, off to go to the woods to be alone for a bit," she said finally.

I felt a mix of emotions- amused at first, and a little embarrassed, but I also felt oddly pleased that she had concocted that particular story to tell King Drest. I fully appreciated that she'd simply been thinking on her feet and was only trying to enable our escape, but I also realized then that I was beginning to really like this brave, quick-witted Pict girl.

"Stop it," she growled from behind me.

"Stop what?" I asked, confused.

"You're *smiling*."

I turned around to face her, very confused now. "How in the world could you know whether I was smiling or not?"

"I can tell," she said. "Stop it. My story was just that. A story to keep us alive. Don't think it meant anything important."

"Very well," I said and turned back to the trail ahead.

"I mean it," she said.

"Very well," I said again, having no idea what else I could, or should say. A grin nonetheless slowly spread across my face that I couldn't suppress.

We rode on for about three hours in silence, finally reaching a river. I decided to tackle that problem in the morning, and we made camp in a nearby grove of trees for the remainder of the night.

# Chapter Fourteen

I woke gradually, first noticing the sound of birds chirping around me, and the sound of the river, not far away. Carys was nearby, munching on some grass. Then I heard Gemma's steady, slow breathing, and felt a faint puff of warm breath against my face with each exhale. Something about that seemed odd, and made me finally open my eyes. Gemma's face was inches from my own, and she was sound asleep.

I recoiled, startled. We'd gone to sleep in the usual manner, back to back but she had apparently rolled over sometime during the night. I stared at her for a moment, noting a lock of her wavy red hair that lay across her face and was nearly in her mouth. I smiled slightly. Asleep, she didn't seem as tough or intimidating as she did when awake. She even looked cute. Impulsively, I lightly brushed the lock of hair out of her face, then sat up and began preparations for another day's ride. Gemma woke up a few minutes later while I was saddling Carys. She pulled her cloak tightly about her to ward off the morning chill, and strode off into the woodline with a loud yawn, eliciting a yawn from myself in response. I mounted up and waited for her, then helped her up behind me.

"Do you know where we can cross this?" I asked her, gesturing to the river.

"The water should be fordable if we follow it north a ways," she said in a husky voice and yawned again, almost in my ear.

I didn't bother to reply, and simply turned Carys north. The sky was heavy with clouds again today, and this close to the river, fog enveloped us. It wasn't quite as bad as the fog from a few days ago, but I could barely make out the far side of the river at times. Within an hour or two, I found a likely spot. From the wide swath of torn up earth and hoofprints, I suspected this was the same spot where Arthur and the rest of the army must have crossed, no more than a day or so previously. I dismounted and walked to the river's edge, examining the site.

The water was clear enough to see the bottom and didn't appear to be more than two or three feet deep. "We can cross here," I told Gemma. "We're going to get wet though." That water looked really, really cold, I thought. We pulled off our boots, in order to keep them dry during the crossing.

"Ye gods, what is that terrible stench?" She asked, gagging as I removed my socks. "Surely that's not your feet!" she exclaimed.

I sighed. "I've not had a chance to bathe in a few days, and haven't been able to change out my socks in the last two. They can't be that bad, though."

"Trust me, they are!" she affirmed as she began to hike her dress up. Then she stopped and stared at me. "Turn around so I can take my leggings off," she ordered.

I did, and took my own pants off as well. My tunic came down to my knees, and the more of my clothing I could keep dry during our crossing, the better. I'd decided that I should walk alongside Carys to make sure the ground was stable. Even though the water didn't look too deep, I decided to also take off my mail shirt. In the event that things went badly, and I ended up in deep water, I didn't particularly want an extra twenty pounds of armor weighing me down. I removed my cloak, my spatha, and belts, then grimaced as I raised my arms over my head. Gemma grunted and tugged at the short sleeves of my mail and helped me slide out of the shirt. I frowned, noticing a tear in the back from where several links had been broken, thanks to the blow I'd received during my fight. We rolled my things up in my cloak. Now I was wearing just my underwear, my thin linen undershirt, and my thick, woolen, long-sleeved tunic. I gritted my teeth, bracing myself, and took my first step into the river.

I was not prepared. I gasped, and nearly jumped out. It was *so* cold! For her part, nice and dry on Carys' back, Gemma exploded with laughter at my reaction. I strode into the water. My heart raced and my legs felt like they were on fire from the intense cold, but I gritted my teeth and endured it, and slowly led Carys across. At its worst, the water reached almost up to my waist. I wanted to just die when the water came that high, and briefly wondered if my ability to ever have children had just ended. At last, I brought Carys and Gemma safely across the river, and collapsed onto my knees, shivering and with my teeth chattering away furiously.

God bless her, Gemma immediately dropped out of the saddle and wrapped my cloak about me, handed me my trousers, then pulled on her own socks and boots. Only the hem of her dress had gotten wet from the crossing, so she quickly gathered up nearby wood for a fire. I tried to get up and help, but my legs, which had nearly gone numb, now felt like they were on fire all over again as they slowly warmed back up.

"Stay there. I've got this," Gemma said. She quickly dug out my flint and iron striker from the saddlebag, and within a few minutes she had a small fire going. I straddled it, letting the blessed warmth thaw out my legs and groin with a happy sigh. Gemma saw me do this as she gathered larger sticks for the fire, and giggled.

"Don't judge me," I grunted.

"Not judging ... just laughing," she chortled.

Once she was sure the fire was burning steadily, she built a small ring of stones around it, to help shield it from the wind that always seemed to be blowing in this region. We sat by the fire, enjoying its warmth for a time. Carys too, came over, and stood by the fire. I used my cloak and gave her legs a rubdown, making sure they were dry. Finally, my own legs felt recovered enough that I was able to stand up and began pulling out some food from a saddlebag. As I did, I looked around, noting the hills faintly visible above the fog. "Are those the Ochail Hills?" I asked, pointing to the ridgeline northwest of us.

Gemma looked where I was pointing. "Yes," she agreed. "The southern end of them."

"How much further until we get to that village at the Forth? What did you call it, Stirlee or something?" I asked.

"You mean Sruighlea. We're more than halfway there, by my reckoning."

"So another couple of hours of riding to get to the village," I calculated. I pulled out my dagger and cut the last piece of cheese in half and gave her one of the pieces. I also fished out my ration of cracked wheat and my cooking pot. Adding some water and a pinch of salt, I turned the wheat into a steaming porridge.

Gemma found my wooden bowl and spoon, and once the porridge was done, I served her up a small bowl. As soon as the pot was cooled off enough, I ate a bit directly from that, as I only had the one bowl and spoon, then offered the rest to Carys as a treat. She lapped it up with gusto. Afterwards, we cleaned the utensils and put them away. Then Gemma turned to me. "Let's see this terrible injury of yours," she pointed to my shoulder.

"I'm fine," I lied.

Gemma raised an eyebrow. "You cringe and whinge every time you have to move that arm. You're not fine. Let me look."

I dropped my cloak, and peeled out of my long, green tunic with a bit of help from Gemma. We did the same with the thinner, linen tunic I wore under that. I stood, shivering, as close to the fire as I could while Gemma moved around behind me to look at my back.

"Ooh, look at that," Gemma murmured. "That's some nice color." Her fingers ran lightly up and down my shoulder as she examined the injury.

"Nice. Now how bad is it?" I asked, trying not to let my teeth chatter.

Gemma scoffed. "It's very black and blue and a bit swollen, I'd say, but the skin's barely broken." There was a pause, then she added, "I'm actually more concerned about the smell."

"It smells?" I asked, alarmed. I'd heard that serious injuries can emit particular odors.

"Yes, the smell," she said. "Your smell! Have I not mentioned that you stink?"

I rolled my eyes, but didn't bother to reply. "We've been over that," I grunted.

"Anyway, if I had to guess, I'd say you'll be fine in a few days," Gemma assured me, patting me gently on the head and giving me a smile. She made a show of pinching her nose with one hand as she handed me my linen undershirt, holding it out to me between two fingers in disgust.

Dirty or not, I was freezing cold, and quickly grabbed my undershirt from her and threw it on, followed by the thicker, outer tunic. I gritted my teeth with each movement, determined not to show any sign of the pain I felt in front of Gemma. I looked down at my chainmail, in a pile off to the side, and rolled my shoulders, realizing that it felt good to have the weight of the mail off of me. Mail doesn't actually weigh much, especially if one wears a belt to help disperse the weight, but I'd been wearing it for about three days straight now. I hadn't realized just how much it had been weighing on me until the moment Gemma helped me remove it. Now I was loath to put it back on so soon, but it wasn't even noon yet, and I wanted to be back at the fort as soon as possible. So I grabbed my chainmail shirt and slid it on, with a bit of help from Gemma. I strapped the sword belt across my chest, followed by my second belt that went around my waist. I adjusted my dagger and the pouches attached to that belt, then started to reach for my cloak. Gemma had already retrieved it however, and draped it around my shoulders and tied the cords.

"Thank you, my lady," I said without thinking.

Gemma's eyebrows rose, then she smiled, and her eyes twinkled, it seemed to me. "Your welcome, my lord," she said. Then she patted my chest and walked away.

I felt foolish. She was no noblewoman, at least not like the ones in Caer Gurcoc, I considered, but maybe she was among the Picts, I reasoned as I checked over Carys' bridle and saddle. After all, she was a chief's daughter, wasn't she? I mulled that over as I finished checking Carys over, then mounted up. Gemma climbed up behind me and I gave her a moment to grab onto my sword belt, then nudged Carys into a trot.

For this last stretch, we were able to ride along the remains of an old Roman road. The fog thinned out as we put some distance between ourselves and the river. I should have felt safe and secure, this close to civilization, but I had a nagging feeling that something was off. Gemma must have felt it too, for I could feel her swivel around to look behind us from time to time.

"What's wrong?" I asked.

"I'm not sure," she said. "I think maybe we're being followed though. Last night I thought I saw a campfire, off in the distance east of us. I stayed awake for a bit and watched, but I didn't see or hear anything else, and eventually I fell asleep. Then a bit ago I thought I saw what could have been riders, coming down a hill towards us."

"How far away?"

"A couple miles or so."

"Well, we should be safe enough soon. The village is just ahead, and my numerus' fort is only a short way past that."

She agreed, but kept checking behind us anyway. Meanwhile, I was mentally fuming at my own stupidity. We should have taken turns keeping watch. Not just last night, after our narrow escape from the Pict encampment, but the previous night. Owain would surely be very disappointed in my oversight, had he known of it. To my relief, we made it across the River Forth and back to the village Gemma called Sruighlea a couple hours past noon. If any Picts were pursuing us for some reason, it had just become much less likely that they would catch up to us now, I figured.

The gate was open to allow people to come and go at their convenience during the day, so Gemma and I didn't need to waste any time talking to guards.

"We should buy a bit of food for the rest of the day, just in case," I told Gemma as we rode in.

"We're only a few hours away," she said. "Don't we still have some bread?"

"A few biscuits only. This won't take long. And where food is concerned, it's better to have and not need, than to need and not have." Gemma conceded the point, and we rode on, keeping an eye out. I knew this village had an alehouse, at least. Having ridden through the hillfort before, I'd seen the broom hanging up on display above the door of one nondescript building.

As I made my way through the main street, heading towards the alehouse, I scanned the narrow lanes for any sign of food. The air carried the scent of smoke and fish, and soon enough, I spotted a young boy standing by a small cart on the side of the dirt road that led past the buildings.

"Fresh dried fish!" he called out to the few passing townsfolk. A couple dozen flat, salted fish lay neatly piled in straw, their silver skins glinting in the midday sun. I approached him, reaching into my pouch for a bit of hacksilver.

"How much for five fish?"

"What are you paying with? The boy asked, eying me up and down. His gaze lingered on my expensive chainmail shirt and sword. He even stole glances at Gemma and Carys, likely assuming she was my slave or servant. Gemma noticed too and shot me a sideways glance. I grinned.

"I have silver," I said, loosening the pouch at my belt.

The little fishmonger's grin widened. "Five fish for half a scripulum of silver seems fair, sir."

I was about to pay when Gemma's hand shot out and clamped onto my wrist.

"Half a scripulum for just five fish?" she exclaimed. "Not on your mother's life, you cheeky little ferret! You'll give us at least eight of those little fishies for half a scripulum!"

The boy held up his hands, looking between me and Gemma. I could see his confusion over who to appeal to, and it amused me. I had the silver, but Gemma was the one glaring daggers at him.

"These were freshly caught, only this morning," he protested. "Six for half a scripulum is totally fair!"

Gemma released my wrist, only to put her hands on her hips like an angry housewife. "I've bought six for half a scripulum of *iron* before! He's paying with *silver*. You'll give us eight, and you'll be happy for it!"

The young vendor finally sighed. "Fine. Eight for half a scripulum. But you'd best remember me next time you come to market." He wrapped the fish up in some cabbage leaves that he plucked from another basket behind him, and handed me the bundle. I took it from him, and handed it to Gemma to put away in the saddlebag. I opened my small pouch and dropped bits of silver onto the boy's scale until he had his silver.

Having secured a bit of extra food, Gemma and I remounted, and continued our journey south. From the village, it was a relatively short ride to the wall. We were able to take the old Roman road for most of the way. Once we were within a few miles of the wall, I began recalling the area, and was able to guide us the rest of the way. Before long, the fort loomed before us, looking just as I'd remembered it. The area smelled a bit like a latrine pit, and I wrinkled my nose, continuing on toward the gate.

"Phew! Peredur was that you?" Gemma asked.

I laughed. "No, but do you see all those holes in the ground to the left and right of the trail?"

"Yes?"

"These serve two purposes. They'll slow down any enemy that charges the walls, since most of these holes have sharpened sticks implanted in them, but the men also use these holes to uh, relieve themselves. As they become filled up, we kick some dirt over the waste, and dig a new hole. The longer we stay here, the more holes we dig, and the better our defense is."

"Gross," Gemma said.

"Maybe," I shrugged. "But it allows us to accomplish two important tasks efficiently."

By this time, I was within about thirty paces of the gatehouse and waved my hand in greeting and to show that my hand was empty of weapons.

"Who goes there?" a guard challenged us.

"Peredur! I'm a rider of Tribune Arthur's numerus!"

"Arthur?" the guard called down. "He and his men returned yesterday. They rested up, then rode out this morning."

"Where to?" I asked.

"Back to Din Pendyrlaw," the guard answered.

I swore softly to myself. "May I enter? I need to speak to whoever's in charge at the fort now. Urgently."

"Oh? Alright, I suppose so. Uh, one last thing though. Who's that girl with you?"

"A villager," I replied. "She has some information the commander needs to hear. Now, please, let me in?"

"A villager?" Gemma asked, behind me.

"You are," I shrugged. "Pict village, Briton village. Either way, you're from a village."

Gemma scoffed.

The gate swung open, and a guard on the ground waved me through. As I entered, I asked, "Where can I find the commander, and who is he?"

"That would be Lord Guinnion, soldier," the guard replied. "He'll be in the great hall, straight on through." I thanked him, and trotted Carys up to the large great hall. Looking around, I saw that many of the levies idling about had fresh injuries, sustained from the fight at the lake, no doubt. Some, I noticed, were filling wagons with equipment, weapons and armor. They were clearly preparing to leave the fort. I felt a twinge of unease at the sight. Gemma and I rode directly to the great hall, dismounted, tethered Carys, and we walked inside. I felt even more worried at having to report to Lord Guinnion. While I'd personally had no dealings with the man, I knew his reputation well enough, and mentally braced myself.

As we approached the entrance to the great hall, I noticed Gemma look at the carved phalluses on the door, and gave me a curious look.

"Don't ask," I snickered, and we kept walking. The great hall was so similar to the one at Caer Lleon, it was easy to determine where Lord Guinnion would likely be. Most of the roof of the great hall in this fort had collapsed years ago, and even some of the walls were torn down or toppled over. That made it even easier to guess which chamber he was likely in. I guided Gemma through the halls, and into the largest chamber of the great hall, overlooking a courtyard. I heard talking inside the chamber, and knocked hard on the door. The voices stopped, and a man barely older than me opened the door. He was well dressed, and looked down at me with a bored expression.

"Can I help you, lad?" He asked.

I introduced myself, and told him I needed to speak with Lord Guinnion. As I spoke, I glanced past the servant. There was a cluster of men in fine clothing sitting around a makeshift table. I saw a man I recognized from several days ago when I'd been on gate guard. The servant looked ready to deny me entry, so I quickly scooted past him. He tried to react by shooting an arm out to block my way, but I was already past him. Gemma ducked under his arm and also slipped past. He spun around, indignant, and made to protest. I didn't give him a chance though.

"Lord Guinnion, I must speak with you," I said, firmly but respectfully.

The middle-aged man turned to look at me, cocking an eyebrow at me.

"Do I know you, young man?"

"No, my lord. My name is Peredur, and I'm one of the Dux Bellorum's men," I said, using Arthur's most prestigious title. "I need to speak with you. Urgently." It had the desired effect.

Lord Guinnion sighed, and waved me forward. He glanced at Gemma curiously, but said nothing.

"Well let's hear it," he said. "I'm a busy man."

"My lord, you need to prepare your men for battle, not for leaving the fort. Within days, there could be thousands of Picts marching south against the Gododdin," I said, getting straight to the point.

Lord Guinnion scowled at me. "Thousands of ... ? Young man, maybe you're somehow not aware, but your own commander already dealt with the Picti

214

threat. There were scarcely thousands, by the way," he said, sounding just a bit patronizing. "Arthur reported somewhere between twelve to fifteen hundred. And they've all been killed, or scattered to the winds. I have a few mounted patrols out, just to make sure there's no stragglers out to make trouble for us, but I'm in a meeting right now, discussing plans to return home in the next day or so, before our food stores run out. Now that's a real problem."

I shook my head. "That wasn't the full army. That wasn't even half of the army the Picts are sending."

"And how do you know this? You've seen this army?" Lord Guinnion asked.

"I've seen a portion of it," I said, then gestured to Gemma. "I became separated from my turma the day before the battle and was lost in the woods for a short time. Gemma here found me. She's from a village in the area and has been hearing for some time that the Picts have been planning an invasion of Gododdin under the leadership of King Drest. I actually encountered him as we made our escape the other night."

Guinnion nodded silently. "Drest, I know of him. Charismatic fellow, by all accounts. And you met him, you say? Seems unlikely, to be sure."

My jaw clenched, hearing this man question my word, but he continued, either not noticing or not caring about my reaction.

"Drest has had his hands full with the Gaels in Dal Riata. I find it highly improbable that in the midst of that conflict on his western border, he'd be able to muster an army as large as you're claiming in order to strike us here in the south. And," Guinnion held up a finger to stop me when I opened my mouth to protest, "You yourself are relying, it sounds like, mostly on the word of this Pict girl."

I winced, and seeing it, Guinnion smirked. "Oh yes, she's obviously a Pict. You see young man, you're not half as clever as you may think you are. For that matter, I also find it interesting that on the eve of battle, you just happened to become lost from your turma, and missed the fight. You seem a bit young to be a soldier, anyway."

"I'm sixteen, and I hope you're not implying that I deliberately avoided the battle," I said slowly. My jaw clenched and my hands subconsciously balled into fists. I glanced around at the other lords gathered around Guinnion. Many of them were also looking skeptically at me. "I may be young, but I was trained to ride and fight by my father, Lord Pelinor. And I am *no* coward." I was seething over the very implication that Guinnion had made against me.

Lord Guinnion shrugged. "It matters little to me whether you are or aren't. Have you personally seen this vast army of King Drest's?"

"As I said, I saw a portion of it," I replied. "And I met King Drest."

"When? Where?" he asked.

"Once I met up with Gemma here, she guided me through the woods and over to Loch Liobhann. We were looking over the battlefield when we saw a horde of Picts approaching from the north. We were nearly surrounded by their advancing scouts, deployed in a screen to shield the rest of their column. Gemma and I hid and watched as they approached, and as we escaped that night, we ran into King Drest.

"Ah? So was it an army that you saw, or simply the families of the fallen, coming to the battlefield specifically to retrieve their kin?" Guinnion asked. "Barbarians they may be, but even the Picts hate leaving their dead lying about for the crows to feast upon."

I glanced over at Gemma, but her face was an impassive mask, and she stood straight and proudly before these men. I have to admit I was a bit impressed with her right then.

"Will you at least send scouts to the lake to confirm my report?" I asked with growing frustration.

Guinnion exchanged a glance with the other lords at the table, then back to me.

"Peredur," he sighed. "The loch is a two day ride from here. I am not sending riders that far north. I have no doubt you saw a lot of Picts returning to the battlefield, but we do have spies here and there throughout the Highlands.

We've heard nothing about troops moving south; not in the numbers that you're talking about."

"Did your spies tell you about the Caledonii and Maeatae warbands encamped at Loch Liobhann?" Gemma startled everyone by asking.

Eyes rolled. "Girl," Guinnion explained slowly, with a patronizing smile, "Spies aren't able to see everything, everywhere, and report everything instantly. Communication does take time."

Gemma's eyes narrowed slightly. "I don't know why your spies have failed you, but they have," she said emphatically. "King Drest made peace with the Scoti at Dal Riata several seasons ago. The tribes have been preparing for this invasion ever since. Stocking up extra food, making weapons. Training."

"This is nonsense," one of the men next to Guinnion said, brushing his hand in the air dismissively towards us. "Send these children away already," he said. "Every day that we're out here in this ruin is costing us enormous amounts of food for the troops and their mounts, not to mention the pack animals. It will be planting season soon, and most of those men need to be ready to get back to work in their fields. We have neither the time, nor the resources to waste, keeping them here. There was indeed a small Picti army. It's been crushed. We're done here."

I looked around the room with a sinking feeling in my stomach as I saw heads nodding in agreement.

"If that's your decision, then I'm wasting my time here," I said, struggling to maintain my composure. It was no use. These men were fools who wouldn't listen to me or Gemma. She was dismissed out of hand for being a barbarian and a girl. As for me, I was young as well, and even my status and lineage had barely earned more than a pretense of respect from these men. I gritted my teeth and left the room, with Gemma hot on my heels. Behind me, the servant closed the door to the chamber, muffling the sounds of the men inside chuckling.

"What do we do now?" she asked, a minute later, almost jogging to keep up with me.

"We ride like the wind, and I'll report to Tribune Arthur," I said. "He'll listen to me, at least."

"And if he doesn't?" Gemma asked.

"He will," I said, firmly. "Arthur is one of the wisest men in Britain. Everyone says so. I don't know for sure what he'll do with the information we have, but at least he'll listen. And he'll believe us!"

Before we left, I found a building, probably an old barracks, that was being used as a stable. I looked around, and saw no guard. I did however, see saddles and other equipment, stacked up neatly at one end. I quickly picked a mare that looked to be in good shape, saddled her up, and gestured Gemma over.

"Here, take this mare," I told her. "We'll travel faster if we each have a horse. You know how to ride?"

"Not well, but I'll manage. Is this allowed?" she asked as she allowed me to help her jump onto the horse and into the saddle.

I shrugged. "There's a saying among soldiers. Better to ask forgiveness than permission. Anyway, I'll figure out a way to return the horse later!" She smiled at me, and I hopped up on Carys' back. Together we trotted off toward the south gate.

The guards didn't particularly care who left the fort, and it was clear from a glance that neither of us belonged to Lord Guinnion's peasant army. I was too well armored, and Gemma was a girl. So they opened the south gate as soon as I approached and told them I needed to rejoin Arthur. Moments later we set off at a canter. They had a lead on us by several hours, but with the wagons I assumed they were traveling with, I was hopeful that we could catch them by nightfall.

# Chapter Fifteen

---

We rode at a canter for a couple miles, then slowed down to a trot for about four. I hoped, by alternating in this way, that we would catch up to Arthur and the Red Dragons. Despite her hesitation, Gemma proved to either be a fast learner, or was in fact already an adequate rider, as she kept pace with me with little difficulty as far as I could tell. We rode the old Roman road that ran parallel to a river north of us for a time. Fortunately, at a point where the river swung around south, there was a stone bridge that allowed us to cross, also made by the Romans, if I was any judge. There were cracks appearing here and there, and vegetation was cropping up in those, but the bridge was at least serviceable. About three hours into our journey, Gemma pointed behind us.

"I see riders," she said.

I glanced over my shoulder, and thought I could make out distant shapes moving, following the same Roman road that we were on.

My first thought was that maybe someone at the fort had taken exception to my borrowing the horse Gemma now rode, but then I remembered the distant fire Gemma had seen the other night, and the riders we'd probably seen on the way to the hillfort.

"If not Guinnion's people, that only leaves Picts," I muttered. "Or perhaps just bandits, but why in the world would Picts bother to follow us all the way south, even risking discovery by Guinnion's forces, or some other random patrol? Surely I'm not that important."

I recalled the young, well armed Pict I'd wounded, the day Gilbert and I had attempted to report our turma's location to Arthur. Was it possible that he'd been a noble- someone important enough that his friends or vassals under his command had decided or been ordered to avenge him? Possible, but it seemed unlikely. Then I considered my riding companion. She'd come to me out of nowhere, ready to throw her lot in with me while knowing absolutely nothing about me, or what might become of her as a result. She had also shown conflicted feelings towards her own people throughout my travels with her.

The woods around us were thicker to our south, so I signaled to Gemma, and we left the road and hid, watching for the riders. This gave our horses a chance to rest and eat.

"I think those are Picts coming up the road," I said, staring at her. "I also think they're following you. Not me. Not us. You." Her face became impassive, as someone does when they are deliberately trying not to reveal their emotions.

The riders disappeared into some low ground, and I immediately told her to mount up. I considered my options as we hid, as deep in as we could be while still able to see the road. I'd taken a gamble that our tracks wouldn't be too obvious in the area where we left the road, which was fortunately quite rocky. The snow we'd had a few days ago was mostly gone now, so it wasn't hard to avoid those remaining patches. I also tried to avoid areas of bare, soft dirt. Hopefully, the people following us weren't expert trackers. If they were, I probably wasn't going to throw them off our trail. I just needed to buy time, even a few hours. The Red Dragons surely couldn't be too far ahead of me and the hillfort of Din Eidyn wasn't too far away. If we were lucky, Arthur would choose to rest there for the night. If he did, I had a good chance of catching up with him there.

I started developing a course of action, in case the horsemen found our trail. There were likely too many to fight, so that was our last resort. I still had my four javelins, and my sling. I had my shield slung over my back, now that Gemma had her own horse to ride, so I also had the three throwing darts attached to the shield. Perhaps foolishly, I hadn't stocked up on javelins or replaced my lost spear while I was at the fort. Nor had I thought to secure any weapons for her. I'd been focused on catching up with Arthur as quickly as possible, and so hadn't thought about rearming. I regretted that oversight now, and wished I'd at least gotten her a shield and spear. Then again ... I glanced her way, thinking again about what I knew about her.

"Alright, Gemma,"I said. "I need to know. Are these men after you?"

Gemma hesitated and fidgeted with the hem of her cloak, then said, "Probably."

"Why?" I demanded.

She hesitated, clearly reluctant. She pursed her lips, clearly working something out in her mind.

"Let me put it this way," I said, growing frustrated. "If all they want is you, one of my options, at least, is to hand you over to them. Can you give me a reason not to?"

"You're alive because I helped you," she protested. "And I have information you need Arthur to have."

"And now I might be killed because you're withholding information," I countered.

She let go of her cloak and sighed. "I've already told you that I'm a runaway slave. When Arthur attacked that village the warband was encamped at, it caused a commotion. I used the opportunity to escape. That night, I found you, thanks to your fire. That's all true."

I considered her story for a moment, then shook my head. "What else is there to your story?" I asked. "Slaves are valuable, but I can't believe your village would have mustered a dozen armed, *mounted* men, just to bring you back."

Horses weren't something most Picts owned, just like with us Britons. That had been another fact that was bothering me about our pursuers. They were really making some effort to track us down, and they had the resources to make a proper go of it. Come to think of it, while she was clearly no expert on horseback, she had at least some familiarity with them. All of these facts just weren't adding up with the story she was giving me.

Gemma flashed a look of guilt this time. "They might, if I burned down half the village as a distraction."

I recalled the column of smoke I'd seen that morning after becoming lost in the woods. "You burned down half the village?" I echoed, shocked.

"I wasn't trying to!" she exclaimed, quickly. "Most of the men were gone that morning. The villagers were out and about tending to the animals with the rest of the slaves. So I grabbed a burning stick from a cooking fire and tossed it up on the roof of my master's house when nobody was looking. It caught fire, but ... then the flames spread and a couple other houses' roofs also caught fire."

I envisioned a cluster of the large wattle and daub roundhouses with their straw roofs and could easily see how the fire must have spread. "Did it kill anybody?" I asked.

"I don't know," Gemma admitted, casting her eyes down. She wrapped her arms around her chest. "I don't believe so. As soon as my master's home began to blaze, I took off. I was nearly a mile down the trail when I happened to look back from a hilltop and saw that two other houses were also burning. I felt bad. I wasn't terribly mistreated most of the time, and I'd not intended to burn down any of the homes, really. I just needed enough of a fire to provide me with a distraction."

I puffed, feeling a bit skeptical. "You didn't want to burn any houses down? Gemma. What exactly did you think would happen by tossing a burning stick on top of a straw roof?"

"It had been raining and snowing the last couple days," she protested. Truthfully, I wasn't even sure the roof would catch fire at all! Let alone go up in flames so quickly!"

I snorted. "Well you truly guessed wrong there."

Gemma looked at me almost fearfully. "You won't turn me over to the riders, will you? I promise, you'll never regret helping me."

I sighed, looked into her pleading eyes, and made a quick decision. "Are you any good with a sling?" I asked her.

She gave me a confused look for a moment, then nodded. I handed her the pouch at my belt that held my sling and a dozen smooth stones. "Here," I said. "If whoever's back there leaves the road and comes for us here, we'll have to assume they're hostile. Nail one of them with the sling as soon as they come into range. Try to target someone important-looking."

Gemma smiled in relief as she took the sling.

Several minutes after we peeled off the road and into the woods, the horsemen finally came into view. We watched them approach from behind some heavy brush.

My heart beat faster in anticipation of the oncoming threat. The riders were too far away to clearly identify, but I could see light reflecting off their weapons and armor to know that at the very least, this was a group of soldiers. They didn't turn off the road, and continued eastward.

"We lost them," Gemma breathed a sigh of relief.

"But now the group is between us and Arthur," I pointed out. "At least they aren't likely looking for us behind them. All the same, we'll avoid the road now, and stick to the edge of the woods for as much of the journey as possible."

*****

We traveled on, riding cautiously along the woodline wherever possible to make us harder to spot. Once, we passed a small village consisting of no more than a few simple roundhouses, and a corral for their sheep and goats. We received a couple of curious glances, then they ignored us as we rode past.

Unfortunately, we didn't cover nearly as much ground now, having left the road. We also had to cross yet another river, scarcely twenty minutes later. We had to follow along the river for over a mile before we found a bridge to cross. It was a simple, crude bridge made of logs, and Gemma and I had to dismount and carefully cross one at a time, but it was sufficient for our needs. As with most of the area I'd seen in this region, the forest was more patchy rather than all-encompassing. The shadows were growing longer, and after crossing, we stopped to give our horses a short rest, and to eat the fish I'd purchased at Sruighlea. We'd scarcely finished eating when we saw the riders approaching again, from the east. They were spread out over a wide area, and clearly on the hunt. At their present speed, they'd reach us within a few minutes.

"Time to go," I said. We got up, and after we saddled up, I brought my shield around, letting it hang against my left side, ready for use. I had a feeling I was going to need it soon. On an impulse, I also plucked out the three plumbatae from their sheaths and handed them to Gemma. They likely wouldn't do *me* any good, after all.

"If you can, use the sling first, should things get hairy," I told her. "If you don't get a chance to stop riding, and they get close to you, use the throwing darts. Are you any good at throwing rocks?"

Gemma nodded.

"Good. Well, these darts aren't much different. You can grab them by the feathered end or by their tips, or even along the shaft and throw them like a small javelin. If your aim is true, chances are the dart will hit its target, tip first. So if you have to use them, focus on your target's chest and aim for that."

Gemma took the darts and thrust them into her belt.

"If we get separated, or anything happens to me, ride east as fast as you can. Find Arthur. Tell him ..." I nearly said "tell him how I fell," but stopped myself. Christian or Pagan, we soldiers have a strong superstition about saying such things aloud. Just like when Aylmer claimed how easy our reconnaissance mission was had annoyed the rest of the turma, I was reluctant to speak of my own death- even as I accepted the very real possibility of it. To give voice to the thought was to make it more likely to happen. Instead, I shrugged and finished my thought another way. "Tell Arthur how you helped me, and warn him about King Drest, if I am unable to."

Gemma nodded, looking deeply into my eyes. She seemed to understand what I wasn't saying. "What's the plan?" she asked.

"The River Forth is north of us. If we swing around that way the riders could trap us. So we'll angle around to the right. We have all the room we need to maneuver around them to the south."

We set off, riding at a canter in open ground, and slowing down to a trot when we had the cover of woods. I understood that the human eye is attracted to movement, as with predatory animals, and if I thought the riders already had a good idea where we were I'd have had us go slower over the open ground, rather than faster. Instead, I was counting on them not knowing for sure where we were, and that their attention would be focused on the road and the immediate area before them, rather than on their flanks. I was fairly certain that they would find our path eventually, though. I hoped that by the time they did, we would have already swung around them, and have a clear path to Din Eidyn. Whether Arthur was there or not, there would be a small garrison there, and that garrison could be our salvation against the warband hunting us.

We caught glimpses of them as we rode up and down the rolling hills and through the patches of trees, doing our best to keep out of their line of sight. We used the low-lying ground between hills to mask our movement where possible. This trick wouldn't conceal us for very long, but my hope was that it would prevent them from riding at us too quickly, for fear that we might change directions and evade them again.

Over the next hour, the plan seemed to be working. They kept to the course we'd originally seen them on, heading due west, while we angled south for a mile or so, then headed back east, towards Din Eidyn. It would be dark within another hour, and I'd begun to hope that we would still make it to the hillfort that night when four riders appeared from behind a hill, only a few hundred paces ahead of us. Gemma and I reigned in our horses, and I scanned around. As I'd feared, another four riders were coming towards us from the right, about the same distance away as the group to our front. At least three more riders were closing in from behind us, though they were still nearly a mile back. They were surrounding us.

My mind worked furiously, but I only saw one solution. "Run for it!" I yelled to Gemma and turned Carys south, leaning forward in the saddle and nudging her flanks with my spurs. Carys bolted into a gallop. The warriors ahead reacted instantly, urging their own horses forward to intercept me. The riders to my left did the same. Gemma raced along behind me, but her lack of horsemanship was becoming painfully obvious. Her eyes were wide and her mouth was stretched into a fearful grimace as she swayed around in the saddle, struggling to maintain a proper form. I assessed her core problem in a glance- she lacked the grip strength in her legs to maintain her balance at the gallop. Outrunning the party wouldn't be an option then.

I looked over at her and gestured to the southeast. "Keep going!" I shouted at her.

"What will you do?" she asked, looking even more frightened.

I grinned at her, in an attempt to calm her down and at least make her think I had things under control. "Something reckless," I yelled over the thundering hooves of our mounts. "Don't worry, I've done this before."

Having said that, I angled Carys towards the closest riders, now only two hundred paces away and coming on fast. They were definitely Picts. If their small, rectangular shields and long, wild hair hadn't given them away, the blue paint on their faces would have. Besides their shields, all four of them were armed with spears. As usual with them, none wore armor, and only one of them had a helmet. My left hand gripped the handle of my shield, my right pulled out a javelin from the case behind my leg. With a rough cry, I hurled the javelin at the centermost rider. He jerked his shield up, and the javelin sunk into it instead of its wielder. The Pict was forced to discard his shield at least, though. There was no more time for javelins so the instant I'd thrown the one, I reached down and drew my spatha from its scabbard. I charged the Pict furthest to their right, holding my sword just above my head. The barbarian angled his spear at me and thrust as I came on. In a tight, circular move, I parried the spear thrust and brought my blade under and inside his guard, slicing deep into his side as I rode past.

The man cried out and dropped his spear, clutching at his wound. The other three spun their horses around and came at me, thrusting with their spears. One hit my shield. Then one of the Picts screamed in pain, arched his back, and dropped his spear. He slowly slumped over and fell to the ground, crying with pain all the while. A throwing dart protruded from his back.

There was a pause as we all turned to look at him, startled. A dozen paces behind him, Gemma was beginning to ride away. At least one of the two remaining Picts looked like he wanted to chase her, so I kicked my heels into Carys' flank and charged into him.

The three of us were a flurry as we exchanged blows. I frantically blocked and chopped at their spears with my shield and sword, while Carys snapped and bit at both Picts and their horses. After one such attack drew blood, a warrior to my left cursed, and having lost his spear, raised his axe with the clear intent of striking at Carys.

"No you bloody don't!" I snarled as I brought my shield up, blocked his attack, and thrust at the man over my shield with my spatha. The long blade took him at the base of his throat, and he collapsed from his horse, choking and clutching at his throat. Two were down, while the first man I'd wounded was off to one side, still clutching at his side. but now the four that had been closing in on the left came thundering up. I swore and disengaged from the remaining Pict I'd initially charged, spurring Carys into a gallop away from the Picts. I looked around frantically as I rode, searching for Gemma. Then I saw her. She was a couple hundred paces ahead of me, riding east at a canter. And she had another of my throwing darts in her hand, ready to use. I smiled grimly.

*Good girl,* I thought. She looked back, and I waved her onward. "Go!" I shouted. She turned back and nodded, and dug her heels into her mount's flanks and took off at a gallop again.

Then I heard a horse's hooves pounding behind me, and instinctively I ducked forward. A spear skittered off my back as a Pict came up beside me on my left, attempting to skewer me! I reigned in hard and Carys reared up as I swept my shield up. The shield smashed into the surprised barbarian's face, and he tumbled from his mount. Carys lunged forward and we took off again. A javelin flew past in front of me, from my right. I spun to look, and saw a Pict with wild red hair riding in my blind spot behind me. It was the man who'd lost his shield to my javelin at the onset of the fight. Again, I reigned in and leaned to the right. Carys followed my lead and an instant later she slammed into the Pict's mount as we galloped along side by side and our legs bumped against each other's. I couldn't use my long blade with the Pict as close as he was, so as he made a grab for my right arm, I brought it up and smashed him above the eye with the rounded ivory pommel of my spatha. This was the Pict who wore a helmet, so my blow wasn't as severe as it might have been, but the impact still rocked him back and I swerved Carys away. As we parted, I slashed at the Pict, cutting him deeply in his unprotected abdomen. He slumped forward with a gasp, his horse slowed to a stop, and I spurred Carys onward, desperate to keep the warband from surrounding me. I looked back. There were at least seven or eight riders behind me, so close I could see the furious snarls on their painted blue faces.

The sun had nearly set now, and in the distance I could see a cluster of torches that surely must be Din Eidyn. I was so close! I caught up to Gemma, who'd dropped out of the gallop and back to her slower, but more comfortable speed.

"Ride!" I yelled as I caught up to her. I pointed at the lights with my bloody sword. "Get to those lights!"

"I can't!" Gemma yelled back, wiping tears from her eyes.

"You must!" I retorted. The Picts will be on us soon. Carys is almost spent. So unless you favor your chances in melee with them," I pointed back at the riders, "Get going!"

"I don't want to just leave you alone!" Gemma cried.

"I can't fight them and protect you!" I snapped. "Now get going, you damned girl!"

I saw the terror on her face fade. She glared at me, then flinched as a javelin sailed between us, landing in the dirt a few paces ahead of us. She gave me a last look, full of emotions I had neither the time nor the inclination to decipher at the present, and she urged her horse back into a gallop.

I spurred Carys into doing the same, but she was becoming exhausted, and though she sped up a little out of sheer determination, it was still barely faster than a canter. I could hear her snorting and panting for breath as she ran. I snarled, and tugged on the reins, angling her back toward the Picts, just in time. The one that had thrown his javelin at Gemma and I was upon me in an instant. He had an axe, and chopped it down at me as he barreled past me. I dodged, and the axe only clipped my right side. My movement, and particularly my armor, saved me from the worst of the blow. Nevertheless the axeblade tore into the mail, and bit into my side, just below my ribcage. I hissed in pain, and swung my sword at his back as he rode by, but the blow had no power behind it, nor even much skill in that moment, and the blade did nothing more than tear his cloak.

I glanced past him, and was relieved to see that although several men were still in pursuit, their mounts too, were tiring. I spun Carys back around to receive the Pict's next charge, and tugged on the reins. Carys reared up, her hooves flailing. She clipped the warrior's mount as it came on, and caused the beast to shy away. I urged Carys forward and she shouldered hard into the Pict's horse. Both horse and rider staggered. The man's right side was to me, as he'd been intending to strike again with that short axe of his. That left him fully exposed to the long blade of my spatha, and I thrust at him, stabbing him through the ribs. The rest of the Picts were some distance away as their inferior mounts struggled to keep pace with my valiant Carys, who outclassed them in every way. I glanced behind me, to the east, and saw to my satisfaction that Gemma was barely more than a distant speck now. Even if I died here, I'd bought her enough of a lead that she should easily make it to Din Eidyn ahead of these Picts. I wasn't ready to die just yet though, so rather than remain where I was and allow them to pile on me, I turned east myself, and nudged Carys into a canter.

Twenty minutes or so later the distant lights grew more distinct, and eventually I thought I could even make out the faint outline of the hillfort itself in the moonlight. Gemma was nowhere in sight. With any luck, she'd made it to the fort. I still rode with my sword in my hand, though my arm was pressed against my side in response to the throbbing pain there. I began to think that I would be able to maintain my lead, and could almost taste the mead I was so ready for. Or mulled wine. Yes. I thought, licking my lips. That's what I would have.

I became complacent, in those last few miles, and it nearly cost me my life. I'd kept my sword in hand, and head on a swivel, but my mind was drifting. I could blame the loss of blood for this carelessness, or the lack of visibility of the night, the proximity to Din Eidyn, or even simply my youth and inexperience. It doesn't matter now. In any case, I rode around a particular grove of trees and Carys stopped dead in her tracks. Somehow, the Picts had gotten around me without me noticing, and now seven men, spaced out in a loose crescent-shaped line of battle, stood arrayed not fifty paces before me. Their spear tips shimmered in the moonlight as they trotted toward me. Their mounts snorted and blew heavily from the effort it had clearly taken them to get around me. Three of them wore helmets and chainmail shirts, I noticed.

I sighed. This was finally it, I figured. I'd survived the patrol that attacked Gilbert and I, days earlier. I'd survived the chase that had lasted off and on all this afternoon and evening. I saw no way out, this time. I glanced back toward the lights of Din Eidyn for what I figured would be the final time, puzzled that they seemed to be bobbing up and down a bit. No matter. I was surprised to realize that it was Gemma's face that kept flashing before me as I gripped my sword in anticipation of the fight and its inevitable outcome.

I was determined to die with honor at least, and so I brought my sword up.

*"Last Hope!* I screamed the Red Dragons' battle cry at the top of my lungs and kicked Carys into a gallop.

I thought I heard "Last Hope!" echo faintly in the distance. Then the fastest of the Picts greeted my charge. He stabbed at me with his spear. I blocked it with my shield, but the force of it sent me toppling backwards from Carys' back! I hit the ground hard, and my sword and shield went flying. I rolled away immediately, and a thrown spear buried itself into the ground where I had just been. Beside me, Carys was a flurry of hooves flying in every direction, neighing loudly all the while and causing the Picts' horses to shy away.

I scrambled to my feet and grabbed the spear the Pict had tried to skewer me with. An armored warrior slashed at me with a sword but I dodged out of the way and stabbed at him with the spear, knocking him off his mount. I spun around, preparing for another attack, but I was too slow. Another Pict bashed me in the head with his shield as he rode past from behind me. I went down again, seeing bursts of light. I shook my head, fighting through the throbbing pain and jumped up a moment later, pulling my dagger out as I did so. One of the armored Picts charged, hacking at me with a sword. I weaved to one side, but the sword still glanced off my chest, spinning me around from the momentum. Another barbarian cocked his arm back, making to throw his spear at me. I braced myself, ready to spring to one side, when the tip of a javelin burst out of his chest from behind! The barbarian gasped in shock, looked down as the spear he'd been about to throw tumbled out of his hand, and he fell to the ground.

Then, I heard a horn blast. The Picts heard it too, and we all realized that it was no Picti horn. I knew the sound, and began to laugh in malicious glee!

"Last Hope! I screamed again.

The sound of dozens of men streaming towards us bellowed in response. "Last Hope!" they roared, and again, I heard the distinctive blast of our lituus. The Picts and I turned to look eastward and saw a rank of horsemen, many carrying torches, galloping towards us. Metal gleamed from polished helms and the tips of javelins as they came on. At their head flew the brass-headed dragon standard. It's long red tail fluttered behind it.

I snatched Carys' reins and sprinted away from the Picts, anticipating the coming storm, and the Red Dragons did not disappoint. A hail of javelins rained down on them and in an instant, nearly every one of the group that had dogged me for the past several hours were cut down like wheat before a scythe. The few remaining Picts attempted to flee, but the Red Dragons cut them down as they swept past.

I whooped and laughed in relief as the horsemen, at least two turmae by my estimate, slowed to a halt and circled around toward me. The first face I recognized in the torchlight was my own decurion, Owain. Beside him was Arthur himself. Further back, Gilbert grinned and waved. They looked down at me, smiling. I brought my right hand up in salute.

Arthur nodded down at me.

"Out for an evening ride, Peredur?" Owain asked.

"Weren't you ordered to report to me about ... five days ago?" Arthur asked.

My own grin slipped, but I looked into their faces and saw the genuine humor in their eyes. "I was delayed a bit," I replied. "But Tribune," I said, suddenly earnest. "I do have information you need to hear!"

Arthur nodded. "Tell me all about it on the way back. Was this all of them? The girl who came riding up to the gate, screaming my name like a banshee a short while ago, seemed to suggest that there was an entire host of barbarians heading this way."

"There are!" I agreed, then seeing the smiles leave their faces I clarified, "But not here. Not yet. I believe these are the last of the Picts who were chasing us for the past few days."

"Well then," Owain said. "Why don't you hop on this horse we brought for you and let's head back to the fort. That little scratch," he gestured to my side, which was stained with blood, "won't be a problem, will it?"

"I can ride," I said. "Preferably on noble Carys though." I scratched Carys' neck affectionately, who turned and nickered.

"Noble Carys has just ridden herself half to death, keeping you alive," Owain remarked. "Ride this spare we brought back to the fort and let her have a much deserved rest."

"Yes, Decurion," I said and did as I was bade.

I smiled as the troops formed back up. I searched around the field for a moment to retrieve my spatha, then mounted the horse offered to me and took my place beside Arthur and Owain at the head of the column. Gemma was safe, I was going to have that wine, or at least some mead, after all!

# Chapter Sixteen

W e rode back in relative silence. Owain pointed out that discussing matters as serious as what I'd implied deserved a better setting than trying to converse while riding in the cold, at night. After all, Din Eidyn was only a few miles away. I didn't protest. My side was throbbing, and now my back ached from when I'd been knocked off my horse.

Din Eiydn was an impressively large hillfort, from what I could see as we approached. It seemed even bigger than Din Pendyrlaw. Granted, it was night time, so I could only go off what I could see in the moonlight. The great hall, a large, unadorned stone structure sat upon the hill's summit, dominating the landscape. Below it were two wooden palisades, built atop berms that encircled the hill, providing a strong defense. Steep trenches protected the palisades against would-be attackers. I saw the roofs of a dozen structures built up inside the ground level of the hillfort. The Red Dragons were currently encamped around the outermost palisade.

We dismounted some two hundred paces before reaching the camp, to give our horses a chance to fully cool down from the hard ride they'd made, however short it had been. As we walked through the camp, and the men who'd come to my rescue began to disperse, I felt a bit embarrassed to see that many of the men were awake and cheered our arrival. Calls of "Welcome back, Peredur!" and teasing comments like "Well, look who finally showed back up!" assailed me. I nodded to faces I recognized.

Beside me, Owain grinned. "That Pict girl came galloping right up to our tents, screaming that she needed to speak to Arthur, and that his man, Peredur, was a few miles away, about to be killed by an army of Picts. Well, Arthur immediately called for anyone who could be ready to ride in a few minutes to form up. The camp looked like a beehive while the lads ran about, throwing on armor and saddling up. Arthur only waited until we had at least a turma's worth, then we rode off. Several more caught up with us as we rode after you."

I looked around, and noticed that indeed, most of the men who'd come to my rescue were underdressed, and looked more like the very barbarians we'd fought, rather than the proud heavy cavalry we actually were. Only a few wore any armor, aside from helmets, which could have been scooped up and donned as they rode. Several didn't even have shirts on, and hurried over to their tents to throw on cloaks before they tended to their horses.

Even Arthur himself hadn't taken the time to don his distinctive squamata, or scale armor. Instead, he only wore his cream-colored quilted subarmalis—a padded tunic commonly worn beneath heavier armor. Designed in the Roman style, Arthur's subarmalis featured decorative strips of cloth that draped over his upper arms and two overlapping rows that covered his thighs. Each strip was further embellished with a brass disc for added decoration.

Pulling off his helmet, Owain addressed me. "Peredur, servants are expecting you at the great hall." He gave my side a pointed look. "Do we need to send you to Tewdrig now?"

I shook my head. "I'll be fine, Decurion. If it's all the same to you, I'd rather get dirty, bloody clothing off me first. Maybe the medicus could meet me here in the fort?"

Owain nodded. "I'll send someone to see if he's busy. Go ahead and wash up. If Tewdrig isn't inclined to come to you, go see him after you've cleaned up. Then you can eat and get some rest. Your contubernium is seeing to your horse and bringing your belongings to your tent. We'll talk first thing in the morning."

"Yes, Decurion," I said with a nod. Glancing from Arthur to Owain, I quickly asked, "Is Gemma, the girl who told you I was in trouble, has she- "

Arthur cut me off. "She's fine. Before we left, I made the same arrangement for her that I've made for you. She's staying in the servants' quarters, beside the great hall. She'll be at the briefing in the morning, as well. We had one of the lads keeping an eye on her to make sure she wasn't up to anything- she's a Pict after all."

I shook my head. "Watch her if you must, but I'm fairly confident that she'll cause no mischief. I believe she's trustworthy."

Arthur shrugged. "Good to hear. And she did play a large part in us getting to you. We'll decide for ourselves what to do with her though, in the morning."

I bade the two good night, and did as instructed. I trudged through the main gate, passing the dozens of houses, shops, and animal pens at the base of the hill where the residents of Din Eidyn lived, and up the winding road to the great hall. As Arthur had said, a servant greeted me at the entrance, and escorted me through the building and into a small chamber. I untied my cloak, and tossed it on the table, along with my sword and belts. He helped me out of my armor and outer tunic. Taking off my undershirt was a slower process, as blood from my wound had seeped onto it, and stuck to my side. The servant gently took a sponge and wetted the area, then we slowly peeled it off. He left me in peace to finish undressing, once I assured him that I could manage from there. There was a large wooden tub, already full of water. It hadn't been pre-heated very well, but it was warmer than the river water I'd waded through on more than one occasion these past few days, and the chamber itself had a hearth, with a fire blazing away. So I gingerly sat down in the tub, and felt almost like I was in heaven and I scrubbed all the dirt, blood, and grime off myself. I chuckled then.

Back home, heaven would have meant a room with a large enough hearth to make the room comfortable. Large rugs and animal furs covered most of the smooth, wooden floors, and the bathtubs would be full of hot, scented water. Servants would have brought a tray of fresh bread, meat, cheese, and fruit available to snack on while my brothers and I bathed and splashed each other or just laid back and relaxed. There would be fresh soft clothing waiting for us when we decided to get out, which we usually didn't do until the water had lost its warmth.

Now, after just a few days in the freezing cold wilderness, even a simple bath of slightly cool water felt blissful. This chamber was small and bare, though it did still have wooden floorboards. I noticed a bit of food on a nearby table, a little dried meat. And there was fresh clothing draped over a nearby chair for me. Simpler clothing than I generally dressed in, but still looked to be of good quality, and warm.

I didn't spend long in the bath. I got clean, dried off, and had only just pulled on some underwear and the woolen trousers when there was a knock on the door.

"Who is it?" I asked as I fastened my belt around my waist.

"It's Tewdrig, the medicus," a voice said.

I opened the door, and recognized the gray-haired healer I'd last seen at Caer Lleon. Behind him was the servant who'd shown me to the chamber. The two entered, and while the servant walked past me and set down a pair of tall steaming mugs, the medicus pulled up a chair beside me and sat down.

"Good evening ... Peredur, right?" Tewdrig said as he opened up his leather satchel. "How's that wound of yours?"

I nodded and turned toward him, carefully lifting my arm for him to inspect.

"Oh, that's a nice one," the medicus murmured. "Axe, was it?"

I nodded. "Yes, sir."

"Well, you're lucky. This is just a flesh wound. A painful one, I presume, but nothing too bad. I'll stitch this right up, put a salve on it, and after a week or so of light duty, you'll be right as rain." As he said this, the medicus moved around me, looking over the rest of my injuries. Besides my newest one I was fairly sure the injury to my shoulder still looked a bit rough. I had several other bruises around my shoulders, both ribs, and my upper arms. My head had begun to throb on the ride to the fort as well, from the hit I'd taken.

"You're definitely a bit banged up, aren't you, boy," Tewdrig said. "Still, nothing serious. I doubt any of these others will even leave scars," he chuckled. "I'd best put some salve on that shoulder, too, though it looks like it's healing fine. That's a nice lump you took to your head, too. Let me guess. A shield?"

"Yes, sir," I agreed with a wince, as he nudged at it.

He gestured for me to have a seat, then he pulled up a chair beside me and pulled out a hooked needle, and threaded it. "The servant here brought some mead. Would you like to drink it first, or should I start stitching you up, now?" he asked.

I took a look at that wicked-looking needle in the medicus' hand, and snatched up the mug beside me. I chugged the contents, then nodded at the man. "Let's do this," I said.

If I'd known how much those stitches would hurt, I'd have asked for at least four mugs of that mead first. As it was, I felt like I would pass out while he worked. Thank God the man was good, at least, and within just a few minutes, though it felt much longer, he had my wound sewn up. He wrapped a clean linen bandage around my waist, then washed the blood off of his hands in the tub at our feet.

"There we are, young man," Tewdrig said. He held up a drinking horn that he'd produced, which the servant dutifully filled from the jug of mead. "Be careful with that side for a few days, eh?" he asked, smiling at me.

I wiped sweat from my forehead and nodded. I was still a bit light-headed. Tewdrig left, and the servant looked down at me. "I'll bring your armor and weaponry down to your tent. Don't worry about your old clothes. I'll see to it that they're cleaned and mended."

I thanked the man and tried to insist that I could carry my own mail, but he was having none of it and scooped it, and the rest of my kit, up before I had even finished pulling on my old boots. "Lead the way, sir," he said with a smile.

Seeing that I'd been outmaneuvered, I donned my new cloak and a fur cap that had also been kindly provided to me, and together, we walked back down the hill, out of the fort, and into our encampment. The sentry on duty guided us to where my contubernium's tent was. My tentmates were all asleep, and many were snoring. I found my blanket already occupying a place reserved for me, and after dismissing the servant with a grateful 'thank you', I went inside. Quietly as I could, I unrolled my blanket and, using my cloak as my pillow, I laid down and was asleep in moments.

*****

It felt like I'd barely closed my eyes when something grabbed my foot and shook it. I sat straight up, my heart pounding. Instantly, pain flared up in my side and back. My eyes shot open, and I looked around. Gilbert was crouched on one knee by my feet.

"Good morning, sunshine," he said with a smile. "Owain says it's time for you to get up and report to the great hall for a council meeting."

I groaned, rubbed my eyes, and slowly pulled on my tunic. "What time is it?"

"It will be dawn soon," Gilbert said. Once he saw that I was fully awake, he went back outside. Apparently, his was the last guard shift of the night.

I looked around, noticing that in the ever so faint light from a nearby campfire, the rest of the contubernium was still sleeping. *Lucky them*, I thought to myself. I finished dressing, then shuffled back up the hill to the great hall. A different servant from the one I'd met the night before stood by the entrance.

"You're Peredur, of Caer Gurcoc?" he asked.

I nodded.

"Follow me, please," he said and led me inside.

He led me up a narrow stairway, through a hallway, and into a large chamber. The chamber had large but very narrow widows interspersed around it, with tapestries decorating the walls in between them. Animal hides lay strewn about the wooden floor. A fire blazed in the hearth, warming the chamber and providing additional light in the room. Oil lamps were set up on a long, rectangular table that dominated the room. Several high-ranking men were seated around the table, with the man I presumed to be the lord of the hillfort at one end in a high-backed chair. To his left and right sat two men on each side, whom I guessed were nobles and advisors.

On the other end sat Arthur, Cai, Owain, Galhault, and a couple of other decurions. Upon my arrival, Arthur and Owain turned to greet me.

"Ah, Peredur. Glad you could join us. Here, have some mulled mead and sit down," Arthur said, pulling one of the empty chairs out from the table.

I did and glanced around the room, feeling very out of place.

"Are we ready to begin then?" asked the man at the head of the table, looking at Arthur.

"We're waiting on one more person, Lord Aled," Arthur responded. I heard the door open behind me, and Arthur, looking over my shoulder, smiled. "Ah, and there she is."

I glanced behind me as well and felt my jaw go slack. Gemma walked in, but not as I'd ever seen her before. Now she was clean, and her wild red hair was neatly brushed and tucked into place with a colorful scarf. She wore a long blue dress, belted at the waist. A striped cloak was draped about her shoulders. Her clothing was simple, nor did she wear any jewelry, but her gracefulness and beauty still caused every man in the room to shut up and turn to acknowledge her, if only for a moment. She bowed in acknowledgment to Lord Aled.

"My lords," she greeted them, then sat down next to me. I caught a faint, flowery scent from her that, combined with her appearance and demeanor, nearly left me reeling. How was this the same girl who'd forded a river with me, helped pull armor off of me, and slept out in the woods next to me?

Suddenly, she elbowed me and gave me a weird look. Her eyes danced around, and I realized she was trying to make me look toward the end of the table. I did, and felt my face burn with embarrassment. Every man there was looking at me. Some looked clearly amused, some annoyed, except Owain. He was studying Gemma, but his expression seemed more thoughtful than anything.

"If you're done gawking at the lady, may we begin?" the man to Lord Aled's right said.

"Uh, certainly, my lord," I said, clearing my throat. I felt like a complete fool and that I would suddenly rather be back in the woods with a dozen Picts chasing me than here in this room, with these people. Well, the people on the nobles' side of the table, at least.

"Thank you," the man said, smiling with exaggerated politeness. "As I was saying," he gestured to Lord Aled, "this is Lord Aled Mywnfawr, the Duke of Din Eidyn. These two here are Lords Cadwallon and Idwal. I am Count Hywel." The Count paused and clasped his hands behind his back. "So, gentlemen," he said, looking around at the rest of the table. "Let's get right to it then, shall we?" He looked back at me and Gemma.

"Now, Arthur has told us that the pair of you believe Gododdin is still in danger from the Picts. Is that correct?"

Gemma and I glanced at each other. When she made no move to answer, I replied, "Yes, my lord." I told him all that had transpired, from the moment I became separated from my turma until the moment I was rescued the previous night. As I'd feared, the looks I received were skeptical, by the end.

"You ran into King Drest himself?" the count snorted, not even trying to hide his disbelief. "A likely story".

"I'd know him the way any of you would recognize him," Gemma said for the first time, gesturing to Arthur.

Steepling his fingers, Owain spoke up. "I believe them," he said. "Have you ever met Drest?" He looked at the northern lords. They said nothing, and the corners of Owain's mouth twitched. "I have. You may or may not know, but I am a cousin to King Domgal of Alt Clut. A few years ago, shortly after he became king, Drest, technically Drest II, once visited my cousin. He offered to stop the raids into our land in exchange for tribute. Peredur and Gemma's description matches my own memory of him."

"Did King Domgal agree to his terms?" one of the lords asked.

Owain looked at him and smirked. "Quite the opposite. He demanded tribute from King Drest as compensation for previous raids made by the Picts."

There were chuckles around the room. Then Owain's face grew serious, and
he looked hard at Gemma. "There's something about your story that doesn't
sound right, though."

All eyes turned to her, and now it was Gemma's turn to flush.

"Where exactly did you say you're from?" Owain asked.

"A village north and west of Loch Liobhann. It was too small to have a name,"
she said.

"Hmm, and yet your accent sounds much more western than northern,"
Owain mused.

"What's that supposed to mean?" I asked, feeling a need to protect Gemma.

"Owain is saying that she sounds more like she hails from Dal Riata rather
than Picti lands," Arthur chimed in. "It's something we discussed earlier this
morning. And I think I agree. I've had my own dealings with the Gaels, to
include a few friends."

He spoke something then to Gemma in a strange, lilting language I didn't
understand, but it caused Gemma to flinch.

"Who are you, really?" Arthur asked.

Gemma glanced at me. I stared at her. Had she been lying to me? Still? I
thought we'd already had this conversation and sorted this out.

"As I told Peredur," she said, "I am ... or was, a chieftain's daughter. Drest's
forces attacked my village, killed my father, and enslaved me and any other
women and children who survived. Later, I escaped."

"Who was your father?" Arthur asked.

"Nobody you'd have known, I'm sure," Gemma said.

"Try me."

Gemma squirmed in her seat. "His name was Hamish." She glanced around,
not seeing any reaction. "See? I told you. Nobody you'd know."

Arthur narrowed his eyes thoughtfully. "Who was *his* father?"

242

Gemma hesitated. "Fergus," she said softly.

"Fergus ... Mor?" Arthur asked.

I didn't know that name either, but the northern lords certainly did. So did Owain. Their eyebrows shot up, and they all sat straighter in their seats or leaned forward.

"Yes," Gemma answered, so quietly that I barely heard her.

"Speak up, girl," Count Hywel said.

Gemma straightened up, and in a loud, clear voice she said, "I am the daughter of the slain Chief Hamish, who was the younger brother to King Domangart Reti, and the youngest son of Fergus Mor, the first King of the Gaels of Dal Riata."

There were gasps around the room. Even I was taken aback. She *was* royalty then, I realized in shock. Gaelic royalty, to be sure, but royalty nonetheless.

Only Arthur seemed unphased by the revelation. In fact, he actually seemed to be smirking slightly. He glanced at a dark-haired, middle-aged man seated beside him. The pair exchanged knowing looks.

"I suspected as much the moment I saw you," he said. "King Fergus came to my father's home at Din Tagel years ago, shortly before his death. He'd brought his daughter, Morgana. She's the same age as me. She looks a lot like him, only smaller and prettier," Arthur grinned. Everyone chuckled. Arthur looked back at Gemma. "You look a lot like Morgana. And not just that red hair. Clearly, Fergus' looks run in the family."

"So it does," the dark-haired man said with a wry smile. "I should have seen the connection, myself, but then, you're much closer to Morgana than I ever was," he smirked at Arthur. To my astonishment, Arthur actually looked flustered and pointedly turned away from his companion, who grinned even more broadly. Clearly, there was a history there.

"So what to do with this?" the Count asked, looking around the room. While they debated, my eyes roved back over to the man beside Arthur, trying to place him. He had the weathered, square-jawed face of a veteran. He was also heavily muscled in spite of his middle age. I'd seen him before, I knew. He'd been with Arthur when the Red Dragons rode up to the fort several days ago. Before that, I'd seen him a few times in Caer Lleon. He rarely wore armor, though.

*Ector!* The name suddenly sprang to my mind. This was Ector Artorius. He was a former commander of the Red Dragons or something like that, and the word was that he'd been Arthur's mentor back when Arthur himself was a youth. To my knowledge he had no official rank within the Red Dragons, being retired now. I supposed he was simply one of Arthur's friends and advisors, like Myrddin.

"My lords," Arthur's voice finally cut over the din, interrupting my private musings. "We can decide how best to deal with Maithgemm later. Right now, we have a more pressing matter! If hers and Peredur's account is true, then we could have thousands of Picts descending on Gododdin in days! That is what we need to focus on."

"And you believe them, I suppose?" The count asked. Clearly, he did not.

"I do, though I admit there could be some exaggeration with the numbers," Arthur said. "But which will be more costly? Sending out scouts and bracing for an invasion that either never materializes or is a bit exaggerated? Or doing nothing and being completely unprepared when an invading force at least as big as the one Peredur and Maithgemm claim is out there arrives at your doorstep? And keep in mind that both Maithgemm and my decurion, Prince Owain, are convinced that the man she and Peredur ran into only a few nights ago *was,* in fact, King Drest! And if he is encamped at Loch Liobhann, that gives all the more credibility to the threat."

"What would you have us do, Arthur?" Duke Aled asked, rubbing at his temples.

"Muster every levy you can," our tribune responded immediately. "Send them to man the forts along the border wall. Post additional lookouts with signal fires along the shore overlooking the Firth of Forth to ensure that the Picts don't try to cross the Forth from there. While you do that, I would bring the

Red Dragons back to the fort we were at previously. Hopefully, Lord Guinnion hasn't evacuated it yet."

"We already have sent hundreds of levies to that fort," the count protested. "Wouldn't it be best to stay here? If there is a Pict army on the way, Din Eidyn will make a far better place to defend from than that old dirt wall," the duke argued.

"It would," Arthur conceded. "But if we do not reinforce Guinnion, we condemn him and all of his levies to death, likely as not." He looked at the count. "Yes, you have sent hundreds of levies there. And a couple dozen of them were killed in the battle in the woods. Twice that number were wounded and released from service. We also suffered casualties. My men number just under three hundred now. There are about nine hundred able men at the fort now. Unless Drest is a fool, which I refuse to believe, then he wouldn't invade without assuming that he will have to fight at least one battle against a heavily defended garrison, whether it is the fort at the Antonine Wall, here, or somewhere else along the Firth. If I were in his shoes, I would want at least three to four thousand men for that. We already found one camp of about a thousand tribesmen and destroyed it. According to Maithgemm, there were only two tribes there, besides a smaller, third tribe who already lived in the region. So if Drest is still coming south, even after that defeat, then he has men to spare."

Arthur was leaning over the table now, fists resting on the wood, and looked around, making sure that he had the nobles' attention. "My lords, if Drest is on the move, they will almost certainly be at the fort soon and will surround and entrap Guinnion and his forces at that fort, or even worse, they'll catch up to Guinnion and his men on the march, on open ground. That will be the end of them." He looked at the count with a severe look. "You say it will be hard to muster up another few hundred levies? Well, how much harder will it be to muster an entire fresh army to replace the casualties Guinnion will suffer if we do not reinforce him?"

245

"It's also possible that Guinnion and his men, who should be leaving the fort soon, will abandon that ruin, march back here before the Picts can catch them, and we can make a stronger defense *here*," the Duke said.

"It's possible," Arthur acknowledged in a flat tone, making it clear what he thought of that likelihood. "I'm not going to have my men just sit here and rely on hope," he said, curling his lip slightly as he said it. "We will ride back to the fort. If we do nothing more than add to Guinnion's number and help secure his flanks while he and his men march back here, so be it, but I suspect we'll have to fight them at that fort, whether we wish to or not. Remember, in any plan of battle, the enemy always has a say in the matter." Arthur glanced sideways at Ector as he said this, and I saw Ector return the look with a slight smile.

Duke Aled glanced at his advisors. They whispered amongst themselves for a moment, then Count Hywel turned back to the Duke. "We can afford to muster an additional four hundred men, but for no longer than a week. We simply will not have provisions for that many for any longer than that. Not at this time of year. We will send them to the fort as well. As you say, hopefully, they will only be needed to create a larger column of troops to march back here and not have to fight at that ruin."

"That should prove sufficient," Arthur nodded. "If there's no other matters that require my attention, I'll get the Red Dragons ready to ride. We can make camp at Guinnion's fort tonight."

We all stood up, and as Arthur and the decurions made ready to leave, Gemma leaned towards me and put a hand on my arm, whispering, "What about me? Please don't leave me with these people." She looked almost frantic, and her eyes jigged back and forth between me and the lords of Din Eidyn.

A jolt of excitement went through me at her touch. I looked down at her small hand, then up to her eyes. "Why not?" I whispered back. "It's safe here."

Gemma gave me a withering look. "Safe? I am a Gaelic-Pict. The Gaels and Picts and the people of this land have been raiding each other for ages! Now, the Picts are in open war with them. How do you think I could possibly be safer here than at that fort with you and Arthur?" she hissed. "At best, they'll enslave me the moment you and the Red Dragons are out of sight."

"Well, how safe do you imagine you'd be at a fort being attacked by Picts?" I countered, forgetting to whisper. Heads turned.

"What's this about?" Owain asked, glancing from Gemma to me.

"She's afraid of what will happen to her if we leave her here," I said to Owain in a low voice, glancing over at the Duke and lords, who were having their own discussion.

Owain looked over, too, then back at Gemma. "Ah. I see your point." He turned to Gemma. "Walk with us back to our camp."

We followed Owain and the others out and walked in silence as we passed by the barracks where the Duke's retinue and the small garrison of Din Eidyn lived, past the gates of both palisades and out to the camp.

"Arthur, a word?" Owain asked.

Arthur and Ector turned and walked over.

"Ector, would you get these men ready to ride?" Arthur asked.

"Sure," Ector said and slapped Arthur's shoulder affectionately as he walked away. "Alright, lads, up and at 'em! We got a hard ride ahead of us!" Ector bellowed as he walked towards the center of the camp.

Arthur must have seen me flinch and grinned. "Got a voice like one of those huge marching horns, hasn't he?"

I rubbed my ear. "Yes, Tribune," I said.

"You should try waking up with that voice screaming in your ear. That man became as a father to me after my parents died, while I was still a child." He smiled, then focused his attention back on me and Gemma. "So what's going on here?"

Owain relayed Gemma's concern. Arthur listened and frowned. "Yes, I see your point," he looked at Gemma. "Could you keep up with the numerus, on horseback?"

Gemma flashed me a quick glance, then replied, "Yes, my lord."

"I doubt you have any experience with weapons, am I right?"

"No, my lord," Gemma admitted. "Except with a sling."

"Your cousin, Morgana, sure did," Arthur chuckled. "Fergus had quite the soft spot for his daughter, so when she begged him to learn to use weapons as a child along with her brothers, he was unable to deny her. She's one of the best archers I've ever seen." Arthur sighed, scratching his short beard as he pondered. "Are you squeamish?"

"Squeamish, my lord?" Gemma asked.

"Yes. Would you be able to handle the blood and mess of a battlefield?"

"She can," I chimed in. "She and I rode through the battlefield in the forest. I think I was more sick than she was."

"Could you assist our medicus, our healer?" Arthur asked.

"I could, my lord," Gemma said without hesitation.

Arthur nodded. "It's settled then. Talk to Tewdrig, our medicus, then go into the village while we pack. Buy yourself some clothing suitable for assisting him in the medical tent."

From a pouch on his belt, Arthur pulled out some bits of hacksilver and dropped them into Gemma's cupped hands.

"Get yourself a bedroll, a travel pack, and a dagger as well. You'll need all of those things if you're going to be riding with us."

Gemma's eyes widened and moistened as she looked at the silver Arthur had just so casually handed her. "Th- thank you, my lord," she choked out.

Arthur smiled. "It's the least I can do. You saved one of my men and might be the reason an entire invasion of Gododdin fails. And on top of that, you're Morgana's cousin. We keep in touch. If she ever found out that I didn't help you when you needed it, she'd have my- well, she'd be very angry with me. And Morgana is not someone I want to have angry at me."

Gemma clutched the silver protectively to her breast and bowed to Arthur, then flashed us a wide grin and headed towards the camp. She stopped and turned back to us just as quickly. "Which tent will I find your healer in?" she asked sheepishly.

Arthur grinned and pointed. Gemma nodded again and took off jogging in the direction he pointed. He put his hand on my shoulder. "Peredur, if she's anything like her cousin, watch yourself around that one."

"Tribune?" I asked, unsure of his meaning.

Arthur laughed. "She's a redhead, boy. You know all the things they say about redheads?"

"Yes, Tribune," I said, though I was fairly certain I did not, but was too embarrassed to admit my ignorance.

"Well, Fergus Mor and his brood are probably the originators of every one of those stories, based on my experience. So good luck with that girl."

I stood there, perplexed and just a little worried, as Arthur walked away then.

"Peredur, come on! Get a move on!" Owain called over to me. I looked over and saw that my contubernium was in the process of tearing down our tent. I quickly jogged over and began to help.

We struck camp and were on the road within the hour. Rations of biscuits, cheese, and dried meat were issued out from a supply wagon as we formed up so that we could eat as we rode. Gemma stowed her gear in the medical wagon, and rode alongside Tewdrig. Thanks to the silver Arthur had gifted her, Gemma had changed out of the nicer dress she'd worn at the council and now wore a plain, undyed woolen dress down to her calves, warm pants, and new ankle-high boots to replace the worn-out pair she'd been wearing when I encountered her in the woods. She kept her old belt but sported a new dagger looped onto it. Her one concession to vanity was her cloak. It had a green and blue plaid pattern and was pinned with a penannular brooch that consisted of a large ring and a long pin that pierced through the cloak. Her curly, fiery red hair was still tied up in the scarf she'd worn at the council meeting.

Many of the men gawked at her when we'd formed up into column formation and passed by the wagons, and I admit, I felt just a bit jealous, though I really had no right to. For her part, she was engrossed in a conversation with our old medicus and scarcely seemed to even notice the attention she was getting. And if she noticed the looks she was getting, she wasn't acknowledging it.

Arthur left two turmae to ride with the supply wagons, and they rumbled and creaked down the road. The others, Arthur led at a fast trot. We took breaks every hour to give our horses a breather and to get a bit of water. Just shy of five hours later, we came within sight of the fort. My stomach clenched into knots at the sight of it. A column of smoke was rising from within. We were still a mile away, so the smoke was too much for simple cooking fires. That could only mean that the fort was either already under attack or, worse, had been attacked, and we were too late!

# Chapter Seventeen

W e rode towards the fort anticipating a fight. When we were within half a mile of it, I heard the quick blasts of the lituus, calling for the numerus to form into a wedge formation. In column formation the Red Dragons rode four abreast, and each turma within the column formed up only two files wide, riding alongside each other. This made the numerus' transition from column into a wedge able to be performed smoothly and quickly, with each turma maintaining cohesion. All that was required was for the turmae on each half of the column to fan out, so within the span of only a minute or two, we made the transition into a wedge formation and were ready for action.

A moment later, the horn blew again, and we sped up to a canter. The red streamers of our draco standards began to extend and flutter as we sped up. Looking upward, it appeared like a flight of brass-headed, red-bodied dragons were soaring above us amidst a forest of spear tips. As we increased our pace, we used the opportunity to create space between the ranks so that at the moment of impact when we charged, the rear ranks wouldn't collide into the backs of the men and horses in front of us.

My turma was on the left flank. I was in the second rank of our turma. In the gaps between the men in the first rank, I saw the situation as we approached the fort. It looked bad. Picts had, of course, swarmed over the border wall itself and were attempting to climb up the eastern and southern walls. I suspected they were attempting to scale the north and west walls, too, but I had no view of those. They heard our horn blasts, and for a moment, the Pict warriors were in absolute chaos. Some continued to climb their makeshift ladders, some dropped back down and turned to face us, and others ran back toward the wall.

Arthur chose the perfect spot to aim our wedge into- the corner where the border wall met the eastern wall of the fort. It perfectly trapped the horde of Picts against two formidable barriers and left them absolutely nowhere to maneuver in order to avoid our charge. At three hundred paces away the horn blew again, giving us the signal to speed up to a gallop and charge! I watched the first rank pull out javelins and throw them into the horde the moment we were in range. This was followed up immediately by the impact of our horses into the disorganized barbarians, still attempting to form some semblance of a battleline. They failed miserably, and whereas a cavalry charge against a proper shieldwall would likely not tear up more than their first two ranks, our first rank penetrated so deeply into them that my own rank was able to follow up and get into the fray!

I'd hoped to get a new spear and helmet from supplies here at the fort, as we hadn't stayed at Din Eidyn long enough for me to do so. Now, I found myself having to go into battle once again feeling a bit under-equipped. I hung back, conscious of the wound to my side, but I couldn't bear to stay out of the fight altogether. Neither could Carys, who charged into the melee almost without any guidance from me. My side felt stiff, and pain flared up with every slash, thrust, or parry, so I quickly shifted my focus to blocking incoming attacks with my shield while Carys assisted me. I praise God for such a horse as Carys! I gave her the freedom to kick and bite and was content, on this occasion at least, to let her take the lead in this fight. And, of course I was surrounded by Red Dragons. One moment, there seemed to be a veritable sea of Picts surrounding me and my companions. In the next, there were none. None standing, at least.

Panting, with sweat and blood streaking my face, I looked around. Red Dragons swarmed around the eastern wall and controlled the entire area between that wall and the border wall to which the fort was connected.

"They're pulling back!" someone cried, and a ragged cheer went up.

I looked around, desperate to see for myself what was going on, but was frustrated to find that aside from the walls looming up around us, all I could see were my companions and our draco standards, which their bearers were waving about in celebration. Commands rippled through the ranks as decurions worked to restore order for in truth, our formation had come undone in the chaos and confines of the fight. The gates were opened, and we were allowed entry into the fort. Thankfully, most of the men inside were manning the walls, or the space within the fort would have been very crowded with so many mounted men riding into it, but we wouldn't be able to stay within the walls indefinitely.

It was nearly as chaotic inside as it had been outside. Levies carried wounded comrades into the great hall. The dead were hauled away and placed somberly near a gate to be buried later. Leaders were calling out to their men and seeing who had fallen.

Once inside, we also saw that the western gatehouse was badly burned, and the gate itself had barrels and other miscellaneous things, even a wagon, barring the entryway. Though the flames were already put out, smoke still rose from it.

"All right, men, fall in! We need a headcount!" Aylmer called out.

The two sections of my turma formed up in two ranks behind our draco standard, with Decani Aylmer and Sawyl on the ends to our right. Around us, the other turmae were having their own formations. In optimal conditions our numerus would have been formed up on line, with each turma formed up by contubernium, five paces from the next turma over. As we were too crowded to do that now, we formed up wherever and however we could fit, and the air was full of decurions and duplarii shouting orders, or calling for absent soldiers.

In front of our formation, Owain did a quick headcount, ensuring that we had everybody. Two of Sawyl's men were seriously wounded, and were already being taken to the great hall for treatment, but none in our turma were dead or missing. While Owain ensured everyone was accounted for, Cornelius walked through our formation, making sure we had all of our important kit and that it was combat ready. He noticed my missing spear and helmet. While spears broke frequently following a fight and replacing that was not a big deal, he gave me a dirty look in regards to my missing helmet.

"It was lost during one of my fights with some Picts, after I became separated from the turma," I expained.

Cornelius nodded. "Make sure you replace it as quickly as possible. Check with our supplies master. If he has a spare, you can purchase one from him. Otherwise, you'll need to find one at some other shop and get a new one as soon as possible."

"Yes, Duplarius," I said with a nod.

Once our headcount and inspection were concluded, Owain gave us permission to fall out but told us to stand by. In other formations, turmae who were missing men immediately went back out to where the fighting had occurred in order to retrieve our fallen.

"Obviously, we can't all stay here, in the fort," Owain told us. "If I had to guess, I would say we'll probably end up deployed the way we did for those couple of days before we rode north. The levies will take the fort, and we'll reoccupy our camps further back in the woods, with lookouts posted along the border wall to watch for the enemy. Make no mistake," Owain warned, looking around to make sure he had our full attention. "This fight has only just begun. We caught them by surprise and gave them a bloody nose. They fell back to regroup, but I'd bet a barrel of ale that they'll be back. Maybe as early as this evening. So stay ready."

"Cornelius," Owain said. "They're yours. I've got to report to Arthur." Cornelius nodded and Owain walked away.

"Alright lads," Cornelius said. "See to your horses, then do what you can to get your kit ready for another fight, and don't forget to top off on water! Once all that's done, if the Pagans haven't come for us again, you can relax until we get the word."

While we prepared, we heard from the levies what exactly happened with the western gatehouse. The Picts had initiated the attack by having archers loose dozens of fire arrows at the gatehouse of the western half of the fort. At the same time, the rest of the horde swarmed the north and east walls of the fort with crudely made ladders. It had almost worked. The western gate caught on fire and was now effectively compromised. A reserve force of Picts, previously hidden, had attempted to rush and batter down the weakened gate but were unsuccessful. The levies had formed a chain, emptying barrels of water on the gate, and the fire was extinguished in time to at least prevent its complete destruction. They had also piled empty barrels, stones, and even a broken wagon up against the gate to block it, so the Picts had been unable to breach the wall that way.

Owain was back in less than an hour. As predicted, we got the immediate word to pack up and move back out of the fort. The Red Dragons were to set up where we'd staged for the incursion into the forest- in the woods to the rear left of the fort. Beside us, to the right, the fifty or so mounted troops of Guinnion's levies set up their own camp. Contubernia of eight soldiers were deployed along the border wall on both sides of the fort, about four hundred paces out, to extend our awareness of the battlespace. Additional, two-man observation posts were established in the woods surrounding both the fort and our camp, creating a large screen line, thereby preventing the Picts from sneaking up on us from any direction.

Since we were only reoccupying the same site that we'd used previously, we had less work to do. Cleared out patches of land were already prepared for our tents, once the baggage carts arrived. So we busied ourselves with making improvements on the large corral for our horses. The entire numerus, except the men on sentry duty, was then put to work felling trees, hacking off branches, and either working on our corral, fashioning a new door for the western gate, or planting logs into the berm.

I was restricted to light duty, to allow the wound to my side a chance to heal, so I was put on sentry duty, along with Gilbert, on the east side of our camp. It had been a minor miracle that, when I'd asked Gilbert to check my wound, he determined that only a few stitches had torn loose, and caused a little bleeding. We fixed that with a fresh bandage around my stomach, and then I returned to my duties. From my position, I actually saw Arthur once. He'd removed his cloak and armor, and was carrying one end of a large log towards the eastern side of the fort. Ector was carrying the other side. Both were dirty and dripping sweat. By that evening, the berm that the border wall had become over the ages was actually beginning to look like a proper wall once more.

Three hours after the numerus started preparing our bivouac site, our supply wagons and the turmae that had escorted them arrived, along with a column of about two hundred additional levies from Din Eidyn. Gemma saw me, waved, and strolled over to where Gilbert and I sat on a log. Skipping the pleasantries, she told us that about a hundred Caledonii Picts had spotted them and attacked, but the turmae guarding the wagons had thrown their javelins, charged, and rode circles around the warband, cutting them to pieces. Very few had lived to run away. The escort took three casualties though.

I'd been watching the wagons come in, and saw the soldiers pull a bloodied, limp body from the wagon and lay it gently down in the grass, just off the road. Two others, clearly wounded, were helped down. One had to be carried, the other limped along. All disappeared through the eastern gate.

"The dead soldier is .... was one of Decurion Tyree's men," I said, watching them. "I don't recognize the other decurion, nor the wounded men. Do you?" I glanced over at Gilbert.

He shook his head. "I barely know anyone outside of the turma," he said.

This wasn't too surprising. I didn't either, though of course, I at least recognized some of the more famous decurions. I suspected that was truer than not for the rest of the men in the numerus, especially newer ones like us.

Gemma stood beside me, staring off back down the road. She had some blood on her hands, and I suspected she'd already begun her duties as Tewdrig's assistant. The girl looked so dejected that on impulse, I stood up and gently put my arm around her shoulders. Gemma leaned into me and rested her head on my shoulder. We stood like that for a few moments, then she pulled away, wiping at her eyes with the back of her hand.

Gemma looked up at me. "Thank you," she said. "I should get going now, though. Tewdrig will likely be needing me soon."

I said nothing, unable to think of anything appropriate to say. So I just nodded to her. She smiled, then walked away.

"Smooth," Gilbert said from nearby, after she'd gone far enough away to not hear. "So will you be giving the rest of us hugs now too, when we're stressed out? Or is she special?"

"Sod off," I said, not wanting to take my eyes off Gemma, even as she walked away. Then, just before she entered the fort, she turned back towards me and raised her hand. I returned the gesture, and she disappeared inside.

A short while later, I saw that unknown decurion again, and watched as he and his turma picked up their fallen comrade by the edges of his cloak and somberly carried him out to the woods. They buried him beneath a tree, some distance outside of our camp's perimeter, amongst a row of other freshly dug graves. A Pict sword taken from the battlefield where he'd died was jammed deep into the earth in place of a headstone.

Later that night, I mentioned what I'd seen to Cornelius. He told me that under better circumstances, like when we didn't have an urgent need to put up fortifications, the entire numerus would have formed up to honor the fallen. The decurions of the fallen would then praise the man, or men's deeds, and commend his soul to God.

As the sun began to set, Gilbert and I were relieved by a couple soldiers in Galhault's turma. Gilbert headed back towards camp, but I decided to go see our armorer about a new helmet. The man I was searching for was Sextus Brocius, a friendly, heavyset man in his late thirties, with brown hair and a trimmed beard streaked with gray. Like me, he was one of the few men in the numerus who could actually read as well as speak Latin. I found him unloading supplies from his wagon. He stopped when he saw me approach, and wiped his brow.

"Ah, Peredur, greetings. You look like you need something."

"Well met, Sextus," I said. "I do indeed. I need to replace my helmet."

"I see," Sextus said. "Well, I do have a variety of options available. I'm cheaper than the smiths in most villages or towns, but not free. You have silver, I assume?"

"I do," I replied.

He smiled, and climbed up on top of his wagon. He glanced around for a moment, then opened the lid of one of the crates. "How's this one? A simple, bronze skullcap style? I also have one with a nasal piece to protect your nose.

"I like the segmented helmets. Do you have any of those?"

Sextus smiled. "Ah, one of the more popular styles. I always keep a few of those on hand. Do you want a plain one, or one with added facial protection? I'd recommend at least a nasal. I even have one with an attachable faceplate, in the Germanic style. Very fierce looking."

"My last helm had cheek guards. I liked those. If I can get an iron segmented helm with cheek guards and a nasal, that would be great," I told him.

Sextus studied me for a moment. "I have a helm like that but, uh, it's not cheap." He reached down and pulled out the helmet. It was iron, though the nasal and the studs riveting the segments of the helm together were brass. As were the hinges that connected the cheek guards. "The market price of this is three unciae of silver," Sextus said. "Because I'm able to purchase large orders of weapons and armor for on-hand supplies for the Red Dragons, I get cheaper rates. So I could sell this to you for, say ... two and a half unciae, even."

"May I try it on?" I asked.

He handed it over, and I plopped it on my head. It was clearly too large.

"I'd need a liner put in," I said. "How much extra for that?"

Sextus rolled his eyes around for a second, thinking. "That'd be ... one uncia of silver extra."

"So much?" I asked, startled.

"That's a lot of extra rivets that have to be put in," Sextus replied. "Never mind the quality leather for the lining itself."

"Three and a half unciae, total," I mused. I hesitated, weighing my options. Literally. I grabbed the pouch at my belt and hefted it. I had about five unciae on me.

"Sextus," I sighed. "If I give you that much, that won't leave me much left. And I'm probably going to have to spend more silver soon to get my mail shirt repaired, as it is. What about if I give you a Pict sword in a day or two?" I asked.

"You have one?" he asked.

"Not yet, but you know as well as I do that we're likely going to be in one vicious battle over the next couple days. I'm sure I can loot at least one. And one good sword would easily cover the cost of the helm and liner."

"*If* you get your hands on one," Sextus pointed out. "How about I hold onto that helm until you produce such a sword."

"Oh come on, man," I argued. "Without that helm my chances of surviving the fight at all are worsened. I suppose I could pay you the silver now, and if and when I find a Pict sword, you can give me my silver right back, plus a bit more, since a Pict noble's sword will almost certainly be worth more than that segmented helm!"

"And what if you die? Or worse, you die, and the helm is damaged?" he protested, then had the good grace to look a little embarrassed at such a terrible implication.

I stared at him, and he dropped his gaze uncomfortably. "If I die, I'm sure you can take up your lost merchandise with someone in my turma," I said. "You can get your bloody silver from them. Or you can loot my corpse yourself, I suppose."

"Oh, come off it," Sextus protested weakly. "You know, I didn't mean it to sound like that... Fine. Take the helm," he sighed. "Once this battle's done, you either produce a sword or give me my silver, though."

"Agreed," I said, and we shook hands.

Sextus leaned over and rummaged through his wooden chest, producing two more segmented helms, also with nasals and cheek guards. "Here, see if any of these fit. If we have to put the liner on that other one it will take a few days for me to get it to you, or else you'll have to wear a thick cap under it until I can get it riveted.

The second one I tried, which already had a liner, felt good. Before I knew what he was about, Sextus pulled out a spear from the wagon and rapped me on the side of the head. Pain from the lump I'd taken against the Picts shot through me.

"Well, the helmet stayed in place," he said, studying me. "How'd that feel?" he asked, totally nonchalantly.

"Like you cracked me on the side of the head," I complained through gritted teeth.

He rolled his eyes. "Oh, don't cry about it. I'm sure you've had your head knocked about before. Did it feel loose?"

I shook my head. "Maybe a little."

"Good, then it fits properly. All you have to do is tie the cords attached to the cheek guards nice and snug, and you're all set. You can take that one."

"Thanks, Sextus," I said. "You're a good man, no matter what they say about you," I grinned, then turned and walked away.

"No matter ... Hey!" Sextus called after me. "What's that supposed to mean?"

I waved back at him but kept walking back to camp.

*****

Once it grew dark, work around the camp and on the fort's walls finally ceased and we were allowed to make cooking fires and have hot supper. Soon the air was thick with the smell of meat- mostly salted pork, and porridge. I ate with my tentmates and showed them my new segmented helm. I asked Gilbert to help me pull my mail shirt off, though I had to be careful not to open up the wound in my side as he tugged on the sleeves, and I wiggled out of it. Then, I sat down on a log and took the opportunity to check over it to make sure it wasn't rusting. After all, this was the first real chance I'd had in several days to do proper maintenance. I had at least two noticeable tears in my shirt that needed fixing- both were nearly wide enough for me to slip my hand through.

Around me, Gilbert and a few of the other soldiers closest to me paused in the various activities they had been performing and looked up, surprised. I turned around, half expecting to see Arthur walking up on us. Instead, it was Gemma.

"May I join you? Is that allowed?" She asked, looking around uncertainly.

I scooted over to one end of the log I'd been sitting to make room for her. "I've not heard of any rules forbidding it," I said. "Please, do sit down with us."

"Thank you," she said and gathered her dress about her as she sat. She held her hands out, gazing into our fire.

"Have you eaten, uh ...?" Gilbert asked, looking from her to me.

"Oh, I'm sorry," I said. "Lads, this is Gemma. She's the niece of the King of Dal Riata," I stressed. The last thing I needed was for anyone to assume she was some camp follower or slave. "She's also been invited by Arthur to assist Tewdrig."

The men nodded to her in greeting as I introduced them to her.

"You're the girl that came screaming for Arthur to come rescue Peredur here the other night, right?" Marcus asked.

Gemma blushed slightly. "Yes, that was me."

"Brave of you. You did a good thing," Marcus said with a smile.

We sat and talked. Gemma was incredibly curious about our lives back south and expressed her excitement at seeing Caer Lleon for herself when we were done here in the north.

"I don't see why you'd want to," Gilbert said, puzzled. "Wouldn't you prefer to go home to Dal Riata? You're some kind of princess, right?"

"Not quite," Gemma clarified. "My father was a village chief, not the King. The King is my uncle. I've only met him a few times. And no, I don't particularly want to go back. King Domangart would just want to marry me off to some old man. The girls in my family tend not to respond well to those kinds of arrangements. Like my cousin, Morganna. Care to know how she got out of an arranged marriage?"

"Tell us," I encouraged her. "But first, would you do me a favor? My saddlebag is next to you. Would you hand me the small pouch from it?" I pointed. "I've got spare links in there."

She dug around for a moment, pulled out a small leather pouch and shook it. It rattled and she tossed it to me. I caught it, and then, one at a time, started repairing the damage to my mail with new iron links.

"So, how did she get out of it?" Gilbert asked. He'd just swallowed down his last bite of salted pork.

"She arranged for an archery contest amongst the suitors that King Fergus and his wife had selected as worthy matches for her. She agreed to marry whoever scored best."

"I didn't know Gaels put much emphasis on archery," Marcus mused.

Gemma grinned. "We don't. That was the point. She didn't want any of the suitors to do well. And most of them failed miserably. Though not all of the suitors were Gaelic, I should add. They were given three arrows each. One couldn't even hit the target at all. Only one managed to hit within the bull's eye. He was a Briton. My cousin was pretty sure that was a lucky hit since his other two arrows missed."

"So, shouldn't she have married that one?" Marcus asked.

"He thought so," Gemma smirked. "But my cousin, Morgana, had one last trick to play. She'd been seated with the King, Queen, and Prince Domangart on a balcony overlooking the courtyard. She stood up and pointed out that the exact wording of the agreement, as stated by the King, had been that whoever scored highest *amongst those present* would win her hand."

Gemma stood up, close to the fire, and was telling the story like a true bard now. "You see," she boasted, "My cousin is an excellent archer. So after she said this, she jumped down from the viewing stand, snatched up a bow and arrow from the table, and before anybody could stop her, she loosed an arrow!"

Gemma paused dramatically, making sure she had all of our attention as she acted out her story as though she were her cousin. We were thoroughly engrossed now. Even a few of the soldiers from nearby cooking fires and turned to listen. She grinned and continued, "Her arrow flew between two of the suitors and struck the bull's eye dead center! And she'd loosed her arrow from several paces behind them"

This earned a bout of laughter from her audience. Gemma held up her hand, signaling for us to calm down. "Well, Morgana threw down the bow and declared, 'I've scored best! Therefore, I have won my own hand!' and stood there daring anybody to challenge her claim."

"How did the suitors ... the King react?" I was greatly amused but also astonished. I struggled to even imagine how such a scenario would have played out if the daughter of my own King, Cadwallon, had done such a thing back home in Gwynedd.

"As the story goes, King Fergus roared with laughter. He thought it was the funniest thing he'd ever seen," Gemma responded with a grin.

"And the suitor who should have won? How did he respond?" Gilbert asked. "Surely, he must have felt cheated."

"You could ask him yourself," Gemma said. "He's here, in this camp."

That got everyone's attention, and the grounds became very quiet, too shocked to say a thing. And everyone was furiously trying to work out who she could possibly be referring to. I could only think of one man in the vicinity who might have been the unfortunate suitor. "Surely not ... Lord Guinnion?" I asked.

Gemma looked at me, puzzled.

"It was me," a rueful-sounding voice startled everyone out of their inner speculations.

We all turned as one, in shock, for the man was none other than our very own Tribune Arthur! He stood well behind the group, with his arms casually folded across his chest.

"You?" I gasped, though likely others did too.

"High King Conanus had hoped to secure an alliance with King Fergus. Conanus was already married, though he had no heirs yet. His father and mine were close friends, so he bade me sail north to attempt to secure Morgana as my bride. And for the record," Arthur said, cocking an eyebrow at Gemma. "Two of my arrows at least pierced the edge of the bull's eye. The third arrow was nearly in the center, but otherwise you are correct. Her arrow flew right past my head and into the dead center of the bull's eye. It nearly split my own arrow."

"So what happened afterward?" I asked, looking from Gemma to Arthur.

"Morgana and I became close friends," Arthur said. "She even sailed south with us without King Fergus' knowledge. He came after her a short time later, but Morgana made it clear that she would die before allowing any man to touch her without her approval or consent. So Fergus gave up and returned home. He was a bit ah... upset by Morgana's antics. She stayed at our family's estate in Dumnonia for a time. Then she met our friend Myrddin and decided what she wanted more than anything was knowledge. And of course," Arthur chuckled and looked around at the rest of us, "If any of you have met Myrddin, there's pretty much no topic in the world that he doesn't seem to know at least something about."

"So what brings you to our fire, Tribune?" I asked. "Was there someone you needed to see? Something we can do for you?"

"No, no," Arthur said, waving for us to relax. "I was walking by and heard Gemma here regaling you all with the tale of my greatest defeat, so I thought I'd come over and hear her version of it." He scowled at Gemma, then gave her a quick wink.

She sat back down on the log next to me as Arthur left to the sound of applause and hoots of laughter from the men. Hearing such an entertaining story and then finding out it included our own beloved tribune was a rare treat!

"Who else has a story?" Someone asked, and from another fire, someone stood up, offering a tale he'd heard from a bard years ago about the duel fought between the Saxon warlord, Horsa, and Prince Catigern of Guarthigern at the Battle of Aylesford fifty years previously.

"Well, he's already getting that wrong," Gilbert grumbled. "Horsa and his brother Hengist were Jutes, not Saxons. I better go over there and help set the record straight after he sits back down," he said and stood up to go sit by the other contubernium's fire. Most of the rest of my tentmates shifted their attention as well, leaving Gemma and I with a moment to ourselves.

I finished weaving the last few rings into my mail while Gemma watched, absorbing every detail.

"They'll need to be riveted together at some point," I said, admiring my handiwork a few minutes later, "But a bit of butted mail is better than no mail at all," I grinned.

"A bit of what now?" Gemma asked.

I showed her my mail shirt. "Most soldiers around Britain only have butted mail, well, of the ones that have mail at all, anyway. The metal links are woven together, with each link connecting to four others, but with butted mail, the individual links still have a small break from where the smiths cut them to slip through the other links." I pulled a link from my pouch and held it up. "See? When the ends of the link are just pushed together, it's called butted mail. It's not bad, but the rings can separate over time, especially since there's usually a tiny gap where the ends meet. Even a lot of movement can cause rings to disconnect. Quality mail is riveted, like this." I held out my shirt for her to inspect. "The ends of the rings are riveted together, closing that gap completely. It makes the whole shirt much stronger. Probably what saved me from that sword cut."

"Nice," she said, nodding appreciatively. "This is lighter than I would have thought. May I try it on?"

I nodded, and she smiled at me. Then she undid the clasp to her cloak, removing it, before wiggling into my shirt, exclaiming "Ouch!" once when her long hair got caught in the mail. After a few moments, she got it on and stood up. She was nearly as tall as me, so the mail actually fit her rather well. The sleeves hung a little past her elbows, and the hem came down to just above her knees.

She rolled her shoulders. "You can tolerate wearing this for days at a time?" she asked, raising her eyebrows. "It's lighter than I'd thought, but I can definitely still feel the weight."

"It's not so bad if you belt it around your waist, then pull a bit of it out and let it hang over the belt," I said. "That displaces some of the weight."

"How do I look?" She grinned and stood tall with her hands on her hips.

"Like Queen Boudica, reborn," I said with a grin.

"Queen, who?" she asked.

"Boudica. She was a queen of the Iceni tribe, down in southeast Britain, who fought the Romans a long time ago."

Gemma looked pleased. Then she reached down, grabbed my shield, and dropped into a fighting stance facing me.

"Put a spear in your other hand, and you'd look rather fierce," I smiled back at her.

Her eyes twinkled, and she reached for my spear, leaning against our wagon. Then, she stopped and peered into the woods. "And who's this lovely thing?" she asked in a cooing tone.

I turned to look, startled.

"Mel!" I exclaimed with a grin. "Where have you been, girl?"

Mel's ears perked up, hearing her name. She stood only a few paces away and sniffed the air, then looked from me to Gemma.

"Mel's a dog that seems to be following me all over these God-forsaken ...." I stopped and looked over at Gemma, feeling guilty.

She glared at me for a moment, then back at Mel.

"What a sweet animal," she admired and walked up to Mel with her hands held out. Mel sniffed at them for a moment, then sniffed up and down Gemma's legs while she giggled. I just sat and watched, dumbfounded.

"Are you kidding me?" I finally asked, feeling simultaneously excited, annoyed, and just a bit jealous. "I've been feeding her and talking to her for over a week now, and she's only come that close to me once, but she lets you just dance right up to her ... and pet her?" I was astonished now, as Gemma was indeed scratching Mel's shoulders and rump, grinning broadly. Mel's tail wagged, and her mouth opened in what could only be described as a smile.

"What witchcraft is this?" I marveled.

"No witchcraft needed," Gemma said. She knelt down on one knee. Mel backed off for a moment, then sniffed at Gemma's face. Gemma grinned as Mel licked her a few times. "We girls just have an understanding, I guess."

I shook my head again, watching Gemma as she scratched away at Mel's flanks. This went on for a few minutes, and then a burst of laughter from my companions a short distance away startled the dog. She jerked her head up, alert, then cautiously loped off back into the woods.

"I like your friends," Gemma smiled, looking back at me.

"They like you too," I said. "Some may like you even more than me," I said, glancing off into the woods.

Gemma laughed. "Help me out of this mail?" she asked.

I did, and she wiggled her shoulders around as she slid out of the armor. "Much better," she sighed.

"Yeah, the weight takes a bit of getting used to," I said.

"Well, I should get going," Gemma said. "It's becoming dark now. I wouldn't want to give people the wrong impression, being seen in the camp so late at night."

I agreed. "I'll escort you to the great hall."

"Get your kit on when you leave the camp," Decanus Aylmer called out after me.

"I'm only walking to the fort and back," I protested.

"Doesn't matter. Arthur's orders. Anyone who leaves the camp, for any reason, does so with their armor and weapons."

I sighed, and Gemma helped me back into my mail. I belted on my sword and dagger, draped my cloak over my shoulders, then slung my shield across my back. Gemma handed me my spear and helmet with a wink.

Fully armed and armored, I escorted Gemma on the short walk to the fort.

"What you said back there about your uncle," I said. "Do you think you'd actually be able to return south with us?"

Gemma walked quietly for a moment, then answered, "What was the expression you said earlier? Better to ask forgiveness than permission?"

I looked down at her, surprised. She saw my look, and giggled. "I'm only a niece. If I were his daughter things could become... problematic? I could ride back with you, then write to him from your home."

"That would take months to send a letter and receive a response," I mused.

"Precisely," she said with a pleased smile.

"Eventually though, you will have to return, won't you?" I asked.

"Does that bother you so much?" she asked.

I felt my face and ears growing hot at the question, and at the intense look this beautiful girl was giving me.

"It does," I admitted.

Gemma stopped and took my hand in hers. By this time we were through the fortress gate and almost to the great hall. She gazed deeply into my eyes, and I looked back at her. Our faces were only inches apart. My heart was racing and I licked my lips, feeling excited, and frightened. Then suddenly, a horn blasted from the first, followed quickly by the second gatehouse along the northern wall, causing us both to jump.

"The Picts are attacking again!" I exclaimed. I turned to run back out of the gate, intent on rejoining my turma, but the guards posted there were already slamming the gate shut. Almost as quickly, from the other side of the northern wall, I heard multiple horn blasts that most certainly did not come from any of *our* instruments. Then came the sound of what must have been thousands of barbarians howling and screaming their war cries as they rushed the fort!

# Chapter Eighteen

Shouts of "To the walls!" and "Here they come again!" reverberated throughout the fort as the Picts charged.

"Get to the great hall!" I ordered Gemma, practically pushing her toward the building. She nodded and ran. Instinctively, I rushed toward the northern wall, toward the sound of the fighting.

There were already at least a hundred and fifty men manning it, with slings at the ready. The instant the Picts made themselves visible in the moonlight and the glow of the torches along the walls, the slingers began unleashing their missiles at the barbarians. Within moments of the alarm being sounded, another three hundred levies who'd all been dozing our lounging about at the base of the walls jumped up and scrambled up the earthen ramparts to man the walls along with me, and the slingers already there.

From my spot on the wall, I looked out at the oncoming horde. The sight that greeted me looked like something out of a nightmare. The entire landscape, at least what was visible, swarmed with Picts. Most had shields angled up facing us to ward off the slingstones being rained down on them by the levies. They sort of looked like an avalanche of multi-colored shingles pouring out of the darkness and surging up and over the outer ditch. It was in the steeper ditch at the base of our wall where the Picts were really getting cut down as they attempted to prop up ladders and climb up the wall to get at us. Just as many gamely attempted to scale it. They paid no heed to their comrades who were dropping left and right to our barrage. The trench around the base of the wall kept filling with more Picts, anxious to get at us.

More and more of our men filled the rampart as well, though, and it bristled with our spears. Then I heard a sickening "*thwack!*" and the soldier next to me fell backward, dead or unconscious. From all along the line, I heard the sound of stones hitting shields, clattering off the wall, and the more unnerving sound of stones smashing into bodies.

I ducked behind my shield just as two slingstones impacted hard against it.

"Get your shields up!" I screamed. The men beside me brought their shields up as stones continued to smack off of them. Few men fell now, but the barrage served its purpose, and suddenly Picts were climbing over the wall, stabbing at us over and around our shields. One spear thrust at me, straight towards my face! I ducked with a yelp and felt the blow impact on my shield. I countered by punching him with the boss of my shield. He staggered back, and I punched him again, knocking him backward off the wall. A spear thrust at me from the side. It was another Pict, still climbing up onto the wall. I knocked the spear aside and thrust at him with my own spear. It skewered him just under the sternum, and down he went, nearly taking my spear with him. I felt a familiar flash of pain in my side, but I pushed it to the back of my mind and focused on the Picts.

We fought desperately for several minutes. Every now and then, as a man grew tired or injured, he backed away from the wall, and the man behind him immediately moved up to take his place. If the man falling back were too injured to keep fighting, he would make his way down the rampart and to the great hall for medical care. Otherwise, he might just tear a bit of cloth from his cloak or the cloak of any dead men nearby, bandage himself up, and be ready to rotate up to the front as needed. Many in the second rank fought as well, thrusting their spears over the shoulders of their comrades in the front rank at any targets of opportunity that presented themselves. As we rotated to the rear, we also pulled our more severely wounded or dead comrades away from the wall and to the back edge of the rampart. We did this not just as a mercy to prevent our wounded from being trampled but also to get them out of our way so we could fight.

On one such occasion that I rotated back to the rear rank of the battleline, I glanced around, trying to get a sense of how the battle as a whole was going. I was near the northwest corner of the wall, so I had a good view of the shorter, west wall. Only two ranks fought along it, and very few casualties seem to have been suffered there. Contrasting that, those of us defending the longer north wall had to fight in three ranks along its entire length. I saw several bodies being dragged away, though whether they were dead or only severely wounded was impossible to determine. The east wall was over a hundred paces away, and so was barely visible in the moonlight. My gut feeling was that the Picts were focusing all of their effort on breaking through our north wall, though.

As my breathing slowed down to something akin to normal, I realized my side felt wet. I transferred my spear to my left hand and reached down, feeling my side. I held my hand up and saw blood. A fresh wave of pain hit me then, and I grimaced. My wound had apparently reopened. Tewdrig would doubtless be annoyed with me when I reported back to him later to have my side fixed up again.

Around me, many of the men were looking ragged and fearful.

"They just keep coming," one man next to me panted.

"We can't fight them forever," another said. I looked around, sensing the mood of the men and not liking it.

Some distance away to my right, the chieftain Garwlwyd fought alongside his men from atop the gatehouse of the northern wall. He was impossible to miss. He had a long sword in one hand and a tall banner in the other. And of course, he wore his wolf's pelt cloak with the head serving as a hood. In the moonlight, it made him appear as a cinbin, a terrifying wolf-man creature said to live in the deep woods. Even as I glanced his way, I saw his sword flash down on the head of an unfortunate Pict who'd been trying to climb over the wall; then he followed the attack by kicking the barbarian back down into his fellows below. Behind me, I saw Gemma assisting a man in putting a wounded levy on a stretcher and taking him back to the great hall. I also saw Lord Guinnion observing the battle from a window of the great hall. He wore a plumed helmet, an ornate suit of armor, and a sword belted at his thick waist. His armor was in pristine condition.

Somebody needed to do something, I thought, but Guinnion was too far in the rear and probably wasn't very inspiring anyway, and Garwlwyd was nearly on the other end of the wall.

"Men of Gododdin!" I called out. A few heads turned my way.

"Men of Gododdin!" I shouted as loudly as I could. My voice cracked from the effort. More men turned my way. In an odd way, the attention of all these men caused me greater unease than had I been in the front rank, fighting off Picts. What was I doing? I thought. I was no orator! But it was too late to shut up now. I held my shield up overhead, partially because it bore the Chi Rho but also because holding up my left arm hurt less than waving my right about.

"Take heart, men!" I yelled. "Look to your chief, Garwlwyd, fighting beside us like a wolf! Beyond the wall, Arthur and the Red Dragons ride against the Picts. They need but a little more time to get set! Would you flee like women when victory is so close?"

God bless her. Gemma heard me, as I'd hoped she would, and from the ground, she shouted up, "Who's fleeing? Not *this* woman!"

I glanced down and gave her a grin before turning my attention back to the men. They, too, had turned to glance down at Gemma upon hearing her voice. Though she was dirty and blood-stained from her work, there was no mistaking her femininity, even in the moonlight. Her long skirt, her curves, and her long hair, tied back though it was, gave her away readily enough.

Some of the men murmured and looked back towards the wall, where their comrades in the first rank were still thrusting away with their spears at the oncoming Picts.

"Think of your families at home!" I reminded them. "If you fail to stop the Picts here, they'll march onward and soon be at your doorsteps! Would you have these barbarians kill and enslave your kin?"

"No!" Many of the men shouted back and raised their spears in emphasis.

I shook my shield overhead. "Then be strong and take heart! And put your hope in the Lord! And at all costs, do not let these Pagans breach our wall!"

The men shouted and cheered and, to my relief, turned back to face the wall. Many of them even squeezed their way up to the front or did what they could in the second rank, thrusting at the enemy over the shoulders of their comrades with their spears. Satisfied that the line would hold, at least for a while longer, I took my own place back in line and watched for an opening.

Barely a few minutes later, I heard the new sound of horns over the din of the battle and heard a rumbling noise off in the distance.

"Is that thunder?" a man in front of me wondered.

I recognized the sound instantly and laughed, patting him on the back. "Only the thundering sound of my numerus!" I grinned at him. Apparently, the Red Dragons, and probably the mounted levy contingent, had circled wide around the Picts and were now doing what the Red Dragons did best- smashing into the barbarians' flank or rear.

I let out a whoop as shouts of confusion and alarm spread throughout the horde at the base of our wall. Oh, how I wished I could have gotten out of the gate earlier and joined them for the assault!

Despite the attack from the cavalry, the horde of Picts was large enough that the assault on the wall didn't let up. All too soon, the spearman in the first rank began calling for relief, and the men in the second rank stepped up to the wall. I stepped forward into the second rank as the man we relieved moved to the rear, bleeding and breathing in ragged gasps.

Once, while in the rear rank, a Pict vaulted over the wall, smashing the rim of his shield into the man in front of me. He staggered back into me. The man to the Pict's left attacked him, but the Pict blocked the spear thrust with his shield, then countered with his sword, felling the levy.

His *sword* ...

Before something intelligent could come to mind, I shouted, "He's mine!" In an instant, I dropped my spear, which would be completely unsuitable in the close fighting I was about to engage in, drew my sword, and lunged at the Pict.

My opponent saw me charge and actually grinned at me. He brought his shield up high and swung his sword low, aiming for my legs. I leaped to my right, evading both his shield and sword. This even gave me an angle on his side, and I thrust at him. He, too, dodged away, and my blade only grazed his side instead of punching through his ribs.

I thrust at him again, aiming for his face. He cocked his head to the side, narrowly avoiding my strike. Twisting the blade, I flicked it toward him in a tight chop. This man wore a helmet similar to my own, and my blade bounced off of it, but the impact staggered him. Seizing the moment, I slammed my shield into him, leaning my full weight into the attack, and knocked him further off balance. He fell to the ground. I made to attack again, but a spearman nearby, seeing the Pict fall, thrust down with his spear and killed the man. I was annoyed, I admit, but understood that this was a battle, not some pre-established one-on-one duel, so I shrugged and bent down to secure his sword, but the blade was kicked away as men shuffled and jostled around in the midst of the melee, and it skittered into a mass of soldiers' feet. I swore but scooped my spear back up and resumed my work on the wall, repelling Picts as they attempted to climb up to us.

After what seemed like an eternity, the Pict assault ended. One moment, they were swarming up their ladders to get to us, then horns from the woodline began blowing, and the barbarian horde that had been seething so relentlessly toward us began to melt back down to the ground and out into the woods. The levies on the wall began thrusting their spears into the air and shouting triumphantly.

I glanced around. Some primitive part of my brain or sixth sense screamed that we were in danger. "Shields up!" I shouted as loudly as I could. "Get your shields up!"

Many on the wall instinctively followed my order, automatically assuming that whoever was shouting orders must have the authority to do so and should, therefore, be obeyed. An instant later, several of the levies, who either didn't hear me or hesitated, began dropping to the ground as another hail of slingstones from the woods tore into our ranks. Our elevated position from the woodline down the hill, combined with partial illumination from the moonlight, allowed the Pict slingers to unleash a barrage on us with reasonable visibility and accuracy.

Now everyone on the wall either crouched down low or had their shields up. We stayed like that for a couple of minutes before, one by one, we lowered our shields, stood up, and looked out. The Picts were gone, but the cold night was not quiet by any means. Here and there, beyond the wall, voices screamed, groaned, or sobbed from the pain of their injuries. The last of our wounded were taken down from the ramparts. Left on their own for a brief time, I saw the men on the wall reacting in a myriad of different ways. Some laughed and cheered and boasted to their friends. Many others simply sat back down on the ramparts, exhausted. A few leaned over the walls and retched. Most picked their dirty cloaks off the ground where they'd discarded them in the heat of battle. As we calmed down, we began to feel the cold again. I heard the quiet sobbing of a few of the other men who'd lost friends or kin or were simply coming to terms with the sheer terror they'd felt during the fighting and suppressed at the time in order to function as they needed to. In the back of all of our minds was the knowledge that this battle was not over yet. Like this afternoon, the Picts had withdrawn, but nobody believed they were defeated.

None of these men were my friends, my cymbrogi, so I ignored them as they did me. I sat alone on the rampart and listened to the cries and moans of the wounded Picts out beyond the wall. I do not think of myself as cruel, and especially after becoming friends with Gemma, brief as my time with her had been up to this point, I found that I did not hate the Picts. Those men out there were my enemies, to be sure, but they were still men, probably not so very different than we ourselves. And so it wrenched at my heart, hearing the cries of the wounded out there in the cold, dark fields. I wanted to go down there and see if there was any aid I could render, but I was also unbearably exhausted. I had been up since before dawn, ridden from Din Eidyn to the fort, and fought the Picts that afternoon. Then, just as I'd thought I would finally be able to go to sleep, the Picts had attacked us again. To add to this, I'd lost blood from the wound to my side. I knew I should see to that, so I stood up and walked over to the great hall. Mercifully, I couldn't hear the moans of the enemy wounded from the hall.

Immediately outside the entrance, I saw a row of perhaps a dozen bodies draped in bloodied cloaks. Inside, at least twice that number of men sat against the wall, cradling injuries, waiting to be seen by the medicus.

"Gemma?" I called out. A few heads turned my way.

"Be with you in a moment!" she called out.

I headed toward the sound of her voice. There was a chamber off to the left-hand side of the dimly lit corridor. I was just about to enter when Gemma, on her way out, collided with me. We both staggered back.

"Hey, watch it," she exclaimed. Then she recognized me. "Peredur!" Gemma's face lit up into a broad smile. "You're alive!" Then she saw the blood at my side and her smile disappeared instantly. "And you're wounded again?"

"Same injury from before. It just reopened," I replied.

From inside the room, Tewdrig's annoyed voice called out, "What's that? Peredur, did you undo my sutures? What's the point of me sewing you up if you're just going to undo my work?"

"Apologies, Medicus," I said. "It wasn't really my intent to do so. Maybe you should take your grievance up with the Picts? They had more of a hand in the matter than I did."

Gemma rolled her eyes, then grabbed my shoulders and looked me up and down.

I did the same with her. She had splatters of blood on her face and hands. The sleeves of her dress were rolled up, and she wore an apron over her dress, which also bore dark red stains upon it. Clearly, she'd been as busy as I had tonight. Though while mine had been spent in the taking of lives, her time had been spent in saving them.

"You're well then, besides that one wound?" she asked, her eyes searching mine.

"Yes, I think so," I replied.

"Good. Then you can go find a place to sit against the wall over there and wait your turn. If your side is still bleeding, hitch up that belt of yours and cinch it down nice and tight over the wound. The pressure should make it stop."

As she'd said this, she turned me around and gently pushed me towards the wall. Before I could say another word, she spun around and went back into the chamber where Tewdrig was working on another soldier.

"Sorry about that, Tewdrig. Now, what can I do?" I heard her ask. She seemed to have fit right in with the Red Dragons, I mused. I found an empty spot as she'd directed and asked a nearby levy to help me out of my mail. I knew it would need to come off eventually anyway when it came time for Tewdrig to sew me back up. After that, I dozed off and on. Periodically, Tewdrig, with Gemma in tow, would come out, walk down the hallway, and assess who needed care the most urgently. They'd help somebody up and escort them into the surgical room. Finally, it was my turn.

"Good. You've already taken off your mail," Tewdrig noted. He offered his hand. I took it, and he helped pull me up. Tewdrig might be in his fifties, but he was a surprisingly strong man, and he fairly hoisted me right up off the ground.

I followed them into the room and sat on the chair Tewdrig gestured at. There was a table with bloody medical instruments on it, an oil lamp, and a bowl of water. A jug of mead was also there, and a small cup.

"Drinking on the job, Medicus?" I asked with a grin.

The old man glanced over at the jug and grunted. "That's for the patients, to help with the pain."

He wiped blood from his last patient on his apron and prepared to tend to me. In the meantime, Gemma helped me pull my tunic and undershirt off. Looking down, my side looked like a bloody mess. Loose bits of thread from the previous sutures poked out, and trails of crimson ran down to my hip.

"Well, it's not still bleeding at least. And didn't bleed too much, relatively," Tewdrig muttered as he looked my side over. "Gemma, if you please?"

Gemma nodded and unspooled a length of thread, deftly prepping a hooked bone needle. She held it up, about to pass it to the medicus, then paused. "May I try this time?" she asked. She sounded almost too eager to take on that particular task, I thought.

"You've been watching me closely, girl?" Tewdrig asked.

"Oh yes," Gemma said with a smile. "It doesn't seem so different from sewing cloth together. Aside from the blood."

"Well then, I don't see that it would be a problem," Tewdrig nodded.

I looked from one to the other. "Do I have a say in this?" I asked.

"No," they both replied at once.

"It's just a simple suture to a flesh wound. You'll be fine," Tewdrig grunted. "Now, lift your arm and hold still. He picked up an oil lamp from the table and held it near my side.

"I want a drink, at least, before she sews me up," I protested.

Gemma rolled her eyes, and the medicus set the lamp back down. He poured me a cup of mead, which I downed at once. Tewdrig picked the lamp back up, and Gemma bent down to my side, needle at the ready. Maybe it was the mead, but the excited gleam in her eye made her seem a bit ghoulish or something. I looked away and focused on not crying or passing out as she sewed.

Tewdrig pointed and gestured a few times while he watched Gemma work. I felt myself grow lightheaded, and my vision dimmed. She finished a short time later, at least when measured by the passing of the moon. To me, it felt more like an eternity.

"There," Gemma said cheerfully. "That wasn't so bad, was it."

"No, not too bad," I lied. My head slowly cleared up, and my vision returned to normal. Tewdrig chuckled and handed me another cup of mead. I took it gratefully and chugged it down.

"Alright, lad," he said. "Off you go. Do please try not to reopen these sutures again."

I nodded and weakly gave him a thumbs-up. Then I slipped back into my clothing, scooped up my mail and sword belt, and went back outside. It hit me then that it was actually a bit warmer than it had been for the past week. I looked around. As before, about a hundred men lined the north wall, a bit less than that manned the others, I guessed. The rest had returned to their tents, set up in the ruins closest to the walls.

I went over to the western gate. The guards were different this time.

"Could you crack open the gate a bit? I'm one of Arthur's men and need to return to my turma," I told them.

"Sorry," the older of the two said. "There's Picts out there, and our orders are not to open the gates for any reason, by order of Lord Guinnion."

"Exactly," I said. "It's regarding those Picts that I need to get out there. I have a message I need to deliver to the Dux Bellorum," I said, shamelessly dropping Arthur's title as the overall commander here.

"The who?" the man asked.

I gritted my teeth. This man was a northerner, scarcely different from the Picts on the other side of the wall. Of course, he didn't know formal Latin titles.

"The Duke of Battles," I tried again. "The man in charge of everyone here."

"Not me. I'm Penteulu Garwlwyd's man."

"Garwlwyd is Lord Guinnion's man. Here on this battlefield, Lord Guinnion is the Dux Bellorum's man," I said as patiently as I could.

"I don't know nothing about that," the guard said. "I'm pretty sure Lord Guinnion only answers to the king. And our king is King Leudon, not Arthur."

Under different circumstances, I might have just gone to the wall, hopped over the edge, and climbed down, bypassing this fool, but I really, really didn't want to risk opening up my wound again. I sighed and fished out a bit of silver from the thick leather pouch at my belt.

"Here," I said. "Here's a piece of hacksilver. Enough to celebrate properly over at the alehouse when this is over. Look, I'm not trying to get you into trouble or risk the lives of anyone in the fort. I just need you to lift the bar across this gate and open it enough for me to slip out."

The man gave me a thoughtful look and eyed the silver in my hand. "Alright," he said at last. "But if word of this gets out, and there's any kind of trouble because I let you out, I'll rat you right out to Garwlwyd, or Lord Guinnion, or whoever asks."

*I bet you won't tell them you took my silver, though,* I thought. "Fine with me," I said. "All I'm trying to do is rejoin my comrades who are just behind the fort a ways. I would have been out there with them earlier, but just as I was leaving the fort earlier, the damned barbarians attacked, and I had to fight in here instead."

"That would explain that nice chainmail and those spurs," he said, gesturing to my feet. "Not many of our lads have gear like that."

I grinned and dropped the silver into his hand. He slipped it into his own pouch and nodded to his companion. The two of them hefted the bar that bolted the gates shut and pushed the large, heavy door open. I slipped out, and immediately, the door shut behind me.

I listened, motionless for a few moments, ensuring that I was indeed alone here in the woods. When I heard nothing, I made my way along the wall, heading south. In short order, I saw the campfires from my numerus' camp. A roving guard called out as I got to within a hundred paces.

"Halt and identify yourself!" the guard said.

I halted and held my hands out. "It's Peredur," I said quickly. "Of Decurion Owain's turma."

"Your name sounds familiar," the guard acknowledged. Then, unexpectedly, he lowered his spear, pointing it towards me. "What's the Tribune look like?'

"Arthur? He's tall. Muscular. Short, light brown hair. Short beard ..."

"Alright, you're a cymbrog," the guard said, relaxing.

I nodded to him and made my way to the camp. I was desperately tired, but I had one thing I needed to check on first. Listening for the telltale stomping hooves and occasional neighing, I made my way over to the large corral.

"Carys," I called out quietly. "Carys?" I said again after a moment. I heard a whinny, and then Carys pushed through the herd, nuzzling my outstretched hand. I smiled.

"Glad to see you again, girl," I whispered. Carys pushed her muzzle against my face. I laughed and scratched at her jaws and neck for a bit. For the sake of peace of mind, I looked her over. She was fine, as I expected, but I had to be sure. I whispered good night to her, gave her a final pat, then found my contubernium's tent. Ducking inside, I carefully moved through the sleeping men until I found an empty space where my bedroll had been left. I'd barely entered the tent when the light patter of rain began to fall on the roof. Relieved that it had waited this long, I quietly set my equipment on the ground beside my bedroll, wrapped myself up in my blanket, and fell asleep.

# Chapter Nineteen

I woke the next morning from such a deep slumber that upon first opening my eyes, I had to think for a second to remember where I was. My father's estate in Caer Gurcoc? No. I heard birds chirping outside as my mind worked, slowly waking up. I heard my tentmates talking around me and yawning. Some of them were also waking up. The barracks of Caer Lleon? No. I was in a tent, not a wooden barracks. I heard someone mention the Celidon Coit. Oh yes, I remembered then. The woods of Caledonia. We were encamped behind the old Roman fort.

I sat up, wincing from the pain in my side. I glanced over at my bloodstained tunic and decided to clean my clothes. After all, I only had a couple of changes of clothes packed away in my bag in our turma's supply wagon. I pulled those out and put on a fresh undershirt, a dark gray tunic, light brown trousers, and my old cloak. Since the pond was just outside of camp, I knew I had to wear full kit, so I carefully donned my mail and armed myself, then headed outside with my soiled clothes draped over my shoulder.

As I stepped out of the tent, I almost collided with Gilbert, returning from his own trip to the woodline. Something about him seemed a bit off.

"Hey, you leaving camp?" he asked.

"Just to the edge of it, to clean some clothing," I said.

"That can wait. Owain wanted a word with you when you'd woken up."

"Oh? What's up?" I asked.

"You got trapped inside the fort last night when the Picts attacked?"

"Yes. Why?"

"So you weren't there when it happened," Gilbert said, shifting his weight a bit. Something was troubling him, and he was clearly reluctant to talk about it.

"What's going on? Is the Decurion mad at me about something?" I demanded. In the back of my mind, I remember how I'd paid off the guard last night to let me out through the gate. Surely that wasn't a problem, was it?

"Aylmer's dead," Gilbert said flatly.

"Dead?" I echoed. I was shocked. How could that be? I'd seen him just last night. Last night ... before the Picts' assault. "No ...." I whispered, stunned.

Gilbert nodded solemnly. "He died last night as we charged into the Picts.

"God have mercy," was all I could think to say for a moment. "Who's the new decanus then?"

"Owain hasn't named one. If I were to wager on it? I'd say it will be you."

"Me?" I was startled. "I've only been in the turma for a few months. Same as you. I would think Aeron or Marcus would get the spot. They've been in for a couple years or so."

Gilbert shrugged. "I don't make the decisions around here. For what it's worth, I think you'd be a fine pick, though."

"Thanks," I said. "Has Aylmer been buried yet?"

"Yes. Last night. We buried him next to the other soldiers who died yesterday. Aylmer didn't die alone. Galhault lost one of his boys. Cai lost two of his."

I walked towards Owain's tent, and Gilbert came with me. I ran my fingers through my hair as I processed the news. To be honest, I had very mixed feelings. A part of me was saddened by the knowledge that three of my cymbrogi, four counting the one who'd died the previous afternoon, were now dead. Another part of me was profoundly relieved that at least they weren't people I'd known and been close to, like Gilbert, for instance. Aylmer was a good enough soldier, and I'd born him no ill will, but he'd also been a bit of an odd one and, honestly, annoying. Everyone in the turma thought so, too. What rattled me the most was how suddenly Aylmer had died. He was there with us just last night; then I went to the fort. The very next morning, I was told he was dead.

"... You do not even know what will happen tomorrow. You are a mist that appears for a little while and then vanishes," I muttered.

"What was that? Gilbert asked.

"Nothing. Just a passage from the letters of Saint James," I said.

"Ah. My people pray to Woden," Gilbert said.

"And you?" I asked.

"Sometimes, but I pray to the Christian God, too. And sometimes I think that Woden and your God are the same."

"I suppose it's possible," I said. "The Romans loved making comparisons between their gods and others. The Holy Church does it, too. That's why the old festival of Samhain is being replaced with All Saint's Day. Other holidays are being merged too, I think."

"And the celebration of the birth of your God's son," Gilbert added.

"Jesus, the Christ," I said.

"Yes. Him. A long time ago, your priests started holding mass to celebrate the birth of your Christ each winter, just after the solstice. Now there's nearly as many Saxons who pray to Jesus Christ as to Woden. And statues of Woden or even Jupiter are repurposed and placed at altars along with the cross of Jesus."

We reached Owain's tent, which was the same size as the ones used by the contubernia but was his alone. Our draco standard was planted firmly into the ground at the tent's entrance. Gilbert wished me luck, then left, leaving me alone at Owain's tent.

"Decurion? Peredur reporting as ordered," I announced.

There was some shuffling from inside, and then Owain appeared, pushing the tent flap aside. He smiled when he saw me. That was a good sign, at least, I thought.

"Peredur, glad you could rejoin us. I understand you got stuck inside the fort with those poor ground-pounding levies last night."

I smiled at his use of the slightly mocking term commonly used among the men of the numerus to refer to infantry, who have to walk everywhere. "Indeed, sir," I said. "I made myself useful, though. I fought on the north wall."

"I've heard," Owain said and looked thoughtfully at me. "I've also heard that on at least one occasion, you ordered the men around you to get their shields up just in time to receive a slinger barrage. You might have saved a lot of lives last night."

I shrugged. "It was nothing, sir. I just did what I thought needed to be done. And there was nobody else giving any orders on that part of the wall at the time."

"So you stepped up," Owain said. "By all rights, being previously wounded, you could have stayed by the great hall and held back. Nobody would likely have noticed."

The very idea offended me, and I recoiled. "Sir! I could never have done that," I protested. "Let the levies fight and just sit back, knowing I was better armed, better trained than they were, and knowing how badly they could use every man available?"

Owain smiled and nodded. "So instinctively, you throw yourself into the fighting when it's presented and take the initiative to lead when you see there's an absence of leadership. And you gave intelligent, timely commands."

"Decurion, I-" I started to protest, but Owain held up a hand.

"No more modest protesting. Humility is a good quality, Peredur, but in excess, it can become as annoying as arrogance. Keep that in mind."

"Yes, Decurion."

"Good. Now, I assume you've heard the unfortunate news regarding the death of Aylmer?"

"I have," I answered.

"His death leaves your contubernium without a decanus. I've conferred with Cornelius, and we're both in agreement that between you, Gilbert, and the others, you show the most initiative and the quick intelligence a leader needs. Not to mention resourcefulness. Maybe this will help dampen that humility a bit,"

Owain added with a slight smirk. "Arthur himself was impressed by your little adventure in the wilderness. You made yourself into a decoy, allowing Gilbert to accomplish your mission of passing on my message to Arthur that night before the battle in the forest. You survived that, you survived the forest, and you managed to find an asset who was able to provide critical information that may have prevented a successful invasion of Gododdin. You did that, Peredur,"

I admit, I squirmed a bit at that. I felt that most of the accomplishments he was praising me for had occurred more to sheer luck and the grace of God than any heroic actions on my part, but I knew the Decurion wouldn't want to hear that, so I stayed silent.

"In recognition of all that, effective immediately, you're the new decanus of your contubernium. When a position opens up, don't be surprised if you end up being made a duplarius."

I was stunned, not so much by being made a decanus. I'd suspected that was where this had all been leading to, but duplarius? Now that I'd not seen coming.

Owain must have read the shock on my face because he chuckled. "Calm down, *Decanus*. Focus on the present."

I nodded. "Was there anything else, Decurion?"

Owain shook his head. "Not right now. You can go back and relax with the rest of the men, but stay near the camp and be ready for action."

"Yes, sir," I said and left.

I returned to my section's tent and told them the news. Nobody was surprised. I passed on the word that we needed to stay nearby and ready for combat, then grabbed my clothes and headed down to the pond to finally clean my clothes. I was nearly done when I heard something moving in the woods, not far away. I jerked my head up, and there was Mel.

"Mel!" I said with a laugh. "Well, I haven't seen you in a bit. How have you been, girl?"

Mel came up to me, whining softly and wagging her tail. She hung back for a moment, staring expectantly at me. It dawned on me. In virtually every other encounter I'd had with her, I'd had food to give her.

"Sorry, girl," I chuckled. "I've no food on me this time."

Mel cocked her head at me. I finished washing my clothes, talking with her as I scrubbed them clean and wrung the water out of them. Mel sat on her haunches and just continued to watch me, occasionally whining and licking her lips noisily. Finally, when I was done, I stood and turned towards camp.

"Well, girl, I can get you food, but you'd have to come with me." I started walking up the slope, then looked back at the dog. "Come on, girl," I encouraged.

Mel whined again and took a hesitant step forward.

"Your choice," I said and kept walking.

I only went another few paces before I glanced down, and there was Mel, walking beside me. I grinned. Like her ancestors ages ago, it seemed that Mel had finally decided to trade freedom in the wild for the comforts of civilization, and a regular supply of food. I did wonder if she would actually follow me all the way back into the camp. With every step I took, I half expected her to stop and go back into the forest as she'd always done, but she didn't, and within a couple of minutes, we were at my section's tent.

"I should probably ask our decanus if I can get a bite of food for you," I looked down at Mel, still right there by my side, and grinned again. "Oh wait, that's me. So I guess it's all right." I chuckled at my own joke and rummaged through the various baskets until I found one with packets of dried, salted pork. I opened the packet, pulled out a single strip, and tossed it to Mel.

"Here's your reward for braving our camp," I said. She laid down and began gnawing on it, with the strip of meat between her paws.

"It's nearly as tough as leather, but it's food. And the flavor's not bad."

As I fed her, Gilbert and some of the others gathered around, staring at her in delight.

"Peredur, you got us a dog on your first day as the new decanus?" he asked with a grin.

"Maybe," I said. "If you lads don't crowd her too close and scare her off! Give her space!"

The men backed off a bit.

"She'll be thirsty after eating that salted meat," Gilbert said thoughtfully. He went back into the tent and came back a moment later with his helmet and canteen. Mel made short work of the meat and stood up, glancing around warily at the lot of us. Gilbert, meanwhile, poured some water from his canteen into his helmet and crouched down.

"Here you go, girl," he said softly. "What's her name?" he asked me.

"Mel," I said.

"Mel? Seriously?" Marcus scoffed. "I suppose it was more original than naming her 'Hound' at least."

I just shrugged and ignored him. I was too happy just to have Mel here, actually in our camp. For her part, Mel walked slowly over to Gilbert, who stayed motionless while she sniffed his hands and around him for a moment, then she plunged her muzzle into the water he offered and messily lapped it up.

As it was closing in on noon anyway, the men pulled out food from the wagon and restarted the cooking fires soon after I brought Mel in. She remained the center of attention, however. First, they tested to see if she would play fetch with the sticks they brought to build their fires. She didn't. Would she fight over a stick? When we tried, she seemed to show some interest, but only minimally.

"I'm fairly certain she's only here for our food," Gilbert chuckled. "And who could blame her? Look at her. You can almost see her ribs."

So, as we boiled up some dried vegetables and made gruel with the wheat and some other ingredients, we took turns tossing her bits of stale bread and cheese. In short order, Mel lost all hesitation about coming over to one or any of us. Once the rest of the men had dipped into the large pot we all ate from and dished up their own servings, I finally helped myself. A downside to becoming Decanus is that as a leader, I was expected to eat last. I had no idea of how other armies did this, but it was something I'd learned the Red Dragons, at least, adhered very strictly to when in the field, as we were now. So I was just starting to dig into my food when Mel, who'd been laying out by the fire, suddenly sat up and barked at something over my shoulder.

I turned to look and then immediately stood up. It was Owain, and behind him, Arthur. "What's this then?" Arthur asked, looking a bit amused. "Recruiting new members into your contubernium, Decanus?" he asked.

I felt my cheeks and ears growing warm. "I hope you don't object to her, sir?"

Arthur laughed. "My own hound is in my tent, sleeping. You remember Duplarius Cavall Magmus Augustus, right?"

I grinned. "I couldn't ever forget him, Tribune."

As we talked, Mel came over and cautiously sniffed at Arthur and Owain, who ignored her.

"We came to talk to you about a mission tonight," Owain said.

"A mission?" I asked. He had my full attention now. I noticed that the two were looking around at the men, and couldn't help but think how this felt just a little bit like a surprise inspection, along with whatever other cause they had to visit me here, rather than send for someone to bring me to them.

"Yes." Owain replied. "We want you and your contubernium to sneak in and take a peek at the Picts' encampment tonight. Think you can handle that?"

"What do you want us to find out?" I asked.

"What's their posture, mostly," Owain said. "They've attacked the fort twice now and been beaten back twice, but last night, they carried off a lot of their dead and wounded, so we don't know how badly they're hurt. For that matter, we only have a loose idea of exactly how big their army even is. We estimate that their first attack might have numbered around four thousand. Guinnion says his men counted about three hundred dead barbarians from yesterday's attack when they piled up the bodies in front of the fort. It's much harder to estimate last night's tally. There were only about fifty or so bodies, but we could have killed or wounded three or four times that number. Or fifty might actually be all the damage we did, though I doubt it."

"So, assess their manpower and determine whether it looks like they'll attack soon or not?" I summarized.

"Yes," Owain agreed. "Oh, and if you can, determine how they're situated on food. This is more the Picts' land than ours, this far north, but even they can't live off the land. Not at this time of year and with an army of this size."

"I have an odd request then, but I think it will greatly improve my contubernium's effectiveness," I said.

"Let's hear it," Arthur chimed in.

"Let me bring Maithgemm along. She-"

"You want to bring along a girl? On a scouting mission? Are you mad?" Owain cut in.

Arthur put a hand on Owain's shoulder, stopping him. "Why?" he asked.

"She speaks the Pict language as well as Gaelic. So she might be able to make it easier for us to get close to their camp. And if we can, she can give us an idea of what they're discussing. Secondly, she can pinpoint what tribes the Picts belong to. That means she can give you an idea of whether that army out there is one massive warband from a single tribe, like the Caledonii, or two, three, or four warbands from as many tribes as the warband you destroyed in the forest was."

"He makes a good argument," Arthur said, glancing over at Owain.

"You've traveled with her already," Owain said. "Can you tell me, honestly, that she won't get in the way? That she can be quiet and keep up?"

"She's not as good of a horseman as us," I admitted, "But she's a quick learner. And she's smart. She talked our way out of that Pict camp when we ran into King Drest as smoothly as a priest collecting alms."

Arthur and Owain smiled. "Would you bet your men's lives on her?" Arthur asked. "Because at the end of the day, every decision you make, from here on out, needs to be considered with that perspective. Can you accomplish your mission, and will your decision make it more or less likely that your men will come back alive?"

"In that case, Tribune," I said, "It is my firm belief that bringing Gemma along on this specific assignment will both aid us on our mission and make it more likely that we will all make it out alive."

"Then that's the end of it. She goes, assuming she's willing," Arthur added. "She's literally not one of my men." Owain and I smiled at the jest.

"She's sworn no oath of fealty yet to either me or any king under High King Conanus," Arthur continued. "Until such time as that, she's under no obligation to us."

"I'll go ask her now," I said. "With your permission?"

"Go. And be quick. You'll need time to brief the rest of your men, though I suspect, based on how quiet it got the moment we showed up, that they've been listening this whole time ...." Arthur glanced around, and I saw a wicked grin flash across his face when he saw my tentmates. I did as well and laughed.

Marcus was slowly brushing Mel and feeding her small bites of cheese, facing sideways to us. Gilbert was sitting on a log, whittling very slowly. The others were playing the quietest game of dice that had ever been played. All of them had the most carefully blank expressions on their faces, having been caught listening in.

Arthur turned back to me, smirking. "I'll leave you to it. I want your contubernium out of the gate no later than dusk." Then he stepped up, speaking quietly, "I want to strike the Picts at dawn and end this fight decisively tomorrow, but whether we attack or continue to sit back and defend the fort will depend heavily on your report. So keep that in mind tonight."

"I won't let you down, my lord. *We* won't let you down."

"I'm counting on you," Arthur told me, and with a pat on my shoulder, he and Decurion Owain strode away.

"Alright, lads, gather around. You can quit pretending to be busy now," I told them. They grinned at me.

"You heard Arthur and Owain, so I won't rehash the mission. Pack what you need. Make sure your kit is secure, nice, and tight. We need to be able to move quickly and quietly. No helmets. No shields. Top your canteens off before we leave. I don't even want to hear water sloshing around. I'm heading out to recruit Gemma for this. You lads have already met her, but just as a reminder, don't get any wrong ideas about her. She's a lady. Treat her as one of us, *not* as some camp follower. Understand?"

The men nodded, and I dismissed them to prepare for our mission while I headed off to the fort. I wasn't overly surprised to see that Mel got up and followed along.

*****

Gemma was delighted to see that Mel was actually with me when I approached the great hall asking for her. The two shared a warm greeting while I told Gemma what I needed her for that night. To my utter lack of surprise, she agreed to come along almost before I'd even finished outlining our plan.

I didn't tell her about Arthur's planned dawn attack. That seemed to be something he wanted to be kept secret. I'd assumed I would need to provide her with clothes she could wear for the mission, but she'd planned ahead, back at Din Eidyn, and once I told her about the mission, she disappeared into the great hall, where she and Tewdrig stayed. I noticed that her hair was in a braid today. That was good- practical for what she'd been doing recently and would be doing this evening. She came back out a few minutes later. In place of her cream-colored dress, she wore a long dark green tunic, belted, and with a dagger at her side. Under this, she wore a pair of gray trousers. What really drew my attention was that over the tunic, she wore a quilted linen shirt of a similar type that many soldiers wore. It was a perfect choice of armor for a slim girl such as her, who was unaccustomed to wearing armor and didn't expect to actually engage in hand-to-hand combat but should have at least some protection. And as a bonus, since it was linen, it was quiet. I examined her armor appreciatively.

"Excellent choice!" I said. "Tewdrig advised you to get this?"

"He did. Even though we didn't expect me to ever actually fight, he thought having some protection against stray arrows or slingstones couldn't hurt."

"Good linen armor is pretty good against blade slashes, too," I added.

"What's in the pouch?" I asked, pointing at a large leather pouch at her hip.

She beamed and listed off the items as she pulled them out to show me. "A sling. A smaller pouch with some stones. A piece of flint. A spool of thread. A few needles for sutures, a roll of linen cloth for bandages, another small pouch with some millefolium plant to make a salve if I need to..."

"Got a canteen?" I asked.

The blank, vaguely panicky look on her face told me she'd overlooked that little detail. I smiled at her. "Don't worry. We probably have a couple of spares in our supply wagon. Have you used that new dagger much?" I asked.

"A bit. I used it to help cut clothes and bandages the other night."

"It should still be sharp enough, then," I said. "Grab your cloak. And tell Tewdrig you'll be gone for the night. You may as well come back with us as soon as you're ready to go."

We returned to the Red Dragons' camp, and after finding a canteen for Gemma, we were all set to work planning our operation. We also provided her with a short spear, just in case. At her specific request, I gave her a trio of throwing darts as well, which she tucked into her belt. We agreed that the Picts were likely camped fairly close, but since we only had a general idea where, we decided to take horses.

"If we knew exactly where they were, I'd say we could walk and maintain a lower profile, but since we don't know their exact location, we need the speed the horses can provide," I reasoned.

They'd attacked us less than an hour after the sun had set the previous night and carried off many of their dead and wounded. And most of their army was on foot. This suggested that they probably weren't more than a few miles away. It was also a safe assumption that they were, broadly speaking, north of us.

We continued to plan. We also rolled up some dried meat to take with us. Gemma gave a short lesson, teaching us a few useful phrases in the most widely used Picti language. Lastly, I spoke with Sawyl and persuaded him to keep his section in the tent beside ours quiet so we could get some rest before our mission. I also asked him to wake us when evening was drawing near. Then we went into our tent and took a short nap. We were going to be in for a long night, after all. The tent was full, so Gemma elected to doze against a tree nearby. Mel curled up not far away from her.

# Chapter Twenty

I t was a typical, cloudy sky that evening, though the sun was thankfully visible, mostly. A cold wind blew across the landscape, but even with that, it wasn't as cold as it had been in the previous weeks. The snow, which Gemma told me had come unusually late, was all but gone, and spring was coming on with full force now. We still wore our cloaks in the colder period between dusk and dawn, though.

I led my unit out of the fort at a canter as the sun touched against the western horizon. Gemma rode beside me, and the rest filed behind us. Owain, Arthur, and Ector were there at the gate to see us off. Owain had me brief him quickly on my plan. It met his approval, and we rode out. About a mile out from the fort, there was a long stream that angled generally northeast. I decided we should ride parallel or "handrail" the stream on a hunch. We slowed to an easy trot and fanned out in a wide skirmish line. This let us cover more ground as we searched for the camp and made us a bit harder to spot than if we'd stayed clustered together. And if the camp was where we suspected, we'd approach it from the west, with the remnant of a brighter sky hiding the ground in darkness. This would make it even more unlikely that guards around the camp would spot us before we could spot them. Once we'd slowed down, I also noticed that not far behind us came Mel, loping along. I smiled but stayed focused on our mission.

One of the things Gemma had also taught us back at camp was the mating call of the cuthag bird. We would use this to signal to the others when we needed to get the group's attention. It had an amusing "coo coo" sound and was easy to imitate. We would use the call of another bird with a funny curved beak, called a gylfinir, only as an emergency. If we heard the cuthag, followed immediately by a gylfinir's "kurr-eee" call, we were all to displace immediately and regroup back at the fort.

The sun was going down fast as it set behind us. Another mile after we began following the stream, Gilbert called out. *"Coo-coo. Coo-cooo."*

The rest of us stopped and glanced over at him. Saying nothing, Gilbert simply pointed off into the distance. I looked, and after a moment, I saw columns of a dozen small fires just on the other side of a large stretch of woods, about a quarter of a mile away. I thrust my spear into the air and made a circular motion with it. That was the visual signal for the men to rally around me. As they did, we dismounted. Only once we were gathered around in a tight circle was I willing to speak.

"That smoke looks like it's just on the other side of those trees," I said in a low tone. "Marcus, you and Aeron stay here with our horses. The rest of you, let's go. Fan out. Have your spears ready in case guards spot us before we spot them. Use the terrain to hide your approach. And stay alert."

I turned to Aeron and Marcus. "If we aren't back within two hours, or if you see the Picts acting up before we've returned, you take our horses and get back to the Tribune. Tell him we found their camp but were probably spotted."

The pair nodded, and then the rest followed me as I headed out towards the woods. A few minutes later, we spotted their screen line. We crouched down into the brush, still a couple hundred paces away. Past them, deeper into the woods, we could pick out the hundreds of tents that made up the Pict army, camped along the stream.

I signaled Gemma and the men of my section, and we cut across to the north and huddled together behind a cluster of trees along the bank of the stream.

"Let's use the stream, follow it up, and get eyes on the camp," I said.

"What about their guards?" Gilbert asked.

"They're spread out. I think we can either sneak past their screen line, but if they're too alert, or the brush isn't dense enough for us to sneak past ..." I looked over at Gemma. "Think you could distract a guard long enough for one of us to take him out?"

Gemma stared hard at me. "Just what do you have in mind?"

"I don't know. That's for you to figure out, but you have a better chance than any of us- we'd be attacked on sight. As a girl, guards would likely want to at least question you first before they did ... anything else," I finished.

"Fine," she grumbled. "Lead the way."

I ignored her less-than-enthusiastic tone and headed off, followed by my seven contubernales, with Gemma in the rear. Unless we counted Mel, who was also following along, not far behind us all. I wasn't that worried about her, though. Mel was a pretty quiet dog, and it wouldn't raise much alarm if she was spotted. Wild dogs weren't too uncommon of a sight.

We crept along slowly, practically on our hands and knees, and being as quiet as we could. I probably didn't need to take as many of the lads with me, but it had been a tough call. Was it better to take fewer men and have a better chance of sneaking up on the camp unseen but being more vulnerable? Or was it better to take more men, have more sets of eyes to watch for threats, and have a better chance of fighting our way back to the fort if we were seen? I'd asked Owain about it. He'd acknowledged the advantages and disadvantages of both options but ultimately left the decision to me. After my experience in the woods, I'd decided I would feel more comfortable having the lads with me.

It was a good thing we'd left our shields at camp, at least. Perhaps taking a javelin or two each would have been better than our long spears, though, I considered as we moved.

I would have to remember that next time. Then I smirked to myself. Next time I happened to need to sneak through a creek bed to avoid being seen by barbarian guards? When was that likely to happen again?

We got a hundred paces closer to the camp. The water from the stream helped mask our movement, though we were making very little noise. Then we came upon a guard. The foliage ahead wasn't very thick, and it wasn't dark enough for us to slip past without being seen. I turned to Gemma.

"You're up," I whispered to her. "Get him to turn his back to us so we can take him out."

She arched an eyebrow at me, and one corner of her mouth pulled back into a slight frown, then she nodded. Since then, I've come to recognize that look all too well. It's a look that warns that she is about to scrap my carefully made plan and improvise. Thankfully, she was as good at improvisation as I was good at planning. We complimented each other well in that way. I didn't know this about her at this moment, however. Not fully. So then and there, I was first confused, then aghast and angry when she grabbed a stick, waved it to Mel, and tossed it into the woods instead of drawing the guard's attention directly.

Mel hesitated for a moment, then bolted after it. The guard noticed the dog and was immediately alert, but his eyes were on Mel. In a moment, Gemma, who must have already had her sling out, had loaded a rock into the pouch and began spinning the sling around. The guard cocked his head. He heard the whirling of her sling, but before he'd had time to realize what he heard, Gemma loosed her stone. It impacted into the guard's head, and he collapsed with a soft grunt. I glared at her, but she wasn't looking at me. She was scanning the woods. By this point, Mel had returned to her, the stick in her mouth and her tail wagging. Gemma ignored Mel, however, and loaded another stone. I glanced out into the woods, then back at Gemma.

"What are you doing?" I hissed at her.

"Distracting the guards for you," she whispered, still not looking at me.

Beside me, Gilbert made a slight snorting noise, as somebody does who is suppressing a laugh. I glared at him. As I did, Gemma spun her sling around again. She loosed another stone. We all turned our heads in the direction she'd sent her stone in time to see a guard who'd been seated on a log, some forty paces away, rock backward and collapse to the ground.

"We should be clear now," she said quietly.

I opened my mouth to chastise her but saw the sorrowful, almost sickly look on her face. So instead, I just asked, "Are you going to be alright?"

She seemed to barely hear me. Instead, she looked at the guards, down at her hands, and dropped to her knees.

"I'm assuming she's never killed anyone before?" Gilbert whispered beside me.

"She probably killed a Pict a few days ago on our ride to Din Eidyn," I said. "But then she only threw a dart as she rode away. A lot was going on then, and she didn't stick around to see the body."

I made my way down the line and over to her. She was breathing rapidly and looked to be on the verge of tears. "It gets easier," I tried to comfort her. Even as I said this, images of the men I myself had killed flashed before my eyes, and suddenly, I wasn't so sure it actually did, but it was something I'd always heard veterans like Owain say. I certainly hoped it was true right then.

Gemma looked over at the guards' bodies, covering her face with her hands. "I don't want it to," she said. "I barely even thought about that Pict on the trail. You were in danger, and I acted on instinct. That ..." she gestured to the guards, "that was harder."

"You did well, at least. Really well."

She dropped her hands and gave me a thin smile. "As a slave, I had to protect our flocks. I learned to get good with a sling. I've killed animals before- some because they would have killed our livestock, others for food. I'd hoped this wouldn't feel any different."

"Next time, stick to distraction and let us do the killing, yes?" I suggested.

Her smile faded. "Maybe," she stressed. I recognized then that her 'maybe' probably meant something more like 'sod off'. Time would prove me correct in this, of course.

"Are you good to keep going now?" I asked. I sympathized with her, but we were in a bit of a hurry." She wiped her eyes, then nodded to me.

"Alright, cymbrogi, let's move," I whispered as I made my way back to the head of the line. "It's getting dark, but it's only a matter of time before those dead guards are discovered."

Gemma took her place back at the rear of our line, with Mel beside her. I resumed my place in the lead, and we continued on. A few minutes later, we came into view of the camp.

It was huge. Virtually all open space for over a quarter of a mile was filled with tents or other improvised shelters. Because tents simply filled up whatever space wasn't too thickly overgrown with shrubbery and trees, I couldn't see the entire camp from our vantage point along the bank of the stream. There seemed to be no uniformity between the shelters and any apparent organization of the camp. I said as much to Gemma.

"Not completely true," she said, surveying the camp beside me. "The camp is made up of various tribes, just as the kingdom as a whole is. Within each tribe are warbands of different villages. This isn't so much one big camp as it is five or six smaller camps, all located together."

Just then there was a rustling in the brush some thirty feet away, and we heard a voice speaking softly. Mel began to growl. Instantly, our attention was on the brush, spears held up and ready to throw. A moment later, a man emerged from where he'd been squatting and was pulling his pants up. He was facing the camp and therefore didn't see us, crouched down on his right.

Myself and two others instantly saw that he was a Pict. He turned and saw us, and with surprising speed, drew a sword and raised it. As his mouth was opening to shout, three spears slammed into him, and he merely grunted instead. Still keeping low against the stream's embankment, I rushed at him, drawing my own sword. He collapsed to the ground, gasping for breath. His eyes darted from me to the camp. I thrust my blade through his throat, ensuring a quick and, more importantly, silent death.

301

My heart was racing, and I looked around, frightened of the possibility that he might have companions nearby or that we had been seen, but the woods were quiet, and within the camp, no alarms were raised. Men talked and laughed as they'd been doing.

I sighed with relief. I thought to secure the man's sword, but when I looked around, it was nowhere to be seen. I rolled him onto his side, checking to see if he'd fallen on it. No sword. Then I noticed how close his hand was to the water. I had a sinking feeling, so to speak, and looked over at Gilbert as he retrieved his spear.

"Did you happen to see where this barbarian's sword went?" I asked.

"He dropped it in the stream when we killed him," Gilbert replied. "Why?"

I sighed. Another chance gone. "I owe Sextus a sword," I muttered.

"I'm sure you'll have more chances," Gilbert smirked.

"Maybe you should forget about collecting swords and focus on the camp over there?" Gemma suggested, sounding a bit impatient.

"Agreed," Gilbert and I said in unison.

We hid the dead Pict's body, then while two of the lads kept a lookout for more unexpected enemies coming from away from the camp, Gemma, Gilbert, and I focused back on the camp. Once again, I found myself unable to distinguish between the different tribal groups, though I did notice that the camps were indeed loosely organized into a few distinct clusters. These clusters, or smaller camps, generally consisted of about two dozen tents and other shelters. There was no uniformity in size. This, in turn, made it hard to determine how many men belonged to each cluster. Were the bigger tents the private quarters of wealthier chieftains within the tribes? Or were they used to shelter numerous warriors? More than likely, the answer was "both", but who could tell which tent was used for warriors and which for individual men of status?

One thing we all noticed, that Gilbert grimly pointed out, was that a few of the tent clusters had poles thrust into the ground, with recently decapitated heads tied to them. Most were certainly from our own numerus or the levies, but a few, older heads, had long, matted hair and were clearly women.

"Barbarians," I growled.

"Which tribes do you see?" Gilbert asked Gemma.

"All of them," she responded dryly.

"None absent?" I asked, surprised.

"None would dare refuse King Drest," Gemma said.

I tried to envision any of our southern kings mustering an army comprised of every single kingdom and failed to. Sure, the Red Dragons had nobles made up from all over western and even central Britain, but to muster troops from all of them at one time? I doubted even our High King, Conanus, had enough clout to force all of the Brittonic kingdoms to muster troops for any kind of common cause. As Decurion Owain had explained to us on our long ride north, we'd ridden north to aid Gododdin for three reasons. Arthur hoped that defending King Leudon would strengthen their ties to those of us in the southern kingdoms. Secondly, if the Gododdin ever grew too weak to resist the Picts, eventually, the barbarians could become a bigger threat to us in the south. We already had enough to deal with from westward expansion from the Saxons and the Gaelic raiders from their western island, Hibernia. The final reason, Owain had acknowledged, was Arthur's familial connection.

We continued to scan the portion of the camp that was visible to us. Men were walking about, talking and laughing. Some chopped down trees from immediately nearest the camp, and others were building fires, in addition to the ones already going when we arrived.

"They seem to be in good spirits for an army that's gotten thrashed twice now," one of the lads, named Ambrose, said.

I agreed. That worried me. Yes, this army was large and could absorb a lot of punishment before it was truly beaten, but still. Watching the men working, socializing, and going about their business didn't give me a sense that they were a beaten army. Not by half.

"I'm guessing that big cluster of tents there ..." I pointed some distance off to what could be the center of the camp, "Is that Drest?"

"Most likely, him and his family members and household guard," Gemma agreed.

"Do you see anything unusual about the camp?" I asked.

"Other than its size? No, not really," she said.

Gilbert pointed at something in the camp. "What are those piles of thin logs there? And there?"

I looked and saw what he was talking about. The two tribal camps closest to us, only about three hundred paces away, had stacks of long, thin longs on their outskirts.

"Fencing, maybe?" I asked. That didn't make sense, though. They were the invaders here. Surely, they didn't plan on building defenses. We continued to watch the camp, trying to glean whatever additional information we could. I began to grow restless. I'd give Marcus and Aeron a time limit of two hours. And there were the guards that Gemma had killed. We couldn't stay here much longer.

Then Ambrose nudged me and pointed at something by the edge of the woods far to our left. Two Picts with axes were cutting down a pair of tall, thin trees. Several more were chopping branches off of some trees that had already been cut down and smoothing them down into usable logs, but usable for what purpose? Another few moments went by, and we saw the Picts taking those branches, stripping them of twigs, and then lashing them across a set of the logs. An uneasy feeling settled over me as I began to suspect their purpose. When they stood their construction up to test the durability of their work, my worries were confirmed.

"Ladders!" Gilbert hissed, making the same observation I had.

With a new understanding, I looked again at the stack of logs by the closest camp. There were a dozen ladders, at least. Same with the next one I looked over.

Dark shapes in camps further away, and harder to see in the fading light, were very likely even more stacks of ladders.

"I think we have our answer, lads. They're planning another attack. Maybe tonight, maybe tomorrow, but that's definitely what they're planning. Let's get out of here."

We turned back the way we'd come and scurried away along the creek bank. We only made it a hundred paces when a voice called out in alarm. As one, our heads turned. There was a single Pict, standing beside one of the bodies and staring straight at us. Gilbert reacted the quickest, bringing up his spear and hurling it at the sentry. The man saw it coming and dove aside, crying out as he did so. Sentries further down had heard the commotion and were shouting their own warnings now.

"Go! Go! Go!" I barked, and the seven of us raced through the woods back to where Marcus and Aeron were standing by with our horses. We ran. The voices grew. Soon, a horn blew. The alarm had been raised. Fear strengthened my legs. It was beginning to feel like that day at the lake all over again.

I looked back, for I was in the lead. Gilbert and Marcus were right behind me, and the others not far behind them. Gemma was lagging behind. Behind her, the woods were coming alive as Picts in the camp grabbed weapons and responded to the alarm.

"Run, Gemma!" I shouted to her. She ran, and as she caught up to me, I grabbed her hand and ran beside her, pulling her along.

By the time we reached our horses half a dozen Picts were sprinting after us, no more than a hundred paces behind us, but then we were launching ourselves into our saddles. The nearest of the Picts had stopped and pulled their spears back, preparing to throw.

"Ride! Back to the fort!" I shouted, and away we went, breaking away from the Picts at a gallop, even as spears and javelins began thudding into the ground where we had just been. I couldn't resist flipping them the middle finger as we rode away. Gilbert and a couple others got a laugh from my taunt and did the same.

Then, our elation at making a clean escape was cut short. We heard a sickening "*Thwack!*" and heard a horse's loud, shrill scream, followed by a crashing sound. As one, we halted our mounts and turned back.

Twenty paces away, Marcus' horse had gone down, either taking a spill or more likely, had been hit by a Picti spear, and Marcus himself had been thrown. He slowly got to his feet, clearly dazed.

"Ride!" I shouted to the others, waving them onward, then angled Carys towards Marcus and gave her the spurs. She raced towards him, and I leaned down with my left arm extended.

"Grab my hand!" I called out to Marcus as I approached, slowing Carys to a canter.

Marcus and I clasped forearms when I got to him, and I yanked him up behind me. I looked back, alarmed to see that a particularly athletic Pict was rushing at us, his spear raised for a throw. Then Gilbert was beside me and beat the Pict to the throw, hurling his own javelin. The barbarian jumped to one side, and Gilbert's javelin sunk into the ground where he had just been. Gilbert swore. The Pict threw his spear, but Gilbert batted it aside with his shield.

"I've got Marcus! Let's go!" I yelled.

Further back, I saw more Picts catching up. I turned away, preparing to take off, but Gilbert remained where he was. He pulled out another javelin from his case and hurled it at the closest Pict, who was pulling an axe from his belt as he came on. He was barely ten paces away by then, and though the Pict raised his shield, Gilbert's missile slammed into and through it, seeming to pin the shield to the man's chest. He grunted and fell backwards onto the grass.

"Ha!" Gilbert barked and jubilantly pumped his fist into the air. Then he turned his mount around and rode up to me. Together, we galloped away, leaving the Picts behind.

We made it back to the camp a short time later. Gemma escorted Marcus to get checked out by Tewdrig, and I told the rest of the lads to relax and see to their horses. I went straight to Owain's tent and made my report, telling him of the size of the camp, their ladder-making, and where exactly they were. I admitted that while I could tell him the size of the camp itself, determining the actual numbers of enemy within the camp was much harder. The same went for their food stores, which were mostly hidden, presumably sheltered within some of their tents.

"Pity you were spotted," Owain said. "I'd like to try and talk Arthur into attacking them tonight, knowing that they have those ladders, but they'll be on edge now and alert."

"They still have to sleep," I pointed out.

Owain smiled wryly. "So they do. Well, go ahead and get some rest. You've earned it. I'll send up your report to Arthur and see what he wants to do next."

"Yes, sir," I said and left his tent.

# Chapter Twenty-One

I t felt like I'd barely fallen asleep when I felt someone shaking my foot. I sprang upright with a start, instantly awake and alert.

"Easy there," Owain said. "Get dressed. Get your men up and in formation. Arthur has a plan."

Owain ducked out of our tent. I heard him waking up Sawyl as I hurriedly dressed, then woke up the rest of my tentmates. In just a few minutes, we were outside, tugging our cloaks around us as more and more of the numerus joined us in formation. Soon, all ten turmae were formed up behind our decurions and draco standards, held by the duplarii. It was about two hours before dawn, by my reckoning.

Arthur, flanked by Ector, strode out in front of us. They were both fully dressed and armored, Arthur in his iron scaled squamata and Ector in an old-fashioned, bronze muscled cuirass. They carried their crested helmets cradled in their arms.

"Good morning, gentlemen," Arthur greeted us.

"Good morning, Tribune," many of us said, though it was a muted greeting, being so early in the morning. That didn't phase Arthur.

"Time to wake up, lads. If all goes well, by the time we break our fast, this fight with the Picts will be over, and we will be celebrating our victory."

That got our attention.

"Yesterday, the Picts spent their time burying their dead and making ladders. Enough ladders to make proper use of their army's size. If we sit back and allow them to come and attack Lord Guinnion's fort, the odds look about even. And those of you who have ridden with me before know how I feel about fighting an enemy with even odds."

This elicited a few chuckles throughout the formation. Arthur continued.

"Fighting fair is for duels or sporting events. In battle, we fight to win. Period. So once I dismiss you all, you're going to get kitted up, mount up, and we're going to go wake up those barbarian bastards."

He dismissed us shortly after that, and our decurions broke down the plan to us. It was a simple one, as most good plans are. We scrambled into our armor, strapped on our weapons, and got mounted up. Within twenty minutes, we formed up in our standard column formation and rode out at a trot, as it was still mostly dark, and we didn't want to make too much noise.

The stream the Picts had chosen to set up camp beside had no doubt been a great boon to them up to this point. It provided them a ready source of fresh water, a place to bathe, and even to fish, to supplement whatever food stores they had brought south with them, but as I had noted on my scouting mission, while it wasn't an absolute barrier, it was just wide and deep enough to create an obstacle, one Arthur hoped to exploit. Similar to his attack in the forest, near the lake, we approached from the south, and once we were within sight of their camp fires, we dismounted, our numerus split into two forces, and positioned ourselves as closely as we could to their camp, while using the trees and rugged landscape for concealment. Cai's force edged around to the east. The moment the sun showed itself over the horizon, he would hit the camp with his four turmae, supported by the bulk of the lighter armored levy cavalry, with the rising sun at their backs.

Arthur's column of five turmae would hold back for a few minutes until the Picts had formed up to repel Cai's forces, then he would strike their flank from the south. My turma had a separate mission. To that end, while Cai and Arthur's forces took up their positions, Owain led us wide around, on a similar path that my section had taken, and approached the camp from the west, then we hung

309

back and waited. It seemed to take forever as the eastern sky slowly lit up. My heart pounded and the chill of the morning air was pushed to the back of my mind as I, along with the rest of my turma, stared at the horizon waiting for that first glimpse of the sun.

Finally it appeared, and our attention shifted focus to the distant woods where we knew Cai's forces were hidden. It didn't take long for him to act. Cai's point of attack was over a quarter mile away, so we didn't hear his charge, and only caught glimpses of his men through the trees, but we certainly heard the Picts' response. Horn blasts and frantic shouts rippled throughout the camp. Torches bobbed up and down, and they all flowed away from us to the southeast.

The sun continued to rise, and just as planned, a few minutes after Cai had launched his attack, Arthur and his turmae followed it up with his own assault. I watched the line of riders from Arthur's formation as they charged into the fray. Sunlight reflected off armor and weapons as they swept down on the Picts. In the clear morning air, I even imagined I could hear them scream our battle cry, "Last Hope!"

Owain had remained dismounted throughout this, watching the battle progress. A pile of kindling at his feet. "Make ready," he told us. "We're going in soon. Everyone have their torches ready?"

I held mine up and glanced at the rest of my contubernales, affirming that they also held theirs ready. Every man in the turma held one in one hand. For our mission, our shields were all slung on our backs, and we left our long, cumbersome spears at camp. Additionally, each of us had several used wineskins that would have otherwise been discarded, but were now full of animal fat from our stores. Normally fat from the animals we butchered and killed was preserved for use in cooking or making candles later, but this morning, it would serve an altogether different purpose.

We heard the screams and shrill neighs of hundreds of horses as Arthur's formation slammed into the barbarians. Owain knelt down with his flint and striker over a pile of twigs he'd made when we first got into position and com-menced to getting a small fire going. As soon as the twigs lit, Owain grabbed the torch that Cornelius handed him and lit it. With this, Owain walked down the ranks and lit our torches. Cornelius held his torch while he mounted, then took it back. As our duplarius carried the draco, he was the only one of us without a torch.

"Turma! Forward, at the canter," Owain barked.

My palms grew sweaty, and my heart began to race as we rode toward the camp. We were following the stream. There were no sentries in the woods now. Every last Pict was focused on Cai and Arthur's cavalry wings as they slammed into the barbarians, withdrew, flung javelins, and charged again when the Picts attempted to counter-charge. And if they were too slow in doing that, I knew Arthur or Cai would circle around behind the battleline and throw another volley of javelins. That was the deadly beauty of cavalry fighting against infantry.

With torches held high so as not to frighten our horses, we galloped into the Pict camp itself, fanning out as we rode in amongst the tents. Our priority target was the ladders, and as we came upon them, we pulled out a wineskin full of animal fat, liberally splashed the freshly cut wood with the stuff at two or three locations, with a focus on the hemp rope that lashed the pieces together, then lit it with our torches. A few of the fires would still surely extinguish before fully catching the stacks ablaze, but not likely all of them. Sure enough, within but a of couple minutes, we had several stacks of ladders burning away merrily as we rode through the camp.

Once, a trio of Picts, already wounded from the battle and who'd been presumably making their way back to camp, saw what we were doing and cried out. Before they could draw any attention to us, however, Cornelius quickly charged at them. In quick succession he cut them down with his sword, and we continued our work unmolested. We swept through the entire camp within only about fifteen minutes and found at least ten stacks of ladders. Cornelius came upon Picts in ones and twos, either fleeing the battlefield out of cowardice or too wounded to continue fighting, and rode them down as he came upon them.

The battle south of us still raged on, with Arthur and Cai's forces gradually pulling back further south in order to prevent the barbarians from encircling them. If that ever happened, the superior numbers of the Pict horde could spell doom to the numerus. That had been the beauty of Arthur's plan, though. The primary goal of this attack was to burn as many of their ladders as possible, and inflict some casualties in the process. Supply stores would also have been a wonderful target, but the Picts didn't do us the courtesy of consolidating them in a centralized location that we could find. Instead, we assumed that each warrior, or maybe each warband's chief, stored their own foodstuffs. So we'd settled on burning their ladders. What we did next depended entirely on the Picts. If our sabotage went unnoticed, as it mostly had, it was possible that Arthur and Cai could drive the Picts back through their own burning camp with a stream to further impede their retreat. If the Picts put up too strong of a resistance, the numerus could slowly pull back and return to the fort and at least we'd have dealt the barbarians a severe blow by destroying their camp.

If our effort was noticed, or the Picts had, for whatever reason, decided to divide their efforts and repel both the numerus and prevent our sabotage, then we could at least harass them with ranged weaponry for a while. No matter how the Picts responded to our attack, Arthur had a plan for it.

Once we successfully lit the barbarians' ladders on fire, we signaled to Arthur and Cai that our mission was accomplished. That signal was the lighting of surrounding tents on fire, and we did that with the utmost enthusiasm, methodically pausing to light each tent we passed as we rode out of the camp. There could be no doubt that Cai and Arthur would see our signal and know the mission had been successful.

As we came to the edge of the camp, we tossed our torches aside into the last tents that we passed by. Then we cantered away, with the Pict camp in flames, and rode south, around the line of battle and back to the fort. Turma by turma,

Arthur and Cai's forces disengaged and joined us. To our surprise, or at least to mine for sure, the Picts gave chase! Of course, we were mounted and so were able to keep ahead of them, but we had to ride hard back to the fort with the Picts only a few hundred paces behind us.

Arthur had prepared Guinnion for this outcome, too, apparently, for as we approached, I saw that the north wall was crowded with levies, their slings and a few bows at the ready. Levies were even lined up on the eastern side of the border wall. The northern gate was opened for us, and we poured through and then rode right back out the western gate, where we lined up in a long battleline of two ranks, facing the wall, ready to charge if the Picts decided to try their luck climbing over it.

They did, and we'd barely begun to catch our breath when the spears and then the heads and shoulders of hundreds of Picts surfaced from behind the wall as they climbed up and over. One of Arthur's red-cloaked riders, a member of his personally led turma, galloped down the line, racing toward the fort. I didn't have time to ponder the significance of that, however.

"I don't think they liked the bonfires we lit for them, boys!" Owain called out to us.

The lituus sounded the call to charge, and almost of their own volition, our horses surged forward just as the faster Picts began dropping down to the ground. My section was in the first rank, with Sawyl's behind mine in support. We slammed into the horde as they swarmed over the berm and tore into them with our long cavalry blades. It was desperate fighting, and just as the numerus had done at their camp, we quickly had to fall back. In anguish, I saw Aeron get pulled off his horse by Picts, howling their warcries, and disappear into their midst. I tried frantically to get to him and Carys, sensing my urgency, flailed her hooves at the Picts in front of her, but more barbarians kept coming over the wall faster than we could kill them. Distantly, I heard our lituus calling for us to fall back, but I was almost at the point where I'd seen Aeron go down. I had to get to him!

Then Owain was beside me, screaming into my ear, "Fall back, damn you! We must stay in formation!"

"Aeron-" I started to object.

"He's dead! Fall back!" Owain shouted.

I screamed in fury at having to abandon one of my comrades, one of my own tentmates, but did as Owain ordered. I wheeled Carys around and saw that the rest of the numerus was falling back, but not straight back. We were angling back, with our line turning as the spoke of a wagon's wheel. To the Picts, and honestly, to myself as well, it appeared that our right flank was on the verge of being turned.

No sooner had we reformed than we hurled a volley of javelins at them. Dozens of the Picts' front rank dropped, dead or wounded, or at the very least without their shields, and they closed in with us again. Then levy spearmen swarmed out of the western gate, shouting their battle cries and fanning out into a battle line as they came. Because of the angle of our own battleline, which had swung away from the fort, the levies slammed into Picts' left flank. Scores fell in those first moments.

In the chaos of the fight along the wall, I'd nearly forgotten about the levies in the fort. I looked up at the walls. There were still dozens of them up there, slinging stones and loosing arrows into the masses. Barbarians struck with these missiles toppled backward over the opposite side of the wall or tumbled and rolled down lifelessly on our side.

The lituus sounded again, and our line fell back again, still angling away from the fort. Those Picts on our left flank, over two hundred paces from the fort, were singularly focused on our men in front of them and pressed forward. The Picts on our right flank and in the center were becoming trapped and realized it. They had us to their front and a growing number of Brittonic spearmen of Gododdin on their left flank and, increasingly, behind them. This sowed confusion among them, and I saw many Picts die while they were still looking around, attempting to determine where the greater threat lay. Some of these confused, hapless barbarians I slew myself, for I was determined to avenge Aeron, having failed to rescue him.

Gaps were appearing in our ranks, too, I noticed. That was one of the reasons we were forced to pull back as often as we did, to close the gaps caused by our own casualties. I feared to discover the cost to the numerus when the battle was done. More horses seemed to be dying than men, it seemed to me, though. I was surprised that Arthur hadn't given us the order to dismount and fight, but he did not, and we battled on. At least thrice over several minutes, we disengaged from the Picts, fell back, and launched javelins or plumbatae at them. The first two times our volleys caught them as they rushed to close with us, and we dropped dozens of them. The third time after we fell back, they halted and instinctively began to form a shield wall. Unfortunately for them, their small shields were entirely inadequate for that, and they only gave us an opportunity to unleash another volley at them. With the failure of their shield wall, they broke out of it and began to charge us again. We beat them to it, however, and counter-charged. This decimated their ranks, and some began to flee. Arthur himself rode up and down the line, visible in his red cloak and tall, red-crested helmet, yelling for us to fight on and occasionally jumping into the rank and fighting beside us.

Then, as if in a dream, a familiar-looking Pict climbed atop the wall, a fur-lined cloak flapping in the breeze behind him. The warrior wore a bronze helmet, a long coat of mail, and a sword belt decorated with gold discs. It was King Drest! An arrow flew at him from the fort, but it only sank into the earth where he'd just been as he slid down the steep berm. A levy spearman met him at the bottom and thrust his spear at Drest, but the king swatted the blade aside with his shield and plunged his sword into the man's stomach. A second and third levy attacked but met similar fates.

"Owain!" I shouted, desperate to be heard over the din of the battle. Only a few paces away, Owain looked my way. "Owain, it's Drest! It's their king!" I gestured frantically with my sword. Owain looked and saw the king, cutting his way through the levies with shockingly ruthless efficiency.

I heard someone bellow, "Last Hope!"

Everyone within earshot echoed the cry, "Last Hope!"

As we did, Arthur appeared from seemingly nowhere, leaped from his horse, and attacked Drest with a flurry of thrusts and cuts nearly too fast for me to even see, and yet the Picti king blocked, avoided, or parried each one. From out of the swarm of men, Cavall, Arthur's hound, darted through, barely more than a gray blur, and he launched himself at Drest. Drest brought his shield up, but Cavall's momentum nearly knocked the king backward and off his feet.

I wanted nothing more than to watch my tribune face off with King Drest, but in that moment, a wave of Picts came rushing at our line, screaming and howling, and I was forced to focus on my own survival. I was only vaguely aware that Gilbert and Marcus fought beside me. I cut down a Pict on my right, then suddenly, I was yanked off Cary's back by someone on my left and slammed to the ground. The barbarian's spear nearly had me, but then there was Gilbert, who leapt from his own mount and onto the back of the Pict standing over me. The pair went down, with Gilbert screaming like a wild animal. I'd heard of Saxons and those of Germanic blood going into berserker rages but had never witnessed it for myself. I was fairly certain this was happening to Gilbert now, and I scrambled to my feet, staring at him from the corner of my eye as I scooped up my shield and faced the Picts. He was dirty, covered in blood, and growling curses at the barbarians. He'd lost his shield and had his sword in one hand and his seax in the other. If Gilbert's manner unnerved me, it must have terrified the Picts, for they actually backed off a pace.

That did them no good, however, for no sooner had they backed away then a shower of javelins flew over our heads and dropped several of them. Then on came the rest of my section, enveloping the pair of us and restoring the temporary break that had been made in our battleline. No more Picts replaced them, and I looked up, taking the opportunity to wipe sweat out of my eyes.

They were facing us in a tightly packed shield wall. They did not retreat but did not attack either. Most were gasping for breath. We were just as tired as they, and held to our own line, content to have a moment to catch our breaths. Beside me, Gilbert looked over at me and grinned. The white of his eyes and teeth were in stark contrast to the grime that covered the rest of his face and much of his helmet and mail, in fact.

"You look terrible, cymbrog," he said in a hoarse voice.

"I can't look worse than you," I retorted and actually snickered.

All the stress, fear, and anger that had been fogging my mind for what felt like an eternity suddenly lifted with that small laugh, and almost involuntarily, I began laughing even harder. Gilbert joined me. We stood like that, laughing like idiots for a minute. Those around us gave us odd looks but said nothing. Then we heard a shout from a point some fifty paces away, followed by an explosion of shouts and cries. Everyone's attention, Briton and Pict alike, swiveled toward the commotion.

In a space between our lines, Arthur was climbing to his feet. Like Gilbert and most of us I suspected, Arthur looked a mess. His helmet was gone, as was his cloak. King Drest lay sprawled at his feet. His chest was heaving up and down, but otherwise, he lay motionless. The tip of Arthur's long sword was pointed at Drest's throat. Cavall stood nearby, snarling and barking at the surrounding Picts, though he stayed at his master's side.

"Your king is beaten!" Arthur shouted, looking toward the Picts. "You are beaten!" He looked down at Drest. "Do you understand my words, barbarian?"

From the ground, Drest turned his head to one side and spat blood. "Yes, Roman. I understand you."

"Tell your men to surrender then. Your camp is burned. Your army is decimated. See the truth of my words." He removed his sword tip and leaned down, holding his hand out to the Pict king. Drest clasped his forearm and allowed Arthur to haul him up. He looked like even more of a mess than Arthur. He looked around. Everyone else began looking, too.

In the fierce melee we'd been engaged in, most of us could only ever really focus on what was happening immediately in front of us, with only occasional insight into what was happening elsewhere. We trusted our officers to maintain the situational awareness of how the battle as a whole was developing. Now, everyone saw that Arthur was correct.

The Pict army was crowded around the base of the Antonine wall in a loose formation that extended some hundred paces in length and was five to six ranks deep. Levy slingers and archers lined the ramparts of the fort's western wall above the Picts. A large mass of levy spearmen were still pressed in against the Picts' left flank, but hundreds of spearmen, two to three ranks deep, now controlled the top of the earthen wall, and another mass of spearmen had wrapped around the Picts' right flank. The Red Dragons still held our own battleline opposite the berm, though we were down to just one rank of mounted Red Dragons. I noticed on a closer look that, like me, a number of my cymbrogi had been unhorsed but were still in the fight. Despite our losses, the Picts were fully encircled and outnumbered, and the levies held the higher ground on two sides.

King Drest saw it, too, and finally spoke. "What are your terms?"

"Surrender. Give up your armor, shields, and swords. You may keep your spears, daggers, and axes so that your people can continue to hunt and work. You will not return to your camp but march straight back north to your own lands. Anyone too wounded to walk of their own accord will remain here. They will be nursed back to health and live as slaves to the people of the Gododdin as reparation for the harm you have caused them these past few months. Finally, you will not allow your people to come any further south than the River Forth until such time as the rulers of the Gododdin say otherwise," Arthur stated.

Drest flinched as though struck. "And if we refuse?"

"We shall slay you here, to the last man," Arthur said coldly. "Then we will ride north and scour the lands north of the Forth of any Picti villages we find and enslave any we come upon until either your people have scattered and hidden themselves too well in the highlands to be worth a prolonged hunt for them, or the Picti tribes are no more."

Oh, Drest did not like that answer. His face contorted with fury, and his hands tightened into fists. Arthur merely stood there like a statue. His sword was still in his hand, but held low, pointed at the ground. The Picti king also looked around at us and at the Gododdin levies all around him and clearly did not like the situation. Whether Arthur could indeed muster an army big enough to invade the highlands and hunt down the Picts as he threatened to do scarcely even mattered, as far as Drest was concerned. What was very clear was that if he refused to surrender, we were absolutely capable of carrying out the first part of Arthur's threat and killing him and all of his men here and now. Even the dumbest soldier, Briton or Pict, could see that. After several tense moments, Drest turned back to face Arthur.

"Would you have me bow and humiliate myself before you, too?"

"No. You're a king. You fought bravely, if not justly. Give me your word that you will honor my terms before the one true God, and you may go in peace."

At this moment, from the wall of the fort, Lord Guinnion pushed through the ranks and leaned down. He still looked immaculate, I noticed. "No! This is not enough! Arthur, you do not have the authority to make terms with this Pagan scum!" He shouted.

Arthur's head whipped around, and he barked at Guinnion. "Be silent, Lord Guinnion! Dictating terms of a surrender fall within the purview of the Dux Bellorum- me! My authority comes from King Leudon and High King Conanus Aurelius. So unless you can produce tangible proof that your authority supersedes mine in this matter, I *will* dictate King Drest's terms of surrender. And you will honor them!"

Arthur didn't verbally threaten Guinnion. I suspect he simply had too much respect for Guinnion's status, if not the man himself, to threaten him openly in front of his own people. His body language, however, made it perfectly clear that he fully expected Guinnion to comply.

Lord Guinnion's mouth opened and closed, but he failed to say anything. Finally, red-faced, he turned and left the wall. Arthur redirected his attention back to King Drest.

"What is your answer, King Drest?" Arthur asked. Compared to how he'd just spoken to Guinnion, his tone with Drest seemed remarkably civil, even respectful.

"You're not leaving me with much of a choice," Drest responded. He practically spat out the words.

"No, I'm not," Arthur agreed. "I detest the notion of slaughtering you and your men, though I will if you force me to. Nor do I want to have to come back north and fight you again."

It seemed to me that Drest almost smiled at that. "I accept your terms," he said bitterly. "And may the gods of this land grant me justice upon a day."

"That's where you err, King Drest," Arthur answered coolly. "There is but one God who rules all the lands of this realm and in Heaven. It is He who delivered you and your army to us. And will likely do so again, should you break your oath."

Drest glared at our tribune but said nothing more. Instead, he turned to his men and began shouting at them. His voice cracked as he spoke, and as he finished, cries and groans of dismay rippled through the ranks and not a few bursts of anger, but they complied. Swords and shields were dropped or thrown to the ground before us. The few among them who wore mail or other armor stripped themselves of it and dropped it to the ground along with their weaponry.

Then came the final, most emotional part. The levies on top of the berm cleared a space, and the Picts slowly climbed back up and over to the far side. Those who were too wounded to do so were forced to remain. The comrades and kin of the wounded wept openly as they said their goodbyes. A few even deliberately sat down next to their comrades, choosing to go into slavery with them rather than abandon them.

"I think Arthur may be going too far with this condition," I said softly. Beside me, Gilbert heard me. "This is justice," he sneered, watching them. "You're moved by the tears of these men? Think on how many homes they burned or would have burned had they won this battle. How many orphans and widows and cripples throughout the borders of Gododdin has this horde already created since they invaded south? How many more still would they have created, had we not stopped them here? And make no mistake. They would have taken slaves as well as looted treasure back north with them, as well. Or, depending on how successful their invasion was, they would have stayed and ruled these lands and simply killed or enslaved the whole population. It's simply the way of the world, Peredur. The Angles, Saxons, and Jutes are doing it all over the eastern half of Britain even now. Long ago, the Romans did it to the whole of Britain, I've heard. More than likely, before the Romans came, the Celtic tribes murdered, enslaved and conquered each other. My own people in Germania certainly did."

"You're right," I admitted, begrudgingly. "It doesn't mean I have to like it, though."

Gilbert patted me on the shoulder. "Ah. Peredur, the Innocent. I truly hope that someday the world can function the way you believe it should." I winced as my shoulder flared with pain. He glanced at me. "Shoulder still hurt?"

"Yes," I grumbled. "My shoulder hurts, my side hurts, along with practically the rest of my body." I looked down at my side. Through the links in my mail, I was fairly certain my tunic was dark with blood, meaning that my stitches had torn loose. Again. Gemma was not going to be happy with me, I mused.

"You're wounded, too," I pointed out to Gilbert and grinned.

"Come on, let's go to the great hall and get Tewdrig to sew us up," he said.

I found Marcus and instructed him to look after our section for the day, then reported to Owain and told him where I was heading. Following that, Gilbert and I joined a long line of wounded cymbrogi. Too many, I thought.

The able-bodied Picts were disappearing over the wall, and levies, along with many of our own men, were already sorting out any weapons and armor worth looting, as well as checking over the Pict bodies.

"Before you scatter out and join the rest in...cleaning up the battlefield," Owain instructed us, "Get accountability of your men. We'll hold formation shortly. Don't let your men take too many spears and such home with us. We don't have enough space on the wagons, and the levies need those kinds of weapons and basic armor more than any of us do. So do not get greedy!"

"What about these?" one man called out. He held up a thick, silver necklace known as a torc.

"Jewelry is fine," Owain said to the cheers of the turma.

I took quick accountability of my men. Aeron was my only casualty, I was relieved to discover. Several others, like myself, were wounded, but not so badly that they were willing to see the medicus before they found some loot. I joined them in that regard and kept my eye out as Gilbert and I walked along the wall, heading for the great hall. Along the way, I snagged up not just one but three Picti swords, a couple of engraved bracelets and torcs that looked to be made of gold and silver, and a nicely painted Picti shield that was still in good shape.

"Why do you want that?" Gilbert asked. He, too, had a growing collection of loot in his hands.

I shrugged. "Souvenir? This might be the only time I travel this far north."

Gilbert shrugged, and we continued on.

I was dismayed at the large number of wounded, seated or lying down around the great hall, waiting for medical treatment. Fortunately, most of them were levies rather than men of our numerus. The fearsome levy chief, Garwlwyd, was among them, I noticed. I gestured to Gilbert, and the two of us joined him. His leg was cut, high up near his hip.

"How are you fairing, Penteulu?" I asked, using his title.

The grizzled warrior looked up at me and nodded. "It's just a flesh wound," he said dismissively, though his voice was taut with pain. "Picti bastard cut me with a sword thrust, near the end of the fighting."

"Good thing you got cut where they did," Gilbert commented. "A twist of your hips the wrong way and you might have lost more than just blood," he commented with a wink.

Garwlywd chuckled and nodded. "A loss my wife would have found even more heartbreaking than my death, no doubt." Then he asked us, "So what happens now, with you Red Dragons?" The warrior asked.

"We ride back to Caer Lleon, though I think our tribune intends to stop by Din Pendyrlaw first. What about you and your people? Do you think things will settle down now?" I replied.

A look of something like unease or uncertainty flashed across Garwlywd's face, but he nodded slowly. "Maybe. Me and my kin will return to our village on the south bank of the Forth. We're mostly fishermen. I love it there. Nothing more relaxing than sitting on a log by the river, with my son beside me and listening to the water rippling, while the wind rustles the leaves of the trees, waiting for a nice, big fish to chomp on your hook." He smiled and half closed his eyes as he spoke.

*Who'd have thought,* I mused. *The most feral-looking warrior in Guinnion's army has the soul of a poet.*

"So, from fighting Picts to being some kind of fisher king, eh?" Gilbert snickered, apparently appreciating the contrast as well.

Garwlywd opened his eyes, looked up at Gilbert and flashed another smile. Eventually, Gemma came and got Garwlywd, deeming his injury more severe than mine or the others still present. When she noticed me among the wounded again, she shot me a dirty look, no doubt annoyed that I would need to be stitched up again. I just grinned back at her. I was in too good of a mood at the prospect of going home, alive and with a small fortune in loot, to be affected by her temper. I helped the warrior to his feet, then Gemma helped him inside the great hall to be stitched up.

As I waited my turn, I sighed, grateful to know that the campaign was over. I'd survived. Most of our men had survived, and we were going home soon, and Gemma would be along for the trip. That thought alone put a wide smile on my face and I closed my eyes contentedly, feeling the warm sun on my face.

# Epilogue

## Caer Gurcoc, Isle of Mona, 549 A.D.

T he old man leaned back in his chair, and his eyes slowly closed.

"Grandfather, wake up!" Rhys said, tugging at his sleeve.

"Finish the story," added little Cadoc.

The old man's eyes flared open. "I wasn't sleeping!" he protested. "I was just ... resting my eyelids for a moment." He yawned.

"Please, grandfather, at least finish the story?" Enid asked. She tried to act more gracefully than her excited younger brothers, but she did still want to hear the rest of the tale.

"Where was I then," the old man mused.

"You and Gilbert were at the great hall at Guinnion Fort to get sewn up," Rhys prompted.

"Oh yes," the old man nodded. He brought his mug up, about to take a drink, then realized it was empty. He frowned and set it back down on the table.

"Well, there wasn't much that would interest you boys after that. One turma kept an eye on Drest's men and made sure they scrambled out of Gododdin and back north. Those of our numerus who were well enough then rode back to Caer Lleon. The lads who were too seriously wounded to travel were taken to Din Pendyrlaw; then they rejoined the numerus as they were able or went home for further recovery."

"What about the barbarian king, Drest? What happened to him?" Rhys asked. "I bet he lied to Arthur!"

"What about your friend, Gemma?" Enid cut in. "What happened with her?"

"Gemma was madder than a wet hen when she saw that I'd reopened my side again. She sewed me back up, but gave me all sorts of grief while she did," the old man chuckled. "Thankfully, I passed out and missed most of it. As for Drest, well, that's complicated, but you're right; we had to deal with Drest again later on."

The old man glanced at one wall, where a row of shields were hung up. Two were distinctly Picti shields.

"But that's a whole new story. And your grandmother over there is giving me that look," the old man grinned.

The children all turned to look at their grandmother, sitting by the fire, sewing, and giving her husband the side eye.

"It's nearly dark, and your parents will be expecting you home soon," she said.

"So, no more stories tonight," Peredur sighed. "Now you really need to get home, but I tell you what. Next time you come over, I'll tell you the story of the time me, Gemma, Morgana, and Myrddin ended up as prisoners of a band of rebels during a second trip up to Caledonia."

"What?" Enid asked, wide-eyed. "You went on an adventure with Morgana the Fey and Myrddin?"

"Yep, we truly did! It all started following the Battle of the City of the Legion after a warband of Gaels came raiding the coast of Rheged ..."

"Peredur," the old man's wife cut in. "Don't you start with that tonight!"

"Uh-oh. I'm going to get your grandmother mad if I tell you another word about that," Peredur said with a grin.

"Good night, Grandfather. Good night, Grandmother," the three children intoned and waved to the pair as they shuffled out the door. The elderly couple waved back. Once the door had closed, the woman turned to look at Peredur and cocked a thin eyebrow at him.

"A wet hen, huh, Peredur?"

Peredur looked at his wife with a grin and reached absently across his thick stomach to scratch at the old scar on his side.

"Come on dear," she said after a bit, as she rose to leave. "We should be going to bed soon as well. You have a chicken pen you need to repair in the morning." Peredur rolled his eyes. She'd been on him about that all week. "I'll be there in a bit, dear. May as well finish this mead first." He stared into the crackling fire blazing away, sipping the last of his meade. In his mind, the fire reminded him of larger infernos he'd seen, on battlefields. The sounds of men screaming in rage and pain, and of weapons striking against wooden shields echoed distantly and a single tear crept slowly down the old man's weathered cheek.

# Author's Note

L ittle is actually known by even the most knowledgeable experts about much of what transpired in Great Britain between the 5th - 8th centuries, commonly referred to as the "Dark Age". What few records that do exist rarely agree with each other. One of the earliest sources to mention Arthur, in the context of being a historical figure, is found in the *History of the Britons*, written in about 828 A.D. and attributed to the Welsh monk Nennius. In this manuscript, Nennius lists twelve battles that Arthur is supposed to have fought and won. Arthur is not necessarily a "king" but is given the title of "*Dux Bellorum*", which means "Duke of Battles," and was a title used by the Romans since the Age of Antiquity. There are no dates ascribed to these battles listed by Nennius, no specified enemy, and the names of the battles themselves do not easily correspond to locations known to us today. This story is based on Battle #7 at Celidon Coit and #8 at Guinnion Fort from Nennius' list.

Historians generally agree, at least, that Celidon Coit most likely refers to the woodlands of Scotland, called Caledonia by the Romans. Guinnion is a wild card. The prefix "Guin" or "Gwen" means "white" in the Welsh language. The suffix, however, is speculative. As for "Guin/Gwen," historians generally believe this is a reference to a location and that "Castello Guinnion" basically means "The White Fort/City," but Guin/Gwen is also used in people's name, as with the famous name of Guinevere/Gwenhwyfar. With so little information to work with, I have crafted a narrative around these two battles that I think is at least believable, if not backed up with any surviving evidence, and hopefully enjoyable.

Peredur's Saga is partially based upon Nennius' *History of the Britons*, *The Anglo-Saxon Chronicles*, and Geoffrey of Monmouth's *The History of the Kings of Britain*. It is not my intention to attempt any kind of definitive story of "the real" Arthur, as I do not believe such an endeavor is possible. Instead, this saga is an attempt to illustrate how the vague and sometimes conflicting narratives presented in classical sources could have unfolded within the context of 6th century Great Britain, with as little "creative license" being taken as possible. That being said, Peredur, of course, is still a latecomer to Arthurian lore and, therefore, most likely fictional. His earliest known literary appearances come either from a series of Welsh tales called the Mabinogion, which feature a character named Peredur, or from the French poet Chretien de Troyes, who also wrote a series of Arthurian stories, which included *Perceval, The Story of the Grail*. Both of these stories appear by the late 12th to early 13th century. My personal belief is that the Welsh story of Peredur came first. Other French and German writers continued to add Perceval to Arthurian stories. Details vary from story to story, as they do with most elements of Arthurian lore, but there are some elements that are generally consistent with Peredur/Perceval. He is nearly always depicted as young, sheltered, a bit of a "Mother's boy," and eager to prove himself to Arthur. He's also frequently sent off on quests.

I have attempted to reflect this general trend in Peredur's treatment and opted to name him Peredur rather than Perceval as the Arthurian story as a whole seems to come from the Welsh, though, as always, there is some debate on that, as with every, other aspect around the legend of King Arthur. I hope in any case that you, Reader, found this story entertaining and will follow along the rest of Peredur's journey as I take him up and down Great Britain as he matures into a full-fledged veteran and leader in his own right under the command and mentorship of the likes of Arthur, Owain, and others.

# Characters List

**A**eron (AH-ron): a member of Peredur's contubernium within Owain's turma.

**Aylmer** (AYL-mer): a member of Peredur's contubernium and later decanus from South-central Britain.

**Arthur** (AR-thur): the son of Riothamus "Uther" the Pendragon. Arthur is a noble and lord of Din Tagel in the kingdom of Dumnonia. He is also the Tribune of the Red Dragons Cavalry and frequently the Dux Bellorum (field commander) in battles he is involved with where troops from other kingdoms are present.

**Bran** (BRAN): a fellow recruit in Peredur's training turma.

**Bedwyr** (BED-wir): the Castellan of Caer Lleon and a decurion of his own turma.

**Brynn** (BRIN): a levy soldier of Gododdin under the command of Garwlwyd. He also serves as a guide and interpreter to Owain's turma.

**Cai** (KAI): the son of Ector Gaius Artorius and foster brother of Arthur. He is the Vicarius and Second in Command/ the Executive Officer of the Red Dragons Cavalry.

**Cadoc** (KAH-dok): one of Peredur's grandchildren.

**Caradoc** (KAH-rah-dok): The Decurion in charge of recruit training at Caer Lleon.

**Cornelius** (kor-NEHL-ius): a decanus and later duplarius within Owain's turma.

**Domangart Reti** (DOH-man-gart REH-ti): a king of Dal Riata of the early 6th century, following the death of his father, King Fergus Mor.

**Drest II** (DREST): a prominent king of the Picts of the early 6th century.

**Drystan** (DRIS-tan): one of Arthur's decurions. Drystan (based on Tristan) is from Cair Wisc (Exeter, UK).

**Ector Gaius Artorius** (EK-tor GAI-us ar-TOR-ee-us): former Vicarius of the Red Dragons while it was under the command of "Uther" the Pendragon. He is Cai's father and Arthur's mentor and foster father. He is from Caer Londien.

**Enid** (EH-nid): the oldest of Peredur's grandchildren.

**Ewan** (YOO-an): a fellow recruit in Peredur's training turma. He is Rhun's younger brother.

**Galhault** (GAL-holt): one of Arthur's decurions. Galhault (based on Galehaut) is from the island of Guernsey (Sarnia), off the coast of Frankia (France).

**Garwlwyd** (GAH-roo-thloo-eed): a Penteulu (tribal/family leader) of some of the levied infantry of Gododdin.

**Gilbert** (GIL-bert): a member of Peredur's contubernium within Owain's turma. Gilbert is of Frisian descent and is from Cair Badon (Bath, UK).

**Idris** (ID-ris): a member of Peredur's contubernium within Owain's turma.

**Leudon** (LAY-oo-don): Gododdin's king in the early 6th century. He is married to Arthur's half-sister, Morgause.

**Maithgemm** (Gemma) (MATH-gemm): a runaway slave of Gaelic father and Pict mother. She is from western Caledonia (Scotland).

**Madog** (MAH-dog): a fellow recruit in Peredur's training turma.

**Marcus** (MAR-kus): a member of Peredur's contubernium within Owain's turma.

**Morcant** (MOR-kant): one of Arthur's decurions.

**Myrddin Wylt** (the Wild) (MIR-thin WILT): an all-around wise man and bard (based on Merlin) who was an advisor to Uther and later to Arthur.

**Nimue** (NIM-oo-ay or NIM-oo-ee): a former protege and sometimes lover to Myrddin. She lives in a cottage at the lake, Llyn y Fan Fach, in Dyfed.

**Owain** (OH-wine): a relative of Domgal, King of Alt Clut. Owain is also one of Arthur's decurions.

**Peredur** (PER-eh-door): the youngest son of Lord Pelinor in Caer Gurcoc on the island of Mona (Anglesey, UK). He is a member of Owain's turma.

**Quintus** (KWIN-tus): a member of Peredur's contubernium within Owain's turma.

**Rhun** (RHIN): a fellow recruit in Peredur's training turma. He is Ewan's older brother.

**Rhydderch** (HRU-thairk): one of Arthur's decurions.

**Rhys** (REES): one of Peredur's grandchildren.

**Sawyl** (SOW-ul): one of Owain's two decanii.

**Sextus Brocius** (SEX-tus BROH-see-us): a merchant who accompanies the Red Dragons and acts as their primary armorer.

**Tewdrig** (TEYOO-drig): the medicus (doctor) of the Red Dragons Cavalry.

**Titus** (TIE-tus): one of Arthur's decurions.

**Tyree** (TIE-ree): one of Arthur's decurions.

# Glossary

## Castellan

Definition: The governor or keeper of a castle, responsible for its defense and the surrounding land.

Singular: Castellan /ˈkæs.tə.lən/

Plural: Castellans /ˈkæs.tə.lənz/

Pronunciation: KAS-tuh-luhn

### Chi Rho

Definition: A Christian symbol made by superimposing the first two letters of the Greek word for Christ (ΧΡΙΣΤΟΣ), representing Christ.

Singular: Chi Rho /ˌkaɪ ˈroʊ/

Plural: Chi Rhos /ˌkaɪ ˈroʊz/

Pronunciation: KAI roh

### Contubernium

Definition: A unit of about eight soldiers in the Roman army who shared a tent and were the smallest organized group.

Singular: Contubernium /ˌkɒn.tuˈbɜː.ni.əm/

Plural: Contubernia /ˌkɒn.tuˈbɜː.ni.ə/

Pronunciation: kon-too-BER-nee-um (singular), kon-too-BER-nee-ah (plural)

### Cymbrog

Definition: A Welsh term meaning "fellow countryman," "compatriot," or "brother-in-arms," often used in a martial context to describe comradeship.

Singular: Cymbrog /'kʌm.brɒg/

Plural: Cymbrogi /'kʌm.brɒ.gi/

Pronunciation: KUHM-brog (singular) | KUHM-bro-gee (plural)

**Decanus**

Definition: A leader of 10 men in the Roman army, often commanding a contubernium.

Singular: Decanus /dɪˈkeɪ.nəs/

Plural: Decani /dɪˈkeɪ.niː/

Pronunciation: deh-KAY-nus (singular), deh-KAY-nee (plural)

**Decurion**

Definition: A Roman officer in charge of a turma, typically a cavalry unit of about 30 men.

Singular: Decurion /dɪˈkjʊə.rɪ.ən/

Plural: Decurions /dɪˈkjʊə.rɪ.ənz/

Pronunciation: dih-KYOOR-ee-uhn

**Denarius**

Definition: A Roman unit of weight equivalent to approximately 3.4 grams of silver, historically tied to the silver denarius coin. It was used for small-scale transactions.

Singular: Denarius /dɪˈnɑːr.i.əs/

Plural: Denarii /dɪˈnɑːr.i.aɪ/

Pronunciation: deh-NAHR-ee-us (singular), deh-NAHR-ee-eye (plural)

**Duplarius**

Definition: A soldier in the Roman army who received double pay, usually due to a promotion or distinction in service.

Singular: Duplarius /djuːˈplɑː.ri.əs/

Plural: Duplarii /djuːˈplɑː.ri.aɪ/

Pronunciation: doo-PLAH-ree-us (singular), doo-PLAH-ree-eye (plural)

**Libra**

Definition: The Roman pound, a unit of weight equivalent to approximately 327 grams, used as a standard for larger transactions involving metals such as silver and gold.

Singular: Libra /ˈliː.brə/

Plural: Librae /ˈliː.braɪ/

Pronunciation: LEE-brah (singular), LEE-bry (plural)

**Numerus Equitum**

Definition: A Late Roman cavalry unit, typically smaller and more flexible than earlier formations like the *ala*. The *numerus equitum* was used for a wide range of roles, including reconnaissance, raiding, and rapid response in battle.

Singular: Numerus Equitum /ˈnuː.mə.rəs ˈɛ.kwɪ.tʊm/

Plural: Numeri Equitum /ˈnuː.mə.raɪ ˈɛ.kwɪ.tʊm/

Pronunciation: NOO-muh-rus EH-kwee-tum (singular), NOO-muh-ry EH-kwee-tum (plural)

**Plumbata**

Definition: A type of throwing dart used by Roman infantry, featuring a lead weight to give it extra momentum.

Singular: Plumbata /plʌmˈbɑː.tə/

Plural: Plumbatae /plʌmˈbɑː.teɪ/

Pronunciation: plum-BAH-tuh (singular), plum-BAH-tay (plural)

**Seax**

Definition: A short sword or large knife used by the Saxons, commonly employed for combat and utility purposes.

Singular: Seax /sæks/

Plural: Seaxes /ˈsæks.ɪz/

Pronunciation: SAX (singular), SAX-es (plural)

**Scripulum**

Definition: A Roman unit of weight equal to 1/24 of a libra or approximately 13.6 grams, often used for precise measurements, particularly in trade and for precious metals.

Singular: Scripulum /ˈskrɪp.ju.ləm/

Plural: Scripula /ˈskrɪp.ju.lə/

Pronunciation: SKRIP-yoo-lum (singular), SKRIP-yoo-lah (plural)

**Solidus**

Definition: A unit of weight equivalent to approximately 4.5 grams of gold or silver, often associated with the gold solidus coin. It was used for high-value transactions.Singular: Solidus /ˈsɒl.ɪ.dəs/Plural: Solidi /ˈsɒl.ɪ.daɪ/

Pronunciation: SOL-i-dus (singular), SOL-i-die (plural)

**Tribune**

Definition: The commander of a Roman military unit, including both infantry and cavalry units like the *numerus equitum*. The *tribune* was responsible for the overall command, strategy, and management of the unit.

Singular: Tribune /ˈtrɪb.juːn/

Plural: Tribunes /ˈtrɪb.juːnz/

Pronunciation: TRIB-yoon (singular), TRIB-yoonz (plural)

**Turma**

Definition: A Roman cavalry unit composed of around 30 men commanded by a decurion.

Singular: Turma /ˈtʊər.mə/

Plural: Turmae /ˈtʊər.maɪ/

Pronunciation: TUR-mah (singular), TUR-my (plural)

**Uncia**

Definition: A Roman ounce, equivalent to 1/12 of a libra or approximately 27.3 grams, commonly used for smaller weights in trade and transactions.

Singular: Uncia /ˈʌn.si.ə/

Plural: Unciae /ˈʌn.si.aɪ/

Pronunciation: UN-see-uh (singular), UN-see-eye (plural)

**Vicarius**

Definition: A Roman administrative and military rank, meaning "deputy" or "substitute," often used to denote someone acting as second-in-command.

Singular: Vicarius /vɪˈkaː.rɪ.us/

Plural: Vicarii /vɪˈkaː.rɪ.iː/

Pronunciation: vi-KAR-ee-us (singular), vi-KAR-ee-ee (plural)

**Wealh**

Definition: An Old English term used by Anglo-Saxons to describe a native Briton, meaning "foreigner" or "slave."

Singular: Wealh /wælk/

Plural: Wealas /ˈwæl.əs/

Pronunciation: WAL-k (singular), WAL-uhs (plural)

# Important Locations

**A** **lt Clut** (AHLT KLOOT)

Modern Location: Dumbarton, Scotland.

Alt Clut was a powerful fortress and the center of the Kingdom of Alt Clut in the 6th century, ruled by the Brittonic-speaking peoples in the Clyde Valley. It was a key stronghold for resisting the Picts and Anglo-Saxons, playing a critical role in defending the western Britons during this period.

**Antonine Wall** (AN-toh-neen)

Modern Location: Stretching across central Scotland from the Firth of Forth to the Firth of Clyde.

Built by the Romans in the mid-2nd century, the Antonine Wall marked the northernmost frontier of the Roman Empire in Britain for a brief period.

**Caledonia** (KAL-eh-DOH-nee-ah)

Modern Location: Roughly corresponds to present-day Scotland.

Caledonia was the Roman name for the land north of their empire, home to fierce, independent tribes, most notably the Picts. Roman attempts to conquer Caledonia were unsuccessful, and it remained a largely unconquered region beyond Roman control, marked by its resistance to Roman occupation.

**Caer Lleon** (KAI-er HLEE-on)

Modern Location: Caerleon, near Newport, Wales.

A significant Roman legionary fortress that remained a major power center after the Roman withdrawal from Britain. It is sometimes associated with the legendary King Arthur and his court.

**Dal Riata** (DAHL REE-ah-tah)

Modern Location: Spanned parts of modern-day western Scotland and northeastern Ireland.

In the 6th century, Dal Riata was an emerging Gaelic kingdom that straddled the Irish Sea, with settlements in both Ireland and western Scotland. It played an important role in early Gaelic expansion, and its kings helped shape the early political landscape of both Scotland and Ireland.

**Din Eidyn** (DIN AY-din)

Modern Location: Edinburgh, Scotland.

Din Eidyn was a major hillfort in the kingdom of Gododdin during the 6th century. It was a center of power for the Brittonic-speaking peoples of the region.

**Din Pendyrlaw** (DIN pen-DUR-law)

Modern Location: Traprain Law, East Lothian, Scotland.

Din Pendyrlaw, now known as Traprain Law, was the primary stronghold of the Votadini tribe in the early medieval period, including the 6th century. It was a key power center in southern Scotland, acting as both a defensive fort and a trading hub.

**Din Tagel** (DIN TA-gel)

Modern Location: Tintagel, Cornwall, England.

Din Tagel, commonly associated with Tintagel Castle, was a coastal fortress and settlement in the 6th century. It held significant strategic and symbolic importance in the kingdom of Dumnonia. Though much of its later fame comes from its association with Arthurian legend, in the 6th century, it was a vital defensive position controlling access to the southwestern coast of Britain.

**Dyfed** (DUH-ved)

Modern Location: Southwest Wales, corresponding to modern Pembrokeshire and Carmarthenshire.

Dyfed was a small but strategically significant kingdom in the 6th century, established by Irish settlers who had gained control of the area. It maintained strong connections with Ireland and was involved in regional politics with other Welsh and Irish kingdoms.

**Dumnonia** (DUHM-noh-nee-ah)

Modern Location: Devon and Cornwall in southwest England.

Significance: In the 6th century, Dumnonia was one of the most prominent Brittonic kingdoms resisting Anglo-Saxon expansion. It was a bastion of Romano-British culture, and its rulers maintained control over a significant portion of southwestern Britain during this period.

**Glywysing** (GLU-wiss-ing)

Modern Location: South Wales, corresponding to modern-day Glamorgan.

In the 6th century, Glywysing was a smaller Brittonic kingdom located to the west of Gwent. It was often closely associated with its neighbors, sometimes forming alliances with Gwent, and was known for its coastal defenses against raiders from Ireland and the Anglo-Saxons.

**Gododdin** (goh-DOTH-in)

Modern Location: The region around modern-day Edinburgh, Scotland.

The kingdom of Gododdin was one of the major Brittonic kingdoms of the north in the 6th century.

**Gwent** (GWENT)

Modern Location: Southeast Wales, corresponding to modern Monmouthshire and parts of Glamorgan.

Gwent was an important Brittonic kingdom in the 6th century, known for its strategic position along the Severn estuary, allowing it to engage in trade and conflict with both neighboring Brittonic kingdoms and the expanding Anglo-Saxons. It was a key center of power in early medieval Wales.

**Gwynedd** (GWIN-eth)

Modern Location: Northwest Wales, corresponding to modern Gwynedd and Anglesey.

By the 6th century, Gwynedd had become a dominant Welsh kingdom, playing a key role in resisting the Irish raids and consolidating power over northwestern Wales. Its rulers, such as Maelgwn Gwynedd, were instrumental in shaping early medieval Welsh politics and culture.

**Hibernia** (hi-BUR-nee-ah)

Modern Location: Ireland.

Hibernia was the Roman name for Ireland, a land they never successfully invaded. In the 6th century, Ireland was a land of powerful, petty kingdoms, known for its warrior elite and increasingly for its growing Christian monastic tradition, which would soon become a major cultural force across the British Isles.

**Loch Liobhann** (LOKH LEE-van)

Modern Location: Loch Leven, in present-day Scotland.

A freshwater lake in the Scottish Highlands, Loch Liobhann (Loch Leven) lies near the traditional boundaries between the lands of the Britons and Picts.

**Powys** (POW-iss)

Modern Location: Mid-Wales.

Powys was a major Brittonic kingdom in the 6th century, controlling central Wales and parts of modern-day Shropshire. Its rulers played a significant role in defending against Anglo-Saxon encroachment, particularly from the Kingdom of Mercia.

**Rheged** (REH-ged)

Modern Location: Cumbria and possibly parts of southern Scotland.

In the 6th century, Rheged was one of the most powerful Brittonic kingdoms in northern Britain.

**Sruighlea** (SREE-luh)

Modern Location: Stirling, Scotland.

Sruighlea, located near the River Forth, was a critical strategic site in early medieval Scotland, serving as a natural crossing point between the Highlands and Lowlands. In the 6th century, it may have been a defensive stronghold for the Britons of Gododdin or the Picts, controlling vital trade and military routes. The surrounding fertile lands further enhanced its importance as a settlement.

While its later fame is tied to events in Scottish history, Sruighlea likely held significant strategic value during the time of Arthurian Britain.

# About the Author

J ason Kyle was born in California and grew up across the United States as the son of an Air Force servicemember. At seventeen, he joined the Army Reserves, transitioning to active duty after high school, and deployed to Iraq in March 2003. Over the years, he completed two more deployments to Iraq and earned a bachelor's degree in History. He is the author of *The Apprentice Mage* (2011), a fantasy novel based on the world and characters created by Reaper Miniatures.

Jason currently lives in Georgia with his son and their dog. He is preparing to retire from the Army and looks forward to a new chapter as a history teacher and writer.

# More From Cannon Publishing

**Join the Crew!**

S ign up for our newsletter for the latest news on new releases and more.

# Follow our authors at their Amazon Pages!

Shane Gries (Dragon Finalist)

Lucas Marcum

Al Hagan

James Copley

Jason Kyle

G. Scott Huggins

Michael Morton

Charles Hackney

Jon LaForce

Jason Weiser

Kal Spriggs

Brian Gifford

Charli Cox

Dan Kemp

Jonathan Shuerger

## More Books from Cannon Publishing

### Irregular Scout Team One

In July of 2016 a plague swept the world, and the civilization collapsed and fell. For a lone National Guard sergeant, a veteran of the wars overseas who had settled down to a new life, the nightmare began on a hot summer evening at the barricades. Orders and chaos, gunfire and being overrun, his unit dwindles away in the face of the infected. Months later, living in the ruins, the thud of helicopter rotors followed by a crash and the rescue of a downed pilot leads Sergeant First Class Nick Agostine back into the arms of the US military. From his experience comes the idea of teams, military and civilians experienced in dealing with the undead and barbarism of the wilds. The first Irregular Scout Team leads the way for Task Force Liberty to advance down the Mohawk Valley in Upstate NY, making contact with survivors and clearing out the infected with stealth and firepower.

*Volume 1*

*Volume 2*

*Volume 3: Civil War*

*Volume 4: Bad Company*

# The Line

When the world descends into chaos and anarchy with an unbelievably swift plague, turning victims into ravenous maniacs, the soldiers of America's storied 1st Infantry are asked to hold the line. From the brutal streets of urban combat to the bloodied, desperate defense on the plains of Kansas, they fight a war against an unrelenting enemy who used to be their fellow citizens. As civilization falls, can they hold the line?

*The Thin Dead Line*
*Dead Storm Rising*
*The Big Dead One*

# Fallen Empire

What's a soldier to do when the war is over? When he's only known conflict his whole life? Since time immemorial the solution has been to find another war, this time for pay. Whoever has the credits and wins the high bid gets the experienced fighter. Sometimes, though, the credits aren't enough to cover the price.Empires rise, but Empires also fall. The Terran Union has spent five centuries under the control of the alien Grausians, like a barbarian tribe under the thumb of Rome. Now, after almost two decades of civil war and succession struggles, the formerly subject races have settled back in their ancient territories to lick their wounds and re-arm, leaving hundreds of settled planets to exist in a political vacuum.Into that space steps the free companies, mercenary units that fight for gold, honor, power and glory. Veterans who can't get the wars out of their souls, new recruits looking for adventure, corporations with their own agenda. Join us in a 27th Century that echoes history.

*The Irish Brigade*

*Overrun*

*Silent Violence*

# Athenaeum, Inc

The Professor has problems, and not just what decades of soldiering did to his back and his knees. His boss just died, leaving him as CEO of the extremely discreet intelligence contractor Athenaeum, Incorporated. His old buddy the Operations Director is a highly skilled Army Ranger veteran but his finance chief is slightly unhinged and spends her money on highly inappropriate work outfits. The surviving old men on the Board of Directors are stuck in the 1970s. Running Athenaeum out of an old Cold War bunker and keeping their roster of experts together is expensive, but the government contracts are drying up or going to bigger, flashier corporate players.

*Door Number Three*

*Doubling Down*

# Off World

When nuclear war erupts on Earth, the American colony in the Alpha Centauri system is left stranded. As the new day dawns, a furious attack by the native inhabitants threatens to overwhelm the colony's defenses. It's left to the thin red line of the US Army's 9th Regiment to stem the tide and ensure humanity's survival in this harsh new world. From two time Dragon Finalist and author of the best selling series "Irregular Scout Team One" and "Invasion" comes a new tale that tells of the struggle for survival on a brutal planet.

Offworld: Ragnarok

Offworld: Expeditions

## Valkyrie

Humanity engages in a desperate struggle with an alien species for this side of the Orion Arm. Space ships die in instantaneous bursts of light and turn into vapor, but on the ground Marines scream and lie wounded in the mud and blood, praying for the Valkyries to come save them. They aren't wishing for death and a Nordic goddess to take them to Valhalla, the wounded are praying for the men and women of the '348th Field Hospital MEDEVAC to dive through fire and hell to come save them. Because they know that ...Valkyries never die!

Valkyrie
Valkyrie: Rebellion
Valkyrie: Attrition

## *High Caliber Awards*

The Cannon High Caliber Awards are an annual contest for new writers. In it we ask them to submit a novella length story of Science Fiction, Military or Fantasy genre to challenge their skills.

2024

2025

## The Wishkiller Saga

While on patrol Captain Aethal Paaling discovers evidence that an ancient terror has reached the rich soil of his home: the Lotus, a prolific growth whose addictive leaves devour their victims from within turning their hosts into horrible, terrifyingly violent mockeries of humanity. Created at the dawn of history by the twisted power of a godly relic called the Well, the return of the Lotus may be a harbinger of even more horrors to come. Carrying the fatal news to the capital, Aethal discovers that even in the face of death itself, the Lords Paramount of Verlaen will fight to keep their secrets and their power. With only the guidance of his legendary Greater Rifle and the aid of the Pheonix Lancers, the soldier must find his way through the halls of a forgotten holy order and into deep dens of crime seeking answers. He must find the truth as quickly as he can, because the Lotus may have already taken root among those he loves... and fighting it may cost him everything, including his soul.

*A Cold and Mortal Spring*

When nine out of ten people in the world have died in a brutal plague, what do those who remain do to pick up the pieces? Does the creed, "Duty, Honor, Country" have a place any more if there's no country left? On his way across the devastated remains of Texas, Marine Corps veteran and survivor Eric Marten rescues a young woman from a vicious attack by men who have turned into savages. As Dani slowly learns to trust him, they try to stay alive in the deathlands that America has become, using all their wits to survive a post-apocalyptic nightmare.

*90% Death Rate: A Post Apocalyptic Thriller*
*Angel of Death: A Post Apocalyptic Thriller*
*The Bloody Princess: A Post Apocalyptic Thriller*

# Hell Train

**A single train carries what might be the last vestige of civilization through a hellish nightmare.** A few hundred alive out of millions, lights going out all across what was once America as the possessed arose from the dead and murdered the living. A few hundred survivors travel across the country in an armored train, seeking some place to shelter in a fallen world. All that remains is a dystopian nightmare marked by rains of blood, impossible horrors, and portals to Hell opening in the skies. US Army Captain Jack Zamora is responsible for their safety, a self-imposed burden that wears on him every day. Fighting off undead, protecting the survivors, keeping the train running and supplied as his team desperately plans their next moves. Starvation and disease threaten. but it gets worse, because the ancient gods have sent their emissaries, horrific beings of myth and legend that walk the Earth. Things that can drain a man's very life essence or even that of an entire city.

*Hell Train: All Aboard*

**Sometimes a hero isn't what you expect, and the one you need comes from the castaways of society.**Nearly broken and at the end of his rope, former decorated scout pilot and prisoner of war, Red has finally accepted the inevitable. He and his kin have no future in the Human Confederation of Worlds, being gene mods and barely human themselves. With the help of his friend he flees Terra for adventure and fortune out in the reaches of the galaxy. Along the way he's dragged back into conflict that calls on all his piloting skills and he learns the deeper meaning of Kin, as his crew becomes his family.

*Path to Freedom: The Path, Book One*

## *Invasion*

More than a decade after the Confederated Earth Forces were defeated, their commanding general, a boyhood protegee, lives in exile and disgrace. His life on an isolated farm is forever changed when two strangers show up at his homestead, and the war comes crashing back down on him. The problem though, remains the same. How do you fight an enemy that is technologically superior and holds the high ground?

Invasion: Resistance

Invasion: Day of Battle

Invasion: Total War

## *Military Sci-Fi/Fantasy Anthology*

The military experience is timeless, and echoes down from our past and into our future. Along the way, not everything is as it seems. Thirteen stories from established and new writers in the field of Military Science Fiction and Military Fantasy bring you tales of the terrors of combat and the even greater fear of the unknown in Cannon Publishing's first Bi-Annual Military Anthology.

## The Hundred Worlds

Fifteen classic Science Fiction stories from both masters of the craft and up and coming new writers!A tyrannical United Nations pulls the strings of its colony worlds, ruling with an iron fist. Corporate interests take precedence, and brushfire rebellions smolder on the edges. One system, home to the only alien species yet discovered, with human allies throws off the yoke and calls itself Independence.

# *MECHA*

*MECHA*

Feedback from the slight pressure of a hand closing sends a powerful mechanical arm smashing into an opponent. A neural link hurls blustering plasma fire from your suit's shoulder mounted cannon. Your reactor levels scream with overload as return fire smashes into your armor, and damage alarms wail while you hurl your twenty ton body sideways for cover.You're a Mecha, a mechanical fighting machine with a human pilot. The guy that the infantry curse at in training and pray for in combat. The machine that the last hopes of your people ride on. The construct that strikes fear deep into alien hearts as they hear your turbines power up. The one able to pass through hell and come out the other side victorious, or die trying.

## Under A Different Sun

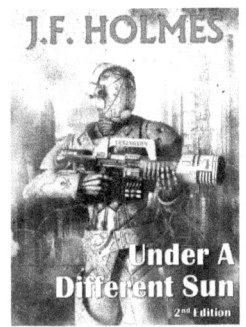

In the near future, massive empires rule the stars, and west of the Reach, they are battling for control of new systems. In the no-mans land between the front lines, Captain Nate Meric and the crew of the privateer Lexington fight for prize money, and loyalty to their ship and their friends. Beneath it all, though, runs a hidden dream. To see America restored, and take her rightful place among the stars.

### *Sea of Fire: Demonrise*

Brian Corel, former slave, gladiator, ex-fiance to an Empress, exiled Captain of the Taland Royal Guard and now owner of the frigate *Widowmaker,* does the best he can to balance the lives of his crew with his own desire to live life as a free man. Skirting the border between being a privateer and an outright pirate, Corel stumbles into a war with a religious cult intent on corrupting the kingdom of an old friend and has to set things right while grieving over his lost love. Along the way he signs a dragon into his crew and has to risk everything to rescue his brother from the grasp of a demon that has destroyed an entire continent.

## Chosen by the Sword

There are some things a PhD doesn't prepare you for, like running two feet of steel through the guts of a flesh-eating monster straight out of a nightmare, while ducking razor sharp claws. Or having the sword critique your fighting style while you do it.Dave Howard had a problem. Last week, he was out looking for a teaching job in the middle of a wrecked job market. This week he was neck deep in green blood and hellfire. Dragged into it by the very sword, his grandfathers' mysterious possessed blade, that was now walking him through hacking up a ghoul without getting his own head cut off. This wasn't exactly what he had gone to school for, and the University he had just taken a job with seemed to be anything BUT an academic institution. More like some kind of monster hunting bunch of weirdo nerds. Maybe his degree in Personality Psychology might be useful there, at least. The fighting though ... as he dodged another swipe of claws and awkwardly tried to follow the instructions the sword was screaming at him, he shot back at it, "Hell, I'm Canadian! Swordplay isn't in my cultural DNA!"

## Beyond the Wall: A Novel of Post-Roman Britain

**The legions are but a memory, the glory of Rome only a shadow of crumbling ruins and broken walls.** A darkening tide of barbarism was washing across Britain's shores and the lights of civilization were slowly flickering out into darkness, only kept burning by the legendary Red Dragons cavalry unit. Led by their Tribune, Arthur, who serves no kingdom but goes where the fight is hardest and most crucial, they wage desperate battles to keep back the tide. The Red Dragons ride the length of Britannia to fight the invading Saxons, Scoti and Picts, wherever they show, from across the seas or down from the Highlands. At sixteen years old Peredur of Gwynedd has listened all his life to the stories of his father Pelinor fighting with Ambrosius Aurelianus. When word comes that his older brother has been slain in battle with the Saxons, his desire for revenge leads him to follow in his father's footsteps as a warrior, becoming a cavalryman with the Red Dragons. Along the way he may either find himself a warrior and leader worthy of Arthur or be left lying forgotten in the dust of history.

## *Hell's Bells: War & Love Downrange*

Two souls collide in the middle of a deadly war.

Sergeant Sylvie Lyons of Her Majesty's Royal Engineers wishes she'd listened to her grandda's advice and stayed away from the military.

USMC Sergeant Hondo Cassidy wants nothing more in life than being a Marine and fighting. Hondo and Sylvie find themselves thrown together when his artillerymen are assigned to provide security for her engineers deep in the desert of Afghanistan.. Amidst death, destruction, cultural misunderstanding and the inevitable that happens when you mix an all male unit of Marines with an engineer unit that is mostly female, Sylvie and Hondo find in each other a reason to live. That is, if they can survive.

## Semper Die

*Semper Die*

**The dead rose expecting a feast. What they got was a firefight.**

Sergeant Alex Slaughter and the Marines of Alpha Squad were on a routine training exercise near Quantico when everything went silent. No comms. No command. No clue.

What they find when they return to base is worse than anything they trained for: a bioweapon has unleashed a zombie virus that has shattered civilization, and now they must survive the Collapse.

But as the squad pushes deeper into hostile territory—through the death-choked streets of Arlington and into the rot-stained corridors beneath D.C.—they discover that the undead aren't the only threat. Desperate survivors, rogue military units, and darker truths buried beneath the weight of secrecy will test their loyalty, their mission, and their very humanity.

Written by USMC veteran Jonathan Shuerger and set in J.F. Holmes's brutal and unrelenting Irregular Scout Team One universe, Semper Die delivers pulse-pounding action, authentic military detail, and a terrifying vision of what happens when duty and apocalypse collide.

If you crave hard-hitting military thrillers, brotherhood forged in battle, and Marines who refuse to die quietly—this is your next mission.

**Lock. Load. Semper Fi. Semper Die.**

# More from the Fae Wars!

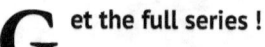

**G**et the full series !

*Onslaught*

What would you do if America and the world were invaded tomorrow by a relentless and brutal enemy? In an alternate 2015, a US Army Special Forces Team, part of the legendary black ops unit "Delta", is in midtown Manhattan to take out a Chinese spy and his handlers, sending a message short of outright conflict. All goes smoothly until they find themselves in a full blown shooting war through the canyons of the City. Portals from another world have opened in Central Park, making a way for figures out of historical nightmare to invade. The

Fae, creatures banished from Earth thousands of years ago and now only part of our legends, have returned with Dragon fire, spell and sword to conquer and take revenge.The first volume of The Fae Wars covers Team Three, G squadron, Special Forces Detachment (Delta) as they fight their way off Manhattan and then join the defense of the refugees as the Fae assault the bridges. The fabled 69th Infantry puts up an epic fight against superior weaponry and then the war descends into the asymmetric hell that the Delta Operators know so well. Along the way they find new allies and old powers that come to their aid

### The Fall

For the first time in two hundred years an enemy has stepped foot on American soil and war has come to our cities. The US military is rocked back on its heels and driven into a fighting retreat as each defense line falls. The foe is unstoppable and ... Fae. Creatures from a legendary past who have come to reclaim the Earth in the name of magic and revenge. In the hills of Pennsylvania a ragtag, devastated army prepares to make a last stand against dragon fire capable of melting an Abrams tank and wizardry that stops fifth generation fighter jets in mid-air. Inevitably it comes down to shining steel verses human will, and Sergeant Oliva Acevedo transforms from a hospital clerk to a hardened fighter. Volume Two of the best selling "Fae Wars" follows the fighting retreat of the US Army as the Fae establish control of a shattered America.

### Futures Past

Two thousand years ago the Fae were banished from Earth and they've spent that time plotting return and revenge. When their portals open around the world and start crushing the human's military with spell encased steel and dragon fire, it becomes a massive stuggle between technology and magic. When the Fae Invasion hammers the West Coast, Captain James Powers and his California Army National Guard artillery battery is caught on its way home from Annual Training. In a running battle the unit is smashed by combat with orcs and elves, leaving their commander struggling to keep his people together and alive. Along the way a dying priest with a strange ability to see the future manipulates people and events to bring Captain Powers to his true calling as a Seer. As they run and fight, the humans gain new allies, Fea tinkerers who love all things mechanical and hate the elves. With their help they begin to take the war to the enemy in a brutal mayhem of ambush and assassination. Book Three of the Fae Wars series following the bestselling "Onslaught" (set in NY City) and "The Fall" (Pennsylvania)

*Tales From the Occupation: A Fae Wars Anthology*

Wars end, enemies are defeated and territories are conquered and the combatants have to return to a life changed. America and the rest of humanity have fallen to the Fae, ancient mortal enemies of mankind. After building their strength for two thousand years, the Elves have claimed their vengeance and now rule Earth with an iron fist and dragon fire. Down but not out, a human resistance is building, but first daily life needs to be lived. An anthology of stories exploring life during the Occupation in the best-selling Fae Wars universe.

*Insurgent*

*Wars come and wars go. Eventually even the most belligerent of combatants will arrive at some kind of living arrangement, either through exhaustion or slaughter. Kill enough, down to the last child, and there will be no more war ... until the next one, of course.* In August 2015, the war started, portals opening up between their world and ours, allowing the Fae to return to our (or their) home world in blood, fire and magic. Conventional forces fought back as well as they could, but the invasion had been planned to hit us in the middle of our civilization. America's military was scattered overseas or concentrated in large bases that were quickly overwhelmed by forces that were dropped right in the middle of their units. The fighting was brutal and horrific, magic overwhelming technology. It took six weeks, and the President surrendered to spare the civilian population. A puppet government was put in place and the Fae started to divide the conquered lands into principalities run by their Great Houses, slowly turning America into a land of feudal slavery. Thing is, though, the Fae had lived in their exile for thousands of years, fighting wars among themselves and against various races that populated their new home. Pitched battles where there was a clear-cut winner and loser. They had never fought an insurgency and had no idea how bloody it could get. Major David Kincaid. United States Army 1st Special Forces Operational Detachment–Delta, soldier of a defeated but unbroken nation, was going to show them. If, that is, he can keep the faith. The follow up novel to the bestselling "Fae Wars: Onslaught" by J.F. Holmes.

*Ghost*

*There are wars, and then there's War. The all-encompassing thing that is fought on many levels, and with many kinds of weapons, many kinds of warriors. Even ghosts.* Alex was no one, a man just trying to get by at his paperwork job at the new Homeland Security. A man grieving for his wife, who had died in the Invasion. Someone just trying to keep his head down while the elves appointed him to do the paperwork of putting their boots on the necks of a conquered American people. Thing is, even a nobody paper shuffling clerk has a weapon, one that had lit the fires of revolution in America hundreds of years ago. His mind, and his words. The internet was still up and running, somehow and someway, and Alex takes to his keyboard. Inspired by his hero Patrick Henry, soon the words of the "Ghost" start inciting attacks on the Fae and the District of Columbia rings with explosions, gunshots and cries of Freedom. The Resistance notices, and Alex is soon assigned a bodyguard and a handler, an ex-police officer who is running from her own hidden past. Together they work to keep the flame of resistance alive and escape from the tightening net of the Fae. The consequences are, as always, Liberty or Death.

*Northwest Front*

**Fae Wars returns on a new front as war rages in the Pacific Northwest!**
Corporal Erik Doherty isn't some kind of special operations super soldier; he's just an infantry grunt trying to get by in what was once the United States Army, now an enforcement arm of the Fae overlords. When orders come down from a chain of command more interested in boot licking their new masters than protecting American citizens, he has to make the choice. To serve and live, or run and die? Ashleigh Greene is a teenage girl with a price on her head, the Fae looking for retribution for the killing of one of their nobles. As her hometown burns behind her, she flees into the mist shrouded forests of the Pacific Northwest, her family killed by dragon fire and her world destroyed. On separate paths, each human comes face to face with a haunting legend that has lived for thousands of years. One that has been waiting, watching, and hating the old enemy that has finally returned. Together, they bring war to the Fae in a battle for honor and revenge. Book seven in the best-selling Fae Wars series!

## Authors

### John Holmes

J.F. Holmes is a retired Army Senior Noncommissioned Officer, having served for 22 years in both the Regular Army and Army National Guard. During that time, he served as everything from an artillery section leader to a member of a Division level planning staff, with tours in Cuba and Iraq, as well as responding to the terrorists attacks in NYC on 9-11.

From 2010 to 2014 he wrote the immensely popular military cartoon strip, "Power Point Ranger", poking fun at military life in the tradition of Beetle Bailey and Willy & Joe.

His books range from Military Sci-Fi to Space Opera to Detective to Fantasy, with a lot in between, and in 2017 two are finalists for the prestigious Dragon Awards.

In 2018, he launched Cannon Publishing, www.cannonpublishing.us specializing in military science fiction, fantasy and thrillers, with an emphasis on works from up and coming authors.

### Lucas Marcum

Lucas Marcum is a critical care nurse practitioner and an officer in the US Army Reserve. When he's not working, or performing his reserve duties, he can be found hiking, reading, attempting to perfect his soft pretzel recipe and spending time with his family.

### James Copley

James Copley is a former Non-Commissioned Officer of the U.S. Army, having served over twenty-one years in both Active and Reserve/Guard units, variously trained as Infantry, Communications, and Ordnance specialties before finally retiring from the Army National Guard in 2016. During his service, he deployed four separate times, twice to Iraq and twice to Afghanistan.

He is currently working as a software engineer in Central California with his wife, two children, and two dogs. Reading was his number one passion from a very young age, and more recently he decided to try writing his own. Feel free to join him on his writing journey!

### Charli Cox

Charli Cox is a best-selling Military Sci-Fi and Horror Comedy author. She also writes Sci-Fi, Alternate History, and Military Fantasy stories.

If you enjoyed Fae Wars: Northwest Front and want to see more stories about Ash and "Gunny," Cannon Publishing has you covered. Burnt Mountain and Sasquatch will be coming to your Kindle later in 2025. Also, please be sure to leave a review!

Representing #teamandmore, Charli's first published short story is in The Phoenix Initiative: First Missions from Chris Kennedy Publishing. She has stories in Bureau 42 and Express Elevator to Hell, also from CKP.

Look for Whistles of the Wendigo, an Alternate History/Military Fantasy novel set in the Joint Task Force 13 universe from Three Ravens Publishing, due to release soon.

Charli's previous experience has been as a Realtor, HVAC Business Manager, IT Office Manager, and freelance bookkeeper. Professional skills such as drafting strongly worded emails transition surprisingly well into writing fiction.

An animal lover and #boymom, she lives in SW Oregon with her Leg husband, two sons, an Arabian mare, and two Husky mixes who think they are hooman.

Learn more about Charli and sign up for her newsletter on her website. Hang out with her on Facebook, Instagram, and/or TikTok.

### Jason Weiser

Mr. Weiser has been a government contractor for the last eleven years, and before that, a writer working odd jobs trying to get by. He has a BA in History from CUNY Brooklyn. Mr. Weiser released his first novel in 2025, with Cannon Publishing, but before that, released a short story in their 2018 Spring Military Sci Fi Anthology.

Mr. Weiser is also an avid wargamer and has been published quite a bit in the hobby, having most recently run "Military Miniature" magazine as it's editor in chief from 2021-2023. Before that, he wrote for EpochXperience (a division of SJR Research) as a contributing writer for their blog on wargaming and military history topics from 2020 to 2021.

He also wrote two scenario books on Cold War wargaming topics, "Red Star, Burning Streets" and "Red Star, White Lights".

Mr. Weiser encourages all his fans to visit Cannon Publishing at their website